# A FAR, FAR *Better*
# PLACE

# A FAR, FAR *Better* PLACE

*Dickens Inn*

*Volume Two*

*a novel*

## Anita Stansfield

Covenant Communications, Inc.

Cover image *Empty Park Bench in Spring* © by Mcfields, courtesy of istockphoto.com

Cover design copyrighted 2010 by Covenant Communications, Inc.

Published by Covenant Communications, Inc.
American Fork, Utah

Printed in Canada
First Printing: February 2010

15 14 13 12 11 10    10 9 8 7 6 5 4 3 2 1

ISBN-13: 978-1-59811-964-0

# Chapter One

*Anaconda, Montana*

Jackson Leeds reached across the desk to answer the phone, and kept sorting papers while he said, "Dickensian Inn. How may I help you?"

"Jackson?" With that one word, he recognized the voice of his sister, Melinda, but he panicked over her frantic tone.

"What's wrong?" he demanded, giving her his full attention.

"Mama's sick, Jackson. She's real sick." He could tell she was crying. "It came on bad in the night. We're at the hospital, but it doesn't look good."

"Do you want me to come?" he asked, ignoring the deep uneasiness he felt at the very idea. He'd not been back to the town where he'd been raised in more than twenty-seven years. In fact, he'd had no contact with his family at all until a little more than two years ago when a fateful incident had brought them back together. He'd kept in touch with his mother and sister since then, and they'd talked about his coming home to visit. But ugly memories of his childhood, and the reasons he'd kept his distance for so long, had made it easy to avoid the subject. His father had been the reason for most of the ugliness, and he'd been dead for years. But Jackson knew he still had difficult feelings buried inside him that he hadn't cared to look at too closely. Now, he had just volunteered in a split second to return to the town he'd once vowed to never set foot in again.

"I think you'd better," she said, and he took a moment to accept the deeper implication.

"What are you saying?"

Because of Melinda's tears, he could barely understand her. "The doctor says it might only be a day or two."

"Until *what?*" he demanded, hearing himself use a tone that had once been common in the squad room of the FBI agency that had been his life. Now he'd retired from that, and he was living a completely different life. He'd not had cause to feel so agitated or impatient in a long time.

"We're losing her, Jackson," Melinda said. "You need to come; get here as soon as you can."

"I will," he promised. "Tell her to hang on."

"I will," she said and ended the call.

Jackson leaned back in the chair and tried to take it in. *His mother was dying.* For years he'd gone without having any relationship with her at all, and he'd convinced himself that the lives of his family members meant nothing to him. But a great deal of healing and forgiveness had taken place between them, and his heart threatened to crack wide open at the very idea of losing her.

Instinctively he did what he had learned to do in the face of any difficult moment. He went to find his wife. It was a short walk down the hall and through the dining room of the restored Victorian mansion where they lived and worked. He'd met Chas two and half years earlier when he'd come to stay at the Dickensian Inn while on administrative leave from the FBI, due to an internal investigation. Chas had been widowed at a young age when her husband Martin had been killed in a military training accident. And soon afterward Chas had lost a baby who had been born with a heart defect. Chas had been raised by her grandmother, who had inherited the family home, and the two of them had embarked on turning the place into an equitable business. The Dickens theme of the place had been due to Granny's obsession with the great writer. Chas had been named the abbreviation for Charles for the same reason. But Jackson had his own fondness for Dickens, and it was for that very reason he'd chosen *this* bed-and-breakfast for his escape. He'd not expected to fall in love and have his life changed so dramatically. Their age difference of twelve years had never been an issue to either of them. In a very short time he and Chas had shared life-altering events, including the death of her grandmother and trauma related to his work that he preferred to avoid thinking about. Right now his mind was most focused on how Chas had been instrumental in helping him heal the relationships with his mother and sister. What had started out as a disaster had ended up as a miracle in his life. Now he had to face another disaster, but he couldn't find any reason to believe that there would be a miracle at the end of *this* path.

Jackson found Chas in the kitchen; she was working on breakfast preparations for the two couples who had stayed at the inn the previous night. Her shoulder-length dark hair was pulled up in a ponytail. The baby was sitting in the little contraption that had become a permanent fixture in the kitchen. Little Charles wasn't yet six months old, but he was sitting up straight and tall, bouncing up and down, making silly noises, signaling his enchantment with all the brightly colored toys attached to the thing he was sitting in that Jackson had dubbed "the spaceship." Jackson glanced at the baby, who looked up when he came into the room. He couldn't hold back a smile when he saw his son grin at him. But his heart returned quickly to sadness. He'd really believed that his mother would have had the chance to see Charles become old enough to at least *know* her.

"Hey there, handsome," Chas said, glancing quickly toward him. She did a double take and stopped what she was doing. "Is something wrong?"

"Yeah," he said. "That was Melinda on the phone. My mother is sick; very sick, apparently."

"No," Chas said, wiping her hands on the full-length apron she always wore while she was working. "What's wrong?"

"She didn't say, but . . ." the gravity in his voice slid into sorrow, "whatever it is, it's not good." His voice cracked. "She's dying." Chas took a sharp breath and put a hand over her heart. "We need to go there . . . now."

"Of course," she said eagerly. "What do you need me to do?"

"I'll use my cell phone to arrange the flights. If you could make some calls on the landline to get everything here covered. I hope Polly didn't have any big plans this week."

"I'll talk to her. We'll figure it out."

Polly had worked for Chas at the inn for many years. She endearingly referred to her as the secretary, slash office manager, slash assistant, but she was also a friend and had often stayed at the inn during challenging times or simply to cover for Chas when necessary.

"Okay," Jackson said. "Then I guess we'll pack and . . ." His voice faded as he headed back out of the room, but he was stopped by her hand on his arm.

"Are you okay?" Chas asked, pushing her arms around him.

Jackson held her close and absorbed the sustenance she always gave him. "I can't answer that right now," he said. "We can talk on the way to the airport."

"Okay," she said. He kissed her quickly and headed back to the office.

Chas called Polly on her cell phone while Polly was driving to the inn to begin her work at the usual time. They were in the middle of their conversation when Polly walked through the door, and they hung up when they were facing each other.

"Okay, I'm here," Polly said. "Everything will be fine. I'll watch the baby while you pack, and I'll catch up in the office later."

Polly was shorter than average and slightly plump, although she had recently been losing weight and was looking pretty good. She had a head full of thick red curls cut short. Chas thought she looked like Little Orphan Annie, and she had the energy of a pinball machine. Like hundreds of times before, she was grateful for Polly's efficiency in working at the inn, as well as her friendship.

Less than two hours later they were on the road to Butte, with Charles buckled into his baby seat, making happy noises. Ten minutes into the drive, Chas said, "You told me we'd talk. You haven't said a word."

"I don't know what to say," he admitted. "I just . . . didn't see this coming. I thought we had years left. She's not *that* old. Granny lived to be *much* older than this. I think I just expected that it would be the same. I kept thinking we would go to Arkansas, spend some time together, and have some fun. This is just . . ." He waved a hand in the air as if that could explain what he couldn't find words to say. "It's just not right," he finally concluded.

"We had some great times when she came here," Chas reminded him. His mother and sister had come to stay at the inn a number of times, including three visits since Charles had been born. It hadn't been difficult to arrange, since Melinda and Jackson both had more than sufficient financial resources, and Melinda was not tied down with work or children; she owned her own business that ran itself, and her children were grown.

"Yes, we did," he said, "but she kept asking me to come home . . . to visit her there . . . and I didn't."

"Is this regret I hear?"

"Yes, Chas," he snapped, "this is regret!" He immediately added in a softer voice, "I'm sorry. I'm not angry with you. I'm angry with myself."

"Okay, I understand. But now that you're here and there's no going back, you're going to have to deal with what you have to work with."

"Intellectually, that makes sense," he said, still sounding angry, "but I'm having a little trouble with processing it that way at the moment. You're just going to have to be patient with me."

"Of course," she said gently, taking his hand. "You were there for me when Granny died. I'm not going to let you go through this alone."

He took her hand and kissed it. "Being there for you when Granny died was easy, Chas. It was no sacrifice."

"And you think this is? I love your mother too. I love *you.*"

"I know that. And I'm grateful. But you had no regrets with Granny, nothing to wish you had done differently."

"No, but I felt that way about Martin," she said, and he took a surprised glance at her face before he turned his attention back to the road. "Things were far from smooth between us a lot of the time." His surprised deepened. "You didn't know that, did you?"

"How could I if you'd never told me?"

"We loved each other, and I always hoped that with the love we shared we could make our marriage better, not worse. But we'd both been very young and naive when we married. It's hard to say how it might have turned out had he lived. Obviously that doesn't matter anymore. But I said a lot of things I regretted. The last time I saw him before I flew back home . . . before the accident . . . we argued. I said some awful things. We talked on the phone a couple of times after that, and I apologized, but . . ." her voice became heavy, "there are some things you can't take back." She looked at her husband. "I know what it's like to feel regret, Jackson. But I also believe in forgiveness . . . and I believe in miracles. I also believe that the end of this life is not the end. Just try to keep that in mind."

"I'll try," he said, but it didn't take long for his thoughts to turn again to regret, and he knew it was easier said than done.

The flight was long, but fortunately the baby was fairly cooperative, and fellow passengers seemed more amused by his antics than annoyed by his restlessness. Then he finally slept through the last stretch of the journey. Jackson felt his inner turmoil increase as their destination drew closer. Chas said little, and he appreciated her allowing him the time to wrestle with his thoughts. Just having her by his side gave him the strength and courage to believe that he could face this and survive it. Even with her there, he had his doubts. But without her, he wouldn't have a prayer.

Looking out the window, Jackson saw the terrain become familiar as the plane eased closer to the ground. He'd not set foot in Arkansas since he'd boarded a plane at the age of eighteen to join the Marines. Even with as much as he'd traveled the country on work-related assignments with the FBI, he'd never returned to any part of his home state. He tried not to think about the life he'd left behind, or the way things had been when he left, but no amount of will-power could keep his mind from taking in the memories—and most of them were not good. In fact, he could hardly come up with a positive recollection at all. Still, he had spent his life learning not to show his emotions and remaining steady and firm in the face of unspeakable horrors. It had been his duty and his occupation. Surely he could apply his skills now and keep himself together. He joked with Chas about how easy it had once been to travel with a single carry-on bag. Now they were waiting with a stroller at the baggage claim for multiple suitcases and a car seat.

"Are you complaining?" she asked with a chuckle.

"Not even a little," he said and gave her a quick kiss as he handed her the baby in order to get their belongings from the rotating carousel.

Chas found a place to change the baby and nurse him while Jackson secured the rental car. Once they were on the road, it was getting dark and Jackson felt exhausted. It had already been a long day, but he knew it was far from over. They drove for nearly two hours, and he felt grateful that it was dark so he couldn't see the land-scape becoming familiar. He just followed the familiar road signs and drove straight to a Best Western that hadn't been there twenty-eight years earlier. He'd checked on the Internet before leaving home to find a place to stay and had made reservations. When they pulled into the parking lot, he said to Chas, "It will never compete with a Victorian inn, but it's a lot better than what they used to have around here. We can be grateful for progress."

"What *did* they have?" she asked.

"There was the tolerable motel, which was actually clean—as opposed to the motel that *wasn't* tolerable."

Chas made a disgusted noise, and Jackson went to the lobby to check in and get the key. With the few steps he took from the car to the door, he could feel the strangely familiar stickiness of the humidity, which was already making memories cling uncomfortably to him. He was glad to be helped by a teenaged girl, fearing he would run into people who had known him. He hoped that he had changed enough to *not* be recognized. For once he was genuinely glad to have gone prematurely gray. Chas had often told him that he looked convincingly younger than his actual middle forties, and his hair didn't detract from that. He believed her, mostly because she'd never lied to spare his feelings over anything else. He felt sure he bore little resemblance to the dark-haired boy who had left here so long ago.

They unloaded their luggage, freshened up a little, and went straight to the hospital. Jackson told Chas that while he'd grown up in a small town, they were fortunate that the hospital that served a large area was located here. He'd called Melinda on her cell phone to let her know they were nearly there, and she met them just outside the elevator near the intermediate care unit. She hugged them both tightly, looking just the same as she always had. Her fluffy blond hair was done in the same style she'd worn in high school, and her flashy wardrobe hadn't changed much either. She still wore too much makeup and jewelry, and her fingernails were professionally done in a way that Jackson considered too long and too bright. But he loved his sister, and in the time since the wounds had been healed in their family, he had grown to respect and admire her for the selfless way in which she had cared for their mother. In spite of her own awful upbringing, Melinda had tried very hard to raise her two children well. She'd done a pretty good job once she'd divorced their deadbeat father. Her kids were adults now, and Melinda was financially independent due to her own efforts, and she was a kind and generous woman. He'd learned a great deal from Melinda about forgiveness and making the most of what life has handed you.

Melinda began to cry once they had exchanged their greetings and she'd made a fuss over the baby and how big he was getting.

"How is she?" Jackson asked frantically, praying his mother hadn't died in the few minutes since he'd spoken to his sister on the phone.

"Mostly sleeping . . . from that stuff they give her to keep her comfortable." Melinda still spoke in the thick Southern accent that Jackson had worked so hard to get rid of. "She's in pain when she's awake, so I guess that's for the best. But there's sure a lot I'd like to talk to her about now that it's come to this."

"So, she really is . . ." Jackson stammered. "This is really . . . it?"

Melinda nodded.

"What happened?" he demanded quietly. "What's wrong with her?"

"I think we should sit down." Melinda motioned toward the chairs in the waiting area where they stood. "She's asleep and not likely to die in the next five minutes. You need to know."

"Know *what?*" Jackson couldn't help sounding mildly angry as it became evident that something had been withheld from him. He felt Chas's hand on his arm, silently reminding him to remain calm.

Melinda took Jackson's hand in a way that seemed to have the same purpose. He saw her drawing courage. "Mama didn't want you to know."

*"Know what?"* he asked again, sounding much calmer than he felt.

"She's got a kidney disease; she's had it for a long time now, even before we came to see you . . . that day." Jackson knew what she meant by *that day.* It was the first time they'd seen each other in twenty-eight years. "I told her that she should tell you what was going on, because we both knew that without a transplant, it was only a matter of time before it took her, but she wasn't a candidate for a transplant with her age and so many other health issues."

Jackson tried to grasp this with his mind, and keep his emotions out of it. "You're telling me that you've both known for years that she was dying, and you never said a word to me?"

"Mama insisted!" she said, but her tears increased with her words. "I thought you should know, but she made me promise."

"Why?" Jackson asked. Melinda hesitated, and he became the man who had once confined himself in interrogation rooms with criminals until he got the answers. *"Why?"* he repeated and felt Chas squeeze his arm.

He saw Melinda swallow carefully, and the truth rose in her eyes before it came through her lips. "She didn't want you to worry, and she didn't want you coming to see her because you felt sorry for her. She wanted you to come home because you *wanted* to."

Jackson shot to his feet, finding it more difficult to keep his emotions in check. He attempted to explain. "My reasons for not coming home had nothing to do with her . . . not the last couple of years anyway."

"She knew that," Melinda said. "We've had a lot of good times together since you've come back into our lives. We're all grateful for that."

"I'm grateful for that too," he said and stuffed his hands in the back pockets of his jeans. He lowered his head. "But I still didn't come home."

"She understands," Melinda insisted.

"Does she?" he countered. "I'm not sure I do." Needing to focus in order to avoid breaking down, he asked, "Where is she? Can we see her?"

Melinda stood up, relieved. "Yes, the nurse on duty even said it would be okay to bring the baby in for a few minutes as long as he's not fussing. I'm sure Mama would love to see him."

Jackson took the baby from Chas when she stood, as if little Charles could protect him from emotions he couldn't face right now. His heart quickened painfully as they followed Melinda down the hall and into a room where his mother was sleeping. She was hooked up to a great deal of equipment and monitors, and she already looked dead. He was grateful to have Chas's hand in his, and grateful that he wasn't still foolishly avoiding his family completely, as he'd been doing before Chas had come into his life. At least he was here. At least they had shared some good memories to help counterbalance the bad ones. Not certain how to feel, or what to say to his mother, he was glad to recall Chas's advice from earlier. *Now that you're here and there's no going back, you're going to have to deal with what you have to work with.* He had to be smart enough not to add to his regret by blowing what little time they might have left together. He could deal with the rest later. He wondered if they would have to wait for her to come around, but Melinda touched Melva's arm, and Jackson held his breath as his mother began to stir. She opened her eyes, and Melinda put her face close to Melva's, saying with quiet excitement, "They're here, Mama."

"Here?" Melva said in a husky whisper and shifted her eyes. Melinda moved aside and Jackson gave the baby to Chas, suddenly needing to be closer to his mother than holding the baby would allow.

Jackson sat on the edge of the bed and took his mother's hand, leaning close to her face as Melinda had done. "I'm here, Mama," he said.

"Oh, my boy. My boy!" she said, exactly as she'd said it when they'd been reunited after twenty-eight years. He saw tears in her eyes just before tears blurred his own vision, and he pressed his face next to hers on the pillow with some semblance of a hug. He eased back to look at her again, and she lifted a feeble hand to touch his face, ignoring the IV line in her arm. "I'm so glad you came."

"I would have come sooner," he said, "if I had known." He knew it sounded like a feeble excuse, but it was the truth. He was well aware of the answer but still had to ask, "Why didn't you tell me you were so sick?"

She offered a gentle smile. "I didn't want you to worry," she said. He knew that was part of the truth, but he had to confront the rest of it.

"And you didn't want me to come home for the wrong reasons?"

"You're home now."

"Now that it's too late," he said, feeling like a child, perhaps like the child he'd never really been allowed to be.

"It's never too late," she said, appearing completely at peace.

"You're dying, Mama."

"I know, but . . . we had some good times, and . . ." She stopped when she heard the baby cooing, and her attention shifted. Her eyes lit up when she saw Chas holding little Charles. "You brought your family."

"I did," Jackson said and took the baby while Chas embraced Melva and kissed her face. He watched while his wife told his mother how much she loved her and how she was going to miss her.

Chas started to cry, and Melva's tears increased. She touched Chas's face and said, "You're the best thing that ever happened to him, my dear. Be patient with him. Take good care of him."

"I will, of course," Chas said, glancing at Jackson. "It's not hard, you know. He's very good to me."

"He's a good man," Melva said, "in spite of me."

Jackson blew out a ragged breath. They all knew she'd been far from the ideal mother, but he didn't want her to believe that such things were even relevant anymore. He was relieved when Chas said, "He knows how much you love him, and he loves you."

"I know," Melva said and smiled. The baby made another noise, as if to demand some attention. Melva let out a weak chuckle and looked at him.

Jackson moved closer and set Charles on the side of the bed where Melva could see him clearly. She chuckled again, and Jackson said in a silly voice, "Tell Granny hello."

The baby made a cooing noise that made them all laugh, then a strange silence fell over the room as little Charles reached out his chubby little hands and put them to his grandmother's face. Melva put her hands over his to hold them there. The infant's eyes connected to the old woman's as if some silent information might be passing between them. Jackson wondered if he was only imagining the sweetness of the moment, then Chas and Melinda both started to cry, as if they too could sense something going on in the room that was beyond their ability to see. The moment was brief but unmistakable. The baby wiggled and cooed, and Melva said to Jackson, "He looks so much like you when you were a baby."

"I don't know how you can remember that far back," Jackson said with a small attempt at humor.

"He *does* look like Jackson," Chas agreed. "He certainly doesn't look like me."

"Thank you for bringing him to see me," Melva said, and her eyes drooped.

"She's getting tired," Melinda explained. "She only has a few lucid minutes each time she comes awake.

Melva reached for Jackson's hand, and he took it. "Will you stay a while?" she asked.

"I will," he promised and pressed a kiss to her brow.

Chas hugged her again, and once more told her how she loved her, and that it had been a privilege to know her. Melva smiled weakly at Chas and said, "You're a very sweet girl." It was something she'd said to Chas a hundred times, and it made Chas smile.

A moment later, Melva was asleep. In the hallway just outside the open door to her room, Jackson asked Melinda to tell him everything the doctors had said. It was great deal of information, but it boiled down to one thing. According to tests results and vital signs, she wasn't likely to last another twenty-four hours. Jackson cried upon hearing the verdict, but quickly pulled himself together. He then reverted to his habit of taking charge under strenuous circumstances. "Chas, honey," he said, "why don't you take the car and go back to the room. You can't stay here with the baby. Just . . . get some sleep and come back in the morning. I need to stay."

Chas considered a protest, not wanting to leave him alone, and not certain Melva would still be alive when she returned in the morning. But a moment's thought and a calm feeling let her know that it would be good for Jackson to have some time alone with his mother—and his thoughts—and she couldn't do any good here. Right now she needed to be a mother and take care of her son. And he was right. Staying here with the baby would be highly impractical and a potential disturbance to others. She nodded and kissed him. "Is there anything I can get you before I go?"

"No, I'm fine. Thank you. Can you find your way back okay?"

"Jackson, it's not *that* big a town."

"Don't I know it," he said. "Call me when you're there safely." He kissed her again.

"I will," she said, and he kissed the baby.

After Chas had left, Jackson turned to Melinda and said, "You look exhausted. Let me sit with her while you get some rest."

"You're exhausted too," she insisted.

"Hey, I've done all-night stakeouts many times in my life. I can handle this. I'll call you if anything changes."

She let out a reluctant sigh. "Okay, but . . . I'm just going to lie down for a while." She pointed to a room down the hall. "They have a couch in there they said I could use. You wake me up if *anything* changes."

"I will. I promise," he said and kissed her cheek. She went back in their mother's room to kiss her brow and whisper something before she hugged Jackson tightly. "I'm so glad you're here. I don't know how I'd get through this without my big brother."

"I'm six years younger than you."

"Still my big brother," she said and left the room.

Jackson took a deep breath to more fully take in what still felt shocking and beyond his ability to believe. His mother was dying, and he didn't feel at all prepared to accept it. He scooted a chair close to his mother's side where he could easily sit and hold her hand while keeping a good view of her face. He was relieved to find the chair comfortable. This was already better than most of his all-night stake-outs. Ten minutes later he felt his phone vibrate on his belt and went out in the hall to answer it, glad to know that Chas and the baby were safely back in the motel room. Charles had fallen asleep during the short drive and was down for the night. Chas told Jackson she loved him and she would see him as soon as the baby was up in the morning and ready for the day.

Jackson returned to his mother's side and made himself comfort-able, taking hold of her hand. For the first hour and a half he pondered the events that had brought them back together, and his role as the prodigal son. He got up and went to the bathroom and found a place in the hospital where he could buy a cup of coffee. He returned to his mother's side and once again took her hand. He spent a couple of hours pondering the work her hands had done, the life they had experienced. He thought of how it must have been for her to live with a man like his father. He'd been drunk most of the time, and he was mean whether he was drunk or sober. He thought of how she'd apologized so profusely to him at their reunion for not being a good mother. They both knew she had done the best she could, that she simply hadn't known any better. She'd admitted that she'd finally figured that out after her children had been raised. And Jackson suspected that it was after his father's death that his mother had finally been able to find herself and make peace with her own life. She was a good woman with a good heart, and Jackson loved her. But he still felt like there was so much more he needed to say to her. There was so much he'd wanted to do with her. It had been common recently for him to think, *I'll have to take my mother there,* or *I should do that for my mother.* And now it was too late. The very most he could expect now were some brief snatches of conversation. But as she slept on, he began to fear he wouldn't even get those.

The night wore away, and Jackson sat by his mother's side for so long that he began to fear she would never regain consciousness, and he would never have the opportunity to say what he needed to say. He found himself praying silently, and had to include in his prayers gratitude for having a woman in his life who had taught him to pray, and to believe that someone was actually listening. He shook his head, wondering where he would be without Chas. He would still be hiding somewhere in a dangerous job, and his mother would have died without ever seeing him again.

Jackson was asking God to allow him a conversation with his mother when Melva began to stir again, and Jackson lifted his head, tightening his hold on her hand to make her aware of his presence. She turned to look at him and offered a faint smile.

"You're still here," she said, and he could barely hear her.

He leaned closer so that she could hear him. "I told you I would stay."

"But it must be so late."

"It doesn't matter, Mama. I want to be with you. And there's something I need to say." She tightened her gaze on him and waited. "I know I said it before, but I need to say it again. I'm so sorry that I wasted all those years . . . that I didn't see you, or call."

"And I've told you before that it's in the past; it doesn't matter anymore. You're here now, my boy, and I'm awfully glad of that."

"But," Jackson heard his voice break and felt his chin quiver, "I should have come home before now. I intended to, but . . . I didn't, and I should have."

"I know why it would be hard for you," she said, her words slow and her voice strained. "I understand." She tightened her hand in his. "Now there's something I have to say, and I want you to listen carefully." She paused a full minute to get her breath, and he could tell it was becoming more difficult for her to breathe.

"I'm listening," he said, leaning a little closer.

He was hoping for and perhaps expecting some piece of advice, some expression of love. He was entirely unprepared to hear, "You need to forgive your father." He wanted to say, *What makes you think I haven't forgiven him?* But he knew it would make him sound like a fool. He knew in his heart that he had ill feelings toward his deceased father, and his mother knew it too. But did she know how deep and difficult those feelings really were? Looking into her eyes, he suspected that she did. How could she not? She'd lived with him too. She'd seen the damage he'd caused. His mother and sister had made wonderful changes in their lives in spite of that damage. And Jackson's life wasn't too bad either—on the surface at least. He owed most of that to Chas. However, he couldn't deny that his inner turmoil was something that haunted him. The way his father's treatment tied into other horrors he'd lived through just prior to his marriage was something that still gave him nightmares. He just didn't know how to face it, and didn't particularly want to. And now it was as if his mother could see his soul. She shifted her head slightly on the pillow and added, "I know how angry you are with him, and you have good reason to be. But you have to let go of it, my boy. You have to forgive him, whether he deserves to be forgiven or not."

"He *doesn't* deserve it."

"I know that, and you know that, but you still have to do it."

Jackson swallowed carefully. His mother was dying. What was he supposed to say? Her anxious expression made it evident she was waiting for him to say something. He cleared his throat and said, "I'll work on it."

"You have to do better than that, my boy," she said. "You have to forgive him. No matter how long it takes, or how hard it is, you have to. Promise me." He hesitated, but she was firm. "It's the only thing I need in order to have peace . . . to know that you will forgive him. Promise me."

He swallowed so hard he almost choked. What could he say? But he knew he couldn't say it if he didn't mean it. "I promise," he said and felt his stomach tighten even as the words came out of his mouth. It would take a miracle for him to be able to forgive his father, but somehow he had to do it. He had just promised his dying mother, and he was not a man to break his word.

# Chapter Two

Melva drifted again into sleep so quickly that she was unconscious before Jackson even had a chance to think what else he might like to say to her. He was so absorbed in pondering what his mother had asked him to do—and the sickness it had provoked—that he was startled when one of the monitors in the room started to beep. A few seconds later a nurse came into the room. She didn't appear panicked, but after she stopped the beeping, made some adjustments, and checked his mother's vital signs, she turned to Jackson and said, "It won't be much longer now. She's getting close."

"What do you mean?" Jackson asked, as if she'd been speaking a foreign language.

She wasn't rattled by his response. She simply said, "Her vitals have changed dramatically since I last checked. She must be ready to go now. You might want to wake your sister."

Jackson coughed to keep from choking and nodded. He left the room and turned the corner of the hall where he leaned against the wall long enough to find a degree of composure. *Ready to go now?* What did *that* mean? Had their conversation been her last item of business to see to before leaving this world? His stomach tightened all over again with thoughts of his father, then he forced his focus on the moment. *His mother was dying.* He managed to remain steady as he found Melinda and woke her, repeating what the nurse had said. She practically ran back to Melva's room. Jackson followed more slowly, his throat and eyes burning hot. He looked at his watch and wondered if Chas would make it back before this happened, but he doubted it was likely. And that was fine. She needed her rest, and she needed to be with the baby. He knew she'd be putting in plenty of time holding him together when she *did* get here.

Less than half an hour later, Melva slipped away while Jackson held one of her hands and Melinda held the other. Melinda cried like a baby. Jackson could only feel shock. They sat there with her long after the monitors had been turned off and the official time of death had been declared. Jackson's mind jumped around in strange memories, as if some kind of coping mechanism was trying to lure him away from the painful reality of the present moment. He thought of all the deaths he'd witnessed in his work, and how much conversation there had been over establishing an official time of death. In most cases, he had been emotionally detached due to having no personal connection to the deceased. He'd also lost a number of people he'd shared some kind of relationship with through the years. It was just part of the job. A person couldn't be in the Marines or the FBI without losing people. There were daily risks involved. Some of those deaths had hit him hard and had been difficult to contend with. But death had never felt like this. There was no tragedy associated with this death beyond the fact that he would have preferred having his mother live several more years. But there had been no violence, no responsible party, no criminal investigation. It was simply the hand of God that had taken his mother here and now— which made him wonder if it was God he should be angry with. But it was impossible to accurately assess how he felt about God when he was so deeply angry with himself.

When there was no reason to stay any longer, Jackson walked Melinda to her car; she was reluctant to leave him but admitted that she needed to go home and get some sleep. They hugged and agreed to meet later in the day in order to begin the gruesome task of funeral arrangements.

Jackson drove to the motel, still blanketed in shock. Dawn turned to daybreak as sunlight erupted over the east horizon, blinding him until he flipped down the visor. Parking the car, he realized that he didn't have a key to the room, but even if he did, Chas would have the deadbolt locked. He didn't want to wake her or the baby, but he certainly didn't want to sit in the parking lot. He called her cell phone while he was walking toward the door. She answered immediately, and he knew she'd been awake. A happy googling noise in the background let him know the baby was awake as well.

"Are you all right?" she asked without a hello.

"In a manner of speaking," he said. "I'm at the door. Could you open it?"

He hung up his phone as the door swung open. Her eyes showed a lack of sleep and asked the silent question that he knew he had to answer. "She's gone," he said, and the shock relented enough to allow a trickle of tears to come through. He stepped into the room and closed the door. Chas immediately wrapped him tightly in her arms, crying against his shoulder. Her tears encouraged his own, and he buried his face in her hair and wept.

"I'm so sorry," she murmured and eased out of their embrace in order to wipe his tears. "Are you okay?"

"No, I'm not okay." He slumped onto the edge of the bed. "I am so far from okay that I can't even . . ." He couldn't finish the sentence.

A happy squeal drew Jackson's attention to little Charles, who was playing on a blanket on the floor nearby. He was still in pajamas, and his spattering of dark hair looked more ridiculous than usual. Jackson rose and picked up the baby, holding him close in spite of his wiggling. The nearness of his son and the very evidence of his life soothed Jackson's aching spirit enough for him to believe that he could get beyond this. Chas wrapped her arms around both of them, and he knew he had much to live for, and great incentive to come to terms with all that weighed on him.

Feeling suddenly as if his grief would burst out of him in uncontrollable torrents, Jackson gave the baby to Chas and hurried to say, "I'm going to take a quick shower and see if I can get some rest. We'll talk later."

Chas nodded, her concern evident. Jackson hurried into the bathroom, glad for the noisy fan that came on with the light switch. In the shower he cried like a baby while he let hot water run over his face. He put on some pajama pants and went straight to the bed to lie down without saying anything to his wife.

"We went to the lobby and had the free breakfast," she said. "I brought you some."

"Thanks," he said, "but I don't think I can eat right now. I just need some rest." She kissed his forehead and left him to it. He wasn't certain he could fall asleep, especially with Chas caring for the baby in the same room. But exhaustion soon lured him into blessed oblivion.

Chas did her best to keep Charles quiet while Jackson was resting, but by late morning the baby became restless and fussy, so Chas took him out in the stroller for a walk. She discovered a quaint hamburger place a block away and got herself some lunch, then she walked on toward a park that she could see up the street. The humidity was uncomfortable, as unused to it as she was, but the temperature wasn't unpleasant otherwise. Charles was asleep before they reached the park, and she found a place to sit in the shade. She'd brought a book in her bag, but had difficulty focusing. When her cell phone rang, she grabbed it quickly, not wanting to wake the baby. While she'd been hoping it was Jackson, she wasn't disappointed to hear his sister's voice.

"I tried to call Jackson," she said, "but it went straight to voice mail."

"He's taking a nap; I assume he turned his phone off. I went for a walk so he could have some peace and quiet."

"Oh, do you think we could talk?" Melinda asked, sounding desperate.

"Of course."

"Where are you? Can I come and get you?"

Chas was surprised, assuming she'd meant a phone conversation. "I don't have the car seat for Charles, and he's asleep in his stroller, but I can tell you where to find me."

"That would be great."

Chas told her she was at the park with the gazebo, and Melinda knew exactly where she meant. Less than five minutes after hanging up, Melinda pulled up in a white SUV and crossed the lawn. They hugged tightly, and Melinda started to cry. They sat down together on a bench and Chas handed her a tissue from the diaper bag. Chas encouraged her to talk through her grief, and she admitted that she was grateful to have someone who would listen. They agreed that Jackson wasn't prone to wanting to talk and analyze his feelings over the situation. Since Chas was an only child, and Melinda only had a brother, it wasn't the first time that they'd expressed gratitude for now being sisters. They had very little in common beyond their actual love for Jackson and his mother, but now they were sharing grief. Melinda had a daughter who was married with children and lived nearby, but she was working at the moment. Melinda's son was in the Army Reserves and was currently away on a military training assignment. Melinda admitted to feeling lost. She'd devoted years to caring for her mother and doing practically everything with her and for her. While Melinda had known of Melva's illness and had been more prepared than Jackson, she still felt the shock and was completely disoriented. Chas encouraged her to take it one day a time and just worry about getting through the funeral. When that was done, they would talk about where to go from there.

When Chas's cell phone rang, she wasn't surprised to hear Jackson's voice. "Where are you?"

"I'm at the park with your sister. Charles is asleep in the stroller. Did you get some sleep?"

"I did, thank you. I'll be there in a few minutes."

"It's the park with the—"

"There's only one park, Chas," he said wryly and hung up.

Charles was waking up when his father arrived. Chas kissed Jackson and commented, "You look terrible."

"Good to see you too," he said, but he almost smiled. Then he greeted his sister.

"Did you get something to eat?" Chas asked as he bent down to greet his son and take him out of the stroller.

"No, but I'm okay."

"Why don't we all just go to my house and I'll fix you a sandwich or something," Melinda said. "We have a lot we need to talk about, anyway."

"I think that's a good idea," Chas said when Jackson didn't say anything at all.

"Just follow me," Melinda said and went to her car.

Jackson buckled Charles into his car seat while Chas put the stroller in the vehicle. While they followed Melinda, Chas said, "I know you're the strong, silent type, Jackson, but it would be nice to have you say something."

"I don't know what to say."

"How about one sentence that begins with 'I feel.'"

"I feel angry, confused, and overcome with guilt. How's that for being psychologically honest?"

"Very good," she said with the same mild sarcasm. "Now, why?"

"That will have to wait."

"Why?" she asked, and he stopped the car.

"Because we're here."

Chas turned to see Melinda's SUV disappearing into the garage of a nice brick home that looked fairly new. "This *is* a small town," she said.

"Not as small as it used to be. But Melinda just happens to live near the park. See, I'm talking."

They found Melinda's home to be comfortable and elegant, albeit decorated a bit garishly. But it suited Melinda's personality perfectly. She guided them past the little front room, through a spacious kitchen area, and into a large living area that looked more lived in than the other rooms. Jackson's eye went immediately to the recliner situated in front of the TV, with a little table that held much evidence that his mother had spent many hours in that chair. He nudged Chas with his elbow and whispered, "Like Granny."

Chas turned to see what he meant and almost stopped breathing. How clearly she remembered her grandmother's comfortable chair where she had everything she could possibly need within easy reach. Chas still missed her, and seeing this place where Jackson's mother had obviously spent much of her time, Chas missed them both and was brought to tears. One look at the expression on Jackson's face heightened her sorrow.

The mood lightened somewhat while Melinda fixed Jackson a sandwich and talked almost nonstop about her business and her kids and grandkids. She fussed sweetly over little Charles and said—not for the first time—what a grand thing it was for her to finally be an aunt. And she promised to spoil him. By the time Jackson was finished eating, Melinda had merged into tender reminiscences of their mother. The positive memories were good, but they naturally slipped into the present reality, and she started to cry. Jackson moved to her side on the sofa and put his arm around her.

"I know," he muttered. "I miss her too, but it's going to be hardest for you. You were taking care of her every day. I'm worried about you."

"Oh, I'll be all right," Melinda insisted, but she didn't sound convinced.

After letting his sister have a good cry, Jackson said, "I hate to face it, but we've got a funeral to plan."

"I don't even know where to begin, or what to do," Melinda admitted. "The only death I've ever dealt with was Dad's. We just did a simple graveside service; the mortuary took care of most everything. But if I dare say it out loud, I think Mama deserves better than what he got."

"Oh, you can say that out loud," Jackson said a little too zealously.

"Okay," Melinda said, "but I don't know where to start. We have an appointment with the mortuary tomorrow morning at ten, but that won't really cover an actual service, will it."

"The funeral for Chas's grandmother was lovely," Jackson said. "Perfect, in my opinion."

"It *was* lovely," Chas agreed.

"You both know Mama never went to church; neither did I. But she believed in God. She prayed all the time, more after Dad died and she knew he wouldn't catch her at it and get angry. I think Mama should have a religious funeral; she'd want that."

Chas looked up to investigate a sudden silence and found both Jackson and Melinda staring at her. "What?" she asked.

"We want a religious funeral," Jackson said. "You're the only one here who has any *real* understanding of religion."

"Okay," Chas said, sensing a great opportunity before her, but not certain of the best approach to take. She felt it was important to point out, "I only know my own religion."

"It's Christian, isn't it?" Melinda asked.

"Yes, of course. But some people don't necessarily agree with or like the way Mormons believe."

"Granny wasn't a Mormon," Jackson said. "Her funeral was lovely. Can't we do something like that?"

"I . . . uh . . . I'm sure I could track down a local bishop and see what we can do."

"Oh, would you?" Melinda pleaded.

Jackson offered a barely noticeable smile with eyes that echoed his sister's plea.

"I'll see what I can do," Chas said, and Jackson watched the baby while she started searching in the phonebook and on the Internet for some contact information. After making a series of phone calls, she finally spoke to the wife of the local bishop. The ward covered a few small towns in the area, and the bishop actually lived about ten miles away in a neighboring community. Half an hour later, the bishop called Chas from the cell phone he carried with him while he oversaw a large chicken farm. She explained the situation and asked if he might be able to help. She emphasized that it might be a great opportunity to serve and share their beliefs of eternity, but stressed that they should be careful to keep the service simple and focus the teachings in a way that could relate to all Christians who might attend.

"Oh, I live here," he said kindly, but with a chuckle. "You don't have to tell me about being careful over such things. I'm certain we can handle it." He took down Melinda's address and all of the contact information and said that he would come by at six o'clock with one of his counselors to meet with the family. When Chas reported the conversation to Jackson and Melinda, they were both very pleased.

During the remainder of the day, Chas sensed that Jackson was struggling far more than he was letting on. His demeanor reminded her of the time following their first meeting, when they'd just been getting to know each other. He'd been dealing with grief then, as well. But he'd also been dealing with a great deal of anger. He'd lost a member of his team in a shooting incident, which had led to the suicide of another member of his team, the man responsible for selling out the FBI to drug dealers. Jackson had felt betrayed, confused, and angry. And it was evident to Chas that he felt that way now. He was managing to make polite conversation with his sister while they traversed between sharing memories and the reality of their mother's demise. But Chas began to feel frustrated, wanting to be alone with her husband if only to insist that he say what he was *really* feeling. As it was, she knew he'd never open up completely with Melinda in the room.

They all shared a simple supper, which Jackson didn't eat much of since he'd eaten lunch so late, and there were moments when it didn't seem at all like there had been a death in the family. Then a reminder of Melva's passing would occur, and Melinda would dissolve into tears. Jackson was full of comfort and reassurance for his sister, but Chas sensed something deeper bothering him, something more than just the loss of his mother. She realized they'd not had a minute to talk since the death had occurred, and she wondered how long it might be until they could have an hour alone.

The meeting with the bishop and his counselor went very well, and before they left, the Relief Society presidency came by to see what they could do to help. Melinda was both surprised and impressed; Jackson was just impressed. He'd gotten used to the way Mormons did things. Chas just hoped that eventually he would be impressed enough to embrace what was most precious to her.

Once the visitors had all gone, they wrote an obituary, and put together a rough draft of the funeral program. Then Jackson and Chas finally returned to their motel room. Charles fell asleep during the short drive, and they put him directly into the crib.

While Jackson was in the bathroom, Chas changed into her nightgown and climbed into bed, leaning against the headboard. When Jackson sat on the edge of the bed to take off his shoes, Chas said, "It's later, and we're finally alone. Talk to me."

Jackson's sigh filled the room. "I appreciate your efforts, Chas; I really do. You're always there for me in every possible way, and there is no way to express my gratitude for that, but . . . I honestly . . . don't have anything to say."

"Your mother died this morning, Jackson."

"Yes, my mother died." He heard the anger in his own voice and forced it down, if only to avoid sounding like a hypocrite. "But that's it; that's all there is to it." His voice broke. "She's gone, and I have trouble believing it's real, but . . . what else is there to say?"

"That's what I'm waiting to hear," she said with perfect confidence. "You said you felt confused and angry and overcome with guilt. So, obviously there's more to it than you're telling me. I know there's something else, something besides the fact that you lost your mother. I won't dispute that losing her is plenty of reason to be upset and grieving, but there's something else bothering you, and the longer you avoid telling me about it, the harder it's going to be."

He glared at her, and she added, "You're giving me that look."

"What look?"

"That . . . you'd rather be getting a root canal than answering my question."

"You're as sharp as your grandmother," he said, but he didn't sound happy about it.

"I'll take that as a compliment."

"And you're sassy like her, too."

"If not for my being sharp and sassy, you'd still be in the FBI, wallowing your life away, completely alone in an apartment in Virginia."

"Yes, I probably would. But I still don't want to talk about it right now."

"Married couples are not supposed to go to bed with unspoken feelings. Is it coming back here that's bothering you? Is that it?" Chas watched her husband turn abruptly to look the other way, and his face tightened. She'd hit on the truth, but not all of the truth. "What else?"

"She asked me to forgive him," he said so abruptly that Chas was startled. It took her a moment to digest what he meant.

"Your father? Your mother asked you to forgive your father?"

"That's right," he said, sounding angry again. "As far as I see it, most of his behavior was unforgivable, but my mother—on her deathbed—made me promise to forgive him." He turned to look at her, and she realized he was even angrier than he was letting on. "Tell me how I'm supposed to live with that."

"I guess you're going to have to find a way to forgive him." Chas saw his anger intensify, but she wasn't afraid to tell him what he needed to hear. "He's dead, Jackson. Holding on to these feelings will not hurt him. It will only hurt—"

"Me, I know," he said snidely.

"I was going to say the people you love."

He straightened his shoulders, and his jaw tightened. "How do you figure?"

"It's a well-known fact, Jackson. You're not so ignorant of basic psychology that you don't know that." She took his hand to soften the blow, knowing he already had plenty to think about. "But for now," she added, "I think you just need to deal with grieving over your mother's death. Let's take on one issue at a time, okay?"

Jackson liked that idea, mostly because he couldn't even comprehend taking on the grief, let alone anything else. He was glad for Chas's permission to push away his feelings toward his father, but doing so urged his grief to the surface, and he felt the threat of tears. She noticed before he could even think of holding them back. She eased closer and wrapped her arms around him. "It's okay," she said gently. "You go ahead and cry; you need to cry."

With that, the full depth of his sorrow broke loose. He dropped his head into Chas's lap and cried like a baby. She held him close and cried with him, and he fell asleep as keenly aware of her love for him as he was of his grief.

* * * * *

Chas came awake to a loud thud and found her heart pounding as a result. She listened for a long moment and heard nothing, then she reached for Jackson through the darkness and didn't find him there. Then she heard him moan in a way that was typical during his nightmares, which were ongoing manifestations of his PTSD. She turned on the lamp and was stunned to find her husband on the floor on the other side of the bed, almost curled into the fetal position, his arms up over his head. His moaning increased, as if the light being on in the room had encouraged his fear. She knelt beside him and put a hand on his arm, startled by the way he retracted from her touch and started speaking in another language. She couldn't understand what he was saying, but she perceived the tone of voice clearly. He was begging. She felt a new level of sickness and horror as she considered what would cause a grown man—an ex-Marine, a man trained and prepared for the worst of circumstances—to be reduced to such behavior. And here before her was the evidence that it had been so traumatic that almost two years after the fact, the trauma still felt fresh to him.

Chas wanted to dissolve into childlike sobbing on his behalf. But she put her own emotions on hold and took hold of him firmly. She said his name loudly enough that she was amazed the baby remained asleep. But Jackson only retracted further and repeated the same words more vehemently. She did it again, holding firmly to him. This third time, he gasped, and his eyes came open. Through his labored breathing she saw him cautiously take in his surroundings and the evidence that he was on the floor and she was there with him. Chas heard her own shallow breathing the same moment he fully focused on her, as if he'd noticed it too. He groaned and cursed, and then he started to shake, as if the reality of the situation left him terrified. Chas noted that the baby was breathing evenly, and she prayed that he would remain asleep until the drama settled. Jackson clutched onto her and put his head in her lap, but his shaking increased. Chas was so stunned that she could only sit there and hold onto him equally tightly. Now that he was awake and the worst of the drama was over, the scene played over and over in her mind, connecting to the logical possibilities of what exactly had happened to him to cause such horrors now. Chas knew bits and pieces, and her imagination had filled in the gaps far more than she'd ever wanted to think about. His insistence on avoiding details was something she appreciated, except that she'd often wondered if her imaginings were worse. What she had just seen gave her a harsh glimpse into how it might have been. It wasn't difficult to connect it to what she already knew, but actually seeing the evidence was shocking. She'd accompanied him out of nightmares before. She'd seen him shaking and heard him express his fears and concerns. She'd heard him call himself broken and completely damaged. But only now did all of those dots connect into a reality that she could hardly comprehend. And what was it exactly that had dredged it to the surface? His mother's death? Or his promise to forgive his father?

Chas didn't realize her silent tears had evolved into sobbing until she heard Jackson say, "It's okay, Chas. I'm sorry."

"You have nothing to apologize for."

"I'm still sorry. I never wanted to pull you into this part of my life."

"When I fell in love with you, it wasn't just a part of your life."

"But it was when you married me."

"We're not going there again, Jackson," she said and took hold of her own composure, knowing she needed to be strong for him right now. They could discuss her own difficult feelings another time. He clutched onto her more tightly, making her aware that his shaking hadn't lessened. "Let's get you back into bed," she muttered gently, urging him to his feet.

He leaned on her until he slipped between the covers, pulling them over himself as if he were freezing. Before Chas could get to her side of the bed, he asked like a frightened child, "Can we leave the light on?"

"Of course," she said and eased close to him, urging his head to her shoulder. She wrapped her arms around him and pressed a kiss to his brow. "It's okay," she whispered and pressed her fingers gently over his face repeatedly. She knew from past experience that the combination of her nearness, her touch, and her voice would bring him most quickly back to reality and away from the memories tied to his nightmares.

He took hold of her and held her closer, muttering near her face, "I don't know how I could get through this without you. I don't know where I would be. Yes, I do. If I'd actually survived this long, I would be suicidal; *drunk* and suicidal."

"For that and a thousand other reasons, I'm glad we're together," she said and kissed him.

He looked into her eyes. "I hate to burden you with this . . . but . . ." his voice cracked, "I'm so grateful you're here."

She put her fingers over his lips. "It is not a burden," she said and replaced her fingers with her lips. She'd learned long ago that her simple expressions of affection were a calming distraction for him. She kissed him again and again, and noticed that his shaking was beginning to settle. It was a long while before he finally became still, and even longer before he slept. Only then did Chas ease away from him and go into the bathroom where she could vent her own emotion. She slid to the floor and pressed a hand over her mouth to muffle what came close to hysterical sobbing. She recalled clearly the weeks that Jackson had been missing in a third-world country, and how full of fear she had been. She'd seen his deplorable condition while he'd been in a hospital following the event, and in the time since, she'd gathered up many hints and clues regarding what he'd suffered. But only now did she feel as if she had any comprehension of what he'd really been through. It felt like the difference between seeing a violent act on a television drama, and actually witnessing it in real life.

Sounds of the baby waking up broke into her shock, and she forced herself to calm down before she hurried to get him, hoping he wouldn't wake Jackson. She changed the baby's diaper, then took him to bed with her so that she could nurse him. She was barely situated when Jackson touched her face.

"I was hoping we wouldn't wake you."

"I wasn't asleep," he said, and she wondered if that meant he'd known she'd been in the bathroom crying. "Why would I want to sleep . . . ever?" Chas didn't know what to say. She could only focus on her attempts to keep from crying again. "Are you okay?" he asked, but she didn't answer, knowing it would give her away. "Why were you in the bathroom crying?"

"I thought you were asleep."

"So, you're keeping secrets from me?" he asked, almost sounding playful.

"I didn't want to upset you."

"I think we're way beyond that. But it was just a nightmare, Chas."

"It was not just a nightmare." She sniffled loudly. "I had no idea how bad it was. I never imagined . . ."

"I don't want you to imagine it, Chas."

"I don't have to." Her voice betrayed the depth of her sadness. "I've seen it now, or at least I've seen what it was like for you."

Jackson leaned onto one elbow, his heart pounding. "What did I do?"

Chas only wondered for a moment if she should tell him. She was sick to death of having this be something they didn't talk about. "You were talking; no . . . pleading."

Jackson's pounding heart quickened further. "What did I say?"

"It was in another language; Spanish, I think."

"Then how do you know I was pleading?" he asked as if he'd like to discredit what she'd said.

"The tone of voice was evident. I didn't know you spoke Spanish." He said nothing, and she added, "I'm tired of the things you don't tell me."

"I speak Spanish," he said blandly.

"And when you were being held prisoner by sadistic drug lords, what exactly were you pleading for . . . in Spanish?"

Jackson looked at his wife's worried face and wondered if a man had ever felt so humiliated and degraded. He rolled onto his back and sighed before attempting to lighten the mood of the conversation. "It's a good thing you're okay with having a husband who is the complete opposite of macho and masculine."

"I completely disagree with that statement." Her voice was brittle. "The fact that you have survived such an ordeal enough to function normally in the real world exhibits more strength and courage than most men could imagine possessing."

"Well, it doesn't feel that way."

"Tell me how it feels," she urged gently.

Jackson didn't want to talk about it. He felt sick just to think of what little she'd figured out about the incident. He reminded himself that he'd been taught through much grueling counseling that being honest about his feelings with a woman he could trust did not necessarily equate with sharing abhorrent details that might poison her mind the way his had been poisoned.

He blew out a long, slow breath and put a hand over his eyes, as if doing so might help buffer the truth. "It feels like . . . a monster that's going to devour me from the inside. It feels like the monster is only growing bigger and more powerful."

"Then we need to find a way to conquer the monster."

He moved his hand and looked at her. "What if that's not possible?"

"Then we will find a way to at least tame it." She reached across the baby, who was now sleeping, and took his hand. "We're in this together, Jackson."

He could never tell her how grateful he was to know that, but at the same time he hated the way this had affected her life. Every time he was assaulted with a traumatic flashback, he couldn't help thinking that she deserved better than this. Still, he admired her commitment and devotion, and he thanked God every day that she had chosen to spend the rest of her life with him.

Since little Charles had fallen back to sleep and there didn't seem to be anything else to say, Jackson carefully picked up his son and carried him back to the crib on the other side of the motel room. He patted his little back and kissed the top of his head before he laid him down and covered him. For a full minute he just watched his son sleep, soaking up the calming effect it had on him, then he went back to bed and tried without success to go back to sleep, but maybe that was partly due to the fact that he couldn't bring himself to turn out the light.

# Chapter Three

Jackson got out of bed at dawn without ever having gone back to sleep. He went out for his habitual, early morning run, glad for the way that pushing himself physically helped push away the memories of his nightmares and the reality of his mother's death. While his feet hit the pavement in a steady rhythm, the scene of his mother's death pounded through his mind with two facts standing out strongly, over and over: she was dead, and he had promised her that he'd forgive his father. Grief, anger, and fear roiled inside of him until it finally bubbled out and he was glad to be on a deserted tree-lined street when he put his hands on his thighs and lowered his head to sob until his chest began to burn and his head felt like it would explode. He was finally able to continue running, but he cried as he did and only managed to get his emotion under control a few minutes before he returned to the motel room, where he found Chas bathing Charles. He was grateful for the kiss from his wife and the distraction of his son as he took over the duty of washing and rinsing the baby's wispy dark hair. He lifted him out of the tub and wrapped him in a fluffy towel, quickly getting in a hug before the baby's wiggling got out of control.

"You okay?" Chas asked when she took the baby to get him dressed.

"I'm managing," he said. "And just so you don't think I'm holding my grief inside, I'll admit that I had a good, hard cry while I was out."

"Good," she said as if he'd told her he'd finally gotten a dentist appointment for the sake of dealing with an abscessed tooth. "Your sister called. We're meeting her at the mortuary at ten. She said you would know where it's at. Why don't you get a shower and we'll take advantage of that free breakfast in the lobby."

"Okay," he said and took hold of her arm. "Are you all right?"

"I think I'm better than you are."

"I'm fine," he insisted. In response to her harsh glare, he corrected himself. "I'm as fine as could be expected under the circumstances, but . . . what happened last night was hard for you . . . and you love my mother too."

"Yes," she said, and tears brimmed in her eyes, "but I also had a good, hard cry while you were out." She reached up to kiss him, still holding the baby in her arms. "We'll get through this together, one step at a time. Right now we're going to get through the funeral and help your sister settle your mother's affairs."

"Okay," he said again and went into the bathroom. Once he was in the shower, he cried again and managed to get it out of his system enough to put on a normal face for breakfast and the meeting at the mortuary. He was grateful for both Chas and his sister being able to think clearly and make firm decisions on the casket, the flowers, and the design of the funeral program. All he had to do was nod and agree, and only once did he actually offer an opinion: he suggested that the casket spray include a variety of colors and types of flowers, since his mother had seemed to find beauty in everything, as opposed to having particular favorites. He said nothing at all to express his strong dismay over the fact that his mother would be buried in the grave next to his father, and they would share the headstone that had been purchased at the time of his father's death. He reminded himself that they were both dead, and their final resting place had no bearing on anything that had happened while they'd been alive. But he still didn't like it.

Jackson felt so tired and drained of strength that it took conscious effort not to doze off while the women were going over details that held no interest for him. He was glad to be able to take Charles to the lobby and play with him, which not only kept Jackson awake, but it also made him smile. How grateful he was for his precious son! The child was living evidence that love could change lives, and that miracles were possible. His very presence offered perspective to Jackson in the face of his daily struggles. His stomach knotted up to think of how those ongoing challenges had escalated since his sister had called him two days earlier. Prior to that, beyond his occasional episode related to his

PTSD, life had been pretty uneventful, filled mostly with daily joy and fulfillment. Now he knew that this disorder that plagued him hadn't yet begun to truly rear its ugly head—or at least it hadn't until last night. Now it had exploded into something worse than he'd ever encountered. He'd dealt with many nightmares, and afterward it wasn't uncommon for him to shake or feel a little panicked for reasons that seemed to make no sense. But what happened last night had truly frightened him. And perhaps worse, it had frightened his wife. He'd rarely if ever seen her so upset. And nothing was harder for him than to see how his own problems affected her. But still, all of this felt secondary to the reality that his mother was gone, and his grief was all tied up in knots of confusion and guilt. The matter of keeping his promise to her was something he couldn't even look at yet. He clung to Chas's advice to take one step at a time and get through the funeral first.

Jackson was distracted from his thoughts by the need to change a diaper. Then the women found him, and Chas declared that they were finished with the funeral plans. They went out to lunch, then to Melinda's home, where she got out a couple of boxes that weren't very big.

"Mama and I spent lots of time going through her things when we sold the house and moved her here. I'm sure it wouldn't surprise you to hear that she didn't have much of value."

"No, that wouldn't surprise me," Jackson said, sitting in his mother's recliner. He liked to think of her sitting in it, but he didn't like thinking of how he never actually saw her do it.

Melinda put the boxes on the floor and sat there to open one. "In the years since she's been here with me, she's been able to get herself some nicer things, but she told me many times that her clothes and stuff weren't going to mean anything to her kids. She had me help her fix these boxes; one for each of us." She glanced quickly through the contents of one of the boxes, then put the lid back on and put it on Jackson's lap. "This one's yours."

"What is it?" Jackson asked cautiously, as if it might blow up in his face.

"Just some odds and ends; keepsakes and stuff."

Rather than opening the box, Jackson put both hands flat on top of it, as if that might keep its contents subdued.

"Aren't you going to look at it?" Melinda asked.

"Later," he said and set the box aside, thinking he'd rather not be in his sister's presence when he faced its contents. He wasn't certain how he might be affected by stirring up *any* memories from his childhood.

Melinda looked like she wanted to protest, but she didn't. Instead, she started talking about their mother's medical costs, insurance, and finances. Jackson listened with half an ear, fixated more on trying to accept the reality that such a conversation was necessary. His mother really was dead.

With a tone of conclusion that caught his attention, Melinda said, "I'm sure it will take a little time to do everything with the bank and stuff, but as soon as I get it all figured out, I'll send you a check."

"A check for what?" Jackson asked, his voice hovering between fear and anger.

Melinda looked astonished that he wouldn't know. "Your inheritance, of course."

"Inheritance?" he echoed with a brisk chuckle.

"It's not a dirty word, Jackson," Melinda said, sounding insulted. "I should think you'd be well aware that Mama had a very nice nest egg put away and she wanted us to have—"

"I did not know any such thing, but I do not want or need my mother's money. *You* should have it. You're the one who's been taking care of her all these years."

"You made your contributions."

"Sending money here and there doesn't begin to compare to the actual care you have given her. And I know you paid for a lot of the things she needed, and the travel she did, and the—"

"I didn't pay for nearly as much as you might think. She had her own money, and she insisted on paying for her own needs most of the time."

Recalling the poverty of his youth, Jackson had to ask, "Where exactly did she acquire so much money?"

"From selling the house, of course. Well," she chuckled, "the house wasn't worth much, but the property brought a pretty penny, what with inflation and all. And it was a big piece of land. It was old Burt Hafen that bought it and built those apartments. He's made a pretty living from the rent. And Mama's had a good time spending the money she got from the land. She put some of it in some pretty sound investments. There's a fair chunk left, and she wanted us to split it equally once everything was paid for. There'll be a few medical bills after the insurance does its part, and the funeral expenses, of course. But she had some life insurance, too, and it's a good policy. We got that right after Papa died, about the same time we sold the house. So, that'll more than cover the burial stuff, and—"

"Melinda," he interrupted. "You're rambling. I get the idea. I'm glad to know everything's taken care of, and I'm glad to know that caring for her has not been a burden for you, at least not financially—"

"Taking care of Mama was never a burden, *at all!*" Her eyes flickered with mild anger.

"I didn't mean to imply that it was. There's still no disputing that you've done a great deal for her that hasn't been easy. I don't want or need the money, Melinda. I want you to keep it."

"I don't want or need it either. But I'm not taking *your* share. I'm certain you could find something worthwhile to do with it that Mama would be pleased with. Don't make this difficult. I'll send you a check when everything is settled. There. That's the end of this conversation. Let's talk about something else."

"I'd like to see where you grew up," Chas said, and Jackson glared at her. He didn't like the change of subject at all.

"As you just heard," he said, "the house has been leveled. There are apartments there now."

"Okay, but I can still see where it is, right?"

"That's a great idea," Melinda said and stood up as if she'd had a sudden attack of nerves and had to move. "Let's go for a drive, and then we'll go to Curly's for supper."

"Who's Curly?" Chas asked.

"It's a restaurant," Jackson explained. "In spite of the name, it's actually pretty decent—at least it used to be. I can't believe the place is still in business."

"Three generations," Melinda declared. "And with food that good, why would they go out of business?"

Following the short drive to the restaurant—during which Jackson completely avoided going to see where he'd grown up—he commented as they were walking inside, "It's not much for atmosphere, but . . ." He let the sentence fade into the delicious aroma of quality cooking.

Dinner was relatively pleasant except for a brief encounter with an older gentleman who passed by the table and stopped to speak to Melinda. He looked vaguely familiar to Jackson as he told Melinda he'd heard of her mother's passing and offered his condolences. The old man was typical of the kind of people among whom Jackson had grown up. He was uneducated and unrefined; stereotypical backwoods redneck farmer. Jackson didn't feel any prejudice or judgment in his assessment. He just hated the memories triggered by the encounter, especially because his father had been exactly this type of person. He was every-thing that Jackson had fought to *not* become. He'd left home at the first opportunity, trained away his Southern drawl, and worked his way into a world that was far from this one—both literally and metaphorically.

Jackson was wishing this man would move on and leave them to their supper when Melinda said, "I'm sure you remember my brother, Jackson." The man turned to him with raised eyebrows, clearly not recognizing him by his appearance. Melinda added, "Jackson, this is Mr. Denny. He lived down the street when we were growing up."

Jackson came to his feet and forced a polite smile and handshake. "Of course," he said, even though his memory of this man was only a vague glimmer.

"You've changed, boy," Mr. Denny said with a smile, and Jackson cringed at being called "boy." It was exactly how his father had said it.

"I'm much, much older," Jackson said, proud of himself for sounding completely light and nonchalant. He figured his years of undercover assignments in the FBI had made him a tolerably good actor.

Jackson was hoping this would end soon—and without drama—when Mr. Denny said, "And ya look just like yer pa."

Jackson turned his head to cough, then managed to say evenly, "It's good to see you again, Mr. Denny. If you'll excuse me. My phone is vibrating and I need to get this call."

Jackson hurried from the restaurant, playing up the lie about his phone by pulling it out of his pocket and putting it to his ear on the way out. Once alone in the shadows around the corner of the building, he leaned against the brick wall and lowered his head, almost hyper-ventilating. Did he really? Did he look like his father? The thought made him sick. Once his breathing became more steady, he reminded himself that he didn't look any different now than he had a few minutes ago. Mr. Denny's comment didn't change who he was or how far he'd come. But it did prick a sensitive nerve that had become more so since his mother's death—or rather, since his deathbed promise to her. He drew back farther into the shadows when he saw Mr. Denny walking toward the parking lot, then he took a deep breath, gathered his composure, and went back in to join his family.

"Are you all right?" Chas asked when he sat down.

"Of course," he said nonchalantly.

"Who called?"

"It's not important," he said, and they finished their meal.

After they'd taken Melinda home and returned to their motel room, Chas said, "You didn't get a phone call, did you."

He felt startled but couldn't see any point in avoiding the truth. "No."

"So, you lied."

"Yes, are you disappointed in me?" Before she could answer, he added, "I thought lying would be preferable to yelling at the man, or having an emotional breakdown in the middle of the restaurant."

"Was it really that bad?" she asked with perfect concern while she changed Charles and put him into his pajamas.

"Was *what* that bad?"

"Being told that you look like your father?" He shot her a sharp glance, and she added, "That *was* the problem, wasn't it?"

"That was part of it," he admitted.

"And the other part?"

"The man reminded me of my father; same type. My dad talked that way, dressed that way, behaved that way. Although, I don't think Mr. Denny was a drunk who beat his kids."

"Not likely."

"My reaction wasn't any personal affront to Mr. Denny, Chas. I just . . . don't like being in this town. I don't like the people. I'm sure that most of them are good and decent. But it all reminds me too much of a time in my life that I've worked very hard to forget."

"Okay, but . . ."

"But what?"

Chas sat down to feed the baby and said with hesitance, "I know you're not in a very good mood. Maybe this is something better left for another day."

"You tell me what you were going to say, and I'll let you know if we need to save it for another day."

"Okay. Fair enough. I just wonder if there's a difference in leaving the past behind and trying to hide from it."

His voice was brittle as he said, "I think you need to clarify that."

"It's perfectly understandable that you wanted—and needed—to move away and make a better life for yourself. And you've done that. But I'm not sure that hiding from the memories is going to help you deal with them. You wouldn't even look in the box Melinda gave you. Most people would have been eager to reminisce with a sibling under such circumstances. I just wonder how you can forgive your father if you don't even look at the portion of your life you spent with him and face it."

Jackson resisted the temptation to throw out a response that was defensive and angry. He took a deep breath and allowed her words to sink in enough to decide whether they were valid, and he couldn't deny that they were. He blew out a slow breath and said, "Maybe you're right, but . . . I don't know what to do about it. Looking at it just feels too . . . hard; too ugly."

"Okay, I'm not suggesting that you have to engage in some deep emotional excavation at the same time you're dealing with your mother's death, but while you're here, maybe you should put just a little bit of effort into facing some of your memories. When the funeral is over, we'll go home and you'll have some distance to sort things out. Tomorrow let's just . . . go for a little drive. I'd like to see these apartments that are where your home used to be, and—"

"It was a house; I refute that it was a home."

"Okay, but it's still where you lived for the first eighteen years of your life, and I'd like to see it. And where you went to school, as well. We need to help Melinda with some things for the funeral, and she asked that you help her look over some papers. But surely we've got time for a little drive."

Jackson sighed and realized he couldn't protest without sounding even more dysfunctional than he felt. "Okay, I guess I can live with that."

"Good." She smiled. "I'll look forward to it."

Once Charles was asleep for the night in his crib, Jackson looked up from the magazine he was looking at to see Chas set the box

Melinda had given him in the center of the bed. "Come on, let's see what's inside," she said as if it were a Christmas gift.

Jackson did *not* want to explore the contents of the box any more than he wanted to go to the dentist, but he didn't want to make any more of an issue of it than he already had. "Go for it," he said and turned his attention back to the magazine.

He heard the lid come off just before Chas said, "Oh," as if she were looking at a new puppy. He glanced over to see her lift out a pair of very old, very faded baby shoes. "Yours, apparently," she said.

"I can't say that I ever remember wearing them," he said, and she chuckled.

Again he pretended to be reading the magazine but couldn't help glancing at her when she said, "Oh, that's so sweet." Now she was holding a silly baby toy that looked a thousand years old and was broken.

"How is that sweet?"

"It was yours," she said. "Clearly, it was sweet for your mother. I'm sure it held sweet memories for her."

"Maybe. But it obviously has no sentimental value for me."

"What about this?" she asked and held up a picture drawn in crayon with his name written in barely legible block letters.

"This is silly, Chas. If you . . ." He stopped when she lifted a black-and-white photograph out of the box. She took a long, hard look at it while he felt his heart rate increasing. She turned it so he could see it, and he felt something akin to coming out of his PTSD nightmares, with memories making his vital signs stretch toward dangerous levels. It was a picture of him as a child in front of the run-down house where he'd grown up. All he could say was, "Please put it back."

"Why?" she asked. "It's just a—"

"I'm terrified to go to sleep as it is," he said, wishing it hadn't sounded so sharp. "I don't need to start dredging up more horrible memories right *now.*"

Chas looked astonished, then concerned. She put the things back and closed the box before she put it into one of the empty motel room drawers. "I'm sorry," she said. "I wasn't thinking."

"It's okay," he said and went back to pretending to look at the magazine while he willed his heart to slow down.

"Why?" she asked, sitting beside him. "Why do memories of your childhood tie into . . ."

"The incident?" he provided, mildly caustic. "I don't know, but they do."

"Don't you think you should figure it out?"

"I probably should."

"Didn't your counselor talk about this when you were initially trying to deal with . . ."

"The incident?" he said again. "You don't have to avoid saying it, Chas. And yes, we *did* talk about it; we talked about it a lot."

"But you never got an answer?"

"Nothing beyond, 'It still may come up some day.' So, maybe I do need to figure it out, but as you so wisely pointed out, I should probably focus on getting through my mother's funeral, and having a *complete* nervous breakdown is not going to make that happen. So, let's just keep the memories where they are for now, okay?"

"Okay," she said. "But can we still go for a drive tomorrow and look at the town?"

"Maybe," he said, keeping his eyes on a magazine ad for cat food.

"Jackson," she said, moving closer. She took the magazine and set it aside, forcing him to look at her. "Are you okay?"

"Not really," he said after a minute of contemplating how honest he should be. The likelihood of him afflicting her with his nightmares in the next few hours tipped the scales toward the fact that there was no hiding his state of mind from her.

She pressed her hand to his face and asked gently, "What can I do?"

Jackson's anxiety fled at the mere thought of all that she did for him. He closed his eyes a long moment and turned to press a kiss to the center of her palm, at the same time putting his hand over hers. "Just being with me," he said, "is more than I deserve."

"Why do you say that?" she asked. "I love you; I want to be with you. It's no sacrifice on my part."

"So you keep telling me," he said. "But it seems to me that just sleeping in the same bed with me is a sacrifice. It certainly doesn't make for a good night's sleep."

"You would do the same for me," she said and kissed him.

"Yes, I would," he said, "but it's a ridiculous comparison, under the circumstances."

Chas decided a distraction from the topic would be the best course. This was a pointless discussion that they'd had more times than she could count. There was nothing to say that hadn't already been said, and no solution beyond the hope that eventually he could find a way to fully face what was going on inside of him and find peace. But they both knew that some people never fully recovered from PTSD. The problem could be a lifetime commitment, but since her hope was that they would be together far beyond this life, she could live with that.

"Hey," she said, smiling at him, "remember the first day you spent at the inn?"

"I remember."

"You went out and shoveled snow because the snow guy was late."

"No, I shoveled snow because I'd only known you a matter of hours and you were making me crazy." His mood had lightened already. "It was like you'd bewitched me, or something."

She laughed softly. "And then I found you in the parlor, looking at Martin's picture."

"That's when I knew I was in trouble."

"In trouble?"

More seriously he said, "I could have passed off being attracted to you as something that would fade with time, but Martin gave us too much in common for me to believe my being there was going to be simple and uncomplicated." He touched her face. "But I never dreamed that I'd end up married to you and living there permanently."

"I'm so glad you came to stay at my inn."

"So am I," he said and kissed her. He looked at her and added, "Did you know that I wanted to kiss you that day?"

"No! Why didn't you?"

"I didn't want you to feel insulted; we'd only met the night before. But I remember standing there in the parlor talking to you and wondering what it would be like."

Chas kissed him. "Now you know."

"Yes, now I know." He kissed her again. "I love you, Chas."

"I love you too," she said and wrapped her arms around him. He held to her tightly and had to believe that he was going to get through this. If only for the sake of his wife and son, he had to get through this.

* * * * *

Since the day they'd been married, Chas had insisted on their praying together before going to sleep every night. At first he'd always been firm about her offering the prayer, since he really didn't know anything about prayer beyond what he'd heard from her. Eventually she'd talked him into taking his turn, even though she still did it much more than half of the time. He'd come to appreciate the habit for many reasons, but after what had happened the previous night, he'd never felt more grateful to hear Chas pray on his behalf. She prayed that his night would be restful and uninterrupted, and that they could find the path to healing and making peace with the past. She asked that angels would surround them through the night, and that he would feel the comfort of the Holy Ghost. He'd never believed in such things as angels before he'd met Chas; he'd never even stopped to consider whether or not he'd believed in God prior to his deep conversations with her on the subject. Now, he couldn't deny that God existed, and he *did* believe in angels. Most specifically, he had no doubt that Chas's sweet grandmother had actually been with him at moments during the most horrid event of his life. But he hadn't connected the most recent turn of events to this theory until he heard Chas pray that Jackson's mother would be with him when he needed her. After Chas had spoken the amen, Jackson turned to look at her with silent astonishment. She just smiled and touched his face, while Jackson tried to take in the fact that losing his mother to death meant that she had passed into another realm where she *could* watch over him. Without warning, he started to cry, but they were tears of peace and comfort mingled with the sorrow he felt over losing his mother. Chas urged him off his knees and into bed where she wrapped him in her arms and encouraged him to cry. His tears accompanied him into sleep, where he had some strange dreams, but he awoke to daylight without having any nightmares and found Chas sitting beside him, feeding the baby.

"You okay?" she asked as soon as she saw that he was awake.

"Yeah," he said and focused his attention on being in this little cocoon with his wife and son. Before he'd met Chas, he'd accepted life as a bachelor. He hadn't been looking to fall in love and end up married, and he'd never expected to become a father in his mid-forties. But he was grateful every minute of the day that it had happened.

After breakfast, Jackson indulged Chas's wish to see the places of his childhood. Pulling up in front of the apartments that now occupied the place where the house of his growing-up years had once stood, he was grateful that it didn't look anything like his memories, and he told her so. They drove past the schools he'd attended, but they had also changed a great deal, and his memories felt detached. It only took about an hour to see most of the town, and much of it held no meaning for Jackson one way or the other. He told her how things had changed, and he actually came up with a few good memories and funny stories from his childhood, although none of them involved his family or being at home with them. He couldn't recall anything good in that respect.

They ended up at Melinda's again, where they shared some soup she had just made. After lunch while Charles took a nap and the women were visiting, Jackson sat in his mother's recliner and listened to them chatter. He started to get sleepy and dozed off. The next thing he knew he'd come awake with a startled gasp, overcome with the same haunting images that had plagued his dreams. Taking in his surroundings, he found Chas and Melinda watching him from where they were both sitting on the couch. He'd seen that look on Chas's face many times, but Melinda's astonishment was unsettling—and embarrassing.

"Are you all right?" his sister asked as if she'd just come upon him following a car accident.

"I'm fine," he said, but it was clear that she didn't believe him.

"You don't *seem* fine," she said.

Jackson cleared his throat and forced defensiveness out of his voice. "I have PTSD, Melinda. You know that."

"Yes, but . . ." She became completely silent, clearly not knowing what to say, or how to ask. She'd obviously never thought too deeply on what exactly that entailed. Either that, or she'd assumed that with the time that had passed since it had come up, he was no longer struggling with it. She finally managed to say, "You look guilty. What have you been keeping from me?"

"Nothing worse than you not telling me that our mother was dying."

"You know why I couldn't—"

"Yes, I know why," he said crisply and stood up. "I need some air." He hurried out the back door, knowing that Chas would offer his sister an explanation that he preferred not to hear.

As soon as she heard the door close, Chas turned to meet Melinda's concerned expression; or perhaps *concerned* was too mild a description. There was no softening the evidence she'd just seen and heard that proved that Jackson had been experiencing perfect terror in his sleep.

"Does that happen often?" Melinda asked, her voice almost squeaking.

"It happens occasionally, but . . ."

"But?" Melinda demanded.

"It's never happened before with a nap . . . at least not that I've known of. Since we've been married, he's had occasional nightmares. Sometimes it wakes me up; sometimes he's pretty shaky for a long time afterward. But . . ."

"But?" Melinda repeated, more alarmed.

"The night before last, he . . ." Tears came as Chas recalled the horror of the event, and she could no longer deny how much it had upset her. "It was worse than it has ever been."

Melinda moved closer and put a comforting arm around Chas. "Tell me what happened, honey."

Chas repeated the incident, glad to be able to share her burden, but also shocked at hearing herself verbalize how bad it had been. She realized she was a great deal more scared than she'd wanted to admit. But Jackson wasn't necessarily receptive to hearing about her fears. He blamed himself for them, and it was always difficult to talk about.

Melinda got a little teary while Chas was talking. But her tears had been close to the surface since she'd lost her mother; it didn't take much to get them started. "Do you know why it happens?" Melinda asked. "Do you know what's going on in his head that would cause such nightmares?"

"He's never wanted to talk about any details. All I know for sure is that he dreams he's in a small, dark room; he's cold, he's in pain, and he's terrified. When he wakes up in the dark, he is apparently unable to separate the past from the present, and he really believes he's there. It's a flashback in his mind, quite literally. He thinks he's there. He . . ." her voice broke, "he thinks they're going to kill him."

"That's just dreadful!" Melinda said, wiping at new tears. "What can be done? Surely there's some way for him to get over this."

"That's what I want to believe. When he finished the initial counseling, he was told that he might hit difficult stages and need more intervention. He was seeing a counselor in Butte a couple of times a month, but then he just stopped going; he said it was a waste of time. And truthfully, the nightmares have happened occasionally, but it hasn't really been a problem that's affected our lives. But now . . ."

"Now, it's worse."

"I've never seen him like that," Chas admitted, hearing the fear in her own voice. "It was so . . . *horrible*. And if that's any indication of what's going on inside of his head, I think there is reason to be concerned, and something should be done. But obviously we need to get through the funeral first."

"You think Mama's death set him off?"

"I think that's part of it."

"What's the other part?" Melinda asked warily.

"Your mother asked him to forgive his father, and he's not very happy about it."

"Oh, I see," Melinda said. "Well . . . that certainly sheds some light, now doesn't it?"

"Does it?" Chas asked. She knew the issues were interconnected, but she knew very little about the reasons. She was hoping Melinda might be able to shed some light that could be helpful. But the baby started to cry in the other room, and Chas had to go and get him.

# Chapter Four

It took Jackson a few minutes to calm the mild panic induced by the bad dream that had invaded his nap. *That* had never happened before. Prior to now it had always been in the deepest part of the night when he was sleeping soundly. It took another few minutes to talk himself out of being upset over the evidence he'd unwittingly given his sister that he was losing his mind. To say that he was embarrassed would be a gross understatement. To know that the women were surely talking about him made it worse. But the idea did encourage him to get a grip and go back inside, if only to put a stop to their conversation.

Jackson stepped into the family room to see Melinda there alone, wiping at tears. That didn't mean anything. She was crying over everything these days.

"You okay?" he asked.

"I'll be fine. It's you I'm worried about."

"There's no need for that." He sat down next to her on the couch and put his arms around her. "I'm going to be fine. It's just been . . . a rough week . . . for all of us. Let's just get through this, okay?"

"Okay." She nodded stoutly.

"I'm worried about *you,*" he said, glad to draw the attention away from himself. "What are you going to do with yourself after we leave? This is going to be a big adjustment for you. Maybe you should come and stay with us for a while."

"That's very sweet," she said, "and I just might do that . . . eventually, anyway. I know that if I need you I'm always welcome."

"Yes, you are."

"Actually, I'm leaving next week to go on a cruise with a couple of friends. They've been trying to get me to go with them for years, but Mama wasn't fond of cruises. So, now we're going."

"That's great," Jackson said. "When you get back, you let me know if you're not ready to be alone yet."

"I will," she said and took his hand. "And you let me know if this problem gets any worse. Don't keep secrets from me."

That statement bristled him, and for a long moment he vacillated between ignoring his reaction, or calling her on it. He opted for the latter. "You're sounding like a hypocrite, Melinda."

"You're upset with me . . . for not telling you about Mama."

"I'm upset that I didn't know it was coming. I would have liked to have had more warning."

"She made me promise, Jackson. What was I supposed to—"

"You could have told me anyway." He felt angry but remained calm. "You should have been able to see that her request was unreasonable. I could have pretended I didn't know, but it would have given me a chance to . . ." He stopped talking to avoid crying.

"Maybe I should have told you, and maybe you should have come to see her anyway. It doesn't matter anymore. What's done is done."

"Well, that's true."

Following some strained moments of silence, Melinda said, "I don't think you were too pleased when Mr. Denny said what he did."

"What did he say?" Jackson asked, pretending nonchalance, at the same time wondering if he wasn't nearly as good an actor as he believed himself to be. He stood up if only to get some distance from her.

"He said that you look like our father." Jackson fought for a straight face but couldn't speak without betraying himself. "And then you conveniently got a phone call. I'm your sister, Jackson. Just because we don't spend a quantity of time together doesn't mean I can't tell when something sets you off."

"Either that or you've been talking to my wife."

"I *have* been talking to your wife." She sounded angry, if only a little. "And why shouldn't I? We both love you, and we're both concerned. But she didn't say *anything* about this. I'm not stupid, Jackson. You hated our father, and—"

"Still do," he clarified and sat down in his mother's recliner, a safe distance from his sister.

"Yes, it's evident that you still do. And with good reason. He was a horrible, horrible man. I'll not argue with you on that point, that's for sure. But he's been dead nigh on twelve years. You haven't seen him for . . . what? Going on thirty years?"

"Something like that," Jackson said with an edge. "But he left a deep impression."

"Yes, he had a way of doing that. And now that you're a big boy, it's time for you to let him rest in peace so you can do the same."

He turned accusing eyes toward her. "Have *you* done that?"

He was stunned by her conviction. "Yes, I have! I still don't like him, and if he was still alive I wouldn't trust him and wouldn't have any desire to see him. But I've forgiven him, which means I'm not carrying around some senseless dead horse on my back that doesn't serve any purpose. It's just a burden and a curse, and you're letting your bitter feelings toward him *kill* you."

"I have PTSD, Melinda, over an event that has *nothing* to do with our father."

"Then how would you explain your worst episode *ever* occurring right after you promised Mama that you would forgive him?"

"It also happened right after my mother died. What makes you think that one thing has anything to do with the other?"

"We *all* know the answer to that, Jackson. There's no good in pretending we don't. Do you want me to say it out loud? Or do you want to keep pretending that this horrible thing that happened to you didn't stir up all the ugliest memories from your growing up years?"

Just hearing her put it like that made Jackson begin to tremble inside. He clamped his hands onto the arms of the chair with the hope that he could keep them from shaking.

"Are you okay?" he heard Melinda say, but it sounded distant.

As if on some kind of cue, Chas entered the room, holding the baby. He realized she had probably heard the entire conversation and was trying not to intrude. He saw her hand the baby to Melinda before she knelt in front of him and took his face into her hands. He could hear himself breathing and knew that attempting to conceal from his sister what was happening would be pointless. He'd many times come out of sleep in this condition. But he'd not had it come on this way since he'd actually been in the hospital during the weeks initially following the incident. His labored breathing turned to gasping, while his mind became absorbed with mixed images of his father and sadistic drug lords. He hadn't questioned his sanity this way since he'd been released from the hospital.

"Look at me," he heard Chas say firmly. "Look at me. Focus on me."

He did as she asked, but still felt his mind torn between the past and the present. The baby started to cry, as if he sensed the unrest taking place. Jackson felt his shaking increase.

"Melinda," he heard Chas say while her eyes didn't divert from his for a moment, "would you please take the baby elsewhere for a few minutes; out in the yard, maybe."

"Of course," Melinda said, and Jackson was barely aware of her leaving the room, mostly because the sound of the baby crying grew more distant and then was gone.

"Jackson," Chas said, keeping a firm hold on his face with both hands. "Look at me; talk to me." She shook his face gently. "Talk to me. Tell me what's going on."

"I . . . I . . . don't know. I . . ."

Chas struggled to remember all she'd read about PTSD, or rather, to recall the information that was pertinent to this moment. Her mind went through descriptions of flashbacks, hallucinations, and paranoia. She prayed silently to be guided to know how to help him, now and through whatever long-term help he needed to get beyond this. She was startled by how quickly an idea came into her mind. It came more in concept than in any specific recollection of something she'd read or studied. *Distract him. Keep him fully in the present. Reassure him of your love.*

"Jackson, I'm here," she said, close to his face. "I'm here and I always will be. No one is going to hurt you. Nothing bad is going to happen. I'm here. Do you hear me?" He nodded slightly, but didn't seem convinced. She eased closer and wrapped her arms around him, but when they broke eye contact, he started shaking more. She eased back to make eye contact again, but it took some effort to get him to focus on her. Again she tried to get him to talk, to tell her what was happening, but he couldn't form even a syllable. She recalled the words that had come to her mind. *Distract him. Keep him fully in the present. Reassure him of your love.* She took his face into her hands and put her lips to his, forcing a passion into her kiss that was motivated only by desperation. For a few seconds he fought it, then she felt him start to soften. She allowed her kiss to gain fervor, kissing him in a way she'd kissed him a thousand times since they'd been married; she kissed him the way a wife should kiss her husband when they were alone together. She felt inexpressible relief at the evidence that it was working when he let go of the chair and took hold of her shoulders. She kept kissing him and eased closer. His trembling settled, his breathing became more steady, his heart rate eased.

"Everything's okay," she murmured against his lips. "I'm here. It's okay."

Jackson felt himself returning from some horrible internal place and wrapped Chas in his arms. He could hear a clock ticking and lost track of the seconds turning to minutes while he consciously pulled himself fully back to the present. "I'm okay now," he finally managed to say and pulled back to look at her.

"Are you sure?" she asked, and there was no hiding the tears trickling down her face. With both her arms wrapped around him, she had no way of trying to conceal them.

"Yeah," he said, "I'm fine. I just don't know what happened."

"Flashback apparently," she said.

"But that's never happened before; not like that."

Chas wanted to point out that obviously his feelings toward his father *did* tie into the incident, more than they'd ever realized. But she didn't want to set him off again. She sensed that he was hovering on a fine line between the past and the present, or between reality and some kind of bizarre hallucination of long-ago events.

"I'm okay now, really," he said and stood up, going briskly into the bathroom.

Jackson leaned over the basin and splashed handfuls of cold water onto his face. He turned off the water and let it drip off his face while he told himself over and over that he was *not* losing his mind. Surely if he believed it with enough strength, he could make it be the truth. He lifted his face slowly to look in the mirror, searching his own eyes as if he could find the answer there about what was going on in his mind that could cause such horrid—and embarrassing—behavior. He hated the way all of this had upset his wife, and now it was upsetting his sister. He grabbed a towel and pressed it over his face to dry it, knowing he had to face them both and that he might as well get it over with.

Chas watched Jackson leave and took a minute to compose herself. Her biggest temptation was to cry like a baby. And maybe she would—later and when she was alone. Right now she needed to help smooth this over as graciously as possible for Jackson, and reassure Melinda that everything was going to be okay. She hoped to be more convincing than she felt. She went outside and found Melinda showing Charles the pretty flowers in one corner of the yard. He was fascinated by the bright colors and was trying to grab them. They both seemed relaxed and calm until Melinda turned to look at her, then Chas saw the panic in her eyes.

"Is he okay?" she asked in a voice that wouldn't upset the baby.

"He's fine," she said. "He just had a flashback." She tried to make it sound like it happened all the time. She was glad for all the studying she'd done, which made it possible to say with some confidence, "They're not uncommon for PTSD, and once the person realizes they are in the present and not in a frightening situation, they're fine."

"But this is worse since Mama died," Melinda stated rather than asked.

"Yes," Chas answered simply, then hurried to put an end to this aspect of their conversation. "And as soon as we get through the funeral and get home, we'll take whatever steps we need to in order for him to get some help. He'll be fine, Melinda; you mustn't worry."

"*You're* worried."

"Yes, I admit that I am. But we have to keep our wits together, and we need to be supportive and loving. The last thing he needs right now is to believe that he's upset us. And I don't think we should talk about it anymore; not right now. I'm going to stay very close to him until we get home and get some help. You mustn't worry."

Melinda nodded. "Okay, I think that's wise; I think you're right." She took a deep breath. "But promise me that you'll tell me what's happening, what's going on. I need to know."

"I'll do my best," Chas said, knowing that the level on which they kept Melinda informed partly depended on what Jackson wanted. She needed to respect his wishes.

"Now," Chas added, "you said there were some papers you wanted Jackson to go through with you. I think that would be a good distraction, and it certainly needs to be done, anyway. I think I should get him home as soon as possible after the funeral."

"Yes, yes. You're right," Melinda said and handed the baby to Chas.

They went back into the house together to find Jackson casually perusing the pictures on the wall, which were mostly of Melinda's children and grandchildren. As if nothing in the world were wrong, he pointed at a picture of Brian and said, "He looks handsome in his uniform."

Melinda beamed with pride as she always did at the mention of her son. He had a good job with a local construction company, and he was in the Army Reserve.

"He must get that from you," Melinda said with equal nonchalance. "Hey, would you mind looking over some of Mama's papers with me since we're not doing anything else? They're real organized, but sometimes I just don't know what's what, especially with the life insurance."

"Sure," Jackson said, glad for a distraction—and for normalcy. He tossed an appreciative glance toward his wife, certain she was responsible for coaching Melinda on that. He hated the feeling that they were ignoring a pink elephant in the room, but not as much as he hated being drilled with questions that he couldn't answer about his mental state. Right now he just wanted to get this funeral over with and go home. He enjoyed his sister's company, but not like this. He sat down at the table and focused on the task, counting the hours until he could be on a plane back to Montana. It was probably naive to think that being home would make the problem go away, but it was a nice thought and he clung to it.

\* \* \* \* \*

The viewing was difficult for Jackson in many ways. He was still trying to cope with seeing his mother's body in a casket when people began arriving to pay their respects. There were absolutely no people there that he knew well enough to actually want to see. There were some people he remembered vaguely, but he had no warm or tender memories in regard to any of them. There were a number of people who fell into the same category as Mr. Denny, the man he'd seen at the restaurant who had reminded him so much of his father. He cringed every time someone told him he looked like his father, but Melinda stayed close by his side and graciously managed to distract such people with clever conversation. A few relatives came, most of whom Jackson didn't remember. There had never been much association with relatives in his childhood. He'd never been close to any aunts, uncles, or cousins. But now, he was surprised to actually have a few pleasant moments when some cousins expressed their love and admiration for Melva. He also heard the same from some of her friends. Apparently, she'd had quite a little group of friends here in town with whom she had met regularly to share lunch and visit.

Melinda's children were there, and Jackson was glad to see them. He'd gotten to know Brian quite well during Brian's two visits to Montana, where they'd spent quite a bit of time together. He'd only met Sasha and her family once when they'd all met at Mount Rushmore for a day. Sasha was very much like her mother, only a little more loud and flamboyant. But she was sweet and had a very nice family. Considering what her grandparents had been like, she was doing great, and he was proud of her.

Jackson was grateful to see his sweet wife hovering nearby while she cared for little Charles. Just knowing she was nearby helped sustain him more than he could ever tell her. When the event finally ended, he was glad to leave the mortuary with his little family and return to the motel room. It wasn't quite time for Charles to go down for the night, and Jackson enjoyed playing with his son and taking charge of getting him ready for bed. While Chas nursed the baby to sleep, Jackson stretched out on the bed beside her and relaxed. He was dreading the funeral tomorrow, but he was grateful for this little reprieve, where it was just him, his wife, and his son in a little peaceful cocoon. He went to sleep with the hope of getting a good night's rest and getting tomorrow over with. But he woke up in the dark, shaking and sweating and talking in Spanish. He was even more dismayed that he woke Chas up as well, then he realized that *she* had awakened *him*. The lamp was already on. He wondered what he would do without her there to bring him to his senses. It was a thought he couldn't even entertain. He was barely coherent and trying to calm down when the baby started to cry.

Jackson groaned. "Did I wake him?" Being in the same room with the baby made the situation more challenging. At home, Charles wouldn't be able to hear Jackson's nighttime fits.

"I don't know," Chas said gently. "It doesn't matter. It's close to the time he usually wakes up anyway."

Jackson glanced at the clock. Just past four. The baby *did* always wake up around this time for a feeding. Having it down to just once in the night was a great accomplishment, but he wondered how his wife could get any sleep between him *and* the baby. If their situations were reversed, he wondered how he could ever go to sleep next to someone who might wake up at any moment and terrify them both. He was glad at least that the nightmare had waited until four. Knowing he'd never be able to go back to sleep, he felt grateful that it wasn't any earlier. At least he had enough sleep to get by on without the risk of drifting off during the funeral and embarrassing himself in front of *everyone*.

Over breakfast, Jackson apologized once again to his wife for making her night difficult, and once again she assured him that she was glad to be there for him and that she loved him. She behaved as if she was not at all worried, but he knew she was just being brave. She was probably more scared than he was of how out of control this could get. And that was pretty scared. As they were leaving the motel room, he asked her to nudge him if he started to doze off, with the threat that if he had a panic attack during the funeral because he'd drifted off to sleep, it would be her fault, and she would be more embarrassed than he would be.

"I'll take responsibility," she said, "but I won't be more embarrassed than you."

He conceded that she was right about that.

The funeral ended up being such a positive experience that Jackson hardly gave any thought to his nightmares and flashbacks. He shed tears when they closed the casket, and struggled with emotion a number of times during the service. But he felt good about the decision to ask an LDS bishop to oversee the service. The musical numbers were beautiful, and there was a peaceful feeling present. Brian read the obituary, filling in more details about Melva's life and expressing his love for her. Sasha spoke of the way she'd seen her grandmother change, and the respect she'd had for her because of that. Both Brian and Sasha got very emotional, and it was evident they'd been close to their grandmother and would miss her a great deal. Melinda talked about her mother's life with more humor, telling stories that made people laugh, easing the tension. She too talked of the positive changes Melva had made in her life, and what a privilege it had been to care for her and to see the example of her loving and forgiving nature. Jackson was glad he'd refused his sister's plea to also speak at the funeral. He was sure he couldn't have handled it very well. The funeral concluded with the bishop giving a brief talk that offered spiritual hope, and he bore a testimony of the resurrection and life after death. He kept his remarks within a format that was appropriate for all Christians, and Jackson heard many comments afterward about what a lovely service it had been.

Being at the cemetery was harder for Jackson. The finality of seeing the casket over an open grave was difficult for him. He believed in life after death, but it all felt vague and hazy to him, and right now he missed his mother. Guilt and regret compounded his sorrow, and he had a hard time remaining composed when it came time to leave.

He was able to relax more as they attended a luncheon afterward that had been prepared by the local Relief Society. The address for the church building had been printed on the funeral program, and nearly everyone who had been at the funeral was in attendance. Jackson recalled a similar event after Granny's funeral, but now he was even more impressed. There was plenty of food, and the ladies serving it were kind and gracious to everyone who was there. He often heard them offering condolences for someone they hadn't even known. He wondered how many hours some of these ladies had taken out of their lives to provide this service, free of charge. He noticed the bishop and his counselors mingling and talking with the people who had known and loved Melva, and he made certain that he spoke to each one of them, expressing his appreciation for their sincere efforts.

After all the events were over, they went to Melinda's home to spend the rest of the day, since they would be flying out the following morning. All of Melinda's family was there, and both Jackson and Chas enjoyed visiting with them. Everyone loved Charles, and the baby got a lot of attention. Jackson especially liked the distraction from his own concerns about facing what was in his head when he returned home. He could leave Arkansas, but he had to take his head with him.

\* \* \* \* \*

Jackson felt indescribably relieved to return home, and there was enough catching up to do that he and Chas were both able to stay busy, so the subjects of death and PTSD didn't come up. On the plane they had briefly discussed the hope that being at home would make things better. Jackson felt sure that Chas was as skeptical as he was on that count, but neither of them wanted to admit it.

The first few days at home went well for Jackson, except for a nagging emptiness over his mother's death. He'd lived twenty-eight years without her in his life at all, and in the few years since their reconciliation, he'd only seen her occasionally, due to living in different states. It seemed natural, then, to feel as if she was still in Arkansas, alive and well. He would often find himself thinking, *I need to tell Mom about this*, or *I wonder what Mom's doing today*. Then the reality would hit him, and he'd feel taken aback. Sometimes it hit him so hard that he had to find a place to be alone for a few minutes in order to cry like a child who had lost his mother. Chas told him that no matter how old a person got, it was difficult to lose a mother. She had never known *her* mother, but her grandmother had raised her, and losing her had been extremely difficult for Chas. Jackson had shared that experience with her, and he was glad to have Chas nearby for him now.

Jackson called Melinda every day just to see how she was doing. She was getting ready to go on that cruise with her friends, and he was glad she had somewhere to go and something to think about.

Jackson was beginning to believe—and hope—that being at home had cured him of his worsening symptoms of the evil disorder. But on the third night home, he had an incident equivalent to that first night after his mother had died. Chas was kind and calm as she urged him back into reality and held him close while he shook violently, but he knew she was scared, and he hated doing this to her. He insisted on keeping the lights on, even though it was just past three in the morning. He also wanted to insist that he go to another room and let Chas get some sleep, but he felt terrified to be alone. As memories of his nightmares ran circles in his mind, Jackson was taken off guard by a sudden assault of emotion. The grief over his mother's death twisted into his present fears, and he sobbed uncontrollably. Chas just held him and offered perfect comfort and compassion until he was finally able to stop crying *and* shaking.

"I'm scared, Chas," he admitted, his voice hoarse.

"I know," she murmured. "I am too."

"I feel like I'm losing my mind."

He heard her take the type of breath that indicated she was gathering some kind of courage before she added, "I think you need to get some help, Jackson. You need to see a counselor; I'll go with you. But . . . we can't fix this on our own. There's obviously something going on that's beyond your control."

Jackson had resisted starting up any more sessions with a psychologist since his condition had been declared "manageable" about the time he and Chas had been married. And he had to admit that it *had* been manageable; not always pleasant, but his occasional nightmares had not been interfering with his everyday life. *This* was definitely getting out of hand. He hated to take this step, but his fear was a great motivator. His concern for Chas added to his incentive. If nothing else, he could do it for her.

"Okay," he said. "We'll start looking tomorrow."

"Okay," she said and kissed him, drawing him closer into her embrace. For the millionth time, he wondered what he would ever do without her.

The following day, Chas volunteered to do some research and seek out a good psychotherapist in Butte, which was nearly an hour's drive. Jackson had seen one there for a while when he'd first moved here, but the appointments had stopped when his condition had been declared manageable. Now that therapist had moved away. Jackson had really liked the therapist that had initially seen him through the worst of the problem, while he'd still been in Virginia. They had done some work over the phone after he'd moved, but she was now retired. Therefore, Chas had no choice but to start from scratch. She was stunned by how many phone calls she had to make, and how many hours it took to finally find someone she believed would be a good match. He was also able to get Jackson in the following Monday, as opposed to waiting weeks for an opening.

Chas felt herself falling into a habit of observing her husband closely, fearing what other symptoms of the disorder might surface. She wondered sometimes if all of her studying in regard to PTSD was helpful, or if it had made her more paranoid. Considering that paranoia was a possible symptom of PTSD, she wondered if the disorder could be contagious.

The nightmarish episodes were becoming more frequent, and they rarely got through a night without one. During the days, Jackson seemed *almost* himself. He was a little subdued and more quiet, but that could easily be credited to grieving over his mother's death. So Chas chalked it up to that and believed if they could figure out how to get the nightmares to stop, they would both be fine.

On the day of their appointment, Chas had her friend Charlotte come to the inn to watch Charles. Polly watched him occasionally, but she had a great deal of work to do in the office. Charlotte had been a good friend of Chas's for many years. They had very little in common, but they had proved to be a good support for each other. Charlotte was a single mother with two children who were both in school. She was gifted at baking and did all of the baked goods for the inn. She did it with such finesse that her breads, cookies, and pastries had become part of the reputation for the inn, especially with returning customers. Charlotte arrived a little earlier than normal with her usual trays of goodies, and Jackson and Chas were soon on their way to Butte. The drive passed mostly in silence, but Chas held her husband's hand, wanting to imply that she would be with him every step of the way, whatever it might take.

Chas felt wary the moment they stepped into this man's office. While she'd been hoping and praying to find someone that Jackson could connect well with, this man seemed to be the opposite. She could sense how uncomfortable Jackson felt through the entire session, and many times the doctor asked questions that seemed so ridiculous she wanted to scream at him and ask if he had any idea what he was doing. In the end, he prescribed something that he seemed to think would solve the entire problem, even though it appeared to be nothing more than a sleeping pill.

Chas was not surprised by the frustration and confusion Jackson expressed once they were alone in the car. They decided they weren't going back to this particular doctor, and they would try to find a different one. They did decide to fill the prescription, hoping it might at least help him get some sleep in the meantime.

That very day, Chas set up appointments with *two* other psychotherapists, thinking it might be better to get more than one on the calendar in case one or the other of them proved to be a disaster. But they had to wait a couple of weeks to get in to see the first one. The second one called back with a cancellation and would able to see him in ten days.

Jackson hated feeling so much hope in taking a pill at bedtime. But he was so physically and emotionally exhausted from this ordeal that he wanted something—*anything*—to help him get a good night's sleep. After three nights of taking the pill, the only difference he found was that following the nightmarish episodes, he was able to go back to sleep. But the dreams were worse, if anything had changed at all.

When Sunday morning arrived, Chas prayed very hard that Jackson might hear something at church to urge him toward a spiritual solution to the problems they were facing. Of course they needed the right tools and intervention, but she knew that true healing could only take place when those things were coupled with spiritual acceptance of the only true source of healing. She'd been praying ever since she met Jackson that his heart would be softened toward the gospel and he would come to a place where he could eagerly embrace it of his own free will. She'd known without any doubt that it was right to marry Jackson, even though he didn't share her religious beliefs. He had promised to always go to church with her and to support her in raising their children with the gospel. She'd wanted a husband and father who actively participated, rather than a passive onlooker. And he'd willingly agreed to that. She had agreed, in turn, that she would never make religion an issue in their relationship. He knew that she would prefer he join the Church, but she would never force it on him or allow it to come between them. When her prayers over marrying this man were so obviously answered, and she'd known it was the right choice, she'd gone forward with the faith that eventually he would come to know what she knew and they could share the joy of an eternal marriage.

Throughout the time since they'd been married, they'd both kept their end of the bargain, but nothing had changed, even a little. Chas wasn't sure what made Jackson so resistant to showing any real interest in what he was hearing. She just kept praying that something would happen to change his heart, and she thanked her Heavenly Father every day that she had a good man in her life, and that he *did* go to church with her. She knew women whose husbands *were* members, but they were inactive and even belligerent. Chas was grateful for what she had.

Chas had hoped that the passing of his mother and the wonderful things that had been said at her funeral by a good LDS bishop would have helped Jackson along a little. But she hadn't seen any change in that regard. He'd commented about how wonderfully the members in Arkansas had taken care of everything, but that had been all.

Driving to church as usual, Chas prayed silently, once again, that this might be the day something was said in one of the talks or lessons to give him a desire to know more, or to even consider the possibility that there was something in this religion that might help heal his pain. At the moment, it was her deepest wish.

# Chapter Five

Chas kept praying on behalf of her husband through the sacrament, and the thought occurred to her that God knew Jackson and knew his heart, which meant that healing would take place in God's time and in God's way. She felt a little taken aback as she wondered if she was trying too hard to figure out the course this might take, when it wasn't up to her at all. She just needed to keep doing what she was doing: being loving and supportive, and allowing Jackson his free agency.

Chas felt some hope when the youth speaker came to the pulpit and said that the topic for the month was forgiveness. She felt certain that if Jackson could do as he'd promised his mother and forgive his father for the abuse he'd inflicted during Jackson's childhood, the rest of his healing would be much easier. Recalling her thoughts during the sacrament only minutes earlier, she reminded herself not to speculate too much, even if the theory made perfect sense. Since his PTSD had worsened dramatically, Chas felt sure it had more to do with his father's abuse than it did with his mother's death. But what did she know? She was only the woman who loved him, the woman who was stabbing in the dark, searching desperately for solutions to the problems and any molecule of hope she could cling to.

Chas's hope merged into uneasiness when she realized that Jackson had tensed up at the very mention of forgiveness. She prayed silently on his behalf and remained discreetly aware of his mood through the meeting. She sensed that he was listening attentively, and she felt hopeful that what he was hearing might have an impact on him. Then in the middle of the final talk, a scripture from the Doctrine and

Covenants was quoted. *I, the Lord, will forgive whom I will forgive, but of you it is required to forgive all men.*

Half a minute later Jackson took the baby from her, got up, and walked out. Chas knew that following him would only bring attention to the fact that his reason for leaving had nothing to do with the baby. When sacrament meeting was over, she couldn't find him, and the car was no longer where it had been parked. She checked her cell phone, which had been left on the silent setting, and found a text message that said, *I'll pick you up after RS.* As concerned as she felt, Chas debated whether to even go to the other meetings. She went outside and used her cell phone to call Jackson, wondering if he would even answer.

"I'm fine," he said as he picked up.

"Now, why don't I believe that?"

She heard him sigh. "Okay, *fine* is relative. I'm fine enough that you should go to your other meetings and not worry about me."

Chas studied her feelings and said, "Will you please come and pick me up, right now?"

Jackson hesitated, knowing there was no way to avoid a conversation about his reasons for leaving the meeting. He couldn't figure how a couple of hours would make any difference, but she obviously didn't agree. "I'll be there in a few minutes," he said and hung up the phone. Chas was waiting for him when he pulled into the parking lot, with Charles asleep in his seat.

As soon as she got into the car, she said, "Maybe we should go for a little drive before we go home, then the baby will stay asleep and Polly will keep covering for us."

"I knew you were going to say that," he said, and he drove in the opposite direction from home. Silence reigned for several minutes before he finally said, "I really am fine."

"But upset enough to walk out of the meeting?"

"I'm not upset anymore." She glared at him, and he added, "Unless I think about it."

"So talk about it," she said, then opened up the conversation with a prompt that she knew would get to him. "Apparently you disagree with what the speaker was saying . . . about forgiveness."

"Yes, I do," he said.

"It's in the scriptures. Don't you believe the scriptures are true?"

"I don't know," he said, and she recognized the obvious. That was a different conversation for another time.

"Okay," she said, "religion aside, any half-decent psychologist will tell you that forgiving is a huge part of healing, and holding on to such grievances will only hurt *you.*"

"You find me a half-decent psychologist who can tell me that," he said snidely.

Chas ignored him, figuring his frustration with his last appointment was irrelevant to the moment. "Even if you are justified in resenting the hurt that was inflicted on you," she said, "you have to let it go."

Jackson pulled over to the side of the highway so abruptly that it startled her. He put the car in Park and turned to face her. "You say that as if I might have never heard it before."

"Apparently it hasn't sunk in yet."

He leaned toward her but kept his voice low so as not to wake the baby. "You have no right to tell me what I have to let go of, any more than that man standing at the pulpit preaching forgiveness . . . as if a person can just snap his fingers and erase all that horror. He has no idea what the world is really like; a man like that has never even had a glimpse of what a man like me has seen, what goes on in my mind, what I have been through. *You* have no idea what I've been through."

Chas managed to remain calm, knowing it would be more conducive to keeping the conversation productive. "You wouldn't tell me," she said.

"Because it was too horrible," he said. "When it's too horrible to even think about, it's certainly too horrible to poison you with."

"I understand that, Jackson; I do. But God knows what happened, and He can take that burden from you."

"How?" he snapped. "If God allows such horrible depravity to even occur, how can He possibly just erase it?"

Chas tried to feel inspired, tried to think of something to say that could keep him talking and hopefully prevent him from getting more angry. She found the courage to say something she'd wanted to say for a long time. "You cannot see God the way you see your father."

"Where did that come from?"

"It's a fact . . . that most people interpret the characteristics of God through those of a parent, usually the father. You might believe at some level that God is kind and good and looking out for you, but maybe at another level—something more emotional and subconscious—you think that God will deal with you the way your father did, and so you can't bring yourself to fully trust Him."

Jackson thought about it and shook his head. "Whatever," was all he said, clearly dismissing the theory.

"Well, when you *do* find a half-decent therapist, you ask him what he thinks of that theory."

"Fine, I will," he said. Then he shook his head as if he could shake out the negative thoughts.

He didn't make any attempt to leave the spot where he'd parked the car, but he did seem more calm, so Chas ventured to say, "Tell me what you're thinking." She reached for his hand at the same time.

"I'm not like those other men, Chas," he said with enough of an edge to his voice that she knew it was something he'd given much thought to.

"What are you talking about?"

"The men we go to church with every Sunday; they're not like me." His tone implied that it was something she should have known, something that should have been obvious.

"Not *like* you?" she repeated. "They're all different and unique, Jackson. How exactly are you not like them, beyond the fact that they're Mormons and you're not?"

He leaned closer and lowered his voice as if he didn't want to be overheard, even though they were completely alone. "How many of them do you think have had to kill people for a living?"

"You make it sound like you did it every day. You *protected* people for a living. The other was just part of the job. I can't say that I personally know whether any man in our ward has actually had to kill someone in the line of duty, but I'm certain there are Mormons *somewhere* who have. How many Mormons do you think are in the military right now, serving their country in the midst of war?"

He apparently had no rebuttal for that, but he *did* add, "And how many of them do you think have been tortured by drug dealers to the point of nearly losing their minds?"

Chas sighed. "I'm certain it's rare," she said gently, "but I do know someone in this ward who has lost two wives to cancer, and I know someone who lost a wife and two children in a car accident. I know someone who is a quadriplegic because of a drunk driver, and I know someone whose son is in prison for committing murder. Do you want me to go on?" He only looked away and she continued. "I will be the *last* person to say that what you went through wasn't high on the scale of horrible things a human being can endure. No one would dispute that, even though most people around here have no idea it ever happened. But just because it happened doesn't make you any less worthy to have the full blessings of the gospel in your life. God is no respecter of persons, Jackson. Any person who comes to Him with a humble heart and righteous desires has the opportunity to take advantage of His greatest blessings. If anything, your experiences have made you more humble, more compassionate to the struggles and heartaches of life. You're a good man, Jackson; Christian in your heart. God made us *all* different. What makes you different from other men we associate with could end up being a blessing to others. Your perspective and abilities are a gift, Jackson. They make you who you are, and God loves you for who you are. He's the one who gave you those gifts, who made you good at what you did, and you used your gifts for good, to protect and serve and defend the rights of the common people. In my opinion, everything that makes you different makes you a hero. *My* hero."

Chas saw his eyes soften over that last comment, but she felt sure that her other heartfelt words had fallen on deaf ears. She could only hope and pray that one day they would sink in.

\* \* \* \* \*

The following Sunday Jackson didn't go to church. He didn't try to make up any excuses; he just said he wasn't going. Chas made no effort to hide her disappointment, but she saved her tears until she was driving to the meetinghouse. People at church asked about him, and she simply said that he wasn't feeling well—which was certainly true. She hated taking care of Charles all by herself, but mostly because she just hated Jackson's absence. And she had a feeling it was going to get a lot worse before it got better.

When she came home from church, he had dinner ready and he was in a pleasant mood. She thanked him for the meal, enjoyed his company, and chose to pray on his behalf rather than engage in conversations that would only make tension rise between them.

Their next appointment with a therapist went better than the last one—until he went off on a tangent of telling stories of how other people had gotten PTSD. When it started to make Chas feel sick, she was grateful to have Jackson interject, "I have done my best to protect my wife from such horrible images. Can you explain what point there is in giving us both more ugly things to think about—regarding people who have nothing to do with us?"

"The point," the therapist said, "is that you need to appreciate how much worse your situation could be."

Jackson felt angry, invalidated, and confused. When they left the office, all he could say was, "I'm not going back to see *him.*"

"Good," Chas said, "because neither am I. What an idiot!"

"Now, is that a Christian thing to say?"

"No, but that's how I feel right now. I feel like I just went to a movie I shouldn't have seen."

"Yeah," Jackson snarled. "I'm sorry about that."

"It's not your fault."

"You wouldn't have been sitting in there if it wasn't for me. Maybe I should do this alone."

"And maybe I should be there with you so that I can know how to help you."

After they'd gotten into the car, he said, "You deserve better than this, Chas."

He'd said it before, and she'd become pretty good at reminding him of her reasons for being committed to him, his life, *and* his challenges. But she'd never heard him say it in that tone of voice. He sounded as if he truly believed it, and there was nothing she could say to talk him out of it. She simply told him she loved him and took his hand, praying that they could find the answers, and that they'd have better luck with the next therapist.

The third time seemed to be a charm. Dr. Leiman was kind and compassionate, and he was a good listener. He expressed hope that they could overcome the problem with time. The big question that arose after seven sessions was *how much time?* It was becoming evident that he had a way of dragging nothing into an hour's session, and they felt like they were paying him for just that. He seemed to be one of those therapists who was interested in dragging out a case if only to keep a patient coming back—and spending money. By the end of the summer, Jackson declared that he was done with therapists; it was a waste of time and money. Chas knew instinctively that they could not solve the problem of his ongoing nightmares without professional intervention, but she couldn't argue with him over the time and money—and hope—that had been wasted. She could only keep praying for answers and keep doing her best to support her husband.

Charles was crawling now, and the purchase of some quality baby gates had become necessary in order to confine him to certain areas of the inn at certain times of the day. The kitchen and bedrooms had been made completely baby-proof, and if they had him anywhere else, they had to watch him especially closely. Jackson and Chas continued with their typical schedule of taking turns watching him so they could each accomplish their tasks at the inn. Jackson usually went out for an early-morning run while Chas was getting ready for the day. He would return and get a shower before Chas needed to start her work in the kitchen. She worked mornings to cook and serve breakfast to their guests and oversee the cleaning of rooms. Jackson worked afternoons, handling the business end of things along with Polly's help. He also maintained the grounds, as well as taking care of any necessary repairs or maintenance. If he couldn't fix something himself, he oversaw arranging to have it done and making certain it happened. They took turns doing necessary errands, or sometimes they went together. It was a good life that kept them both busy, but not *too* busy. With the help of Polly and Charlotte and a couple of girls who came to clean rooms as needed, the inn ran smoothly without undue stress.

Ever since Chas had initially been through the temple, a year after her baptism, she had driven once a month to Idaho Falls to attend the temple. It was a four-hour drive each way, which made for a very long day. But she had done it with conviction and few exceptions. Sometimes she had to change the planned day due to bad weather or some unforeseen circumstance. But there had been very few months when she hadn't made the trip. Jackson was accustomed to this habit, and he always watched Charles for the day. Polly and the other girls took over Chas's tasks, just as she'd arranged it long before Jackson had come into her life.

"Why don't you come with me?" Chas asked her husband the day prior to her scheduled September drive to the temple. "It's a pleasant drive; we can talk. The grounds of the temple are beautiful, and the weather should be perfect. You can watch the baby for a couple of hours while I do my thing, then we can . . . I don't know, do whatever we want. Maybe we could even spend the night; get a room there. What do you think?"

Chas's hope to do something to break the routine and ease the tension of their current challenges dwindled with his long list of reasons why it wasn't a good time and why he needed to stay home. She just smiled and thanked him for watching the baby so that she could go.

Throughout her long drive, Chas prayed and pondered and pleaded with God to make something change, to spur this problem out of its rut. She found peace in the temple, but no specific answers. Following her long drive home, she was glad to see her sweet husband and beautiful son, and she had to admit it had been a good day, even if she hadn't shared it with them.

The next morning, Jackson found her in the kitchen and said without any explanation, "Something isn't right."

"What do you mean?"

"There's . . . something not right . . . here in the house."

"You mean . . . it's haunted?" she asked and couldn't hold back a little chuckle. He gave her a disgusted glare, and she added, "Maybe it's Mr. Dickens."

"Very funny," he said in a tone that indicated he didn't think it was.

"What do you mean, Jackson?" she asked with sincerity. "Tell me what you think is going on."

"I don't know what's going on, I just . . . know that something isn't right. It's that feeling I used to get when I was on a case . . . and I knew that something wasn't what it appeared to be, or someone was lying to me, or something was going to go wrong."

"Your gut instinct."

"That's right."

Chas knew that his instincts had made him a great agent. She'd told him more than once that it was surely a gift he'd been given that had made him so good at what he'd done. But that was then, and this was now—with PTSD thrown into the mix. And he was no longer an agent; he was an innkeeper. Just as Chas needed Jackson to trust her, she needed to be respectful of his feelings, while at the same time trying to keep perspectives clear.

"Okay," she said, giving him her full attention, "let's talk this through. We lock the outside doors at dark. The guests have to get in with a key. There is nothing visibly missing or out of place. Tell me what you mean by . . . something's not right."

"I don't know," he said with marked impatience. "I just . . . feel like something isn't right."

Chas weighed how much she should say and how to say it. She decided that this couldn't go unsaid. "Jackson," she said gingerly, "forgive me, but . . . I can't help but wonder . . . and I have to ask, because . . . if it was the other way around . . . you would do the same, and—"

"Just say it."

"Is it possible that . . . there is nothing wrong? That this is just . . . a symptom?"

It took him a moment to realize what she meant, and then he felt angry. "A symptom? You mean . . . losing my mind a little more? Paranoia? Is that what you're saying?"

"You can't possibly expect me *not* to bring it up as a possibility."

He sighed and forced himself to calm down. "No, I suppose I can't. But I can assure you this is *not* a symptom. I am perfectly in control of my senses when I'm awake."

Chas kept her next thought to herself. *Except for that time at your sister's house when you freaked out over her suggestion that the horrible incident you were having nightmares over was stirred into your ugliest memories from growing up.*

"I'm fine," he insisted. "My instincts are as sharp as they ever were, and I'm telling you that something isn't right."

"Okay," she said. "Who am I to argue? We'll just . . . keep a close eye on . . . everything, and . . . see if we can figure out what's wrong."

"You're patronizing me."

Chas tried to be honest. "I'm not saying you're right or you're wrong. I'm keeping an open mind. Fair enough?"

"Fair enough."

Through the next twenty-four hours, Chas saw nothing out of the ordinary, nothing that would make her think something wasn't right. But Jackson mentioned it twice more, and she felt a growing concern.

That night, the evening routine went as normal, and they went to bed after sharing the usual prayer, which Chas always insisted on, and therefore Chas was usually the one to say it.

Chas was just beginning to feel relaxed when Jackson sat up abruptly, and she asked, "Is something wrong?"

"Yes," he said with perfect confidence. "There's someone in the house." He turned on the lamp and pulled on his jeans. She was astonished by his intensity.

"I hate to point out the obvious, Jackson, but we live in an inn. There are guests in our home."

"This is different," he said and pulled open a dresser drawer where he reached beneath a stack of folded T-shirts and pulled out a handgun.

"You have a *gun?*" she asked, not disguising her panic.

"It's not illegal, Chas," he said and dug in a different drawer to pull out a clip that he efficiently popped into the firearm. It was a sound she knew well from watching TV, but she'd never personally heard it before.

"What are you doing?" she demanded. "You can't just . . . shoot someone because—"

"Shoot someone?" he echoed, sounding offended. "I have never, nor will I ever, *shoot* someone unless they first make it evident they intend to harm me or someone else."

"Okay, but . . . you do not need a gun for whatever it is you think you heard."

"What I *think* I heard? I *know* what I heard."

"That someone is in the house? A guest could have gone out to their car because they forgot something. Or they could have been getting food out of the snack fridge. What are you going to do? Go stick a gun in the face of one of our guests because you heard someone in the house?"

Jackson took in her panicked expression and the logic of what she was saying. He weighed that against the gut instinct that something wasn't right, and the decision was difficult. The point that tipped the scales was his own realization that he'd been oversensitive about certain things that could very well make his present behavior appear border-line crazy. He didn't feel crazy; in fact, he *knew* that he wasn't. For all of his nightmares, and the panic attacks that followed them, he'd never *really* felt out of control of his mind. But Chas's plea of logic compelled him to eject the clip and put it away. "Okay," was all he said before he put the gun in the drawer of the bedside table and went back to bed. He ignored Chas's expression and body language that clearly said she was terrified—but not by a possible intruder. She was terrified that something was wrong with him. He probably should have made some attempt to explain himself, but when it came to such matters he hadn't had any need to apologize for his gut instinct through the course of his entire adult life.

"Let's get some sleep," was all he said before he turned off the lamp. It was another minute before she climbed back into bed, and an hour later he was still staring at the ceiling through the darkness, listening for any unusual sound, trying to avoid certain memories that jumped around in his brain. While he listened and sorted his thoughts, he was well aware that Chas was still as wide awake as he. He separated his preoccupation from the present reality that he was no longer a special agent with his life in danger. He was an innkeeper with a wife and son. That didn't change what his instincts were telling him, and the need to protect his home and family was stronger in him than any instincts that had guided him through protecting complete strangers for years. But it did remind him that nothing was more important than his relationship with his wife, and given some distance from the moment, he knew he owed her an explanation. She wasn't a member of his team; she was not someone who was expected to obey his orders without question. She was his wife.

Chas didn't keep track of the minutes it took for her heart to stop pounding after she'd crawled back into bed. The scene that had just transpired between her and her husband was like something out of a movie—a scary movie. She'd certainly known his profession and a fair amount of what it had entailed long before she'd married him, but the reality of seeing him with a gun in his hand—and apparently intent on using it—had shaken her and left her unsettled. Or perhaps the incident itself might not have been quite so unsettling if it weren't for his recent behavior. She'd been concerned and on edge already. Now she could hardly breathe as she considered what to make of the situation. Given the information she had, she wondered if she should be concerned to the point of needing to take some kind of action. Did he need counseling in spite of his reluctance to get it? Medication? Medical attention? Or was she just blowing the whole thing out of proportion because the incident with the gun had taken her so off guard?

Lying there in the dark, unable to even relax, let alone sleep, she prayed for guidance and understanding in order to be able to do what was best for Jackson, for all of them.

"You okay?" she heard him say without first bothering to ask if she was awake. Obviously he knew that she was.

Chas considered her answer. She would never be dishonest with him, but she also didn't want to bring too much attention to the level of her concern. Or perhaps she did. Perhaps he needed to know. They certainly weren't going to solve any problems by pretending they didn't exist or by avoiding any related conversation—which was how it had mostly become lately. "I'm trying to decide," she said if only to give herself a few more seconds to think about the best response.

"It's been over an hour. You haven't decided?"

"It took forty-five minutes for my vital signs to return to normal."

"Surely you're exaggerating."

"Maybe," she said. "A little."

Jackson tried not to feel defensive. She deserved an explanation, not an apology. But he had to remember that what had been a normal part of his daily life was likely something uncomfortable for her. He decided to get more information before handling it at all. "Why don't you tell me how you feel."

"I will if you will," she said and took his hand beneath the covers. She squeezed his fingers and he squeezed hers in return.

"Deal," he said and rolled onto his side to face her. He wondered what he'd ever done without her. His more frequent memories of the horrors he'd lived through prior to settling into this life with her made his appreciation deeper.

Chas turned toward Jackson and touched his face, which she could barely see through the darkness.

"I'm waiting," he said, glad to feel the tension dissipating between them. She had a calming effect on him, and he realized that he should have started talking a long time ago. Now that his adrenaline wasn't pumping, it was easy to say, "Come on, tell me."

"Truthfully, you scared me," she said. "I didn't know you even had a gun in the house."

"I thought you knew, or perhaps just assumed you would know me well enough to know that I would."

"I just assumed you would have left it behind."

"I left my government-issue firearm behind. I own this one, and I have a license to carry a concealed weapon that has nothing to do with my job—or retirement."

"Isn't it dangerous to have it around?"

"That's why it's never stored with the clip in it, or even *with* the clip. When we have children old enough to get into drawers, I will lock it up or store it higher. When our children are old enough to understand, I will teach them how dangerous it is. Ignorance and carelessness are at the root of accidents, not the actual presence of the gun."

"Okay," she said again, realizing she was fine with that. Moving on, she added, "I've never seen you like that. How could I not be overwhelmed?"

Jackson thought about that for a long moment before he said, "It was a way of life for me for a long time. It's like breathing. When my instincts tell me something's not right, my training tells me to draw my weapon. My intention was not to alarm you, Chas."

"Okay," she said, still trying to merge the man with the gun into the husband she knew.

Somewhat facetiously he said, "You did know I was in the FBI and the Marines before I married you, right?"

"Of course," she said with less humor. "But I guess imagining you that way and actually seeing it are very different. My only exposure to such things has been TV, and I don't watch that much TV. I wouldn't expect that what I've seen is an accurate depiction, anyway."

"Some of it is," he said, "not that I've ever watched much TV myself."

"I did know *that* about you, too," she said. "I suppose I always imagined that TV depictions were overdramatized. I knew you carried a gun, but I guess I thought you wouldn't have used it much."

"Depends on what you mean by *used*," he said. "Any person who needs a gun to carry out their job always hopes they don't actually have to fire it, but it happens. Having a weapon drawn for protection when going into unknown situations was very common. Like I said, if anything didn't feel right—anything at all—we went in with weapons drawn."

Chas pondered what he was saying and found that she could settle all of that into what had happened—except for one thing. She wondered if she should bring it up, but her conscience demanded that it could not be ignored. "Your instincts told you there's danger in the house?"

Jackson wondered if she was worried about the danger or questioning his instincts. Considering that she had talked him out of taking any action, he knew the answer to that question. But he answered it straightly. "Not danger, perhaps, but something not right. And when something doesn't feel right, I don't question whether or not it means danger until I've proven otherwise." She said nothing, and he asked, "Are you questioning my instincts?"

Chas thought of a careful answer. "I can only say that I didn't feel the same thing."

"You haven't seen what I've seen, Chas. You don't have the training I have."

"But your training and experience don't automatically make noises in the house mean that something is wrong."

"No, my instinct tells me that," Jackson said and studied the silence that followed. "You *are* questioning my instincts." Still she didn't say anything. "So, you're worried that I'm losing my mind. Is that it?" He tried not to sound angry, but that's how he felt.

"Now, don't get all defensive. I'm your wife and we need to be honest with each other. You cannot fault me for such concern in light of what you've been struggling with, Jackson. Forgive me for stating the obvious, but you have been officially diagnosed with PTSD—for good reason—therefore I am far from ignorant of the symptoms. And one of them is paranoia."

Jackson rolled onto his back, feeling like he'd been slapped. For about ten seconds he wondered if what he'd been feeling was some form of mental illness, and he came to the firm conclusion that it was not. But how could he convince his wife of that?

"I'm not losing it, Chas," he said with conviction, careful *not* to sound defensive, knowing it would make him sound more guilty. "But there's no way I can convince you of that when you can't see inside my head, and you don't know what I was feeling. So you're just going to have to trust me."

The silence became strained before she said, "I have no reason not to trust you, Jackson."

"Except your fear that I'm losing my mind."

"If you did lose it, would you know?"

"Do you have any idea how many hours of counseling I've endured for PTSD?"

"I have some idea, but none of them were very effective since your relapse."

"My relapse?"

"Are you going to try to pretend that it's not gotten worse since your mother died? I know it's hard when you don't know what to do about it, but that doesn't mean we can ignore it—or at least we shouldn't. Don't forget that I'm the one lying next to you in this bed when you have nightmares and panic attacks. How do you *know* you're not losing it?"

"I just know."

"Okay, explain it to me."

"I'm not having hallucinations or delusions, Chas. Difficult memories do not make me automatically unable to define the line between reality and my imagination. My issues have nothing to do with my instincts."

Chas took a deep breath and tried to accept what he was saying as opposed to giving in to her fear. "Okay," she said, "but I want you to promise me something."

"What?" he asked, sounding only slightly defensive.

"I want you to promise me that when—if—something starts to feel weird, you will tell me and not try to push the feeling away. If you have even the slightest notion that your instincts are crossing into your issues, I need to know about it. Can you promise me that?"

"Yes, I can promise you that," he said with no hesitation. He hoped it would never come to that, and prayed that if it did he *would* know the difference.

Deciding he'd had enough of this for one night, he turned toward her again and said, "I know how to settle this." He kissed her, and she responded eagerly.

"You think you can just kiss and make up and everything will be fixed?" She laughed softly and kissed him again.

"I don't know if it will be fixed, but it can't hurt any."

"No," she said, and he kissed her again, "it can't hurt any."

"Besides," he eased her into his arms, "I had no intention of stopping with a kiss. "Before we got married, you always made me stop with a kiss, but I *did* marry you, so . . ."

"I'm so glad," she said and eased closer to him.

"Me too," he said, and his kiss gained fervor.

Later, Jackson held his wife close to him and whispered in her ear, "I love you, Chas. I'm sorry you have to put up with all the . . . challenges I brought with me."

"I love you too, Jackson, and I will gladly take on whatever it takes to have you with me. You never know. I might just get even one of these days."

# Chapter Six

Over the next few days, Chas saw her husband become short-tempered and snappy. When they'd initially been getting to know each other, he'd admitted that he wasn't known among his peers as being necessarily warm and friendly. He'd told her that she'd changed him, that she'd warmed his heart. During their years together she had seen an occasional glimpse of the old Jackson Leeds, but never like this. Not the kind of woman to tolerate being addressed that way, she quickly reached her limits and called him on it when they crossed paths in the parlor later that afternoon and he barely acknowledged her. With the baby asleep and no guests at the inn, she knew she'd get no better chance to bring up what she knew had to be said before it got completely out of control.

"Is it possible that you could speak more than ten words a day to me?" she asked.

"What would you like me to say?" he asked like a snotty teenager.

"I don't even know who you are," Chas growled. "You're the father of my child and I don't even know who you are."

"*Still* the same man."

"No," she insisted. "The man I married was kind. He was a nice guy. *You* are a stranger."

"Actually," he took a step closer and she could see the anger in his eyes deepening, "the man you married was the stranger. I walked into your life and became somebody I didn't even know."

"You said I changed you."

"Well, maybe I was wrong. Maybe the change was only temporary. Maybe this is the *real* me, and maybe it's all you get."

"I don't believe that. I've seen the *real* you, and this isn't it."

"Maybe you're deluding yourself. Maybe you married the wrong man."

"I don't believe that, either. I prayed about it, and I know the answer I got was real."

"Maybe you should question the source of your inspiration. Or maybe God misjudged me as much as you did. All I know for certain is that I can't pretend to be something I'm not. This is it, Chas! So, live with it, or kick me out."

"Oh, you'd love to put it on me, wouldn't you! If I kick you out, then you can spend the rest of your life brooding and feeling sorry for yourself—alone. It's not gonna fly! I love you enough to stick it out. I'm not giving up on you—or us—that easy. But I'm not going to put up with this kind of garbage. So, you have baggage! Who doesn't? And maybe you have more than your fair share. So be it. I'm not going to leave you to face it alone, but I *will* make sure you face it. We're in this together, and I'm not backing out just because *you* think the past is stronger than you are. I don't buy it. We are going to get through this—together. So, buck up and act like a man. Act like a Marine! A Marine doesn't abandon his post just because the battle gets tough. And I *know* that's who you are at the core, and you know it too."

Jackson felt like he'd been kicked in the stomach. She had him there. He took a step back and slumped onto the couch. She was right. "I'm sorry," he said. "You're right, of course."

"What's going on, Jackson? We've been busy the past few days, but obviously something is really eating at you."

He sighed and hung his head. "The dreams are . . . horrible."

"I know."

"It's wearing on me, and I know it's wearing on you."

"Maybe we should try again . . . to find someone who can help you."

He glared at her. "I really don't want to go through that again."

"There's got to be a *good* therapist out there."

"The only good ones I knew have either moved or retired. It's okay, really. I'll be okay."

"Should I feel convinced?" she asked, and he said nothing. She picked up on the obvious. "What else is wrong?"

"Else?"

"I know the nightmares are hard on you, but something else is going on. You need to tell me. You promised."

He hesitated, not wanting to add evidence to her theory that he needed help, when he didn't want to have to deal with that. But he *had* promised that he would share his feelings with her, and he couldn't deny what he was feeling. "Something's not right here, Chas. I know it sounds crazy."

"Okay," she said, "can you give me anything to go on other than your instincts? Anything that might . . ."

The phone rang and Chas had to answer it; they were running a business. It was a customer wanting to make reservations. By the time she'd finished on the phone, Jackson was mowing the lawn, probably glad to have an excuse not to finish the conversation.

The remainder of the day was typically silent between them, and Chas felt baffled about what to say or how to bridge this gap. And if she dug deeper, she felt confused, frustrated, angry, and mostly afraid. She sincerely believed everything she had told him earlier. She knew in her heart she'd married the right man, but this was not going at all how she had expected. And she didn't know what to do about it. Considering that her husband was a free agent, she could do very little. She recommitted herself to be loving and supportive, but added the mental reminder that unconditional love did not equate to allowing him to treat her badly. She *could* control her own boundaries of what she would and would not put up with in a husband and father. She prayed that she would be guided in establishing those boundaries and declaring them appropriately.

At bedtime they knelt to pray together as they always did, but he boldly refused to be the one to offer the prayer when she asked. At first she'd been the one to offer the prayer all the time, then when he'd become more comfortable with it, they had started taking turns. But since the incident at church that had set him off, he'd grudgingly knelt beside her to pray, but hadn't wanted to actively participate. Sometimes she wasn't even sure if he spoke an amen. In her prayer Chas expressed love and appreciation for her husband, and that they were together as a family. She hoped that Jackson would be able to get that message, even if he had a hard time hearing it directly.

They'd only had the lights out a few minutes when he said, "Did you hear that?"

"What?"

"A noise."

"I . . . wasn't listening; I don't know. It's an old house. It creaks."

"I know what the house sounds like when it creaks," he said and got out of bed. He turned on the lamp, pulled on his jeans, and took out the gun.

"Jackson, what are you doing?"

"There is something not right in this house," he said, finding the clip and shoving it into the gun. "And since there are no guests here tonight, you don't have to worry about me shooting one of them." He said it with angry sarcasm, and Chas swallowed her temptation to respond with a snappish retort in the same tone.

"So . . . what?" She grabbed her robe and threw it on over her pajamas. "You think someone broke in? We would have evidence of that, wouldn't we? I don't understand." She took a quick peek into the baby's room to be assured that he was safe and sleeping.

"I don't understand either," he said, "but I'm going to figure it out." He took a little flashlight out of the drawer of the bedside table that they kept there in case of a power outage. He opened the bedroom door slowly and peered around it as if someone might shoot at him if he wasn't careful. She wanted to tell him that he was scaring her. She wanted to tell him that she feared he *was* losing his mind. She wanted to insist that he stop playing FBI agent for the fun of it. But she felt it was best to humor him, and when he realized there was nothing or no one there, they could talk about these feelings of paranoia.

Chas was startled by the way he poised the flashlight in his left hand, and rested his right wrist over the top of it, gun in hand. The gun went around the corner before he did, and it led the way as he crept up the long hallway. He peered around corners into empty rooms, but he didn't bother opening closed doors. Chas followed close behind him, biting her tongue to keep from telling him this was ridiculous and insane. Instead she just whispered, "I don't know what you think you're going to find. The inn is locked up tight."

He whispered back, "Why don't you just stay in the bedroom and let me handle this."

"I am *not* staying there by myself," she said, proud of herself for not saying, *I am not going to let you out of my sight.*

When it became evident that there was nothing out of place and no intruders were on the main floor, Jackson went to the door that led into the cellar. It was the one place in the house that felt as old as it was. When the inn had been remodeled years earlier, the supports had been strengthened, and every available space had been set up for storage. It was organized and clean, but it always had a musty smell that Chas didn't like. There was one room for emergency food and water storage, another for keeping boxes that included holiday decorations, extra dishes for parties, and other seasonal items. And there was another room that Chas used as a sort of overflow pantry. Food and household items that she used frequently had a stockpile there that guaranteed she wouldn't run out of the important things should they have a bad storm, or if for any other reason she couldn't get to the store. There was also a root cellar, a room that actually had a dirt floor and walls, where fruits and vegetables had been kept in the original days of the house in order to maximize freshness through the winter months. Now, Chas kept a supply of potatoes in there, but not much else.

When Jackson paused at the door to the cellar, Chas felt creeped out just to think of going down there in her bare feet. She kept it fairly clean, but she still didn't like it. And she knew Jackson didn't like to go down there. He'd often joked about not being fond of confined spaces, and he didn't like the cellar. But apparently his own distaste of going down there was not on his mind at the moment. He pointed the flashlight at the doorknob and whispered, "Did you leave that open?"

Chas looked down to see that it wasn't latched. She *always* kept it closed tightly. Her heart quickened while she told herself it was simply an oversight or coincidence. Occasionally Polly went down there to get things for her. She had probably not closed it tight. Chas just shook her head, not caring to share her thought processes with Jackson. He opened the door quietly, peered around it, and pointed the flashlight—and the gun—down the stairs ahead of him. Chas followed close behind him, feeling scared—and angry with Jackson for making her feel that way. He was so convincing that he nearly had her convinced that something *was* wrong. She wanted to have this futile search over with and be able to prove that he *was* growing paranoid without just cause. While Jackson looked carefully into each of the storage rooms, Chas didn't pay much attention. She just wanted to go back to bed. Then he nudged her with an elbow. She looked at his face, and he put a finger to his lips to indicate that she stay quiet. She wanted to ignore his request and scream instead, appalled by this ridiculous cloak-and-dagger. Then he pointed to the floor of the food storage room, and she sucked in her breath. Her stream of thoughts did a sharp reverse while a voice in the back of her head called her a presumptuous hypocrite. There was bedding on the floor. Someone had been sleeping there! In her storage room!

A noise came from somewhere else in the basement, and Chas gasped. Again, Jackson silently cautioned her to remain quiet. She followed him to the old wooden door of the root cellar but stayed back a reasonable distance as he threw it open and pointed the gun and flashlight into the little dirt room.

"Don't shoot me!" she heard a voice say, and she nearly collapsed onto the floor. Instead she backed up against the closest wall in search of some support.

"I'm not going to shoot you," Jackson said firmly. "Just come out with your hands up and we'll talk."

"Okay, okay. I'm coming. I'm coming."

Jackson backed up, and Chas watched in amazement as a boy stepped out of the root cellar, pale with terror. She guessed that he couldn't be more than ten or eleven.

"What are you doing here?" she demanded, now that the silence edict had been lifted.

Jackson lowered the gun and snapped, "Well?"

"I . . . I . . . I was just . . ."

"Out with it!" Jackson insisted, flipping on the light switch. The boy looked dirty and a little scrawny, with dark brown hair that was badly in need of a haircut.

"I was just hiding here 'cause I don't wanna go home, and . . . I'm real sorry. I'll pay you back for the food I took, and . . . I'm real sorry. Please don't call my dad."

"How old are you?" Chas asked, calming down a little as it became obvious that their intruder was no threat to their safety.

"Twelve and a half," he said proudly, as if that fully justified his living on his own in someone else's basement.

"Come along," Jackson said, taking the boy by the back of the collar. "Upstairs, right now."

Once in the main hallway with the cellar door latched tight, Chas expected Jackson to ask him some questions. But he grabbed the inn's master keys and practically dragged the boy up to one of the smaller guest rooms at the very top of the house. He took him inside and said, "You can sleep here tonight because I'm too tired to call the police right now. Take a shower before you get in that bed, and behave yourself. If you're nice it will go better for you tomorrow. I'm locking the door so you're stuck in here until breakfast, and you're too high in the house to think of climbing out the window. It doesn't open far enough for you to get out anyway. Sleep well. You're going to need it."

Jackson didn't give the boy a chance to respond before he closed the door and locked it with the key. Each room could be locked this way to keep open-house guests from going into any particular room, but it also prevented someone from leaving—although Chas had never *once* in all her innkeeping days entertained the thought of locking a guest *in*.

"You could have been nicer to him," Chas said to Jackson as they were heading back down the stairs.

"He's been hiding in our basement, eating our food, destroying our marriage, and pushing me toward a nervous breakdown. Why should I be nice to him?"

"He's just a kid."

"A kid who needs to take accountability for his actions," Jackson said. "He's a runaway, and whatever the reasons for it, he needs to spend the night afraid of what the consequences might be. *Tomorrow* I'll be nice to him . . . maybe . . . depending on his attitude. I gave him a nice bed to sleep in, didn't I?"

"Yes, you did," she said, unable to deny his logic.

Jackson checked the front and back doors to be sure they were still locked, while Chas looked in on the baby to find him sleeping soundly. As they climbed back into bed, Chas said, "I owe you an apology."

"Yes, you do," he said, but his tone was light. "You really thought I was losing it, didn't you."

"I admit I was concerned. Now it's evident that you were right. There's nothing wrong with your gut instinct, and obviously yours is a lot more in tune than mine."

"Apology accepted," he said and kissed her, seeming more like himself than he had since he'd first mentioned that *something wasn't right*. She wondered how many days this boy had been hiding in their house, how he'd gotten in, and how he'd managed to keep himself so well hidden when someone was around almost all of the time. She had trouble falling asleep while it all rolled around in her mind, but finally exhaustion overruled her perplexity.

Chas woke up to daylight and had a sense of something being wrong, then she realized that Charles had not awakened her in the night. Not since he'd been born had that happened. She rushed into his room to make certain he was all right. She found him still asleep, his breathing even. She heaved a sigh and went back to bed to find Jackson stirring.

"Guess what?" she said.

"What?" he asked groggily without opening his eyes.

"Charles slept through the night; he's still asleep."

"Oh, wow!" he muttered. "That is amazing. You know what's equally amazing?"

"What?"

"I slept through the night too."

"So you did. What a great night!"

"Barring the discovery of a stowaway in the cellar," he said.

"Oh, I'd forgotten," she admitted. "Do you suppose *he* got any sleep?"

"I guess we'll see . . . later. We have no guests. You don't have to cook breakfast. The baby is still asleep, and I intend to stay right here for as long as I can get away with it."

"Good plan," she said and kissed him, grateful to be with the Jackson she knew and loved. She knew that a good night didn't mean the problem was solved. But they'd unraveled one mystery, and she felt some peace knowing that his instincts *were* sharp. She was glad to be able to cross paranoia off the list of possible symptoms he was experiencing.

Chas had Charles dressed and fed before Jackson went up the stairs with the keys to release the prisoner. She was scrambling some eggs for an easy breakfast when Jackson brought the boy into the dining room.

"You hungry?" Jackson asked, and Chas peered around the corner from the kitchen to see how the child looked in daylight. He appeared much cleaner, except that he'd clearly put on the same dirty clothes.

"Yeah," was all the kid said.

"Stay right there and I'll get you some breakfast," Jackson said.

The boy had barely started eating when Polly came in to get started on her work in the office. Chas found her there and told her the story, which was received with amazement and even some laughter. Polly wanted a peek at the boy, simply out of curiosity, then she went back to work.

After the boy had eaten a huge plate of scrambled eggs and four pieces of toast, the interrogation began. Jackson sat down across the table from him, leaned back, and crossed his legs. Chas removed the dishes from the table and wiped it off. She sat on the other side of the room, glad that Polly had offered to let Charles play in the office while she worked. A large playpen and toys were kept there as a standard practice. He wouldn't stay content for more than a little while there, but it worked for short periods of time.

"I want to know everything," Jackson said. "If you're honest with me, then I will do everything I can to work this out in the best possible way. You understand?"

"Yes, sir," he said. At least he was respectful.

"I ran away from home. I couldn't stay there anymore. I packed some clothes and stuff, and I was going to ride the bus to Butte."

"What were you going to do once you got there?" Jackson asked. It was typical of runaways to not think beyond the actual getting away.

"I don't know," he said as if it were nothing. "I was walking past here and saw the sign that said you had an open house every day for a while, and it was during that time. I'd seen the sign before and thought I'd like to look inside. I really like this house. It's big and old. I like it. So I came in, but I didn't see anybody. I could hear some noise in the kitchen, so I figured somebody was in there. Then I thought it might be good for me to hide until it got dark so that the police wouldn't find me or something and make me go back home 'cause I can't stay there anymore. So, I went down to the basement, and when I found some extra blankets and pillows and all that food, I just didn't feel so much like riding the bus to Butte, so I just stayed." He emphatically repeated, "I'm sorry. I'm real sorry. I'll pay you back for the—"

"And how exactly did you plan to do that? Do you have a job? Do you have money in the bank? What exactly were you planning to do once you got caught living in my basement? You knew you would get caught eventually, right?"

The boy made no comment.

"What's your name?" Jackson asked.

He hesitated. "If I tell you my name, you'll make me go back, won't you."

"Listen to me," Jackson said in a voice so tender that it touched Chas. He *did* know how to be nice when he needed to be. "I can't legally keep you here. You're under eighteen, and that means you need to be with your legal guardian, whoever that is. If there's a problem at home and you're not safe there, then we can make other arrangements. I can help you with that, but not unless you're honest with me. Now, I need to know your name."

The boy hung his head. "Wendell."

"Last name?"

"Davis," he said as if saying it would bring him to inevitable doom.

"Okay, Wendell Davis, we have some more questions. First of all, how many days have you been here?"

"Five nights before you found me," he said proudly, as if they should be impressed by his skills.

Jackson glanced at Chas. That was about how long he'd been feeling that something was wrong.

"And how exactly did you manage to stay hidden?" Jackson asked.

"I was fine down there 'cause I could hear when the door came open and I could hide if someone came down. The only reason I had to come upstairs was to use the bathroom. I'd just wait on the stairs until it was real quiet, then I'd open the door real slow and careful, and if no one was around, I'd sneak into the bathroom right around the corner. Then I'd sneak back downstairs. I brought stuff to read and stuff to do so I wasn't real bored, most of the time anyway. I was real careful when I ate food downstairs not to make a mess, and I kept a list of what I ate so I could pay you back."

"Okay, fair enough," Jackson said. "Now, why don't you tell me *why* it is that you were so determined to leave home, and why you can't go back there." For the first time since Wendell had realized Jackson wasn't going to shoot him, the boy looked scared. "Out with it!" Jackson said just firmly enough to get the boy's attention.

"My mom died," he said without looking up. Jackson and Chas exchanged a concerned glance. "And my dad just . . ."

"Did he hurt you?" Jackson asked.

"No!" Wendell said with firm sincerity. According to Jackson's instincts and experience, the boy didn't seem to be lying or hiding anything.

"Then why didn't you stay with your father, Wendell?"

"He just . . . didn't seem to want me around," Wendell said. "So, I left."

"How long has it been since your mother died, Wendell?" Jackson asked with gentle kindness.

"Two weeks and four days," the boy said, lowering his head farther, while sniffling at the same time.

Jackson sighed. "Do you think it's possible," he asked, "that your father was just having a difficult time adjusting to your mother's death? You know, dads aren't like moms. Most of the time moms are pretty good at keeping track of their kids, but dads have a harder time with that kind of thing. I'd bet that your father is desperate with worry about you, and he'll be very glad to get you back. And if he's not, we can talk about what other possibilities there might be for you, now that your mom is gone."

Wendell nodded, seeming okay with that, but he was still sniffling.

"That's pretty tough," Jackson said, "losing your mom. I lost my mom not so long ago."

"But you're old," Wendell said. "I'm just a kid."

"Yes, you are. And no kid should have to lose his mom. I'm very sorry that happened. But you seem like a pretty great kid. I bet you're going to do just fine. You'll probably always miss her, but I bet you're going to do what you know she'd want you to do. What do you think she would want you to do now?"

"Let my dad know where I am, probably," Wendell said.

"Do you have brothers and sisters?"

"My sisters are older than me. They don't like me around, either."

"Well, I think we've talked about everything we can before I call the police."

"The police?" Wendell was astonished. "Are they going to arrest me?"

"Not likely. But I'm sure they're looking for you. Don't worry. I used to be kind of a policeman. I know how to handle these things. You go downstairs and get all of your things. Clean everything up so it's just the way you found it. The bedding you used will have to be washed so take it to the laundry room."

"While you're at it," Chas said, "I want all of the clothes you brought with you—and the ones you're wearing—in the laundry room, as well. I'll wash everything for you. I think it might not hurt for you to shower again, and I'll get you something to put on until your clothes are dry. If nothing else, you're going to be clean."

"Yes, ma'am," he said and hurried down to the cellar to do as he'd been told. His speed made it evident he was relieved to be done with the interview.

Chas gave him some pajamas of Jackson's and some safety pins to make the pants fit tolerably while his clothes were being washed. Once Wendell had done everything he was supposed to do, Jackson put him to work in the kitchen, peeling a pile of potatoes. He told him it was a start toward earning all that food.

"What are we going to do with all those potatoes?" Chas asked Jackson in a whisper after she'd peered around the corner to see that he was still busy at it, looking rather silly in oversized pajamas.

"I don't know. We could make lots of that cheesy potato stuff you make with the ham in it and send some with Wendell for his family."

"That's a great idea, as long as you're the one to put all those potatoes through the food processor for me. But there will still be some left."

"Hash browns for breakfast."

"Okay, I can live with that. Have you called the police yet?"

"No, I'll do it now. I wanted to give him time to actually be dressed in clean clothes before he has to face anybody."

"You're just an old softy at heart," Chas said and kissed him.

"When it comes to kids, I am. You should see me with the bad guys. I don't think 'softy' would come to mind."

She smiled and kissed him again, then she went to get Wendell's clothes out of the dryer so he could make himself presentable.

* * * * *

Jackson sat down in the office and dialed the local police department. He simply asked, "Do you have any runaway boys still missing? I think I may have found one hiding in my basement."

He was connected to a particular officer, answered a few questions, and twenty minutes later a pair of officers was at the door, along with Wendell's father. Pete Davis introduced himself to Jackson, then asked frantically, "Do you have my son?"

"I believe so," Jackson said. "Please, come in and sit down." He guided them all to the parlor while he said, "Wendell should be down in a few minutes." He told them all briefly what had happened, then Chas brought Wendell into the room. Pete Davis started to sob as he went to his knees and took his son in his arms. Wendell cried too and held tightly to his father, apologizing profusely.

"It's okay," Pete said, taking Wendell's face into his hands. "Just so you're safe. We're together now and it's okay. Just promise me you'll never do that again."

"I promise," Wendell said and hugged his father again.

Pete composed himself and wiped his tears on his sleeve as he stood, keeping an arm around Wendell. He held out a hand to Jackson and said, "I can't thank you enough, Mr. Leeds. I realize you didn't know he was here, but thank you for giving him a safe place to be."

"I'm glad it all worked out okay," Jackson said.

"I must reimburse you for whatever Wendell might have used while he was—"

"I'm sorry, Mr. Davis, I can't let you do that," Jackson said. Then he turned firm eyes on Wendell, "I will, however, need Wendell to come and do some work around the inn until the amount is cleared. Apparently he's kept track." Jackson winked at Pete while Wendell was looking sheepishly at the floor, and Pete smiled enough to make it evident he'd caught on.

"I think that's an excellent idea, Mr. Leeds. You're not too far from the school. Perhaps he can come here after school until it's taken care of, and I can pick him up on my way home from work."

"We'll be watching for him," Jackson said.

"Here are your things," Chas said to Wendell, handing him his small suitcase and backpack.

"Do you have something to say to Mr. and Mrs. Leeds?" Pete said to his son.

"Thank you for being so nice to me," Wendell said. "I'll be here tomorrow, and I promise to work hard."

"I'm sure you will," Jackson said. "And you're welcome."

After they had all gone, Chas said to her husband, "Well, that was an adventure. Nothing to break up the monotony of life like harboring a runaway."

"Yeah, great fun," Jackson said. "We didn't send them home with a casserole."

"Well, you haven't even shredded the potatoes yet, Mr. Leeds."

"Okay, I'll get right on that," he said and went to the kitchen.

They were able to find the address for the Davis family in the phonebook, and they took a hot ham-and-potato casserole to their home. Mr. Davis was surprised but very appreciative.

That night Charles slept through the night again, but Jackson didn't. The nightmare he experienced was as bad as it had ever been, and the panic he felt afterward felt completely beyond his control. He left Chas to get some sleep and went to one of the unused guest rooms. He had to leave the light on, and it took him a long time to calm down. He knew he could have handled it better if Chas were there to help him, but at least he felt less guilt for depriving her of her sleep.

The next two times it happened he did the same thing, then he announced one evening after prayer that he was just going to sleep in another room. Chas protested, but he did it anyway. And he slept with the light on. He hated being alone when he came awake in terror, but he was glad to know that his wife was getting uninterrupted sleep. He just wondered how long he could go on this way before he became completely undone. A part of him desperately wanted help, wanted a solution, wanted to be free of this. But another part of him felt certain there was no help that could solve this problem, and he just had to learn to live with it.

# Chapter Seven

Jackson was sitting at the big desk in the office when the phone rang. He glanced at the caller ID and recognized his sister's number. They talked every two or three days, and he found they'd actually become closer since their mother's death. She often asked how he was doing, and he knew she meant his nightmares and the associated challenges. He always told her he was no better and no worse, and there was nothing to worry about.

He answered the phone, glad to hear from her and needing a break. But as soon as he'd said his usual greeting, he realized his sister was in a panic.

"What's wrong?" he demanded, hating the way his memory immediately went to her phone call informing him of their mother's impending death.

"It's Brian," she said, and Jackson's mind conjured up images of possible horrors that could have happened to his nephew. Had he been in an accident? Did he have some dreadful disease? Was he dead?

"What about Brian?" he asked when she cried more than explained.

"You know he's in the Reserves."

"Of course."

"He's been called up," she said, and Jackson slumped into his chair from relief.

"Okay," he said, trying to be compassionate. "I can understand why you're upset, but you really scared me."

"Sorry," she said and sniffled. "It's just so . . . hard."

"I understand," he said, "but it's not an automatic death sentence. Odds are it that he'll be just fine."

"But there are no guarantees."

"Of course there are no guarantees. There's no guarantee that one of us won't die in a car accident tomorrow, but we're not going to get worked up over the possibility."

"This is different, Jackson!" She sounded angry. "The odds of him getting hurt or killed in a war zone are a lot higher than the odds of him getting killed in a car accident in the United States of America."

"Yes, of course," he said, "but—"

"I really didn't expect you to be this insensitive, Jackson."

"Insensitive? I'm just trying to point out that—"

"I need to go," she said and hung up.

Jackson looked at the phone in his hand, wondering why his sister had become so difficult to talk to.

A minute later he was still pondering the phone call when Chas came into the room.

"Something wrong?" she asked.

"Melinda called."

"Oh, no."

"It's not *that* bad," he insisted. "Brian's been called up."

Chas let out a startled gasp and put a hand over her heart. "Oh no!" she repeated in a panicked tone; the same tone Melinda had used on the phone. "That's horrible!"

"Is it?" Jackson asked, wondering what he was missing.

"Yes!" she said, astonished by his question. As if she'd pegged him instantly, she added, "Obviously you've never looked at this from a woman's perspective."

"Obviously."

"I'm certain that when you joined the Marines you gave little thought to how it affected the loved ones you left behind."

"I didn't have any reason to believe that my loved ones cared at all."

"You know differently now. Obviously they *did* care."

Jackson thought of conversations with his mother and sister, many years after the fact, that verified what Chas was saying. He felt enlightened—and foolish—even before she continued to explain.

"I can't think of anything more terrifying than sending someone you love into a war zone. I can't imagine how upset Melinda must be."

Jackson hung his head and sighed. "Okay, so . . . maybe I *was* insensitive."

"What do you mean?"

"Melinda told me I was insensitive. I take it you would be in agreement."

"What did you say to her?" she demanded as if he were a teenager.

"I just thought she was overreacting a little and . . ." He allowed the sentence to fade and admitted instead, "I think I need to call her back."

"Yeah, I think you'd better. Beyond her children, you're the only family she's got."

"She's got you."

"Yes, but you're her brother; you're blood."

"But you're a woman. I'm sure you're much better equipped to offer understanding and compassion than I am."

"Oh, I'll give her understanding and compassion . . . later. Right now she needs her brother. Call her."

Chas left the room, and Jackson hesitated a long moment before dialing his sister's number from memory. He apologized to her, admitting that he'd never stopped to consider this from the perspective of a mother, and he did his best to offer compassion. They ended up talking a long while, sharing some of their feelings in regard to his joining the Marines at the age of eighteen, and leaving home with very little warning. He could see now that it had affected his mother and sister far more than he'd even realized from conversations prior to this one. He apologized for the grief he'd caused her, and asked what he could do to help her now.

"I would really love to have you come and visit before he has to leave," she said. "I know it's short notice, but I'd love to have us all together . . . just to visit and relax and have some good meals. If you could bring your family and come . . . just for a couple of days . . . it would mean so much."

"Of course we can do that," Jackson said. "I'll talk to Chas and call you back."

Jackson wasn't at all surprised by Chas's eagerness to accept his sister's invitation. Arrangements were quickly made for their travel and the care of the inn. Wendell came that afternoon, and Jackson gave him a list of chores that he could work on that day and throughout the days when they would be gone. Chas insisted on giving him an after-school snack before he started his work, and he met Polly, who would be watching out for him while Jackson and Chas were in Arkansas. In the few days when Wendell came and worked prior to Jackson's leaving, he was pleased with the boy's work and found him to be polite and respectful. Apparently he was doing fine at home, and Jackson and Chas concluded that his running away was probably more a rash response to his mother's death than anything else. They felt sure that in time, Wendell would be fine, and they were actually glad to have an opportunity to give him some structure and friendship along the way.

Jackson hated going back to Arkansas, and he admitted as much to Chas. During the flight, they talked of ways that he could shift his thoughts of Arkansas to pleasant things in the present, as opposed to the ugly memories of the past. He tried very hard only to think of pleasant visits with his sister, and the fact that a lovely apartment building now sat where the home he'd loathed had once been.

After renting a car, they checked into their motel room, then drove straight to Melinda's where she had supper waiting. She was so glad to see them that the long flight already felt worth it.

The following morning they all went to the cemetery where Melva's death date had been added to the stone over her grave. They left some lovely flowers, but Jackson didn't want to stay long. He still cringed to see his father's name engraved next to his mother's, and he hated the idea that they were buried together.

Their days in Arkansas were spent almost entirely with Melinda's family, either at her home or on some outings. Jackson had some private conversations with Brian concerning what he might expect from his military service, and how he was feeling about it. He felt some gratification in believing that his own experience and wisdom had given his nephew some peace of mind and perspective. Chas shared some private conversations with Melinda and her daughter, where they cried and talked through all the tender feelings of sending Brian away under such circumstances. They had a family picture taken, shared some good laughs, and made warm memories. Jackson had only one nightmarish episode while in Arkansas, and he and Chas were both grateful it hadn't been worse. Chas declared that it was nice to be sharing a bed with him in the motel room where they stayed, since he'd taken to sleeping in another room all of the time at home.

"I just want you to get your sleep," Jackson insisted, not for the first time.

"I would rather be there to help you through," she insisted, just as strongly.

"If I snored like a freight train you probably wouldn't object to my sleeping elsewhere. I dare say it would be conducive to a better marriage."

"That's different," she said. "You need me, and I need to be there for you."

Chas thought she had him convinced, but when they arrived home he went off to his *other* room as soon as they had prayer. Chas was at least grateful that they were still praying together each evening. It seemed like the only spiritual connection they had left. He'd completely stopped going to church, and any discussion about his reasons—or anything at all remotely related to religion—always created tension between them. So, Chas had stopped bringing it up altogether, and just kept praying that he would find peace and be drawn to the things that were so precious to her.

They had returned to find that all was well at the inn, and heard a good report in regard to Wendell. The boy seemed pleased to see them again, even though he assured them that Polly had fed him well and been good company.

After Wendell had been in their employ for a couple of weeks, Jackson told him that he'd adequately paid off his "room and board," but he could keep working there for an hourly wage if he would like. The boy eagerly agreed, and Jackson added, "There's something I want you to have. Come into the office with me."

He went to a large set of shelves where there were books and other paraphernalia that they offered for sale as part of the theme of the Dickensian Inn. They had multiple copies of all of Dickens' novels, and had to regularly restock the supply. Because the rooms were themed around certain characters, many people enjoyed purchasing books as souvenirs of their stay at the inn. Jackson pulled down a paperback copy of *A Tale of Two Cities*. "Have you ever read anything by Dickens?" he asked Wendell.

"I don't think so."

"You would remember if you had. Have a seat." They both sat down on the little couch in the office. "I was near your age, I think, when one of my teachers gave me a copy of a Dickens novel, and it changed my life. It wasn't this book, but this is the one that's always meant the most to me. If you will actually read this book, I would love to give it to you. But if you're just going to take it home and let it collect dust, then I'm going to save it for someone else."

Wendell took the book and thumbed through it. "Wow. It's a pretty big book."

"It is, but I know you like to read."

"I've read all of *Harry Potter,*" he said proudly.

"Then you can surely handle Dickens. Because he wrote it a long time ago, the language is a little hard to understand, but if you read closely, you'll start to get used to it. I think you'll find that Dickens is amazing at creating characters and situations that make you feel like you're there, and you can't stop reading. Are you willing to give it a try?"

"Sure, why not? I have to read something for school anyway. The teacher doesn't care what, just so we're reading every day."

"Okay, I want to point out a couple of things. I want you to read the very first line to me."

Wendell opened the book to the first page and read, "'It was the best of times, it was the worst of times.'"

"What do you think that means?" Jackson asked.

Wendell thought about it. "There's good stuff going on, and bad stuff too."

"Exactly. And I think that this statement describes our time, as well. There are lots of really awful things going on in the world, but there are some really great things too. It's a great time to live, but it's also a very hard time. Would you agree with that?"

"Yeah, I guess so."

"With that much said, I want you to think as you're reading how the lessons the characters learn through the story might apply to us today, not just to them during the time period in which the story takes place."

"Okay." Wendell shrugged.

"Now, I want you to go to the very last sentence of the book. I promise it won't give anything away. Read starting right here."

He pointed to the spot, and Wendell read. "'It is a far, far better thing that I do, than I have ever done; it is a far, far better rest that I go to than I have ever known.'"

"Now, since you don't know the story, you don't know exactly what he means. But I want you to think about it as you read, and when you're done, we'll talk about it, and I'll tell you the story of how those words at the end changed my life."

"Okay," Wendell said eagerly, as if hearing that story gave him more incentive to read the burdensome book.

Jackson told Wendell a little bit about the French Revolution with the hope of having the story make more sense, given some historical background. Wendell seemed genuinely interested, and Jackson hoped that this endeavor would prove worthwhile.

Wendell came back a couple of days later and told Jackson that when he'd informed his English teacher that he was reading Dickens, she told him he'd get extra credit if he actually finished the book before the end of the school year and could give her a report on it. Since a comprehensive book report on a classic novel was a regular assignment that had to be done in the spring anyway, Wendell figured it was a pretty good deal, and he was excited to keep going. It would also give him plenty of time to read it slowly enough to understand it. He'd read a couple of chapters and admitted that he was starting to get the hang of it.

Chas enjoyed having Wendell around. He was an agreeable child who knew how to work fairly hard with only occasional urging. She liked seeing Jackson interact with him, and knew that her husband was, and would continue to be, a good father. She sensed a growing unrest in Jackson, however, and couldn't help but feel concerned. She could easily attribute his tendency to be more testy and impatient to the fact that he wasn't getting good sleep, and she knew it—even though they no longer slept in the same room. They still shared an intimate relationship and spent time together doing things outside of the "everydayness" of running the inn, but she still felt a chasm growing wider between them. Most of the time he was polite and appropriate, but she often felt that he was having to use great self-discipline to be so. His sour moods were becoming more common, and there were times when she was glad to have him find chores in the yard or the garage that needed doing, if only to have a little space and distance. She didn't like feeling that way, especially recalling how it had become their habit to work closely together during much of the day and never get on each other's nerves.

By the last week of October, Chas began to wonder what kind of vicious cycle they had gotten into. At least once a day she had to hold herself back from snapping at him or screaming demands that he get some help and stop pretending that everything was all right. This was *not* the man she had married, but reminding him of that hadn't done any good—quite the opposite, in fact. It seemed that her every effort, no matter how gentle or appropriate, to get him to open up, or seek help, or even acknowledge the problem, was only encouraging him to retreat further from her emotionally. He went about his work at the inn as he always had, but only Chas and Polly were allowed to see his testy side. And he'd only let Polly see it because she was simply around far too much for him to hide it in her presence. She could usually tease him out of a bad mood in a way that Chas was no longer able to do. Chas wondered when she had become the person to whom Jackson was the least kind. Still, he was never unkind enough for her to call him on it. He was well aware that she wouldn't tolerate certain behavior, and he was careful not to cross those lines. But he certainly hovered close to them sometimes, and Chas was becoming increasingly concerned.

On a blustery day less than a week before Halloween, Chas finally acknowledged a recent suspicion and took a pregnancy test that she had purchased along with groceries the day before. She hadn't said a word to Jackson or anyone else about the recent symptoms, wanting to be sure before she shared the news. Looking at the positive indicator, she sat down alone in her bedroom and tried to imagine how this would change their lives. Charles wasn't quite a year old yet, so these children would be very close together. Of course, having lost a baby many years earlier due to a genetic heart defect, she also had to acknowledge that with every pregnancy there was the fear of that happening again. But she couldn't think about that. She was pregnant, and she was going to expect a perfectly healthy baby until she was told otherwise. She wondered how Jackson would receive the news, and hoped with all her soul that this would have a calming effect on him, and perhaps inspire him to take some steps toward putting their marriage—and his emotional health—where they needed to be.

Chas hid the pregnancy test evidence and got to work, mentioning to Jackson in passing that there was something she needed to talk to him about when they could have a few minutes alone. He was on his way out the door to do some errands and simply said, "Okay; later, then."

"Of course," she said and kissed him. He seemed almost surprised by her affection, and she wondered why.

In the afternoon, Chas and Polly were working in the office while Charles slept in his room. Chas had the baby monitor nearby, as always. Jackson came into the office to go over some papers. He said very little to either of the women, but the office felt very small with him there. The three of them had often worked there at the same time and managed just fine, but today Jackson's mood was a little more sour than usual. Chas felt some relief when he finally gave up on what he'd intended to do and left the room, saying, "There are some things I need to take care of in the garage."

Chas breathed a sigh of relief after the door had closed, and she focused on the paperwork in front of her. Polly cleared her throat ridiculously loudly, and Chas looked up to see if she was all right. She appeared to be fine, except for a penetrating stare that seemed to have some hidden message. Chas glanced around the room to see if there was some hint Polly was trying to give her. She looked back at her and said, "What?"

"It's probably none of my business, but I'm trying to figure out if you're really that oblivious, or if you just don't care."

"I have no idea what you're talking about."

"You honestly have no idea why your husband goes out to the garage every time he gets uptight?"

"No," Chas drawled, her heart quickening at the implication.

"And you haven't noticed that when he comes back in, he's much more relaxed . . . and has really great breath?"

"How do you know?" she demanded.

"He's always leaning over the desk to double-check something or answer a question. You would expect somebody to have that fresh mouthwash smell right after they've brushed their teeth, or something. But since when does he keep mouthwash in the garage?"

Chas rose to her feet with a stab of panic, then she had to just stand there a minute and let it soak in. Polly encouraged her overwhelming sense of stupidity when she said, "You really hadn't noticed."

"Am I really that . . . dense?"

"Maybe you just weren't looking for it because you never believed he would resort to that."

"Well, that's true," she said, hearing anger in her own voice. Better that than bursting into tears. She grasped onto the anger and pushed down the deep hurt and sorrow bubbling inside of her.

Rushing out of the office, she heard Polly say, "Good luck."

During the short walk to the garage, Chas had to work hard to suppress the urge to cry, and even harder to put her anger in a place where she wouldn't explode and make the matter worse. She couldn't believe it! She had to check herself and remember that she was only going on Polly's suspicions. Perhaps there was another explanation. Perhaps it wasn't what it seemed to be. By the time she opened the door, she'd almost convinced herself that it wasn't as bad as it seemed, that this was all just a silly misunderstanding. But there he was, pouring liquor into a glass. He froze at the sound of the door, then he set down the bottle, picked up the glass and turned around, leaning casually against the workbench while he took a long sip. She was glad that he didn't try to hide it, but his nonchalance made her angry.

Chas closed the door and leaned against it. "Apparently you were hoping I'd find out."

"Not hoping, necessarily. But wondering why you hadn't."

"Apparently I'm not very sharp."

"Or you give your husband more credit than he deserves."

"Does that make me a bad wife?" She was amazed at her even tone of voice when she felt her hands shaking. Since her influence in his life had been the biggest reason he'd *stopped* drinking years earlier, she had to wonder what the implication might be now that he'd started again. He'd told her then that she inspired him. Apparently the inspiration wasn't there anymore.

"No." He took another sip. "I think you are the best wife in the world. I don't believe a woman could be more patient, or kind, or good than you."

"But you betray me?" The anger crept into her voice.

"Betray you? This has nothing to do with you."

"You will never convince me of *that*. If you don't consider it a betrayal, then why were you trying to hide it?"

"I knew you would be disappointed in me." He set the glass aside and folded his arms.

"You've got that right." She crossed the room and stood to face him. "Why, Jackson? I don't understand. Why would you regress to this? You're better than this and we both know it."

He chuckled bitterly. "I don't know what you think you know, but I do not agree with that statement."

"Which is the heart of the problem. Why can't you simply accept that you can't solve this without help? Do you really think that drinking on the sly is going to make anything better?"

"You know what? I don't think you really have any idea what's going on here, so why don't we just—"

"Only because you won't tell me; you hardly talk to me at all anymore—about anything. So, it's easier to go to the liquor store than to talk to your wife?" She saw the muscles in his face tighten. "Talk to me," she pleaded. "Tell me how you feel."

"Fine." The word burst out of him with a hiss. "I can't keep up with you, Chas. I don't have your faith, your optimism, your undying belief that everything will be okay. I have no reason whatsoever to think that it will *ever* be okay. I can't do it. I can't compete."

"Compete?" Chas felt completely baffled. Had her gentle, careful suggestions been taken with such defensiveness? Did the way she simply lived her life feel like some kind of threat to him? She couldn't believe it! "When was this ever a competition?" she asked. "I never asked or expected you to—"

"You know what?" he said again, sounding more angry. "I can't help wondering if we made a mistake. Maybe I'm *not* the right man for you. You deserve better."

Chas sucked in a loud breath and couldn't let it out. She couldn't believe what she was hearing. She finally managed to mutter, "What . . . are you saying? You . . . can't be serious."

"If you had any idea what's going through my head right now, you'd send me packing and figure it was good riddance."

"Don't tell me what you think I would do or how I would feel. I would *never* feel that way; I would *never* want you to go." He glared at her with silent challenge, but she was willing to take it on. "What *are* you thinking?"

His expression implied that once she heard what he had to say, he believed she would renege on what she'd just said. He leaned toward her and clenched his teeth. "When you talk like that to me, I want to *hit* you, the way I saw my father hit my mother every day of my life."

Chas wasn't nearly as surprised as he seemed to think she should be. She knew about the environment in which he'd been raised. She just held his gaze and said, "But you wouldn't."

"How can you be sure? Especially if I've been drinking."

"I know you better than that. You would never lower yourself to that."

"Like you thought I would never regress to drinking again? A man can do ugly things when he's drunk."

"Then you're going to have to stop drinking."

"And if I don't? I know for a fact that you would never tolerate it."

"You're right; I wouldn't."

"Then I should go." He moved past her toward the door.

Again Chas was stunned. "You would choose drinking over me? This life? Our son?"

He paused and turned to look at her. "You both deserve better than what I can give you. I should have left a long time ago."

"Jackson!" She ran after him. "You can't be serious."

He said nothing as she followed him into the house and to their room, and Chas didn't want to say what she was thinking when they were anywhere near where Polly might overhear. Once in the bedroom with the door closed, she realized he was packing and she was overcome with unbridled terror. "Jackson, no!" Tears came with her words. "You want me to beg, I'll beg. Please don't leave like this. We can talk about this; we can work it out."

"I'm sorry," he said coldly. "I really am. But I can't do it." He just kept packing and wouldn't look at her.

"Please, Jackson, I—"

"Enough, Chas," he said harshly. "I have to go. It's best for all of us, and there is nothing you can say to convince me otherwise. I'm glad you know the truth; I'm tried of hiding it. And now it should be easy to see that our being married is ridiculous. I can never be the man you need me to be."

Chas felt so desperate that she took hold of his arm to try to stop him. He turned and lifted his other hand as if he would strike her.

She cried out, and his hand stopped midair. Their eyes met fiercely, and he dropped his hand, saying in a stony voice, "I need to go before I hurt you more than I already have."

Chas didn't let go of him. "I know what you're doing," she cried. "You're trying to convince me that I made a mistake, but I didn't. I know I didn't. We're supposed to be together, and there is nothing you can say to convince me otherwise."

She saw his eyes turn sad, but his voice turned cold. "Then it would appear we're in serious disagreement." He shrugged her off, grabbed a few more things that he stuffed into a bag. Chas could only stand frozen, watching as if from a distance while he closed the bag and left the room. She heard the door close, but she couldn't move. A sudden weakness in her knees compelled her to sit on the edge of the bed, where the tears finally burst out of her. Polly found her there minutes later, and Chas hadn't even heard her come into the room. She was trembling and in shock, and her tears had given way to a numb kind of terror.

"What happened?" Polly asked, sitting beside her.

"He . . . left," Chas said. Hearing the words urged a single, intense sob out of her lips. "He . . . he packed and . . . he left."

"No, it's not possible!" Polly said. "He wouldn't!"

Chas dissolved into tears again with Polly's arms around her. She cried until the baby started making noises to indicate that he was waking up. He usually played in his crib for a few minutes before he demanded to be picked up, and Chas tried to pull herself together.

"Is anyone else in the house?" Chas asked, hoping no one else had heard their arguing—or her sobbing.

"No, it's just us," Polly assured her. "And for what it's worth, I just don't think he's gone for good. Where's he going to go? He loves you; he loves the baby. He could never live without either one of you. I'd bet that if you just give him a day or two, he'll come to his senses and apologize. We both know he's having a hard time, but at heart, he's really a great guy. You know he is; we both know it."

"Yes, he is a great guy," Chas said and took a deep breath. "Oh, I hope you're right, Polly. I just . . . don't think I can live without him." She let out a weighted sigh. "Martin and I were married so short a time before he was killed, and I spent so many years alone." She started to cry again. "I can't go through that again, Polly; I can't."

"You know what," Polly said with kind firmness, "I think you can do whatever you have to do. I think you're a lot tougher than you think you are. But I really don't believe it's going to come to that. It might get worse before it gets better, but I am not going to believe that he's really leaving you for good until it's signed, sealed, and delivered. He won't do it; he just won't. So take care of the baby, be patient, say some prayers like you always do, and give it some time."

"Okay," Chas said. "Thank you." She took a deep breath and realized that she needed to share her burden, and Polly was her most trusted friend. "Polly, there's something else."

"What? Tell me."

"I'm pregnant."

Polly gasped. "When did you figure that out? Is that why you've been so tired lately?"

"Probably, and I just did a test this morning."

"Good heavens! Jackson doesn't know."

Chas felt a fresh rise of tears and shook her head. "No, he doesn't know. If he knew, do you think it would make a difference?"

"Well, it won't change his problems or what he needs to do to fix them, but it might give him more incentive to do the right thing. You'll know when it's right to tell him."

"If he'll talk to me at all."

"He will; I'm sure of it."

"Talking isn't his strongest trait."

"No, but he has others that make up for it."

"Yes, he does," Chas said and sighed. "For now, this is between you and me."

"Of course. Who would I tell?"

"I don't want Charlotte knowing. She's a good friend to both of us, but . . . I'm not sure I even want her to know Jackson is gone; not yet anyway. I love Charlotte, but she . . ."

"She would see it completely differently than you see it," Polly said. "I know. And she would give you all the wrong advice. I get it, believe me. It's okay. I won't say a word to anyone until you tell me to."

"Okay, thank you, Polly. I don't know what I'd do without you."

"You'll never have to wonder."

Chas did as Polly suggested, going about her normal routine with a prayer in her heart that Jackson *would* come to his senses. She needed him! She needed him so much.

# Chapter Eight

Jackson quickly drove toward Butte with the intention of getting a motel room while he took some time to decide the best way to go about dissolving his marriage in a way that would bring Chas the least possible grief. She'd already suffered so much on his behalf. He just wanted to remove himself from her life and be done with it. He was amazed that he'd finally done it. The idea of leaving had circled around in his mind for weeks, until it had felt as if he'd had no choice but to just do it. But now that he actually had, it didn't seem quite so cut and dried as he'd made himself believe.

While he drove, Jackson's thoughts took an entirely different direction than he'd anticipated. A voice inside his head seemed to ask how he would feel if it were the other way around. How would he feel if Chas had left him, even with the supposedly noble intentions of wanting his life to be easier? He realized in the space of a heartbeat that he'd made a mistake. He couldn't remove himself from her life, not completely anyway. He was the father of her child. They deserved better than what he was giving them now, but removing himself from their lives completely was not *better;* it was far, far worse. And he was a fool to have ever thought otherwise. She deserved a man who would stay with her and be a decent husband and father. How could he have even considered that leaving her was an option when she'd lost her first husband and struggled through so many years of loneliness? He kicked himself to think of how he had one more black mark against him in this marriage, one that he would have to live down. But somehow he had to change this course and make it up to her.

By the time he actually arrived in Butte, Jackson knew what he had to do; there was only one possible course of action that could ever begin to mend everything he'd torn apart. Almost against his conscious will, he found himself arriving at a specific destination. While a part of him knew it was necessary and inevitable, another part of him was terrified. But he had to think of Chas. She deserved better. He had to do this for her. And maybe by the time Charles was old enough to really know what was going on, Jackson could be the kind of father the boy deserved.

Jackson sat in his vehicle in the parking lot for nearly an hour. He was parked as far from the building as he could possibly be, as if the distance might make it easier to make the decision. But it was already made. There was no other possible course.

He nearly dialed the number of the inn more than a dozen times, holding the cell phone in his hand as if it were a lifeline. And yet he felt terrified to make the connection. He kept hoping that Chas would call him, but he couldn't figure why she'd want to. She was probably *furious* with him, and in her gentle wisdom was giving herself time to cool down before talking to him. Well, *his* time was running out. He had to do this before he lost his courage, and he had to talk to her before he did it. He finally dialed the number and was relieved when she was the one to answer.

"It's me," he said, and Chas offered no response, but he couldn't blame her. "You don't have to say anything. Just listen."

"Okay." At least he knew she hadn't hung up on him.

"I need to say that I'm sorry. I'm sorry for bringing this into your life. I'm sorry for not handling it very well. I'm sorry that I let you down . . . that I disappointed you. I'm so sorry, Chas."

Chas was immensely relieved to hear his voice, to hear him apologize, to hear some humility. But she still had no idea if this was simply leading up to more justification for his leaving her. Following more than a minute of silence, she spoke in a voice that made it clear that she'd been crying. "So, you're sorry. Is this phone call meant to be 'I'm sorry. Good-bye.' Or 'I'm sorry and I'm going to do something about it?'"

"I was going to check into a motel once I got to the city," he said. "But I thought, 'Then what?' I don't want to be away from you, Chas, but I know I've really messed things up. While I was driving, I remembered what you said to me before we were married . . . about commitment. You said that marriage was about commitment, and trust, and respect; that we had to trust each other enough to work through whatever came up, and that the commitment had to be stronger than the challenges. How could I be foolish enough to walk away from a woman who believes in such things?"

Chas swallowed hard. "Okay, so you'd be a fool to walk away, but . . . are you going to? I need to know."

Jackson felt the words he wanted to say pass through his heart before settling in his head. He felt like a hypocrite for saying them, but perhaps that was the first step to understanding the problem. "If you can forgive me, Chas . . . if you still think I'm worth the trouble . . ." His voice broke. "I need you, Chas. Please . . ."

Chas absorbed the relief into herself, finding it difficult to stay upright as her fears of him leaving her rushed up all over again. She forced a firm voice, knowing what had to be said. "I love you, Jackson; I love you more than life. And I can forgive you. But you need to understand that love does not equal trust, and forgiveness does not equal trust. You have my love and forgiveness, regardless of anything else. But the trust between us has been broken. Would you agree?"

"Yes," he said, so relieved at the prospect of being forgiven that he had no problem admitting to the truth.

"You're going to have to earn back that trust, and I'm not going to make it easy for you. But as long as I see evidence that you are working to earn it, I will be beside you every step of the way, no matter what it takes. Do you understand what I'm saying?"

"Yes," he said again.

"So, what are you going to do about it?"

"I told you I'd decided against checking into a motel."

"Then come home."

"I can't do that; not yet."

"Then where are you going to—"

"I'm at the hospital, Chas. I'm checking myself into the psych ward. That's what I called to tell you. I have to go now, before I talk myself out of it. I love you. I love you so much. I'll call you when . . ."

"When what?" she demanded, suddenly fearing the distance between them in regard to his intentions.

"I don't know," he said. "I need to get past this. Just . . . be patient. I'll call you when I have something to tell you that isn't the same old garbage. I love you. I need to go."

He forced himself to hang up before she could even comment. He wasn't sure he could handle any course the conversation might have taken from there. He pressed his head to the steering wheel and groaned. He wiped away a few stray tears, then he turned off his cell phone and put it in the glove box before he got out of the car, locked it, and walked through the hospital doors. It took him a few minutes to find the psych ward. But it was a locked section, and he couldn't actually get to the desk there. So he found a nurses' station nearby and said, "I'd like to check myself into the psych ward. How would I go about that?" Seeing the dumbfounded silence on the faces of every nurse within earshot, he added, "Is that crazy?" Then he chuckled, and they all did as well.

A nurse said she would make a call and asked him to have a seat in the hallway. It was nearly twenty minutes before she found him and said, "I finally got in touch with the right person. Dr. Callahan is coming out to meet you, and you can talk to him."

"Thank you," Jackson said and found himself praying silently for the first time in many months. He'd never learned to pray until he met Chas, and then it had become a habit to turn his thoughts to asking God for this or that, or offering thanks for something good in his life. However, he'd completely stopped doing it, without fully understanding why. But he was tired of trying to solve this on his own; it obviously wasn't working. If he'd ever needed God's help, he needed it now. His most urgent request to God was that Chas would be all right in his absence, and that they could really put their marriage back together. And next on the list was a prayer that this Dr. Callahan—or whoever they might turn him over to—would be a decent therapist; someone who could truly help him. The very thought of dealing with doctors like those he'd previously encountered tied his stomach in knots. He focused more on prayer and the hope that came with it, and he was startled to hear a man say, "Jackson Leeds?"

"Yes," Jackson said, coming to his feet.

"I'm Ross Callahan," he said with a smile, extending his hand.

Already Jackson liked him better than the previous therapists. He was probably in his middle thirties, average height and build, with sandy brown hair and a pleasant appearance. He wore jeans with a gray button-up shirt and a dark blue tie. His collar had been loosened, and his sleeves were rolled up haphazardly. He looked completely relaxed and at ease, and a spark of curiosity flashed in his eyes.

"I was told," he went on, "that you're wanting to check yourself in."

"That's right," Jackson said. "Are you a therapist?"

"I am," Callahan said, "although there are some days when this job really makes me crazy." He laughed at himself as if he'd been surprised by what he'd said. "No pun intended." He motioned with his hand, saying, "Let's walk, and you can tell me a little bit about what's going on, and then we can decide the best course."

"Fair enough," Jackson said and picked up his bag.

"I'll start. I was born and raised in New York City, grew up in a crazy family that made me want to get out and become sane. Somewhere in the midst of all the counseling, I realized it suited me. Now I'm the head of this department. I have a wife and two kids, and I'm very fond of Montana—especially with the distance from New York. Now it's your turn."

Jackson was amazed at how easy the doctor was making this. "I grew up in Arkansas in a severely dysfunctional family and joined the Marines at eighteen to get away. I got a degree along with my service and eventually ended up in the FBI. I retired from that a couple of years ago when I got married and took up innkeeping. My wife and I run a bed-and-breakfast in Anaconda. We have a son who's nearly a year old."

Callahan made an interested noise and motioned Jackson into an elevator. He felt a little confused since they'd been on the floor of the psych ward. They were the only two people in the elevator, and Callahan said, "So, what's wrong with you that requires such intense psychiatric care? You don't *look* crazy."

"I disguise it well," Jackson said. "I'm not actually *crazy* . . . exactly."

"Okay."

"I have PTSD."

"Really?" the doctor said as if he'd been told that he'd won an all-expense-paid vacation.

"Is that significant?"

Callahan smiled. "Do you believe in serendipity?" At Jackson's confusion, he explained, "It's a kind of phenomenon where certain things or people come together for reasons that have no logical explanation."

"My wife would call that a miracle."

"Call it what you like, my friend, but you should know that my special expertise is PTSD."

"Really?" Jackson said in the same tone the doctor had used. "Then why didn't I know about you a couple of years ago?"

"I just came to this hospital a little over a year ago. That crazy family I mentioned . . . one of the big problems was my dad's PTSD; he was in Vietnam, and it was ugly. Of course, it wasn't understood nearly as much back then. But his situation was at least part of my motivation to go into psychology, and I've always had a certain fascination with it." He motioned elaborately with his arm. "And here you are."

"Yes, here I am."

"Not doing well, I take it."

"No, I'm not. It's out of control; it's messing up my life and making me do stupid things. I need help before I hurt someone, or myself."

"Okay," the doctor said, looking at him as if he were a rare and precious specimen.

They were silent as they stepped out of the elevator and went down a long hall. The doctor seemed to be contemplating the problem, so Jackson left him to it. Then he realized they were going into the cafeteria.

"You hungry?" Callahan asked. "I'm starved. Come on, I'm buying."

Jackson just had a cup of coffee, and his offer to pay for the doctor's late lunch was adamantly refused. When they were seated across from each other, Callahan said, "So, tell me how you got PTSD. The Marines?"

"No, I got through that pretty well, actually."

"FBI, then?"

"It started out as an FBI assignment, yes."

"I'd love to hear about it."

"Are you going to be my doctor? Because if you're going to assign me to somebody else, I'd rather just wait and tell the story once."

"I would be honored to be your doctor, Mr. Leeds. You're the most sane person I've talked to in days around this place—and I include most of my staff in that statement." He laughed at himself again, and Jackson joined him. "First I would like to assess whether or not you really *need* a doctor."

"Oh, I do."

"Okay, but we could do out-patient counseling. Maybe you don't really need to be admitted to the psych ward. Let's talk about it."

Jackson looked around to be assured that no one was sitting within hearing range. It was a slow time of day preceding the dinner rush.

"First give me the nutshell version of the incident that triggered the problem. Or is there more than one incident?"

"No, just one."

"Then give me a nutshell version of your symptoms. And we'll go from there."

"Okay," Jackson said, hesitated, then asked, "You really want to hear this over your chicken fettuccini?"

"I really do . . . unless you're not comfortable with that; we can wait until—"

"No, it's okay," Jackson said, actually liking the man's informality and comfortable nature. He was just surprised to note that the doctor was okay with it too.

Jackson only had to think for half a minute before he found words to meet the doctor's request. *The incident* had become such a fulcrum in his life that he knew it backward and forward. Summarizing was not a problem.

"I was nearly ready to retire from the FBI when I was sent on one final mission."

"You knew it was going to be the last one?"

"Yes. It was the one I'd been waiting for; it would wrap up everything that felt undone to me."

"Okay, I've got you."

"The mission went fine, but it required my going undercover in South America, assuming the identity of a drug dealer. Our target had never met the man. I pulled off pretending to be someone he had communicated with only through email and text messages. It worked, and we sent our bad guy to prison."

"Cool," Callahan said with his mouth full.

"But apparently the man I was pretending to be had a lot of enemies. I was dragged out of my bed, locked in a concrete cell with only one small window that was too high for me to reach. I was given very little food and water, and what they gave me was disgusting. I was only dragged out of that room to be beaten and tortured, but since I couldn't give them the answers they wanted, they just . . . kept at it."

"Wow!" Callahan said, setting his fork down. "And you survived."

"I'm here talking about it."

"Which is remarkable. I mean . . . really. A hundred other men who had been through something like that would be in a padded room."

"Don't patronize me, Doctor."

"I'm not a patronizing kind of man, Mr. Leeds, because I learned a long time ago that even the craziest crazies can see through that. I know you wouldn't trust me if I were patronizing you, and I know it would be impossible to help you if you don't trust me. I mean it when I say that you obviously have some inner strength that we need to acknowledge. You survived, and you're sitting here talking about it. That's a couple of big hurdles. How *did* you survive?"

"The FBI found me; fellow agents got me out."

"How long were you there?"

"Three and a half weeks."

"Wow," the doctor said again.

"I was in the hospital at least that long. On top of the injuries, I got a nasty parasite. The counseling after that was . . ."

"Worse?" Callahan guessed. "Worse than recovering from the physical injuries?"

"Yeah, it was worse. I hated it, even though my counselor was pretty good; at least I think she was. I felt comfortable with her, and I felt like she knew what she was talking about. That was in Virginia. I did some phone sessions with her after I moved here, and I saw another counselor for a while."

"But you stopped?"

"Yeah. The symptoms seemed under control. I was managing. Now one of those counselors has retired, and the other one has moved. I tried three counselors earlier this year; they were all disasters."

"So, you don't have a lot of faith in my profession."

"I'm here, aren't I?"

"That's true. What changed?"

"What do you mean?"

"Your symptoms were under control; you were managing. But you've been rummaging through counselors. What changed?"

"It got worse . . . worse than it's ever been . . . when my mother died . . . in May."

"What *are* the symptoms, Jackson? May I call you Jackson?"

"Sure. I have nightmares. I wake up in a full-blown panic attack and it takes a long time to get my blood pressure to come back to normal."

"Do you ever hallucinate when you're awake?"

"No."

"Have you ever had a panic attack that wasn't the direct result of a nightmare?"

"Only once."

"Do you know why? Was there something that triggered it?"

"Yes, and yes. But I'd rather save that conversation for somewhere besides the cafeteria."

"Agreed. Do you ever have feelings of paranoia?"

"No," Jackson said, glad to mentally note that such feelings had all been legitimate.

"Have you ever had a flashback while you're awake, when you've actually believed you were back there?"

"No."

"Have you ever hurt or threatened anyone?"

"No. Other than the argument I just had with my wife, no. But I didn't hurt her."

"Are you depressed?"

"Yes, and I'm exhausted."

"And why do you feel that this warrants checking yourself into the hospital?"

"Because I started drinking again when I haven't done so for years. It's ruining my marriage. And I just can't handle it anymore. I have good insurance, and I can afford to pay the difference, whatever it may be. I actually like you, Dr. Callahan. And I think I can actually trust you. Will you help me?"

"Sure. Why not? But I might have to exaggerate a little on the paperwork to get them to keep you. I don't think you're nearly as bad off as you think you are. But . . . let's get you admitted and settled in, and we'll talk some more in the morning. After you spend a night in the ward, you might change your mind." He chuckled and picked up his tray to take it to the conveyor belt that went into the kitchen. Jackson threw away his empty coffee cup and picked up his bag.

"Your timing is good, if nothing else," Callahan said as they walked back toward the elevator. "We actually have a couple of free rooms; that's not always the case."

"That's good, then," Jackson said.

In the elevator, the doctor asked, "So, what does your wife think of this checking yourself in? Usually the spouse comes along."

"I left the house; we were both upset. I called to tell her what I was doing."

"And she's okay with it?"

"She's okay with whatever it takes to have a normal life, I'm sure."

They stepped out of the elevator. "How has she been about the whole thing?"

"She's very patient, very good to me; couldn't be better."

"That's another hurdle you've passed. Some people with this condition have spouses that are not handling it well at all, or they're not very supportive or understanding."

"I'm here to do something about it before it gets to that."

"Okay." Callahan took the ID card hanging from a lanyard around his neck and swiped it through the card reader next to the locked double doors. A light went from red to green, and the door unlocked. As they stepped through the doors, the doctor took Jackson's bag. "I'm afraid we'll need to search this, and we may be holding on to some of this stuff for you." At Jackson's obvious alarm and confusion, he added, "You might not be a threat to yourself or anyone else, but there are other people staying here that are, and we have to be very careful. If you're going to stay here, you'll have to put up with it."

"Fair enough," Jackson said.

He waited while Callahan spoke quietly to a couple of people, then he left for a little while, and a woman asked him about a thousand questions while she made check marks and notations on a clipboard.

Another woman took different information and copied his insurance card. It was Callahan who brought him some papers to sign. All of the personal information had been put into the computer and printed off on forms that required signatures. Callahan handed him a pen and said, "You came here of your own free will, and you can leave the same way—whenever you decide you're ready. Although, once you sign these papers, you are relinquishing a certain amount of power to our staff, and you won't be able to check out without going through some procedures. The only exception to your checking out would be that while you're in our care you exhibit behavior that gives us solid grounds to keep you here until there is some improvement. Make sense?"

"Yes."

"You're also agreeing that you can be observed for evaluation. There are cameras in the room where you'll be sleeping, and our sessions will be videotaped. It says here that you only give permission to our highest level of staff to view these recordings, and they will be kept completely private otherwise. If you're okay with all of that, then sign away."

Jackson didn't even hesitate. He felt better already to just know that he was taking some steps in the right direction. He prayed that the outcome would be good.

Once the paperwork was taken care of, Callahan led Jackson down the hall, saying, "My shift is over in a few minutes, but you'll be in good hands. They'll feed you and make sure you have what you need. I've got most of tomorrow morning clear, and we'll have a good, long talk after breakfast, barring any emergencies that need my attention."

"Okay, thank you," Jackson said.

Callahan stepped into a small room and said, "Here it is. Not real cozy, but it's all we've got."

Jackson stopped in the doorway, feeling an unexpected panic. The room was small and very clinical looking. Callahan turned to investigate his immobility. "I . . . have a hard time with confined spaces."

"Frequently?"

"No . . . just now, or . . . worse now than ever before."

"Why?"

"I . . . am not sure," Jackson admitted. "I don't really like going to the cellar at home. Beyond that I've never had a hard time going into a room before, but I don't like this one."

"Does it remind you of where you were confined?" Callahan asked, and Jackson's heart began to thud.

"Yes, only that was much worse. It was just a . . . concrete room; small, cold."

"Okay, change of plan," Callahan said. "Eventually we need to face that and deal with it, but not tonight. Let me see what I can do."

Half an hour later Dr. Callahan had gone home for the night, and Jackson had been put into a normal patient room down the hall from the psychiatric ward. It was a little more spacious with nice curtains and some minimal decor. He didn't know why it made a difference, but it did. He spent the evening watching TV and missing his family. He resisted the temptation to call Chas several times, believing it would be best to talk to her when he had more hurdles behind him. He slept with the light on and was glad that when the usual nightmare woke him it didn't arouse the attention of anyone outside of his room. It occurred to him that if he'd spent the night in the psych ward, his waking up in a panic would have been observed via camera. He didn't like that idea at all, but he'd signed the papers and he needed to see it through. He could certainly walk out right now if he chose, but he thought of Chas and his son and knew that he had to go through with this. He recalled Chas once telling him that he needed to act like a Marine. A Marine wouldn't abandon his post just because the battle got tough. Like him, he figured most Marines would rather face real battle than this kind of madness, but it was a battle still the same.

\* \* \* \* \*

Chas was grateful that Polly had agreed to stay at the inn for the night. They shared supper and watched a chick flick together after Charles had gone to bed. By then Chas was exhausted and able to sleep. She felt a deep relief to know that Jackson was determined to work things out, and she was inexplicably grateful to know that he was getting the help he needed. She didn't know why he'd chosen to shut her out of the process, but she didn't have much choice beyond waiting for him to reach out to her. She knew from trying it several times that his cell phone was turned off. By the time she'd thought about making some calls to see if she could find him, it was too late in the evening, but she set her mind to doing just that in the morning once she'd fed her guests their breakfast.

Chas woke up feeling well rested and glad that Charles was still sleeping through the night most of the time. When she recalled that her husband wasn't in the house, she started to cry, certain her pregnancy wasn't helping much in that regard. Then she was confronted with a wave of nausea and had to hurry into the bathroom. She went in search of some crackers to ease her turbulent stomach and was feeling a little better by the time the baby woke up. She was soon busy with her day and grateful for Polly's help with the baby while she prepared breakfast for the occupants of four rooms. It wasn't until the baby was down for his afternoon nap that she had the uninterrupted time to make a call to see how her husband was doing. She called the hospital she knew he would have gone to and asked to be connected to the psych ward. Her heart beat painfully hard while she waited on hold, almost fearing that she'd be told that her husband wasn't really there, which would mean that he'd lied to her and left her, after all. On the other hand, hearing evidence that her husband was in the psych ward would be difficult to comprehend and hard to face. But at least it would mean the problem was being faced.

"Hello," she finally said when someone answered, "I believe my husband is a patient there. Jackson Leeds."

"Yes," Chas heard, but nothing more.

"Could you please tell me how he's doing?" she asked.

"I'm sorry," the woman on the other end of the phone said, "I can't give out that information."

"This is his wife."

"I understand that already. But unless the patient has given permission to share information with you, privacy laws dictate that we cannot do it."

Chas felt frustrated but tried to be polite. "And what if he wasn't in his right mind enough to know who should and shouldn't have information about his condition?"

"Then it would be up to the person who had checked him in. Clearly it was not you. Forgive me, Mrs. Leeds, but I can't help you."

Many minutes after hanging up the phone, Chas paced and worked herself into a frenzy. Polly got her to calm down, and they had a long talk. The inn was quiet that evening, with only a few guests who were either out or holed up in their rooms. Chas and Polly worked together to fix supper and eat it, and again they watched a movie. Chas appreciated the distractions and Polly's company, but her heart ached for her husband, and she wondered how long she would have to wait and wonder.

* * * * *

Jackson was inexplicably relieved when Dr. Callahan came to get him. He was bored out of his mind and longing to accomplish something.

"How was your night?" Callahan asked as they walked back toward the psych ward.

"Typical," Jackson said. "How about yours?"

"No nightmares, so I guess that makes it good." Once past the secure entrance, he added, "I thought we'd just visit in my office a while and see what the afternoon brings."

They entered an office that looked more like a cozy den with a small desk in one corner. They sat in comfortable chairs across from each other, and Callahan said, "I've got my morning cleared, which was surprisingly easy to do. I think that's a good sign. With the understanding you already have of PTSD, and your desire to get beyond it, I'm actually thinking if we just jump in headfirst, we can make some progress rather quickly. I have some ideas that I've been pondering that we can discuss later on, but first I'd like you to start at the beginning and tell me the detailed version of what happened. When things come up that make you especially uncomfortable, I want you to take note of that and tell me. I also want to know more about the details of your life before and after."

"Okay," Jackson said and went back to the point where he had gone to the Dickensian Inn while on administrative leave. He reached the occurrence of the incident within just a few minutes, then it took him well more than an hour to repeat everything he remembered up to the time of his rescue and ending up in the hospital. He then skimmed very quickly over the events that had happened since then.

"That's an amazing story," Callahan said. "Again I have to say that it's amazing you survived and that you're as together as you are."

"I don't feel together."

"I don't want to minimize what you're experiencing, by any means, because it's horrible and you have good reason to be upset and to want it to go away, but I've seen PTSD so much worse than this that's been caused by events much less severe. So, we're going to acknowledge the suffering and the challenge, but it's good to keep perspective as well and look at what you have going in your favor." He drew a thoughtful breath. "I find it interesting that you told me that story with absolutely no emotion. Why do you think that is?"

"I . . . don't know. I never thought about it."

"Initially . . . did you have emotion?"

"I did. I recall crying like a baby, and . . . well . . . screaming, getting angry a great deal during counseling sessions."

"That's good. It's good to get those feelings out. But obviously there're still more inside of you. Do you think it's venting into your nightmares?"

Jackson shrugged. "I don't know. You're the shrink."

"I don't know either, but I hope that we can find out. Which reminds me, you said yesterday that you'd only had one panic attack that wasn't the direct result of a nightmare. You said you didn't want to talk about it in the cafeteria. How about now?"

Jackson shifted in his chair and tried not to let on how his heart rate had increased just at the thought of repeating the events that had led up to *that* moment. It was a simple thing. He'd been sitting in his sister's living room. But he remembered far too clearly what she'd said and how she'd said it—and how his physical and emotional response had been completely beyond his control.

"Whoa," Callahan said while Jackson was distracted by trying to think of a way to say it that might not reproduce the effect. "You're suddenly very . . . agitated. I was beginning to think that you are far too composed to have anything wrong at all."

Jackson had to give him credit for being sharp, because he knew it wasn't *that* obvious. Throughout his career, Jackson had learned to read subtle signs that hinted at various emotions. He couldn't deny his added respect for this man, because he knew it wasn't necessarily easy to read him, but at the same time he was tempted to feel angry. He reminded himself that he had come here voluntarily, and he'd agreed to do whatever it took to get well. But in that moment, he realized more than he ever had that *the incident* was only a part of the problem, and the other part certainly *did* make him agitated.

"Are you going to tell me what's going on?" Callahan asked, "Or should we skirt around it and waste time?"

Jackson continued to ponder what to say and felt himself growing more agitated. Trying to hide it became pointless.

Callahan leaned closer. "What's going on, Jackson?" He couldn't answer, and the doctor added gently, "You know *exactly* what's wrong, don't you." It wasn't a question. "There's an emotional trigger here that you're not telling me about, and you know *exactly* what it is. Tell me, Jackson. Let's cut to the chase and get it out in the open."

Jackson nodded, then he had to stand up and turn his back while he contended with his own fear of how deeply this was affecting him—and how good he had become at ignoring this point, shoving it into parts of his brain where he couldn't think about it. Had the doctor pegged it? Was it venting into his nightmares? He took a deep breath and was able to speak in a fairly even voice. "When I initially got counseling, this issue came up, and the counselor suggested that it might come up again, might cause problems. But it all felt . . . stuck at the time . . . I suppose. It felt like there was nowhere to go with it. It just . . . was."

"I hear you. Then something happened to trigger it?"

"Yeah," Jackson chuckled with no hint of humor. "My mother died."

"Why was your mother's death so hard on you?"

"It *was* hard on me, but that's not what triggered it."

"What then?" Callahan asked.

Jackson turned to look at this man whom he'd come to trust completely in a matter of hours, and said what he'd been trying to forget ever since that last conversation with his mother. "She made me promise to forgive my father."

"Oh," Callahan said, dragging the word into two long syllables. "You haven't told me *anything* about your father."

"I'm sure we'll get to that."

"And talking about your father is harder than talking about the incident?"

"Probably."

"Were you talking about your father when you had that panic attack?"

"My sister . . . said that . . ." Jackson sat back down. "She said that . . . there was no point pretending that . . ." He cleared his throat very loudly. "She said that . . . this horrible thing that had happened to me had . . . stirred up the ugliest memories of . . . my growing up."

As soon as he said it, his chest tightened and his breathing became shallow. Callahan said calmly, "Now, there's the emotion I've been waiting to see."

As if something in his subconscious latched onto this validation, taking it as permission to feel, something volatile and ugly erupted from his deepest self. Chas always tried to calm him down and bring him back to normal. Callahan taunted it into the open, like a street bully wanting to fight. Jackson wanted to run from the room and never come back, but he knew there was nowhere to run where he wouldn't take this pain with him. So he took the bait and started spilling all of the horrid memories from his childhood that he'd never said aloud to anyone. And as he spoke them aloud, more tumbled out from places dark and dusty and crusted over with pain. Memories spilled out that he hadn't even consciously remembered, things he'd stuffed away and protected himself from feeling. And as it all spewed out, accompanied by heated anger and helpless tears, Jackson began to understand better than he ever had why Melinda's statement had been brutally true.

# Chapter Nine

When Jackson's emotion finally exhausted itself, he felt like he'd been hit by a truck. Callahan told him to lie down on the couch, and he'd go get some lunch for both of them and bring it back so Jackson wouldn't have to face anybody. While they sat together in the office and ate together, Callahan initiated small talk about their wives and children. He made no comment about the dramatic episodes of the morning beyond simply asking, "You okay?"

"Yeah," Jackson said, feeling the need for some time to process what had happened. But maybe Callahan knew that, and that's why he was avoiding any reference to it.

After lunch, Callahan declared that he had other patients to see and business to attend to, but he would see him again the following morning at the same time. He assured Jackson that the staff would take very good care of him, but he said he believed that Jackson needed to stay in the ward that night. He took him to a different room that was a little larger, with two beds, and a bathroom adjacent to it.

"The room is all yours and you can sleep with the lights on; I think I'd recommend it for tonight, actually. Do you think you can handle it?"

Jackson felt wary but couldn't argue. "I'm sure I'll survive until morning, especially since I can look forward to another delightful discussion with you." His sarcasm made the doctor chuckle, but if nothing else he liked the way this man didn't try to tiptoe around the sensitive points. Jackson addressed his next greatest need regarding the hours between now and their next session. "Is there anything to read around here?"

"Sure, I can get you something," Callahan said. "You have any preferences?"

"Dickens," Jackson said. "Anything Dickens."

Callahan made a noise to indicate he was impressed. "Dickens it is. Sit tight, and I'll see you in the morning."

The moment he was gone, Jackson opened the curtains as wide as they would go, noting that the window would not open. Suicide prevention, perhaps. At least he could be grateful that his thoughts had never gone *there*. He knew things could be a lot worse, and he *was* grateful for this perspective.

Jackson stood for a long while gazing out the window, watching people and vehicles down below, his mind getting lost in the violent emotions he'd experienced that morning. He marveled at the way dots had connected in his mind, things he'd never been able to consciously quite put together before. He understood better than ever why his childhood experiences were linked to his PTSD, but the reality was sickening. The idea of ever being able to forgive his father felt more impossible than it had before, and he wondered if he'd ever be able to keep his promise to his mother. He wondered how Chas and the baby were doing, and if everything was all right at the inn. He felt a desire to call her, to tell her that he loved her. But a quick glance assured him there was no phone in this room, and he'd left his cell phone in the car. He doubted they'd allow him to have it anyway. He was sure he could ask to use a phone, but since a part of him felt a little afraid to talk to Chas, he found it easier to put it off with the hope of being able to actually say something positive when he did.

A woman wearing bright purple scrubs came into the room and handed Jackson a couple of books. "Dr. Callahan said to bring you these."

"Thank you," Jackson said, delighted to see copies of *Great Expectations* and *Oliver Twist*. They were like old friends to him, and he could get lost in their pages for many hours. Without them he felt sure he *would* lose his mind.

"Can I get you anything else?" she asked. "Are you doing okay?"

"I'm fine, thank you," he said.

"I'll bring you some supper when it's time," she said and left Jackson to his reading. He propped himself up on the bed, stretched out, and dug into the story of Pip and the mentally unstable Miss Havisham. Jackson enjoyed the book as much as he enjoyed the memories of how it had taken him out of his own ugly world as a youth. Having it in his hands now felt akin to miraculous. He paused at that thought and had to admit that connecting with Dr. Callahan and being able to spend the entire morning with him were likely miraculous, as well. Perhaps Chas was praying for him; she probably had been all along. The thought brought tears to his eyes as he considered how much he'd hurt her. He might not have had any control over what the PTSD had been doing to him, but trying to drown it in liquor was one of the stupidest things he'd ever done, especially when he knew how much it had meant to Chas when he'd *stopped* drinking. And rather than facing up to it like a man, he'd run liked a scared rabbit. She'd said that she would forgive him, that she would always love him, but that he would need to earn back her trust. He knew she was right; he only hoped that such a thing might be possible.

Only Jackson's "great expectations" kept him from going insane. Supper was a nice diversion, and it wasn't too bad for hospital food. But he'd realized that just being in the hospital was bringing back awful memories of the weeks following the incident.

At bedtime a nurse brought him a sleeping pill. "Dr. Callahan ordered it," she said. "He said that after you wake up in a strange place, he wanted you to be able to go back to sleep."

She asked if there was anything else he needed, and then he was left alone for the night.

\* \* \* \* \*

Chas woke up and tried to count how many hours she had gone without hearing a word from her husband. She *hated* this. Even though he'd told her not to expect a call, she had still hoped that he would need to hear her voice the way she needed to hear his. If only she had any information at all, any indication that something good was going on. She called the hospital again, just to be certain that he was still there. At least she knew where he was. She'd told herself to be patient. She'd tried to hold on to the hope that the outcome would be worth the waiting and the anxiety. She'd tried to replace her fear with faith. She'd prayed for help on all counts, and she'd prayed for him; nearly every minute of the day she found herself silently asking God to help Jackson find healing and peace.

By the end of the day, Chas had become so upset that she had to wonder if Jackson wasn't the only one having problems with emotional stability. More than once, Polly had to work very hard to get Chas to calm down. The third time it happened, Polly pointed out, "Maybe *you* have PTSD. Maybe it's contagious."

"What do you mean?" Chas snapped.

"It's as plain as day. Jackson is falling apart because he's having flashbacks of the time he was missing . . . held captive. It seems you're doing exactly the same thing."

Chas was so stunned that she couldn't speak. Then the truth of Polly's words crept into her spirit and she dissolved into helpless sobbing. Polly wrapped Chas in a familiar, tight hug.

When Chas finally calmed down, Polly asked with gentle kindness, "What are you afraid of, Chas?"

Chas hesitated while her mind sifted through a deluge of thoughts to find the answer. Polly added, "It is about fear, right? Isn't that what all of this is about: fear? As I see it, you need to figure out what you're afraid of, so you can figure out whether or not your fears are realistic or blown out of proportion."

"Maybe they are . . . realistic, I mean."

"You think you'll never see him again?" Polly asked, perfectly pegging Chas's conclusion of her worst fear, even though it hadn't been verbally expressed.

Chas wiped her face with her apron and admitted, "I don't know. I keep telling myself that he'll come back, that he'll be all right, but . . . how can I be sure? When he called he said all the right things, but when he left he was *so* irrational. How can I be sure which side of him will dominate when this is over? But you're right, Polly; that's exactly how it was then. I was terrified that I would never see him again. Now I know that he's physically safe, but what if I lose him emotionally? What if his mind never recovers? Or what if he chooses not to come back? How can I . . ." Her words faded into a new burst of tears.

"I don't understand all of your religious stuff, Chas," Polly said, "but I wonder if you shouldn't have those priesthood guys come over and do their prayer, or whatever it is they do. I'll call somebody if you need me to."

Chas wondered why she hadn't thought of that, and she found it easier to calm down with the knowledge that a priesthood blessing *would* help give her the comfort and guidance she needed.

"No, that's okay, Polly," she said. "I can make the call. Thank you . . . for thinking clearly when I can't . . . and for everything else. I'm so grateful that you're willing to stay here with me. I don't know what I'd do otherwise."

"Glad to do it," Polly said. "Now I'll watch the little dude while you make that call."

Chas's home teachers were there in less than an hour. She was glad to share her burden with these good men, even though she only told them minimal details. The blessing was brief and simple, but Chas *did* feel better. She went to bed that night reminding herself once again to replace fear with faith, to trust in the Lord, and to be patient. But oh, how she missed her husband and longed to have him back!

\* \* \* \* \*

Jackson followed the doctor's orders and left the lights on when he went to sleep. He came out of nightmares three times, which was more than usual, but he *was* able to go right back to sleep and didn't wake up until a nurse brought breakfast into his room. He ate and got cleaned up and had barely picked up *Great Expectations* when Dr. Callahan came into the room.

"You okay?" he asked, sitting on the other bed.

"I vacillate between bored and overwhelmed."

"Okay. I get that. Have you thought much about what happened yesterday?"

"No more than I absolutely had to."

Callahan chuckled. "I like you, Jackson. If all the crazies were as straightforward as you, we'd sure make a lot more progress around here."

"Are you including me in that? Am I one of the crazies?"

"You're in the psych ward, aren't you?" he said with a facetiousness that made Jackson chuckle. More seriously he added, "I hope you've spent enough time with me to know that I'm not disrespectful of my patients or their problems, but I think we need to laugh at ourselves a little, or we'll all go mad trying to help people who are going mad. It's a crazy world we live in, and I've seen some pretty crazy stuff. Sometimes it's very discouraging work, but I've seen some happy endings along the way. Those are the things that restore my faith in the resiliency of human beings." He stood up and added, "How about we go to the office and chat."

"Sounds delightful," Jackson said with sarcasm. While he dreaded the possibility of another painful and embarrassing episode, he felt anxious to get beyond whatever he needed to do in order to go back to his wife and son with some dignity and peace of mind. And perhaps his efforts would go a long way in earning back the trust of his wife.

Once seated in the office, Callahan asked directly, "Do you believe in God, Jackson?"

"Is that psychologically relevant?"

"Actually, yes. There isn't a right or wrong answer, but it's important for me to understand *your* belief system in order to accurately assess what's taking place."

"Yes, I believe in God."

"So, you're a religious man?"

Jackson cleared his throat and shifted in his chair. "Not really, no."

"What does that mean, exactly? No means no. What does 'not really, no' mean?"

"I never even considered or cared whether God existed until I met Chas. *She* is actively religious, not just on Sundays but in the way she lives her life. Through my association with her I had to admit that I *did* believe in God, but I don't share her enthusiasm for religion. And there are concepts that I just . . . don't like."

"You seem very fervent on that. May I ask what?"

Jackson didn't hesitate even a moment. "They teach absolute forgiveness; that we should forgive *all* people for *all* trespasses against us. With what I've been through, I think that's too much to ask."

"I think your feeling that way is understandable."

"But . . ."

"But what?"

"There must be a but there."

"Do you have doubts about your attitude on forgiveness? Do you think it might be possible in spite of how you feel? Or is that just what you hope for?"

Jackson felt too agitated to respond; even borderline angry.

"What do you hope for, Jackson?" Callahan went on. "Isn't it your greatest desire to be free of all this pain and confusion?"

He had no trouble answering that. "Yes, of course."

"Do you want to know what I think about forgiveness?"

"Is this still a religious conversation?" Jackson asked.

"Let's take religion out of it, shall we?"

"Yes, let's," Jackson said, recalling how angry he'd felt the last time he'd gone to church. "Are *you* a religious man?" Jackson countered, suddenly feeling it was important for him to know, perhaps to understand exactly where the doctor might stand when removing religion from an issue.

"I think I'm much the same as you," Callahan said. "I *do* believe in God. I've seen too many things in my life that couldn't possibly make sense without acknowledging a higher power, but I'm not religious. I did read a book once about the Bible and psychology. It was very fascinating. But that's a conversation for another day." He paused and looked hard at Jackson. "Do you want to know what I think about forgiveness? Or do you want to talk about something else?"

"Let's have it," Jackson said.

"It's not exclusively a religious term, you know. It's a psychologically sound principal that is vital to any kind of healing. To forgive means to give up resentment. I have *never* seen any victim of any kind of abuse or violence be able to fully heal and move on until they were able to give up their resentment and bitterness."

Jackson felt like he'd been kicked in the stomach, but he remained steady. "Are you saying I should just be able to snap my fingers and forgive the men who beat and tortured me? Forgive my father?"

"No one could ever just snap their fingers and let go of that kind of pain. It takes time and effort. It's tough. But I believe it is a necessary part of healing."

Following a strained minute of silence while Jackson tried to take that in, Callahan said, "I want to tell you about a psychiatrist I did a rotation with many years ago. He was one of the wealthiest men I've ever known in the profession. I quickly figured out why. He had a sure-fire way to keep his patients coming back, to keep them spending their money on his services. He encouraged what he called the scapegoat theory. He taught his patients in essence to lay blame for all of their pain on other people. He encouraged resentment rather than the letting go of it. His patients never got better. He loved having them reliant on him. It fed his ego *and* his wallet. Now, after working in this profession for several years, I have seen much evidence of the opposite. Holding on to resentment toward someone who has wronged you is like carrying around a bag of rocks. If you give up the resentment, you can stop carrying it around. But don't mistake me. Forgiveness does not mean that you aren't holding them accountable for their wrongdoing. It doesn't override justice. It just allows you to be free of the responsibility of holding them accountable. Your father is dead, and you will never again encounter these sadistic drug lords. They are entirely unaffected by your resentment. But *you* . . . and the people you love . . . are affected by it every day."

Again, silence prevailed until it became excruciatingly uncomfortable. Jackson felt laid flat. He'd grown to trust this man in a very short time. But what he was hearing rankled him beyond description. It was taking every ounce of discipline he could extract from every part of his being to remain seated and to maintain a composed countenance. He felt sure Callahan could see through his façade, to the truth, but he wasn't about to throw another fit like the one that had happened yesterday.

"You look like you have a lot to think about," Callahan finally said.

"Yeah," Jackson managed to say.

"So, I'll give you a few minutes." He stood up to leave the room. "I need to check on something that slipped my mind earlier."

"Okay," Jackson said and heaved a deep sigh when he was alone; then it occurred to him that there might be a hidden camera in the room. He'd agreed to be observed. He stood to look out the window while he frantically tried to process new information and allow it to confront very old, very set feelings. He realized that he couldn't pick and choose which concepts to believe in. Either he trusted Callahan, or he didn't. And he did. He couldn't deny that the rational argument he'd been given on behalf of forgiveness made perfect sense. But his emotions were not accepting it as rational at all. How could he? How could he possibly forgive what had been done to him? It was completely beyond comprehension to him. He reasoned that he needed to give it time and effort as Callahan had already said. He wasn't being asked to declare forgiveness here and now.

Jackson turned around when Callahan came back into the room. "You okay?" he asked.

"I'm working on it."

"Good answer." The doctor sat down. "Do you want to talk about forgiveness some more, or move on?"

"I'll definitely vote for moving on, even though I know that means we'll come back to it eventually."

"That's a good answer too. You're very easy to work with, by the way, which could perhaps explain my own selfish motives for canceling all of my other appointments for the day."

"Why?" Jackson asked, wondering what horror he might escort him through that could take *all day*.

"Not canceled, exactly. I've just delegated them to my staff. They're great. They can handle it. And they all owe me *big time*. I like you, Jackson. You fascinate me. I think I could learn a lot from you."

"As in . . . I'm like a rat in a maze and you're going to see if I can get out?"

Callahan chuckled. "I would love to see you get out of this maze. I think that would be very fulfilling for both of us. But I would never reduce you to a rat. I think you're a pretty remarkable human being, and I think we can beat this thing . . . together. I also think with some strong focus and devoting some serious time to it, we can beat it fairly quickly and you can go home to your family. Sometimes this job calls for twenty-four/seven involvement to get through tough stages. That kind of intensity can be hard, but it is usually rewarding. As a doctor, I see this kind of attention to one patient the same way a surgeon would who needed to do extensive repair to wounds received in an accident, for instance. There are times when people are in surgery for many hours, or several subsequent surgeries over a brief period of time. You're not an emergency in the respect that you will die without immediate treatment. But you're here, I've got the time, and I say we just . . . fix you."

"You really think I'm fixable?"

"Absolutely!"

"You really think I can stop having nightmares and panic attacks completely?"

"I do," he said, "*if* you are committed to doing what it takes. Some emotional problems may never be solved in this lifetime. But I believe a lot more of them would be if people would be fully committed to facing the problem and dealing with it. There are a lot of people out there hiding from their problems with the hope that they'll just go away. The fact that you are here, that you have such a keen awareness of your issues and the reasons for them makes me believe that this is solvable, and maybe a lot faster than you might think. You're just that kind of guy. So, what do you say?"

"You haven't told me what you want me to do yet."

"I'll get to that. Are you willing to be committed to getting better if I'm willing to devote as much of my time to you as it takes to get through it?"

Jackson thought about it a long moment and knew there was no other option. This doctor's willing, straightforward attitude made him certain he'd be a fool not to take hold of this opportunity with all his soul and jump in headfirst. "I'm with you," he said firmly.

"Okay," Callahan said as if they were making plans to go on safari together. "I'm going to just lay out the textbook treatments for PTSD, so you know exactly what I'm doing and why."

"Okay." Jackson liked that. He felt *less* like a rat in a maze by knowing the methodology behind what was going on.

"One option is medication. There are some antidepressants and anti-anxiety drugs that have been very effective with the treatment of PTSD. You told me that you *had* been on some medication at one time, then did fine without it. I know you'd rather avoid drugs if you can, and I am in agreement with that. I prefer to go with the other methods, and after we've exhausted all other possibilities, if you're still having problems, we know it's an option. I'm aware of some pretty new research in that area that might make a difference. But that's for later . . . maybe."

"Okay," Jackson said again. "I'm good with that."

"Now, it's also widely accepted that support groups can be helpful. Again, I would say in your case . . . maybe . . . later. For some people it's very validating and helpful to be surrounded by others who are having similar challenges and experiences. In your case, I don't know. So, we'll move past that for the time being. Now," he leaned forward and put his forearms on his thighs, "there are two other methods that I have given a lot of thought to in relation to your case, Jackson, and I think they could serve us well. The first is called Cognitive Behavioral Therapy, which seeks to alter maladaptive thought patterns. In plain English, what this means is that if your thought patterns are false, we want to teach them to be correct."

Jackson wasn't unfamiliar with the concept of trying to change his cognitive thinking. He'd learned the concept previously, but no counselor had proposed it in terms that could actually be applicable. Now, Dr. Callahan was explaining it in a way that made more sense than the explanations he'd heard before.

"You simply need to change the way your thoughts respond to the stimuli that set you off. For instance, when you wake up in the dark, you're seized with fear because you don't know where you are, and it takes you back to multiple traumatic events. We need to find a way for you to quickly know that the present is not the past, and to change your thoughts in relation to waking up in the dark."

"Okay," Jackson said. "It makes sense in theory, but I need something more to go on. If you've got any ideas, I'm listening."

"I notice you play with your wedding ring a great deal."

"Do I?" He looked down to realize he was doing it. "I hadn't thought about it."

"You miss your wife?"

"I do."

"You were married after the incident, were you not?"

"That's right."

"So, you didn't have that ring on your finger when you were being held captive."

Jackson thought about where this was headed. "No, I didn't."

"It's just an idea, but if you can feel that ring on your finger, you should immediately realize that you're in the present, not the past. As soon as you know you're wearing a wedding ring, then you know that you have a wife and you're safe."

"Provided she'll still want to be married to me after what I've put her through."

"Are you really worried about that?"

Jackson had to think about that. "No. She's very patient and forgiving. And she's big on commitment. It was me who threatened to bail. I thought she deserved better."

"You told me you called her before you came here."

"I did, yes."

"And what did she say?"

"She said she could forgive me. She said it would take time to earn her trust."

"Do you think that's a fair statement?"

"More than fair."

"Then your wedding ring represents many good things. Love, commitment, solving problems rather than running from them. And most importantly in what we're trying to accomplish, it's tangible evidence that you're far beyond the events that traumatized you. And the ring will always be with you, no matter when or where you have a flashback or feel panicked. So, why don't you work on that and see what happens?"

"Okay, I can do that," he said, but it sounded so simple; *too* simple. Was he going to send him home at the end of the day with this solution?

"Now, this is the biggie," Callahan said. "This is where you're really going to need to trust me."

"Okay," he drawled, instinctively wary.

"You are terrified of confined spaces, especially in the dark."

"That's right."

"I would like you to try a process we call immersion, or it's sometimes called exposure therapy. The idea being that patients are exposed to their trigger in large doses and taught coping and relaxation skills throughout the process. In other words, you expose yourself to what you're afraid of in such large quantities that the fearful relationship to it begins to get diluted."

"I'm not following you."

"For example, I had a patient, a woman who had been assaulted in a parking lot. The event was life-threatening and truly horrible. She was terrified to be alone in a parking lot; any parking lot, anytime of day. She started spending a ridiculous amount of time in parking lots. At first it was very difficult for her, but it didn't take terribly long for her to realize that simply being in a parking lot did not mean she was in danger. She's doing great now. She still has some challenging moments, but for the most part she's leading a normal life. She recognizes that she *could* be assaulted again; no one can guarantee that it will never happen. But she takes reasonable precautions that don't impede her life, and she's learned to be careful, not scared. For you, there's an advantage in knowing that your father is not going to come back from the grave and harm you *again,* and it's not likely you will be kidnapped and held hostage *again,* under the circumstances. You have a long list of reasons why that's highly unlikely. So, when you can replace the unreasonable fear with reasonable thinking *and* immerse yourself into the situation that frightens you, the fear can become manageable."

"So . . . you want me to spend *lots* of time in dark, confined spaces . . . and use my wedding ring to remind me that I'm in the present."

"That about covers it. And I want to start today, right now."

"What do you mean?"

"I came up with this plan yesterday, actually. I've already talked it through with my staff, made some special arrangements, and my wife knows that I won't be home for a few days, maybe more."

"A few days?" Jackson echoed, astonished.

"So, are you ready to hear my plan?"

"I'm thinking about being ready."

Callahan gave him a sidelong glance and a kind smile.

"Okay. What have I got to lose?"

"As I see it, nothing. And you may have a great deal to gain."

"Oh, I hope so," Jackson said and thought of his family. He realized he was playing with his wedding ring again—or still—and he hadn't even realized it was something he did. With any luck, this grand plan would work, and he could go home, very soon. Even better, he hoped to go home a better man.

Once again Jackson shared lunch with Dr. Callahan in his office. They'd spent the remainder of the morning talking through the issues that had come up previously, but going into more depth. Jackson was beginning to hate these lengthy sessions, especially when they were so emotionally draining. But he kept thinking of the surgery metaphor. His spirit had been as badly damaged as a human body could be from a serious accident. He could be glad that he had a doctor he trusted who was willing to devote the time to helping the process move on more quickly. He was already getting stir crazy and wanted to go home, but he knew he couldn't face Chas until he'd made enough progress to have something positive to tell her.

"Are you ready for this?" Callahan asked as soon as they'd finished eating.

"As ready as I'll ever be," Jackson said.

"Just to be sure, I want to go over what we talked about."

"So when I freak out, I'll already know the rules. Yeah, I got that."

"We'll be staying in a standard two-patient room, but the window has been sealed up and covered so no light will come through. It will be impossible for us to remove that covering without tools, which we won't have. The room will be air conditioned, so we won't be too hot or too cold. There is a bathroom attached to the room. There's nothing in there but soap and towels, and that window too has been covered. There will be nothing in the room with us beyond the beds and bedding. Our meals will be brought in when I call for them."

"So, *you* will have a cell phone."

"Yes, but you don't know the code to unlock it, so *you* can't use it." He smiled. "Any questions?"

"I don't think so. Maybe I should ask, 'Are *you* ready for this?'"

"Oh, I'm ready. My family knows I'm out of town, in a manner of speaking. We are going to conquer this, once and for all. My hope is that when we complete this exercise, you will never be afraid to wake up in the dark again. I'm hoping it will reduce the nightmares, but I think that even if you have a bad dream, it won't come with you into consciousness when you don't freak out over being in the dark."

"It makes sense in theory. I have the same hope that you do, but I admit to being somewhat skeptical. I guess we'll see."

"But you're willing to do it . . . you're committed to seeing it through?"

"You've asked me that about six times."

"I need to be sure, and so do you."

"Yes, I'm ready. Yes, I'm committed to seeing it through."

"Okay, supper will be brought to us in our room. Oh, one more thing. And this is important. It will be impossible to know when it's night and day with the windows covered. There's a clock, and we'll go by that. But I've also made arrangements for the lights to be disabled during the night. They're going to pull the fuse, so to speak, so the lights don't work. Once it's dark, it's dark, okay?"

That stipulation was harder for Jackson to accept, but he trusted Callahan and knew it was necessary.

"You don't seem sure."

"It scares me, but that's the whole point, right?"

"You trust me?

"I do."

"I'm not going to leave until you're okay with me going. We won't go to phase two until you conquer phase one, and I'm your bunkmate for every minute of phase one. Okay?"

"Okay."

"You want to call your wife?"

Jackson hesitated long enough to see if he'd changed his mind. "No; not until it's over. I think I can face her better when it's over."

"Okay, let's go," he said, and they returned to the same room where Jackson had slept the night before. But now it felt more closed and clinical with the darkened window. Once he got used to that fact, he realized that his reading material had been removed by Callahan's orders.

"We'll both die of boredom!" Jackson protested.

"You can have it back in a few days . . . maybe," Callahan said without apology.

"I assume there's a reason for this. *You* have surely got to be a lot more bored than I am."

"Oh, no. I can play mind games with myself for a long time. I bet you can too. You probably do it without even realizing it. You *must* have learned some mind games while you spent those weeks in confinement."

Jackson just made a disinterested noise, and Callahan added, "Come on, Jackson. What did you think about all those hours alone in the dark?" Jackson didn't answer and he concluded, "That would be the reason. If we're re-creating the situation, you didn't have anything to read. You only had dim light from a tiny window during the days, right?"

"Right."

"So, that's what we're getting. You can't read in that kind of light. And if you have a distraction, something to occupy your mind with, it won't be an accurate re-creation of your experience."

"Great," Jackson said with intense sarcasm. The door was closed and locked, and a minute later the lights were dimmed significantly, obviously from a control outside of the room. Jackson knew immediately that this re-creation theory was working. He felt terrified.

# Chapter Ten

"How you doing over there?" Callahan asked Jackson through the darkness. They were each stretched out on their beds, but it was still too early to go to sleep. The tiniest bit of light leaked through the crack under the door. It was just enough to keep the room from being too black to even see enough to get in and out of bed and to the bathroom.

"I am bored out of my mind," Jackson said.

"That's better than being just out of your mind."

"Give it time."

"What are you thinking about?"

"I thought this was supposed to be an accurate re-creation of my experience. There was no one in the room trying to coax my feelings into the open."

"Well, a little counseling session here and there along the way won't hurt any. Besides, I've been meaning to talk to you about something that's stuck in my head. I meant to bring it up when we were talking about God, but we got onto other things. But I can't help wondering if your issues with religion have anything to do with the issues with your father."

"I have no idea what you're talking about."

"It's very common, actually, for people to project the characteristics of a parent onto their interpretation of God."

Jackson wanted to say that he'd never heard the concept before, but he recalled Chas saying very much the same thing, and he'd completely dismissed it.

"So, what do you think?" Callahan asked.

"I'm thinking that my wife is a lot smarter than I am."

"Excuse me?"

"She once told me the same thing; she said that any half-decent therapist would know the theory. Since I'd had trouble finding a half-decent therapist, I blew it off. She said when I *did* find a half-decent therapist I should ask about it. I'd forgotten. But here you are, proving my wife right."

"Is she?"

"I don't know; maybe."

"You think you project your father's characteristics onto your interpretation of God?"

"I don't know; maybe," he said again. "I've seen evidence in my life that God is merciful and kind; obviously my father wasn't."

"Okay, but it's possible that at some subconscious level, you believe God has a mean side, and maybe that mean side is why He allowed you to be born with such an awful father, or why He allowed you to be tortured and beaten. And if God has a mean side, how could you possibly trust Him enough to make religion an active part of your life? Don't get me wrong. I'm not out to sound like a hypocrite, because as I've told you, I'm not a religious man myself, but I know *why* I'm not religious. I just wonder if you've ever stopped to ask yourself *why*, especially when your wife is, and you know it means a lot to her. Mostly it's just something I would like you to think about. And while you're at it, I'd like you to keep thinking about that forgiveness thing. Maybe the two are linked somehow. I don't know. I'm just speculating. It's *your* brain."

"Yeah, my very messed-up brain."

"Give it time, my friend." Callahan sighed loudly. "Okay, I think I'm going to sleep now . . . unless there's something else you want to talk about."

"Not at the moment," Jackson said with mild sarcasm. "You're not going to give me a sleeping pill?"

"Not tonight. You didn't have any medication when you were there."

Jackson left it at that. He had way too much to think about, and much of it was in the realms of provoking uneasy feelings and memories to the surface, which was exactly what he *didn't* want to do before he fell asleep. This experiment had all sounded very logical and reasonable—and it was. But being here, now, he wondered what he'd agreed to. He felt more afraid than he'd dared admit. Realizing that indulging in such fear would *never* allow him to go to sleep, he tried to imagine what it would be like to go home to Chas and the baby. He imagined himself stronger and more healthy and capable of being a normal husband and father. He recalled in detail the day he'd met Chas; how he'd driven from Butte in a blizzard, and her calls to his cell phone had guided him through a power outage to the inn where she'd left lanterns burning on the porch to show him where to go. Focusing on pleasant memories and sweet hopes, he finally drifted to sleep, praying the night would not be too long.

\* \* \* \* \*

Jackson woke up in the dark, gasping for breath in a way that was keenly familiar. He was cold with sweat, and his heart was pounding. With the darkness surrounding him, he couldn't discern whether or not he had something to be afraid of, but his habit was to be afraid. And he was. He rolled over and reached for Chas. She wasn't there. The bed felt different. His panic grew. In a frenzy he struggled to reach for the lamp he hoped he'd find on a table beside the bed, but the table wasn't there, and the bed was smaller. He hit the floor with a painful thud. The hard, cold floor left him certain he was truly still in that hellish prison, starving, cold, and beaten. All of the memories of events that had occurred in the time since then felt illusionary and imagined. His life was the hallucination. Fear and imprisonment were the reality.

"Hey, Jackson. Jackson!" a male voice shouted, but it only drove him deeper into his panic. In his mind he could hear men shouting, threatening him, ready to strike, to inflict more pain, more suffering.

Jackson didn't know how long it was before he finally realized that he was in the hospital, and it was Dr. Callahan on the floor with him, trying to talk some sense into him. Once the realization hit him, he struggled to bring himself back to reality while his breathing and heart rate remained shallow and fast for more minutes than he could count. Now that he was reasonably coherent, Callahan helped him to his bed, but rather than going back to his own, he sat next to Jackson and kept a hand on his arm. He told Jackson to touch his wedding ring and make certain it was there. He asked him about Chas and the baby and made him talk about them. He guided him through relaxation and breathing techniques to move past the panicked reaction his body was enduring. Jackson finally admitted, "I'm okay now. Thank you. You can go back to sleep."

Callahan moved back to the other bed, saying, "Do you think either of us can sleep now?"

"I know I can't."

"Well, look at it this way. We'll have plenty of time for a good nap tomorrow. Nowhere to go and nothing to do."

"I'm so excited," Jackson said caustically.

Callahan started talking nonchalantly about trivial things until Jackson found he was actually getting sleepy. He knew he had drifted off when a nearly perfect replay of the previous episode happened again. By the time he had calmed down again, the dim lights were turned on and breakfast was brought in.

"At least the food is a lot better than I had there," Jackson said. "And I really like the clean, running water nearby."

"Yeah, that's nice. We should be more grateful for the simple things in life, don't you think?"

"Absolutely."

After they'd finished their meal and they'd both cleaned up, Jackson said, "Thank you."

"It's my job. No problem."

"I think this goes above and beyond the call of duty. I wish there was something I could do for you . . . but I could never repay you."

"Oh, you'll get the bill," Callahan said, and Jackson laughed. "But my services are probably not as expensive as you might think. It's all negotiable."

"It's okay. Whatever it costs, it will be worth it."

"Do you believe that?" the doctor asked. "I mean . . . do you really believe it will get better enough to be worth it?"

Jackson thought about it. "I guess at this point . . . I believe it because you believe it. I would say for me that I more . . . hope it."

"That's more than good enough for now. You're doing great, really. And you know what, after you survive the night a few times without ever turning the lights on, you'll start to realize that you can be in the dark and not feel afraid. I don't know if the nightmares will stop completely, but I think they'll decrease, and I think you'll be able to recover from them more quickly and easily."

"That's what I'm hoping for," Jackson said, then he added, "When you and your wife need to get away for the weekend, I know a great place you can stay. We'll give you the best room in the house for as long as you'd like to stay."

"That sounds great!" Callahan said.

"Maybe it will help make up for your wife loaning you to me this way."

"Wouldn't hurt."

Dr. Callahan didn't leave Jackson alone for about sixty-eight hours. During that time Jackson had twelve severe panic attacks, all induced by nightmares. Callahan was there with him every minute, although he didn't attempt to coddle and reassure Jackson through it as much as he just made it clear that Jackson was not going to die before daylight. Sometimes the doctor wasn't very kind, but apparently he knew what he was doing. He had a way of urging him to be tough and strong in a way that didn't invalidate how weak and vulnerable he felt. It was after the seventh episode that Jackson realized he was recovering more quickly, and on the eleventh, it only took him a minute to take hold of his wedding ring with his right hand, quickly assess his surroundings, and know that he was okay. By the twelfth time, he was able to go back to sleep within a short while. That was when Callahan declared that it was time for phase two, and he needed to be left on his own, but he was also given back his books and some hours during the day with adequate light to read. All things considered, Jackson was beginning to believe he might survive this ordeal.

\* \* \* \* \*

Chas answered the phone with the usual greeting and heard a man say, "Is this Mrs. Leeds?"

"Yes," she said anxiously, wishing she'd bothered to look at the caller ID.

"My name is Ross Callahan. I'm the doctor who's been working with your husband."

"Is he all right?" she asked, not even trying to disguise her panic.

"He's fine," the doctor said. "Without his written permission, I can't legally tell you what's been going on exactly. I know he's been concerned about you, and I don't think he'd mind my calling to just let you know that he's fine and he's making progress. I don't know when you'll see him or talk to him. He needs to feel ready to make that step. That's all I can say, really. I hope you're doing all right."

"Better now," Chas said, and it was evident she'd started to cry.

"You take care now," Dr. Callahan said.

"Thank you for calling. Give him my love . . . if it's possible."

"I will," he said and ended the call. Chas sat down and had a good cry, silently thanking God for giving her something to hold on to. She wondered how long it might be before Jackson was able to come home, and she prayed that all would be well, and back to normal, before too long.

* * * * *

Jackson was pleased when Callahan told him that he needed to merge back into a more normal daily experience. Jackson spent another three days in solitary confinement, with brief visits from the doctor a couple of times a day. He had more nightmares, but they weren't as intense and he didn't feel lost and terrified when he woke up. He finished *Great Expectations* and was almost through *Oliver Twist* before Callahan came to his room and asked, "Are you ready to get out of here?"

"Out of the room, or out of the hospital?"

"Both," the doctor said. "I'm thinking you should go home tomorrow. We'll give it one more night, and then I've set aside some time to spend with you in the morning and we can evaluate and see how you feel about where you're at. Of course, it's still going to take some time and effort; you've got some things to deal with that you're just going to have to work through on your own. But I think you've got the tools to know how to manage it, and I really think you're going to be fine. We'll keep doing some outpatient counseling for as long as you feel that you need it."

"Okay," was all Jackson said. It sounded reasonable, but he felt afraid to go home for reasons he couldn't fully define. But he figured they could talk about that in the morning, after he'd had some time to think about it.

As Callahan was leaving the room, he added, "Oh, I hope you'll forgive me for calling your wife."

"You called her?" he asked, more surprised than upset.

"I just thought she needed to know that you were okay. I didn't tell her anything more than that. I hope it's okay."

"Yeah, thank you," Jackson said. "I probably should have done that before now."

"I think she'll understand. She said to give you her love. You take care, and I'll see you in the morning." He chuckled. "Sweet dreams."

"You too," Jackson said, and Callahan closed the door.

\* \* \* \* \*

The following morning when Jackson walked out of his confinement, he felt a little more disoriented than he'd expected. His lengthy session with the doctor went well, but they both decided he needed another day or two in the hospital for a more comfortable transition. Jackson finished *Oliver Twist,* and Callahan found him a copy of *Bleak House.*

"Sounds cheery," the doctor said facetiously.

"It has a happy ending," Jackson declared.

He was glad to be able to sit in his room with the windows now unblocked so that he could read by sunlight, and he was even more glad to get through a night without any major drama *or* trauma. He wasn't sure what had happened exactly, but it seemed that his mind *had* been trained to realize that he was still safe when daylight came. Apparently in his case, the steps he'd been taking to alleviate his anxiety had actually encouraged it to continue. By rescuing himself with turning on the lights, he had convinced his mind that he needed light to know he was safe. And the theory spread into deeper, more intricate parts of the issue. Now, remaining in the dark had proven that the darkness didn't equal some unexpected pain or suffering.

After twelve nights in the hospital, Dr. Callahan informed Jackson that he needed to go home.

"I can't do any more for you here," Callahan said. "But you've got my number, and I'll be seeing you every week for as long as you need." Jackson didn't comment, and he added, "Tell me what's on your mind. Are you concerned about going home?"

"I guess I am."

"Well, let's talk about it. Don't you think she'll be glad to see you?"

"I'm hoping, but . . ."

"Tell you what. As soon as you eat some lunch, why don't you just brave it and go home. Have a long talk with your wife and bring her up to speed. If it doesn't go well, you call me and we'll talk it through."

While Jackson was finishing up his lunch with the doctor, he turned to look out the window just as it started to snow. Callahan said, "If you leave soon maybe you can make it home before the storm gets too bad."

"Is it supposed to get bad?" he asked. He hadn't heard a weather report for as long as he'd been there.

"I don't know." He peered more closely at the sky. "But it looks like it could get that way."

Jackson's mind wandered briefly to the horrible snowstorm he'd driven through that first time he'd gone to the inn. It seemed somehow appropriate that it would snow today. He suddenly felt like he could do it. He was ready, and he needed to see his wife and son.

"Okay." Jackson stood up and offered his hand. "I guess I'm off, then. I can't thank you enough."

"It was a pleasure," Callahan said, then shrugged and chuckled. "Well, *most* of it was a pleasure. The results are very fulfilling."

"Yes, for me too."

They ended up sharing a brief embrace before they walked down the hall together to complete the paperwork. Jackson was given all of his things and escorted to the door of the ward. It felt strangely disorienting to go past the little world where he had confronted the problems inside of him. But the moment he stepped out into the snow, the fresh air rushed into his lungs, bringing with it a deep relief in knowing that it *had* been worth it; he *had* made progress. He knew he had a long way to go, and some of the remaining issues would be more challenging than others. But he'd learned a great deal. His burdens felt significantly lighter. And Chas was only as far away as the drive to Anaconda. He hurried across the parking lot to where he'd left the SUV nearly two weeks earlier. He got in and pulled his cell phone out of the glove box. Of course it was dead, but he plugged it into the car charger and was able to turn it on. Thirty-two missed calls, and every one of them from Chas. He put the voicemail on speakerphone and started driving while he listened to the seven messages she'd left. They were all much the same. She didn't know if he couldn't answer, or if he just wouldn't, but she wanted him to know that she loved him, she was praying for him, and she would be waiting for him to come to his senses and come back. Jackson wiped away a couple of tears as he drove and listened. His regret for the circumstances surrounding his leaving came back to him more freshly, and he could only be grateful that she was a woman devoted to commitment and willing to forgive him. And most of all, he was grateful to know that she loved him. He wasn't certain why a man like him had been so fortunate in having the love of a woman who was so good, but it was something he would never take for granted again.

The snowstorm was more beautiful than dangerous. Jackson had no slowdowns at all, since the roads were mostly clear, and visibility was fine. He felt nostalgia nearly to the point of tears when the inn came into view. It had an almost ethereal appearance with everything covered in fresh snow, and airy flakes still falling on and around it. He parked the car and just sat there for a minute, taking in the familiarity of being here, combined with a certain strangeness in regard to all that had happened since he'd left here in a fit of selfish anger. The realization that Chas was only a few steps away urged him out of the car and to the back door. He stepped inside and shook the snow off before he peered into the office. Polly was behind the desk, waiting to see who had come in. She smiled when she saw him and he put a finger to his lips to indicate she should not give him away. She whispered, "In the kitchen, I think. No one else is here."

"Thank you," Jackson said. He set his bag down and removed his coat and hung it up. Noting the snow on his shoes, he took them off as well and left them where they could dry. He felt like a teenager in love as he crept toward the kitchen, wanting to surprise Chas, anticipating her reaction. Hearing her phone messages had increased his hope that she would be happy to see him, and he was counting the seconds until she would be in his arms. He knew she would have heard the door, but she would have expected Polly to deal with whoever it might have been, since she was in the office.

Jackson stepped quietly into the dining room and stopped. He had a clear view of Chas standing by the counter, carefully drying goblets with a white dishtowel. The simple image was familiar and filled him with comfortable warmth. Seeing her made him realize that he'd been in some degree of denial over how much he'd missed her. He was wondering what to say, or how to bridge the distance, when she abruptly stopped what she was doing. He knew he hadn't made any noise, and he wondered if she could sense his presence. She turned her head toward him with an expression that clearly said she feared her imagination had deceived her. He heard her draw a sharp breath and saw her set down the towel and goblet very carefully, as if she feared she might drop them otherwise.

Chas was overcome with a bizarre sense of déjà vu, and nearly two years slipped away. She was taken back to the moment when he had come here following the incident that had damaged both their lives so deeply. Prior to that moment, she had only seen him once following his captivity. But an hour sitting in a hospital room in Virginia had hardly compensated for all the grief that had occurred during their separation. Then, just as now, her heart leapt with the thrill she felt. And her hope blossomed. Unable to read his expression, Chas's stomach dropped as if she'd just fallen from the peak of a roller coaster. What if he'd just come home long enough to get his things? To say good-bye? She felt so panicked that she doubted her ability to keep breathing. She wanted to run into his arms, hold him close, beg him to stay with her, to be hers forever. But she felt frozen, hanging over the edge of a cliff. He had the power to either pull her to safety or to push her over the edge.

"I hear there's always room at the inn," he said, and she was able to ease back from the edge just a little.

"There is for you," she said, wanting to believe that he was hanging on her words as she was his. When he said nothing more, she added, "I've been waiting for a phone call; I've been praying."

"I knew you would be. The first time I saw you, you told me you'd been praying for me. I don't think *anyone* ever prayed for me before that night."

Chas appreciated the sentiment, but the suspense was killing her. She needed to know where she stood, if only to ease the pounding of her heart, which was becoming painful. She forced the needed words out of her mouth. "Are you here to stay, or—"

"If you'll have me," he said so quickly that she wondered if he'd been waiting for some kind of cue from her.

Jackson held his breath. This was the moment he'd feared. But he had to wonder only for a tenth of a second if she was happy to see him. She rushed toward him and practically catapulted herself into his arms. He held her tightly against him and lifted her feet briefly off the floor. The embrace they shared was long and breathlessly tight. He heard her whimper and knew she was crying. She pressed her face to his throat for a long moment, then drew back to look in his eyes for an even longer one. She laughed through her tears, then kissed him as if he'd been off to war. In a way, he had been. He couldn't hold her close enough, or kiss her long enough. He was home, and it seemed that she was all he needed.

Chas took a deep breath to assimilate the fact that he was really here. She'd had no idea how long it would be, and the uncertainty had been torturous. Now he was here, and she felt hope that a new beginning was reaching out to her.

"Oh, I missed you so much!" she said, taking his face into her hands.

"I missed you too!" he said and kissed her again.

"Charles just went down for his nap, so you'll have to wait to see him."

"That will give me something to look forward to," Jackson said, "and perhaps some time for us to talk. Are you busy?"

"Not too busy to be with you," she said and hugged him tightly again, not wanting to let him go. "Just give me a minute."

Chas reluctantly let go of him and went to the office, knowing that she had a grin like Oliver Twist with a full stomach. Polly mirrored the same expression when she saw her.

"I told you he would come back," she said.

"I know," Chas said. "And thanks to you, he didn't come home to find me having a complete nervous breakdown." She paused to allow a spontaneous laugh to escape her. "If you think you can hold the fort, I believe I need a long talk with my husband."

"I'd say!" Polly chuckled. "Need you even ask? Talk away. I have nowhere I need to go for the rest of the day."

"I don't think it will take *that* long," Chas said and laughed again. "Thank you . . . for everything."

"No prob," Polly said and waved her out of the room.

Chas found Jackson unpacking his bag. She closed the bedroom door and leaned against it, just wanting to watch him do so, as if it could completely reverse the impact of watching him pack when he'd left. She took in his countenance, especially when he glanced toward her and smiled, and she knew that something *had* changed. His eyes had lost a cloudiness that had become common; his aura was more calm, less agitated, more at peace than she had seen in a long time.

"You're really here," she said.

"So are you."

Chas crossed the room and took both his hands. "This can wait," she said and urged his arms around her again. She put a hand to one side of his face, and pressed her brow to the other. "Oh," she said, "I missed you." She eased a little closer. "I remember the first time you held me close. I felt this way then."

"How is that?" he asked, wrapping her tightly in his arms.

"It had been twelve years since Martin died. I'd forgotten what it was like to even be close to a man. I'd never had a father or brother." She rubbed the side of his face. "I love the stubble on your face, and the way you smell . . . like the aftershave you used this morning, only it's subtle; it's you." She put her hands on his shoulders, moving them down his arms and back again. "And you feel so strong when you hold me." She put her arms around him, and he tightened his embrace. "I missed you; I'm so glad you came back."

"I'm glad that you're glad," he said.

"Were you worried?"

"Yes." The word came out on a stilted chuckle. "Should I have not been worried after the way I behaved?"

"But you apologized. You were willing to make it right."

"I hope I *can* make it right," he said earnestly. He took her hand, and they sat cross-legged on the bed to face each other. "We have a lot to talk about . . . a lot to catch up on."

"Yes, we do."

"Please bear with me. There's a lot I need to say, and I've tried very hard to plan how I would say it."

"I'm listening," she said, taking his hand.

"I need to tell you what we figured out these past several days."

"We?"

"Me and . . . well, a number of people, but . . . mostly Dr. Callahan."

"He called me."

"Yes, he told me . . . after the fact. I'm glad he did. I know I should have, but . . . it's hard to explain why I couldn't."

"It's okay; I think I understand. You're here now. Just . . . tell me; tell me everything."

"Dr. Callahan was there when I checked myself in, and I think I became his pet project. He spent a ridiculous amount of time with me. I'm sure we'll get the bill."

"Whatever it costs, it will be worth it."

"I'd like to think so," Jackson said. "He was quite remarkable. Perhaps it was just that we seemed to connect in a way that . . . well, I didn't ever feel this comfortable with the other shrinks. Not even close. He seemed to understand me without much explanation. Turns out his dad had PTSD from the Vietnam War. So Callahan grew up with it. He said that it was at least part of his motivation to go into the field, and it certainly gave him more incentive to study this branch of psychology more extensively than any other."

"And he just *happened* to be there when you checked yourself in?"

Jackson gave a sideways smile that Chas hadn't seen in a long time. That alone bathed her in joy and hope. "Yeah, well," he said, "I'm thinking maybe Granny had something to do with that."

"Or your mother."

"Or both; imagine what those two could conjure up together."

"Yes, I can imagine," Chas said, "but remember, whatever angels might do to help us mortals, it's all in God's control and under His direction. If miracles are taking place, it is Him we have to thank for them."

"So you tell me," he said, but he sounded more respectful than cynical.

"I'd like to tell you how I know that, but we'll save that conversation for another day."

"Fair enough," he said. "I'll look forward to it."

Chas hoped that meant he wouldn't avoid it as he usually did any conversations of a spiritual nature. "Now, tell me what this Dr. Callahan taught you. Did his father get better?"

"No, after suffering with it for more than twenty years, he committed suicide."

"That's horrible!" Chas said and tightened her hold on Jackson's hands as if that alone might prevent him from ever facing such a dreadful outcome.

"Yes, it is. But Callahan made it clear that it doesn't have to come to that, and it should *never* come to that. He told me that we understand it a lot more than we did then. He said that what few men are still living from World War II are probably still coping with some form of PTSD; the same with veterans from every war since. But the good news is that now they're learning more effective ways of treating it, and they're seeing some great success. But he says it takes commitment on behalf of the patient, and many of them seem to prefer denial or hiding from the disorder, as opposed to facing it and being committed to conquering it. I want you to know that I am no longer in that category."

"I am *so* glad to hear that."

"I thought you might be."

"Tell me what happened. I want to know everything."

Jackson told her in detail about the theory of adjusting his cognitive thinking to replace the old habits of thought with new ones, and about the concept of immersing himself into the situation that most frightened him until it didn't become frightening anymore, and how he had put the principle to the test.

"What are you saying?" she asked.

"I spent most of the last week in a small room, in the dark most of the time."

"And you're okay?"

"I wasn't at first. But before I went in there, Callahan and I had talked it through and had agreed that I wasn't going to come out until

I could get through twenty-four hours without any anxiety. It felt impossible, but at that point I believed that if I couldn't accomplish that, I might as well spend the rest of my life shut away in a padded cell anyway. At first I freaked out worse than I ever had. I *really* felt crazy, and I didn't think I was going to survive it. I really didn't. But . . ." he paused for composure, "Callahan didn't leave for nearly three days."

"Not at all?"

"Neither of us left the room except to use the bathroom. Our food was brought to us. He told his wife what he was doing before we started. He didn't talk to anyone or see his family until . . ." He lost his composure for a minute or so. "Until I could sit in that room and believe that no one or nothing was going to go wrong."

"And?"

"Well . . . he finally said he had to go, and assured me that I was going to be fine. The first day or so without him was hard, but not as bad as I'd expected it to be. He stopped by occasionally for a few minutes."

"And?" she said again.

"And, Callahan wasn't about to let me back down on my side of the bargain." Jackson shrugged. "I spent the last twenty-four hours of my confinement terribly bored, but I felt completely calm."

"Oh!" Chas uttered a small cry and threw her arms around him. "You did, really?"

"I really did." He hugged her tightly, then took both her hands in his. "I don't know how it worked, but it worked. Obviously, there's no good reason for a grown man to be afraid of the dark or confined spaces. Spending several days there apparently taught my brain that the dark and the confinement were not the cause of the fear, and I could switch my thought processes in relation to that. I may not ever *prefer* dark, confined spaces, but I don't think they're going to freak me out."

"And if they do?"

"We worked out other methods I can resort to in order to keep myself in the present; mental processes, so to speak. So, for instance, if I became trapped in an elevator during a power outage, I could talk myself through it and stay calm."

"It's a miracle," she said with tears glistening in her eyes.

"Yes, I believe it is. And for the record, I did a lot of praying through all of this. It was you who taught me to pray, and I want you to know I'm grateful for that. I *do* know God has helped me get through this."

Chas smiled, and the tears spilled down her face. "He's helped us *both* get through this."

He held her close while Chas's mind rushed to a fact that had become lost in other things. She knew she couldn't wait another minute.

"Jackson," she said, looking at him squarely, "there's something I need to tell you."

"Okay," he drawled, feeling nervous. In spite of all his efforts, would she tell him that she couldn't live with the problem anymore?

"Do you remember . . . the day that everything blew up . . . that morning I said that I needed to talk to you about something?"

He thought about it. "I figured it was going to be about my drinking; I thought you'd figured it out. When you came outside and caught me, I thought that was it. That wasn't it?"

"No, that wasn't it. I have some news, and it has nothing to do with anything else we've been dealing with."

"What is it?" he asked, unable to imagine what could be urging fresh tears into her eyes. "Chas, what's wrong?"

"Nothing's wrong," she said. "Everything's fine; at least it is now."

"What? Tell me."

"I'm pregnant, Jackson."

Jackson couldn't draw a breath. He couldn't believe it! It only took a long moment to process a whole new slant on his recent challenges and how they had affected his wife. He couldn't even imagine how Chas must have felt to have him walk out on her when she knew another baby was coming.

"Oh, Chas," he said and wrapped her in his arms. "I'm so sorry."

"What?" She pushed herself away to look at him. "You're sorry?"

"Not that you're pregnant," he said, alarmed that she might think that. "It's wonderful. I'm just sorry for all I've put you through. I had no idea." He laughed softly. "Good heavens. Another baby? Isn't it a little soon? They'll be so close together."

"Yes, they will. But I'm sure we'll manage . . . now that you're back, and everything's okay. I didn't exactly start motherhood at a very young age. We haven't got forever to have a family, you know."

He sighed deeply to take it in. "It's wonderful, Chas; truly. Are you feeling all right? Are you—"

"It's the same as last time. I'm tired, and I feel somewhat nauseous, but I'm okay." She touched his face and got teary again. "Now that you're back, I'm okay."

He sighed again. "I wish I could say that my issues aren't going to come up again, but I fear it will continue to give us both grief."

"But you've come so far. We just have to keep working at it . . . together, in a positive and productive way. Promise me."

"I promise."

"You won't shut me out. Promise me."

"I promise," he said earnestly.

"No more drinking; not even a little."

"I promise," he said even more fervently.

"And don't you ever . . ." She sobbed and gently shoved him in a mild gesture of anger. "Don't you *ever* walk out on me again. Don't you ever leave me . . . or threaten to leave me . . . ever! Do you hear me?"

Jackson took her into his arms and held her close. "Never," he said. "I promise. I'm so sorry."

"I forgive you," she muttered and returned his embrace, soaking his presence into every parched and depleted part of her. She refused to ever live without him again.

# Chapter Eleven

Chas was grateful for the baby's long nap and the uninterrupted hours with her husband after a long separation. When Charles finally began to make noises they could hear on the baby monitor, Jackson rushed into his room to get him. In his simple way, it was evident the baby recognized his father and was glad to see him. Jackson held his son as close as he could manage, given all his wiggling, and wondered how he'd ever believed that he could live without his family. They were all he had that really mattered in this world.

Following a diaper change, they went together to the kitchen, where Jackson put Charles into his high chair for an afternoon snack. Jackson and Chas decided to have a snack with him, and they sat down to share some apples and cheese and some of Charlotte's fresh-baked bread that she'd brought in that morning. While they were sitting there, Wendell came in after school, grinning when he saw Jackson there.

"You're out of the hospital?" the boy said with such pleasure that Jackson felt some guilt for how little he'd thought about Wendell while he'd been gone.

"I am," Jackson said, wondering how much he knew.

"Chas told me you were sick and had to be in the hospital. Are you feeling better?"

"Much better, thank you," Jackson said. "And how are you?"

"I'm fine, thank you," Wendell said with practiced politeness. He sat down at the table, and Chas put a snack in front of him, something that had obviously become a habit.

"And how's the work going?" Jackson asked.

Wendell looked to Chas as if seeking approval. "He's been doing very well," she reported, and Wendell looked pleased.

"I've been reading that book you gave me," Wendell said.

"Great!" Jackson gave him a playful punch on the shoulder, as if he'd made a touchdown. "What do you think?"

"It's kind of hard to understand sometimes, but I think I'm getting used to it. Chas let me borrow the movie, and I watched it with my dad. She said it might help and it did, except now I know how it's gonna end, but that's okay 'cause I get the story better now."

"Good," Jackson said. "I'm proud of you. I read *Great Expectations* and *Oliver Twist* while I was in the hospital."

"You did?" Chas asked.

"I had a lot of time on my hands. I started *Bleak House* but didn't finish it, and I had to leave that copy there."

"I suspect we can find one around here," Chas said with a touch of humor.

Wendell darted out of the room, leaving them to wonder if he'd just realized he needed to use the bathroom, but he came back in less than a minute with a paperback copy of *Bleak House* from the office.

"Thank you," Jackson chuckled. "Now, if I can just remember where I was."

"'Bleak House,'" Wendell said with a wrinkle of his nose. "It sounds kind of depressing."

"That's what my doctor said . . . in a roundabout way."

Wendell finished his snack and went to look at the list of chores that Chas had started keeping for him in the office. Jackson's eyes were drawn immediately to Chas, and he was delighted to find her looking at him. She leaned over the table and kissed him. She whispered, "I'm so glad to have you back," then she kissed him again.

"Me too," he said.

Charles started slapping his hands on the tray of the high chair, and they both laughed before Jackson picked the baby up and tickled him, making them all laugh.

Since Chas needed to get groceries, Jackson went with her just so they could be together. They left Polly in charge of both the inn and Wendell. Chas decided to stock up since Jackson was there to help with all the lifting and hauling. By the time they had everything put away at home, it was time to cook dinner. Polly came into the kitchen to announce that her work was finished for the day and she was going home. Seeing that she had a suitcase, Jackson realized she'd been staying there while he'd been gone. He thanked her and gave her a hug. She said it was great to see him looking so well, then she left Jackson and Chas to prepare their meal. There was only one occupied guest room that night. The couple had checked in while they'd been at the store and hadn't come out of their room. The inn was quiet beyond the laughter and productivity in the kitchen. After sharing a simple supper and cleaning up the kitchen, Chas saw to the preparations for breakfast for their guests while Jackson played with the baby, and then it was bedtime. Once Charles was down for the night, Jackson had to admit he was exhausted. He felt liked he'd lived two separate days in one, since the first half had been in a completely different world.

Chas was delighted and thrilled when it became evident Jackson wasn't intending to sleep elsewhere. He joked about this being the ultimate test, to see if he could get through the night without disturbing her. She was so glad to have him back that she would have gladly taken on any disturbance that went along with him, and she told him so.

Jackson fell asleep contented and hopeful, with Chas's head on his shoulder. He came awake with a start and gasped. His right hand fumbled to find his left, and he fingered his wedding ring. His dream had been disturbing and ugly, but it only took him a moment to assess the familiarity of his surroundings. The sound of Chas's even breathing made it clear that he hadn't disturbed her. It was easy to roll over and go back to sleep.

Waking up next to his wife was a privilege Jackson hadn't enjoyed for a long time. Weeks prior to going to the hospital, he'd chosen to sleep elsewhere, justifying this by telling her that it was for her benefit. Now he could see it had made some things harder for both of them. It took no effort to settle back into his normal routine, and he was glad to once again be living the life of an innkeeper, and sharing that life with his family.

Jackson went for an early-morning run, even though it was cold. He enjoyed the exercise and being back into his routine. Back at the inn, he took a quick shower before he went outside to scrape the snow that had continued falling into the night. Now the sun was out, and the day sparkled. He was able to remove much of the snow with an ATV rigged with a snow blade. Some of it had to be done the old-fashioned way, with a shovel. The work and fresh air felt good, but not as good as going back into the inn and knowing this was home. He would grow old and die here, and he was determined to do it in a way that honored the life he'd been blessed to live.

While Jackson was sitting at the desk in the office, it occurred to him that he hadn't spoken to his sister for a couple of weeks. He found Chas and asked her, "What did you tell my sister?"

"The truth, of course," she said. "Although I didn't share any details that would have embarrassed either one of us."

"Checking myself into the psych ward wasn't embarrassing for both of us?"

"Not at all," she said. "Melinda and I both admired your decision. I gave her a quick call this morning to let her know you were home. You can call her and catch up when you have a chance."

Jackson called Melinda after lunch, and they talked for more than an hour. He gave her the nutshell version of his therapy, and she told him about the letters she'd been getting from Brian. He was apparently doing well, but just the fact that he was in Iraq made Melinda fearful every day. Jackson did his best to validate her concerns, but also to offer reassurance.

Dr. Callahan called later that afternoon to see how Jackson was doing, and it was nice to be able to give him a good report. They had an appointment scheduled in five days, and Callahan told him to call if anything came up in the meantime. In the days leading up to the appointment, Jackson had a few bad dreams, but he wouldn't qualify them as frightening enough to be nightmares. He'd had no panic attacks. He'd not awakened Chas once. And he had no desire to sneak out to the garage for a drink, although Chas made it clear that she had dumped out all of the liquor. He would have been disappointed if she hadn't. But he made it clear that he would never go there again, and he meant it.

On the morning of the appointment, Chas announced that she was leaving Charles with Polly so that she could go into Butte with Jackson. She was hoping to be able to meet Dr. Callahan, and then she would take care of some errands while Jackson had his session.

Chas was glad to be able to shake the hand of the man who had made such a profound difference in her husband's life, and in her own as a result. And she told him so. He assured her kindly that Jackson had been one of his greatest accomplishments in life. He invited Chas to stay, saying that he'd intended to have her attend a session somewhere down the road anyway, and there was no reason they couldn't put that on the agenda today. The three of them spent an hour reviewing and assessing and discussing ways they could work together to continue making progress, or at least to keep Jackson from ever backsliding. Chas felt completely comfortable bringing up the intense anxiety that she'd experienced during Jackson's absence. Callahan explained that, technically, PTSD was qualified as resulting from a life-threatening experience, but a similar kind of fearfulness or anxiety was certainly common for many people experiencing difficult situations. This lesser version was called *adjustment disorder.* Chas could understand why Jackson had connected so easily with this man who respectfully listened to her concerns, kindly validated her feelings, and gently reassured her that she was handling the situation just fine.

When they were finished, Chas went to find a ladies room, and Callahan said to Jackson, "I have to ask if you've made any progress with the forgiveness thing."

Jackson bristled at the mention of it. He looked the other way and admitted, "Nope. Sorry to disappoint you. That's a tough one."

"Okay, well . . . give it some thought."

"Yeah, I'll do that," he said, unable to control the subtle sarcasm. Callahan smiled, and Jackson knew he wasn't at all fooled; he could see right through him.

Jackson went with Chas to do her errands, then they went out to lunch. She commented more than once on how much she liked Dr. Callahan, and how grateful she was for all he'd done.

"You and me both," Jackson said eagerly.

In the car on the way home, Chas said, "I have an idea about what we could do with that money."

"What money?"

"Your inheritance."

"Oh, *that* money. Is your idea something besides sending it back to my sister?"

"She won't take it, you know. And since she got the same amount—and was already well off to begin with—she doesn't need it any more than we do. I know I don't have to tell you, but I'm going to say it anyway. Our needs are more than met, and we could manage just fine without it. But it did come from your mother, and I'm sure it meant a lot to her to know that she could leave something for you. Maybe it helped her feel like she was making up for some of the heartache of your childhood a little bit. Of course, she would know that money can never change such things, but I still think it would have meant a lot to her."

"I never thought of it that way."

"So, I think your mother would be pleased to know that you've graciously accepted her offering, and that you've found something to do with the money that will have lasting value and make a difference for you and your family."

"Okay," he drawled, already feeling more relaxed about the conversation.

"Well, you know how we've worried about the baby being noisy when we have guests; and now we'll be having another one."

"Yes," he said, wondering if her idea was to build onto the inn. The possibility had come up before, but the yard surrounding the inn wasn't big enough to do anything about it. The logical thing to ask was, "Are you thinking about remodeling?"

"Not exactly," she said. "I'm thinking that the house next door is for sale."

"What? That little shack thing where the crazy cat lady lives?"

"She's in a care center; I just heard this morning. The house is being sold. Of course, the house is old and small, but . . . the property . . ."

"Good heavens!" Jackson said and chuckled as he perceived her idea, liking it immediately.

"As I see it, with the amount your mother gave us and what we have in savings, we might still need to borrow some, but not so much that we couldn't pay it off in just a few years. We could buy the property, level the house, and build an addition to the inn that would provide completely separate living quarters for our family. We'd never have to worry about our kids making noise, or leaving messes. And with the addition, we can put in a fenced yard so the kids will have a place to play outside. We'd have a place to barbecue and live like a normal family. But the house would still be attached to the inn, so that we can be right here. We can have the doors wired to signal us when we're not in the inn; stuff like that. What do you think?"

Jackson chuckled again. "I think it's the best idea you've had since you decided to marry me."

"Wow, you like the idea that much. I was hoping you would."

"I especially like that part about being a normal family."

"Yeah." She squeezed his hand. "Me too."

When they arrived back at the inn and walked to the door, Jackson had a feeling come over him that they were being watched. He discreetly looked around while he held the front door open for Chas, but he saw nothing to make him believe that the sensation hadn't been imagined. He brushed it aside and changed his clothes so that he could take care of some odds and ends that needed minor repairs.

Three more times in the next two days, Jackson had that sensation that he was being watched. It always happened when he was outside. More than once he noticed a vehicle across the street that wasn't common to the neighborhood. But that didn't mean someone hadn't purchased a different car and was now parking it directly across the street from the inn. He debated whether to tell Chas. He felt like he should, but the day was busy and he found it easier to avoid bringing it up.

The following day, Jackson and Chas went to town to finalize the purchase of the property next door. The entire transaction went quickly since they had cash to pay the asking price. On their way back to the car, Jackson saw that same vehicle nearby with someone sitting in it, reading a book. He knew he had to say something.

As soon as they were both in the SUV, Jackson said, "See that car across the street; the gray one? Please don't make it too obvious that you're looking."

"Yeah, okay. I see it."

"It's been parked across the street from the inn several times, and . . ."

"What? It's a gray sedan, Jackson. You think there aren't at least a dozen cars that look similar in this town?"

"I'm trained to pick up on subtle differences in vehicles. I know it's the same car."

"Okay, so what about it?"

"I promised to tell you everything, no matter how crazy it sounds."

"Okay," she said, sounding more concerned.

"I feel like we're being watched . . . followed."

"In other words . . . you feel paranoid."

"It's not paranoia if we *are* being watched," he insisted. "I don't feel any more crazy over this than I did when I knew there was something wrong at the house and we had a stowaway in our basement."

"Okay, you got me there. I'm not going to dispute your instincts, Jackson. But . . . who would follow us?" When he said nothing, she added with mild panic, "Could this be something to do with the FBI? Is there some warped criminal out there who would go to such lengths to hunt you down for some kind of . . . what? Vengeance? Payback?"

"I'm sure it's not as dramatic as that."

"Then what could it be?"

"I don't know, Chas, but there's no good in getting all paranoid." After the word came out of his mouth he chuckled. "Listen to me, calling *you* paranoid."

"Well, maybe I am. But it's not paranoia if someone's out to get you."

"Chas, seriously. If someone really wanted to do me or my family harm, they wouldn't be parking across the street and following me on errands."

"Okay, that makes sense."

"And I'm not that easy to find. Beyond not changing my name and the fact that I keep in touch with my sister and a couple of guys in Virginia, I almost live in witness protection. I think we just need to give it some time and see what happens. We'll both stay alert and listen to our instincts."

"Mine aren't nearly as sharp as yours."

"No, but I don't have that gift of the Holy Ghost thing. I'm sure if God wants to warn you, He'll warn you. In the meantime, we're going to go on and behave normally and not live in fear."

"Do you think we should call the police?"

"No. Not yet, anyway. If the police start canvassing the street, we may never find out who it is or what they want. I'd prefer to give it a little longer. I can't explain why, exactly; that's just how I feel."

Chas took a long moment to weigh her concerns against her trust in Jackson and the logic behind his years of experience with such things. And he was right. He didn't begin to fully understand the workings of the Holy Ghost, but he was aware of the concept. And she *did* know the gift; she knew it well. If she prayed for her home and family to be protected—and she did that every day—then she would surely be prompted to take action if any were required. She just had to pay attention and be willing to act without questioning any prompting, however insignificant it might seem.

During the brief drive home, they started talking about their plans for the addition to the inn, and Chas forgot about her fear of being tracked by hardened criminals. They couldn't actually begin the project until spring, but they could get the plans drawn up and make as many arrangements as possible so that the old house they'd just purchased could be cleared away at the earliest possibility in order to make room for construction to begin on their new home. They decided it could be built mostly for practicality, since they could continue to use the parlor and elegant dining room in the inn for any formal events or parties. They wanted a comfortable common room with kitchen facilities at one end, a dining table in the middle, and a living area at the other end; a room where children could eat and play, and where the family could interact together comfortably. Beyond that they needed bedrooms and bathrooms adequate for raising a family. They wanted the exterior to blend into the inn as much as possible, and the yard would be surrounded by a high fence so that toys and playing children would not detract from the inn's elegant and professional appearance.

At his next appointment with Callahan, Jackson told him about his belief that someone was watching him. The doctor was surprisingly unalarmed. He said there was no way he'd suddenly developed the kind of schizophrenia that would make him hallucinate people and vehicles. He agreed with Jackson's logic in how he was handling it, and just told him to pay attention. Jackson promised to call him the moment something felt even mildly crazy, and he also promised to keep telling his wife everything he was feeling, because a second mind and opinion was always helpful in reasoning out things that might seem strange.

"Changing the subject," Callahan said, "I've had a thought concerning your situation that just keeps nagging at me; that means I need to bring it up."

"Okay, I can't wait," Jackson said wryly, and Callahan chuckled.

More seriously the doctor said, "I wonder if you've ever stopped to consider what it means that *you* were the one held captive for three and a half weeks."

"What do you mean?"

"You've said more than once that you felt you stayed in the FBI too long, that if you'd retired sooner, this wouldn't have happened. I'm wondering if you've ever asked yourself what might have happened if that were the case. You would have gotten married sooner, avoided this horrible incident, and you never would have suffered with PTSD. But who would have gone in your place? When everything came together for this mission, if you hadn't been there, who would have gone, and how might it have turned out?"

Jackson felt sick to his stomach. That aspect of his ordeal had never occurred to him. He knew who would have likely gone in his place; at least he could narrow it down to a couple of possibilities. He couldn't even imagine how he might have felt to learn that one of these men he'd worked with and respected had endured something like that—when he might have stayed longer and been the one to go through it. Callahan had once said that a hundred other men who had been through something like this wouldn't have come through it so well. Jackson had often felt that *he* wasn't handling it well at all. But after living in the psych ward for a while, he had gained the perspective that it could be much worse.

Callahan interrupted his smoldering thoughts. "Do you think it's possible that your upbringing made you tougher than some men? Do you think an ex-Marine might be better prepared for such an ordeal? Do you think it's possible that it was better for *you* to be there, than for someone else?"

Jackson swallowed hard and fought the urge to cry like a baby. For the first time since it had happened, he actually felt *grateful* that it had happened the way it had. In all his wishing that he'd made different decisions, it had never occurred to him that doing so might have brought grief into someone else's life.

All the way home he pondered this new perspective. He'd had every intention of discussing it with Chas at the first opportunity, but when he drove into the parking lot of the inn, he noticed that same vehicle parked across the street. The problem wasn't the frequency of someone using a parking place. The problem was that the driver of the car was sitting behind the wheel, wearing a baseball cap and reading a newspaper. It wasn't the first time he'd seen this exact thing; same vehicle, same man. He knew a stakeout when he saw one. He might have wondered if some kind of criminal activity was going down in the neighborhood, but he absolutely knew now that he'd seen the same vehicle more than once in town when he and Chas had been out on errands. As soon as Jackson got out of the car, the vehicle drove away. He'd gotten a good look at the license plate, and he wondered if he *should* call the police and report what he'd seen. But the FBI agent in him wanted to wait a little longer and see what transpired, which would give him more evidence to go on. Instinctively, he truly didn't feel that they were in any kind of danger, but he did feel wary. He wondered if it was really possible that an episode from his past might have caught up with him, although he honestly couldn't imagine what it might be. His worst fears concerned those drug dealers who had tortured him, but they had believed he was somebody else. Since it had been a matter of mistaken identity, they certainly wouldn't be looking for Jackson Leeds.

That night when Jackson was trying to go to sleep, his conversation with Callahan suddenly came back to him. He'd honestly forgotten about it during the course of a busy day, but now it haunted him. He could clearly see the faces of the men he'd worked with, and he knew that one of them would have been assigned to do the job if he'd not been there to do it. His emotional response to the theory implied that examining this alternative more fully could go a long way toward his being able to heal more completely. But there were other issues related to this same concept that he didn't want to look at—at all. Specifically, forgiveness. Each time he saw or talked to Callahan, he brought it up. But Jackson just couldn't go there. Exhausted as he was, he put *all* issues neatly away in a corner of his mind and went to sleep. He woke from a dream that was closer to a nightmare than he'd had since he'd left the hospital. And for the first time since his return, his dreaming awakened Chas. He calmed down quickly, and she didn't seem at all ruffled, but he felt a sense of regression that he didn't like.

The following morning after breakfast, Jackson acted on a hunch and told his wife he was going to town to take care of a few odds and ends. He drove away from the inn, pleased to glance in his rearview mirror and see that he was being discreetly followed at what his pursuer surely believed was a safe distance. He drove to a particular shop downtown and parked the SUV. He'd chosen this spot for two purposes: one, because of its location in light of what he was hoping to accomplish, and two, because this little shop had a back door. He went inside, looked around for less than a minute, and went out the back, down the block, across the street, and behind a couple of buildings before he found what he was looking for.

Jackson came up quietly behind the object of his quest, glad to note that the sounds of traffic coming from the street swallowed up what little noise he made. He had him right where he wanted him. A camera with a telephoto lens hung around the guy's neck, and he was peering around the edge of the building toward where Jackson had left his car parked. Jackson silently slid his pistol out of the holster beneath his jacket, and for the best effect, he cocked the gun not far behind the guy's head, which provoked a sharp gasp. Jackson then pushed the barrel between the man's shoulders, which immediately caused his hands to go up.

"Remove the camera slowly," Jackson said, "with your left hand, and give it to me."

"Oh, man," the guy said in exasperation as he did what he was told. "I *knew* this was gonna happen."

"Higher," Jackson said after he had the camera strap around his own neck, and the guy's hands went up a little more.

"The minute I found out you were ex-FBI, I knew this would happen."

"And yet you kept following me," Jackson said. "How did you know I wasn't the kind of man to shoot before asking questions?"

"Because I'm good at what I do," he said.

"And what exactly is that?" Jackson asked.

"Listen, I haven't done anything illegal. I have a license to carry the weapon and—"

"Give me the weapon," Jackson said, "and then I might consider hearing what you have to say." Before the guy could move, Jackson reached around him and pulled the pistol from inside his jacket. He removed the clip with one hand and let the gun fall into one of his jacket pockets. He dropped the clip into the other. "Okay, I'm listening. Turn around." Jackson wanted to see his eyes. "You'd better talk fast. And remember, I'm *ex*-FBI; I don't have to answer to anybody." The guy turned around, and Jackson was first taken aback to realize how often he had seen this guy from a distance, and secondly how his eyes were open and trusting, even though he had a gun pointed at him.

"My name is Max Tykert," he said. "I'm a private investigator. You can do any background check on me you feel you have to do. Like I said, I haven't done anything illegal, and I have a license to carry the gun. I have no ill intentions here. I'm not out to hurt anybody."

"Who hired you?" Jackson demanded.

"That information is confidential and—"

"And how do you know the person who hired you doesn't have ill intentions? Maybe they know something you don't know; maybe they *are* out to hurt somebody."

"He wouldn't. I know why he hired me, and it's legitimate, but I'm not at liberty to tell you that, and I—"

"Call him," Jackson said, taking his own cell phone off his belt and handing it to the guy. "Call him now. I want to talk to him."

The moment Mr. Tykert had dialed the number, Jackson took the phone from him and heard ringing, then a man answered.

"This is Jackson Leeds," he said. "I have a gun pointed at your private investigator. Do you want to clear this up? Or should I shoot him?"

"I would be happy to clear this up," the man said with a voice that sounded kind and calm. He wasn't surprised by calm, but kindness didn't equate with the situation. "Why don't you have him bring you to me, and we'll talk."

"How do I know that I'm not putting myself in any danger by doing that?"

"You'll have to trust me," the man said, and Jackson let out a sardonic chuckle. "Or," the man added, "you have the advantage of having a gun in your hand. I promise you that I mean no harm to you or your family, but obviously it's time we met face-to-face and talked. I'll see you in a few minutes."

Jackson heard a click and dropped the phone into his pocket. "Okay," he said to Mr. Tykert, "let's go. Take it slow and easy."

"I'm slow and easy," Tykert said, and Jackson followed him to a car parked nearby. The vehicle was the same one he'd recently seen a great deal of, either in his rearview mirror or parked near the inn. There was no one around that made it necessary for Jackson to conceal the gun as they got into the car. He left it pointed at Tykert as the man drove less than five minutes to a *different* bed-and-breakfast.

"So, he's supporting the competition," Jackson said facetiously as Tykert parked the car.

"Well," Tykert responded in the same voice, "he thought that staying at your place might be a little too obvious."

Jackson hated to admit that he actually liked this guy. If they weren't on opposite sides of a gun, they might have had something to talk about.

"He actually lives in Butte and only came to town last night. I believe he was intending to contact you in the next day or so."

"I see," Jackson said, glad to be a step ahead of this guy, whoever he was.

"He's in the only room on the right on the second floor."

"That's great," Jackson said. "Lead the way. I'd like to keep an eye on you until we get this cleared up. I'm sure your client won't mind paying you for the extra time and inconvenience."

"I'm sure he won't," Tykert said with sarcasm.

Again they didn't encounter any other people as they got out of the car and went inside and up the stairs. As they approached the only door on the right, it came open. A distinguished white-haired gentleman appeared and motioned with his arm, saying kindly, "Hello, Mr. Leeds. Please come in."

"Thank you," Jackson said as if he didn't have a gun pointed at the man entering the room with him.

"Nolan Stoddard," the man said, holding out his hand.

Jackson put the gun in his left hand to shake this man's hand. He'd expected some kind of typical white-collar criminal. But this man didn't fit any stereotype of the sort of person he might have expected to hire a private investigator to follow him.

"I guess you know who I am," Jackson said.

"I do," Mr. Stoddard said. "Shall we sit down?"

They all took a chair, and Mr. Tykert looked completely relaxed, perhaps bored. Jackson set the gun against his thigh but kept hold of it. His instincts told him there was no danger here, but he preferred keeping an upper hand in that regard.

"Apparently you're upset, Mr. Leeds," Stoddard said.

"Yeah, I'm upset," Jackson said.

"I can assure you that my intentions were not to upset you or your family. I simply needed some information. Now that we've been found out and there's no harm done, I hope that we can just—"

"Allow me to clarify something first," Jackson said, "and then we'll determine whether or not any harm was done. Not long before you started spying on us, Mr. Stoddard, I spent several days in the hospital; the psych ward to be exact." Both men looked surprised, and Jackson added, "Your investigator could use some work on his skills, I think. He missed a big piece of the puzzle. If you're going to stalk someone, you should know everything about them. Since you obviously *don't* know that part, I'm going to tell you. I was being treated for PTSD due to an incident that happened some time ago, but since my mother's death, it had worsened immensely. So, I finally checked myself in to deal with the problem, and I was told I'd made marvelous progress. Then, just when I think I'm handling it pretty well, I realize that someone is stalking me. My wife thinks that maybe I'm suffering from paranoid hallucinations, and I'm trying to make myself believe that my worst fear is not coming to pass, that something I stirred up during my years in the FBI hasn't come back to haunt me."

Mr. Stoddard's eyes widened in horror. Mr. Tykert closed his eyes and shook his head.

"So, has something come back to haunt me, or not?" Jackson demanded.

"I sincerely apologize, Mr. Leeds," Stoddard said and seemed to mean it. "I had no idea. Obviously my timing was very poor."

"Obviously," Jackson said with stout sarcasm. No one commented further, and Jackson said, "I want to know who you are connected to, and what they want from me. And I want to know now."

"I am not connected to anyone or anything that has to do with you or your past, Mr. Leeds," Stoddard insisted.

"And why would I believe that?" Jackson demanded.

"Apparently your line of work has given you many reasons for paranoia," Tykert said, and Jackson wanted to hit him—except that it sounded exactly like something *he* would have said in the same situation.

"You have no idea," Jackson said.

# Chapter Twelve

Jackson glared at both of the men in the room and felt the need to say, "It's not really paranoia if someone is actually out to get you, now is it?"

"I can assure you," Mr. Stoddard said firmly, "that I have *no* connections with anything to do with you or your career. I have lived in Butte for most of my sixty-three years, where I worked as a project manager for a large firm. I'm a respectable businessman, Mr. Leeds; nothing more or less. I retired a couple of years ago, about the time my wife got cancer. She's been gone about a year."

"I'm sorry," Jackson said, having to admit that he was developing some level of respect for this man; under the circumstances, there couldn't be any other explanation for his offering sincere compassion.

"I *did* know about the matter of your disappearance some years back while on assignment," Stoddard went on, "and I knew about your hospital stay afterward. And I knew you'd retired from the FBI and come here. But that's *all* I knew. You see, I wasn't so much interested in you. It's your wife that I hired Mr. Tykert to investigate."

"My wife?" Jackson repeated with barely suppressed astonishment. "What has my wife got to do with *anything* that would warrant such a—"

"I am more than happy to explain everything, Mr. Leeds, if you will just be patient."

"I'm listening," Jackson said, not feeling patient at all. The mysteriousness of this was almost as upsetting as the thought that someone felt it necessary to stalk his wife.

"Of course," Stoddard said, "in order to learn as much as we could about your wife, your current habits were certainly of interest to me, which would explain why Mr. Tykert often followed you when you left the inn, but it's Chas I need to know about."

"Why?" Jackson asked, making no effort to subdue his anger. With his own life's experience, his mind naturally went to criminal activity and witness protection. He couldn't imagine Chas having any level of involvement in anything that would warrant such attention. And even if she *had,* she never could have kept something like that a secret from him for so long. He knew everything about her. *Everything!* Or at least he hoped he did. "She's lived a simple, quiet life here in Anaconda for *most* of her life. What could she possibly—"

"Mr. Leeds," Stoddard interrupted, "I'll just get straight to the point and then explain, so that your concerns can be laid to rest. Chas is my granddaughter."

Jackson was stunned into silence. He mentally tallied what he knew of Chas's grandparents. He had known her maternal grandmother very well, and Granny's husband had passed away many years earlier. It only took a second to bring to mind the obvious facts regarding Chas's paternity, but he felt the need to say them aloud. "Chas never knew her father; she never even knew his name. He was . . ." He found he couldn't finish the sentence in light of who this man claimed to be.

"He was a low-life, degenerate criminal, Mr. Leeds. He brought more grief into my life than I could ever recount, even if I cared to. I wish I could understand what went wrong, but I don't think I ever will. His mother and I raised four children, and the rest have led respectable and responsible lives. He was the oldest and got into trouble at a very young age. My good wife, may she rest in peace, cried many tears over that boy. I was mostly just angry. He spent a lot of time behind bars off and on, but it was what he did to Chas's mother that was the final straw. He died in prison before he completed his sentence. I don't know if I should be ashamed to admit that I was relieved; I never had to worry again—not about him, not about anyone he might hurt if he ever got out."

Mr. Stoddard paused and let out a heavy sigh, as if the words he'd just spoken had been as difficult to hold all these years as they had been to utter. Jackson took the silence as an invitation to comment, but he couldn't think what to say. He only removed the clip from his gun and holstered it.

"Again I apologize," Stoddard went on, "for causing you grief through my hiring Mr. Tykert. The last thing I would want is to bring any trouble to Chas or her family. I owe you an explanation, and I'm prepared to give it."

"I'm listening," Jackson said in a much kinder voice than the last time he'd said it.

"My children all live out of state. We keep in close touch, but I don't see them very often. When my wife passed away, I had to step back and look at things a little differently. She'd often wanted to find the child that had resulted from our son's criminal act. As heinous as his crime was, we knew a child had resulted, and we'd often wondered about that child. My wife was the one who wanted to make that connection; I was never interested. I felt sure that being born to a single mother under such circumstances would have surely resulted in a difficult life that had probably not turned out well. I didn't want to know. On her deathbed, my wife made me promise to find our grandchild and make certain all was well." Jackson stiffened at the mention of a deathbed promise, but he said nothing. "What could I say?" Stoddard said, and Jackson silently echoed the sentiment. There was no disputing the pressure behind a promise made in such a moment.

"It took me some time," Stoddard went on, "to get past grieving over her death enough to be willing to look at what I'd promised her I would do. It wasn't as difficult to track your wife down as I thought it would be. Until a month ago, I didn't even know if the child was even living, or whether it was male or female. Apparently it's well known among the older generation in this town that the old woman who had owned the Dickensian Inn had raised a granddaughter who was the product of a rape. Having access to my son's court records and putting the dates together made it obvious."

"Are you sure, then? Are you absolutely sure that Chas is your granddaughter?"

"Not as sure as I would like to be. I *feel* sure, and it all fits together. But I would like to do a DNA test to make certain."

"And if it is?" Jackson asked. "Then what? And why the private investigator stalking us?"

"I'm getting to that," Stoddard said. "I must admit that with the grief I'd experienced over the way my son lived his life, I was hesitant to just let someone I didn't know into my life in any way. What if I just announced to this person that I was their grandfather? If this person was anything like my son, I could have expected manipulation, begging for money, calls from jail in the middle of the night, and vandalism to my property. I had no reason to believe that would be the case, but I also didn't know otherwise. I don't know why some people behave that way in spite of a good upbringing, but I knew that this child had my son's genes, and I also had to assume the upbringing could have been challenging due to the nature of her birth. I simply had to know what kind of person my granddaughter was before I could make a decision as to whether or not to announce myself as a relative. Of course, I've now realized that Chas is a wonderful woman. And today was supposed to be the last day that Mr. Tykert was going to be working for me. I had intended to write Chas a letter and just see what happened from there. I don't know if I'm making any sense, and I'm certain it must sound crass, but . . . I can't deny my fears or the reasons for them. I can assure you that I have no ulterior motives. Now that I know what I know, I would simply like to get to know Chas and her family, and maybe I can make some kind of positive contribution to her life that might make up for the absence of a father." He took a deep breath and added with perfect humility, "I hope you can forgive me, Mr. Leeds, for any grief that I've caused you through my methods and my poor timing. I hope that you'll be willing to allow me to meet your wife, and—"

"Have you taken into consideration how this might affect *her?* Maybe she doesn't *want* to have anything to do with her father's family."

"I've considered that a great deal, but I think that decision should be up to her. I think it's only right for her to at least know that I exist, and that I'm aware of her existence. If she meets me and decides she doesn't want me in her life, I will respect that, and neither of you will ever see me again. But if she's willing to give me a chance, I would like to be a part of her life as much as she chooses, without imposing myself."

Jackson pondered the situation and tried to consider the possible effect this might have on Chas. He realized that he couldn't make such decisions on her behalf. Mr. Stoddard was right: any decision regarding this needed to be up to Chas, but she couldn't make a decision without being given all of the pertinent information.

Tykert interrupted the silence by saying, "This is very tender and all, but now that I'm not being held at gunpoint, I think I'd like to go drum up some work that's a little less dangerous."

"You weren't really worried, were you?" Jackson said lightly.

"Not after the first minute, no," Tykert said. "But I have had better days."

"Thank you for your help, Max," Mr. Stoddard said. "You let me know what else I owe you."

"I think we're more than good on that," Tykert said as he stood, reaching a hand toward Jackson. "My camera?"

Jackson handed it to him, saying, "You'll delete those pictures, I assume?"

"It never happened," Tykert said. Jackson handed him his gun and the clip as well, then Tykert held out his hand again. Jackson stood and shook it. "It was nice to be watching someone who was actually leading a decent life. You should consider it a compliment that I couldn't dig up any dirt on either of you."

"I'll think about that," Jackson said. "Good luck."

Tykert shook Stoddard's hand as well and left the room, closing the door behind him. Mr. Stoddard sat back down, but Jackson moved to the window, contemplating how he should handle the situation. He finally turned to face Stoddard and said, "I have one stipulation."

"You want to do a background check?"

"Should I?"

"You're welcome to, but you won't find out anything I haven't already told you."

"Okay, but that's not what I was thinking. I want a DNA test without her knowing. It sounds very likely that you're right, but I think we should be sure. Before we go through with this . . . sensitive reunion, I'd like to know for certain that you *are* her grandfather. I assume that you would like to know that, as well."

"I would, yes. I can certainly live with that. How exactly do I go about something like that?"

"If you'll give me some of your hair, I can take care of it. I believe I still have some connections—some favors I can call in."

"Okay, then," Stoddard said. Opening a drawer, he found an envelope that was part of the complimentary stationery that came with the room. He pulled a couple of strands of hair from his head and put them inside, handing it to Jackson. He then took out his wallet and retrieved a business card, which he handed to Jackson. "I'm retired, but my contact information is all the same. I'm going back to my home in Butte. Let me know when you have the results."

"I'll do that," Jackson said and held out his hand. He didn't know for certain if this man *was* Chas's grandfather, but he couldn't help respecting him—and liking him. They shared a firm handshake, and as Jackson took hold of the doorknob, he suddenly remembered something. "I rode here with Tykert. I'm going to need you to take me back to my car."

"I'd be happy to," Stoddard said, and they left the room together.

In the car, Jackson broke the awkward silence by saying, "So . . . where are your other children?"

"I have a daughter who lives in northern California with her husband. They have three children, all grown but none of them married yet. They're attending various colleges. I have another daughter in New York. She's divorced, didn't have any children. But she's got a good career and she's happy."

"That's great; that she's happy, I mean."

"And I have a son in Florida. He lives with his wife, and they still have a daughter at home; in high school. They have a son who just got married recently. I might get some great-grandchildren one of these days."

"Or maybe you've already got one," Jackson said.

"Perhaps," Stoddard said.

Jackson sat for a long while in his SUV, contemplating what he'd just learned and how it affected him. He felt indescribable relief to know that he wasn't crazy or subject to paranoid hallucinations. He hadn't really been worried about that, but he hadn't felt entirely comfortable over it, either. But then, someone *had* been watching and following them. How could he be comfortable with that? He felt reassured to know that his instincts were still good, on behalf of his family as well as himself. Of course, he felt immense relief to know that his being stalked had nothing to do with his past. He could scratch that off of his list of things to worry about. And most of all, he felt a little in awe of and overwhelmed by his encounter with Nolan Stoddard. It was certainly the last thing he'd expected to find at the end of this trail. He wondered how Chas would react to what he now knew. Or if the DNA test was negative, he wondered how Stoddard would react, knowing that all of his efforts had been in vain. Jackson felt pretty certain this man was genuine, however, and he didn't believe he would have spent well-earned retirement money to hire a private investigator if he hadn't been fairly sure.

Jackson finally returned home, acting as if he'd done nothing during his outing beyond some normal errands. Chas was busy and didn't question him about the time he had spent in town. While she was occupied in the kitchen, he pulled some strands of hair from her hairbrush and put them into an envelope, tucking it away with the one Stoddard had given him.

That night while lying in bed, he felt so tempted to tell Chas what he knew. Instinctively he believed that she would be pleased. The lack of extended family in her life was something she'd commented on many times. But still, he couldn't be sure if she'd be happy about it. The story behind her existence wasn't a pretty one. She'd never expressed any negative feelings toward her father, or rather what he'd done to her mother, but that didn't necessarily mean she didn't have them.

The following day while Chas was out doing her visiting teaching and Charles was asleep, Jackson took some mail out to the box just before the mail lady picked them up for delivery, then he sat down behind the desk in the office and called the number for the office where he'd once worked in Norfolk. He was told that Special Agent Veese was out, so he dialed Veese's cell phone. Without any hello, a familiar voice answered, saying, "Is that you, boss?"

"I don't think Lambert would appreciate you still calling me boss."

"You'll always be my boss."

"Since I owe you my life, you can call me anything you want." Jackson thought for a moment how it might have been if Veese had been held captive and tortured in his place. He felt so grateful that it had been him he almost felt tempted to cry. He forced himself to stay focused on the moment.

"I will. So what's up, boss?"

"What makes you think something's up? How do you know I didn't just call to see how you're doing? It's not like I never have."

"No, but you have a different tone of voice when you call to shoot the breeze than you do when you want to talk business."

"But I'm not in the business anymore."

"So, I'm guessing you need a favor."

"You *did* work for me too long," Jackson said, and Veese chuckled.

"Maybe. Or maybe not long enough. We still miss you."

"I miss you too. But I don't miss the work."

"Can't blame you there. Why don't you get to the point and tell me what I can do for you."

"I'm just wondering if I still have enough clout to call in a favor."

"With me, you do. If it's in my power, I'll pull any string I can. What's up?"

"I need a DNA test."

"Is that all? That's easy. The new girl in the lab owes me *lots* of favors. Do you mind if I ask why? It must be personal, unless you've taken up solving crimes on the side."

"No, I'm done with the crime business. And yes, it's personal."

"You want to find out if your father was really your father?" he asked lightly.

Jackson chuckled. Veese knew him well enough to know that he didn't like his father, even if he didn't know the reasons. "With all the people in Arkansas who think I look like him, I'm afraid I could never hope that might be a possibility. This is about Chas. I've met a man who claims to be her grandfather."

"Really? How can you not already know whether or not you're someone's grandfather?" Jackson gave a brief explanation, and Veese said, "Wow. It would be cool if he *is* related. He sounds like a nice guy."

"Yes, I believe he is. Anyway, I'm sending hair samples from both of them. I've already mailed them."

"Before you even knew whether I could do it?"

"Ah, I knew you'd find a way."

Jackson became busy with his usual work routine and quickly lost track of how many days it had been since he'd spoken to Veese on the phone. He was meeting regularly with a local architect who was designing the addition to the inn, taking into consideration all of their requirements. Then, out of nowhere, the dates on the calendar jumped out at Jackson, and he had to go into town to make some important purchases. He'd known that Charles's birthday was coming up on Monday. They'd been making plans for a party at the inn with some friends and ward members that Chas was close to. Melinda was even flying in Monday morning for a couple of days. But at least as important as the baby's first birthday was the need to acknowledge the Sunday before Thanksgiving. Charles had actually been born on that day, which had been ironic, considering its significance in other respects. Two years before his birth, Jackson and Chas had met on the Sunday before Thanksgiving, and twelve years before that, she'd received word that her first husband had been killed. Jackson knew that for Chas, the tragic anniversary had turned into a joyful one, and he also knew how important it was to remember this day for both reasons. He respected and admired Chas's first husband, who had lost his life in a military training accident. And the day he'd met Chas had proven to be the most important day of his life.

When Sunday morning came, Jackson was well prepared. He'd been able to sneak his purchases into the house the previous afternoon and hide them in the cellar. There were a number of ways he could surprise her, but when he woke up before she did and realized she was still sound asleep, he got dressed quietly and managed to sneak down to the cellar and back again before she had even stirred. He laid the huge bouquet of multi-colored roses on the side of the bed where he'd been sleeping, and set a card and a little box beside them. He then sat down where he could see her and waited for her to wake up. When she didn't awaken right away, he stood up and leaned over to kiss her, just enough to get her stirring. Then he sat back down. He wasn't at all disappointed by her reaction when she opened her eyes to see the flowers. Then her eyes shifted to him and she smiled.

"Oh," she said, sitting up, "I only got you a card."

"Which is more than sufficient."

"But you got me . . ." She made an elaborate gesture, then picked up the roses, closing her eyes to breathe in the fragrance.

"It's been a tough year for you," he said. "I just wanted you to know how grateful I am that you stuck it out with me."

She opened her arms, and he knelt on the bed to hug her. "Happy anniversary," she said and kissed him.

"Open the card," he said. "It's the best part."

"Better than this?" She smelled the roses again.

"Cards are always the best part," he added, and she laughed softly. They'd started giving each other cards early in their relationship, and they each had a significant pile tucked in a drawer.

Chas opened the card to see a silly cartoon drawing of a mouse sitting on a bench wearing dark glasses and holding a white cane. Next to the mouse was a comically hideous monster, covered with warts. "How romantic," Chas said with sarcasm. At the bottom it said, *They say love is blind* . . . She opened it to read the printed words there, *Lucky for me.* Beneath that, Jackson had written, *Every day since I've met you has been lucky for me. Thanks for loving me. All my love, Jackson.*

Chas threw her arms around his neck, still holding the card in her hand. "You're the best thing that ever happened to me," she said and kissed him. "Now it's your turn," she said and jumped off the bed to open a drawer.

"You're not finished yet," he said, holding up the little box.

"A present too?" she asked, pulling a sealed card out of the drawer and closing it.

"Come on, open it," he insisted and took the card from her as she took the gift from him.

Chas unwrapped and opened the little box, fearing he'd gotten her something expensive. But inside she only found a key. It was just a basic key, and it looked brand new. "What is this?" she asked.

"A key," he said, and they both laughed. More seriously he said, "It's the key to our new house." She looked confused and he said, "I bought the doorknobs and locks yesterday. Very soon, instead of me living in your house, I will be able to build you a house."

She smiled and hugged him. "As long as we're together, who cares?"

"*I* don't care. I just felt like giving you the key. When the house is done, we'll have a formal unlocking-the-front-door ceremony, or something."

"I can't wait," she said, then motioned toward his card. "It's your turn."

Jackson read the tender, loving message that Chas had written in his card and had trouble holding on to his composure. He hugged her tightly and told her how he loved her, then she said, "There's something else in the envelope."

Jackson pulled out another smaller card. He opened it and read, *This silly little card is good for an all-expense-paid vacation to Virginia.*

"What?" he said and looked up at her. "Are you trying to send me back?"

"No, of course not." She laughed softly. "You've said many times you should go back and visit your friends. Every time Veese calls for you, he tells me that I need to talk you into coming back. And, well . . . the thought occurred to me a while back that it might be good for you . . . to reconnect a bit. I'd go so far as to say I was inspired. Whether anything profound comes of it or not, it will be fun. You can show off your son."

He smiled. "And my wife." He kissed her. "It's a wonderful idea. Thank you."

"Well, you can't really thank me for anything but the idea, because my money is your money and your money is my money, but since you have more than I ever did, you'll really be paying for it yourself, but . . . you're welcome anyway. I've already bought the tickets and made reservations."

"What?" he said again.

"It's all arranged. We're leaving next Tuesday; nine days to get ready."

"Wow!" Jackson said. "Does Veese know we're coming?"

"Yes. He helped me."

"Well, you two are pretty sneaky," he said and recalled the conversations he'd had with Veese about Chas. How did Veese feel to be handling secrets from both sides?

The baby woke and the day began. Chas was hoping that with all the good things that had happened, Jackson would go to church with her, but he didn't. He had a nice dinner ready for her when she came home, and she tried not to show how disappointed and hurt she felt over his choosing not to share this aspect of her life with her at all. She tried to count her blessings and remember all that was good between them. Perhaps with time he would take more steps in a positive direction.

The following morning they went to the airport to pick up Melinda, and that evening they had a birthday party for Charles that surely had no meaning for the baby whatsoever. But everyone who loved him was thrilled to be there. They shared good food, lots of laughter, and they all enjoyed watching Charles eat cake with his hands. For Jackson, it felt like a celebration of his own life. He'd spent many years believing he would be an eternal bachelor. Having a son gave him more joy than he knew how to hold. Knowing another baby was on the way added to his contentment.

Melinda stayed until Wednesday. She was spending Thanksgiving with her daughter and needed to get back. While she was there, Jackson found it easier not to think about the emotional issues he was trying to avoid. Occasionally he recalled that Veese was doing DNA testing for him, and he wondered what the results might be. But they kept busy with their traditional Thanksgiving celebration. Jackson loved indulging in the present as much as he loved exploring memories of his first Thanksgiving here. He'd only known Chas a few days at the time, but he'd already been falling in love with her. It was Thanksgiving Day when he had first let her know he was attracted to her. Now, three years later, they were a growing family; they had shared more life together in these years—both good and bad—than he'd ever thought possible. On all counts, it was certainly a day to celebrate all that he was grateful for.

The following morning, Jackson was in the office just putting a few things in order when Veese called. Jackson's heart quickened while they exchanged greetings, then Veese came straight to the point. "Hey, I've got the results. You want me to fax them so you can see for yourself?"

"Yes," Jackson said, his heart quickening, "send them now." Chas had gone out for groceries, so the timing was perfect. He gave Veese the fax number, then sat where he could watch the machine. "Don't keep me in suspense," Jackson said. "In spite of wanting to see for myself, I'd prefer that you tell me."

"It's the real deal. He *is* her grandfather."

"Wow," Jackson said, then he chuckled. "That's amazing. I mean . . . I was ninety percent sure, but it's good to know."

"Yeah, it's pretty cool."

"Thanks for your help."

"A pleasure, as always. It's good to hear from you."

"And you. I understand you've been conspiring with my wife."

Veese laughed. "I have. I wasn't sure if the secret was out yet, but since you're coming Tuesday, I knew she'd have to be letting you in on it soon."

"That's very clever. Little does she know we've been keeping secrets from her too."

"Yeah, that's weird," Veese said.

"Now that I'm coming back for a visit, you'll have absolutely no excuses left for not coming *here*. When are you going to come and get away for a weekend? All you need is a plane ticket. We'll put you up and feed you."

"So you keep telling me, but you know what it's like to get time off around here."

"Yeah, I know. Keep at it. Let me know when you're ready for a break. You'll love it here; you won't want to leave."

"You mean like you? I don't think it's real likely that *two* of us are going to find a wife and a reason to retire in Montana."

"You never know," Jackson said and chuckled. They talked for another twenty minutes, catching up on the news concerning mutual acquaintances and happenings in the office, and discussing their plans for the coming week. Jackson was actually looking forward to the trip, and was glad that Chas had thought of it.

Jackson got the fax while they were talking, and he felt a secret thrill at seeing the evidence for himself. As soon as he got off the phone, he found Nolan Stoddard's business card and called his home phone number in Butte.

"Mr. Stoddard," Jackson said as soon as he answered. "It's Jackson Leeds."

"Please . . . call me Nolan."

"All right, Nolan. I have some news."

"I assumed that you wouldn't bother calling without something to tell me."

"So, I'll get to the point. The DNA was a positive match. Chas *is* your granddaughter."

"Oh, my," Nolan said, and then there was silence. It took Jackson a moment to realize that Nolan was emotional. His voice was still a little shaky when he said, "I think that's good news. I hope you feel the same way."

"I do, actually. I want the chance to tell her first, and then you can meet her."

"Okay," Nolan said. "I'll just wait for your call and—"

"There's no need for that. Why don't you just come over for Sunday dinner. Chas will be in church until noon, and we eat at about two o'clock. If you don't hear from me before Sunday at ten, just come about two, and we'll go from there."

"Okay." Nolan now sounded pleased, even thrilled. "If you're sure."

"Of course," Jackson said. "We'll see you Sunday."

"Can I bring something?"

"No, of course not. Feeding one more isn't a problem, honest."

"Well, perhaps a bottle of wine, or—"

"Actually," Jackson drawled, "that's very kind, but . . . we don't drink. Chas because of religious preferences, and me because, well . . . I'm kind of a recovered alcoholic. Therefore, none at all is better."

"I understand."

"But if you prefer wine with dinner, you're welcome to bring some, and—"

"No, it's fine. I don't drink much myself; I've just known it to be a social courtesy for some people." He paused. "I should have known . . . should have remembered. Chas is a Mormon, and they don't drink, do they?"

"No, they don't drink. And you knew she was a Mormon because . . ."

"Private investigator."

"Of course. It's too bad he didn't actually go in to the church. They might have converted him."

Nolan chuckled. "Actually, I think he *did* go in to the church, but only to use the restroom; I think that's what he told me." He paused. "And you're not a member?"

"No," Jackson said, wondering why he felt uneasy admitting it. He never had before.

"I'll see you Sunday, then," Nolan said. "And thank you."

"Hey, I'm just glad you weren't some mob boss out to get even with me."

"I'm very glad we got that cleared up."

Throughout the remainder of the day, Jackson wondered how he would go about telling Chas. He realized he just had to start at the beginning, even though it was going to be a very strange story.

At supper, he said to Chas, "After we get Charles down for the night, is there any reason we couldn't have some time to talk?"

Chas looked up at her husband, wondering about his intended subject matter. His expression was serious enough that she assumed it had something to do with his ongoing issues. But at least he was willing to talk, and even making an appointment to do it.

"That should be fine," she said. "I'll make sure everything's taken care of before he goes down."

"That would be great," he said. "Let me know what I can do to help."

"The usual will be fine," she said. "You *always* help."

He gave her a lingering kiss on her forehead, and Chas wondered where his thoughts were. She couldn't wait to find out.

# Chapter Thirteen

Once they were done eating, Jackson cleared the table while Chas cleaned up the mess Charles had made with his food. Since their guests had gone to bed for the night, everything was locked up and in order up by the time Charles went down for the night. With the baby monitor in hand, Chas sat down on the couch in the parlor. She was only there for a minute before Jackson found her there and sat at the other end of the same couch. He turned to face her and folded one leg on the couch.

"What is it?" Chas asked, feeling a little nervous.

"Something happened last week," he said. "I didn't tell you about it at the time, because . . . well, that will all make sense once I've told you everything. I needed more information before I told you what happened. Now I have all the information, and you need to know what's going on and why."

"Okay," she said, her nerves turning to worry. They had agreed to be forthright with everything, and she hoped he had a really good reason not to be, or she was going to be ticked off. But she sensed he knew that. He seemed more composed than nervous, so she just listened.

"I'm pleased to be able to say that I was *not* imagining that we were being watched and followed."

"What?" she countered. "How on earth did you find *that* out?"

"I followed the guy that was following me."

"Are you out of your mind? You could have been hurt! Does this have something to do with the FBI? Why didn't you tell me before now? I cannot believe that—"

"Chas," he leaned toward her and put a hand over her mouth, "please hear me out. Contrary to your concerns, I believe my sanity is intact. I had seen enough evidence to know that we were being watched, even if you didn't see it. So I set the guy up. It was a simple strategy. I knew he was following me. I went into a shop that had a back door. I walked around the block and came up behind him while he was waiting for me to come back out."

She gasped. "I can't believe you did that. You could have been hurt."

"Chas, I was in complete control. I was not in danger. Turned out the guy was a private investigator, and he made it clear that he wasn't doing anything illegal, and he had a permit to carry the gun."

"He had a gun?"

"Yes. I had a gun, too. I don't think he would have been so forthcoming with information if I *hadn't.*"

"You took your gun and—"

"Chas, please hear me out. Remember that I also have a permit to carry a gun, and I was very careful. Okay?"

"Okay," she said, roiling inside with the danger and mystery of this situation.

"I had him take me to the man who had hired him. He was staying at that *other* bed-and-breakfast." His facetious comment didn't lighten Chas's mood at all. "He was an older gentleman; very kind, even though I wasn't. I told him how I felt about being stalked, especially considering my recent hospitalization. He apologized and told me his reasons."

"Does this have something to do with the FBI?"

"That's what I wanted to know; it was the obvious assumption. But actually, it didn't have anything to do with me at all. He was trying to get information on you."

"Me?" she shrieked loud enough that Jackson was glad that Charles was way down the hall. He hoped that their guests hadn't heard. "Are you sure?"

"Chas, do you think I've just fabricated all of this, or something?" She didn't answer, and he said. "You're really wondering, aren't you?" He couldn't help sounding defensive. "You think I've become schizophrenic all of a sudden, that I'm seeing and talking to people who don't exist?"

Chas realized how ridiculous that sounded, but no more so than someone hiring a private investigator to get information on *her*.

When she still didn't say anything, Jackson said, "I realize it sounds strange, but there is a perfectly logical explanation."

"Which I'm waiting to hear."

"This man's name is Nolan Stoddard, and he is your grandfather."

Jackson watched as her brow furrowed with confusion; then her eyes widened with enlightenment. She stated the obvious. "But I never even knew who my father was. I wouldn't have wanted to."

"I know," he said gently. "This man knew his son was responsible for what happened to your mother, and he knew there had been a child. Did you know your father went to prison for his crime?"

Chas leaned back, breathless and a little light-headed. "No, I didn't know."

"He died there. I don't know how or why."

"I can't believe it . . . any of it."

"I know this is a lot to take in, Chas, so I'm going to hurry and tell you what's pertinent, and then you can have some time to get used to it all. Okay?" She nodded absently and focused on him. "Mr. Stoddard seems like a very good man, Chas. When his wife passed away, she made him promise that he would find you. He had a desire to get to know you, but he didn't want to make himself known if . . ."

"If what?"

"Apparently his son was—"

"My father."

"Yes, although I think we would all use the term loosely. His son brought a great deal of grief into a great many lives, not the least of which were those of his parents. Mr. Stoddard knew nothing about you. He didn't want to announce himself as a relative if you had turned out anything like the man who fathered you. So . . . he hired a private investigator to find you and to learn more about you."

He fell silent as he waited for her to take in what he had told her so far. "And you knew someone was watching us," she said, and he was glad to hear her acknowledge that without any suspicion of insanity.

"I did."

"Your instincts are pretty sharp, apparently."

"I'd like to think so."

"Why did you wait so long to tell me? Did you say this happened last week?"

"It did. I wanted a DNA test done before we took another step."

"And you did that?" She was astonished.

"I sent hair samples to Veese. Mr. Stoddard *is* your grandfather."

"Good heavens," she said, breathless again. "I can't believe it."

He talked for several minutes, telling her more details of his encounter with Nolan Stoddard, his impressions of the man, and his evident sincerity in wanting to get to know Chas without imposing on her life. She listened with a distant look in her eyes, then said, "I don't know what to think, Jackson; I don't know how to take it in."

"I wouldn't have expected anything else. Tell me what I can do."

"I don't know; I can't even . . . think." She stood up abruptly. "I need to be alone."

"Okay," Jackson said as she rushed from the room. He heard a door in the distance that indicated she'd gone outside. He'd expected her to be shocked, and he hadn't known whether her response would be positive or negative. But he hadn't anticipated her leaving. Now that he was left alone, he felt a little disoriented and not certain what to do next. After a few minutes he peeked in the baby's room to be assured that he was sleeping soundly, then he walked out the kitchen door to find Chas sitting in one of the garden chairs on the little patio. Jackson sat down on one of the other chairs and crossed his ankle over his knee.

"If you really want to be alone," he said, "then say so. Or if you can tolerate my company but prefer me to be quiet, I can do that. But I think you need to talk about it. I don't think you'll be able to figure out how you feel until you talk about it."

She said nothing at all for several minutes, and Jackson just sat there, waiting to either be told to leave, or to listen to anything she had to say. "I don't think I want to meet him," she finally said, and he was stunned. He'd never expected this kind of response.

"He's your grandfather, Chas," he said gently, while he wanted to demand that she tell him why she was being so stubborn and presumptive.

"Under the circumstances, I don't know if that's valid." She sounded angry in a way he'd rarely if ever heard. "I think this whole thing is ridiculous, and I don't know if I want anything to do with it."

"You haven't even given yourself ten minutes to think about it."

"Maybe I don't need to think about it."

"Now, that does not sound like you, *at all*. Maybe you should stop and consider what's making you so uncomfortable before you jump headlong into a decision that isn't reasonable."

"How do you know whether it's reasonable?"

"I know you, and you're sounding like a hypocrite."

She made an astonished noise and glared at him. "I refute hypocrite."

"You think for a minute about the day my mother and sister showed up here and I didn't want to see them. You practically forced me to stay and face them, and I was sure it would be a disaster. It turned out to be one of the best things that ever happened to me. Now, listen to yourself."

"This is entirely different."

"No, not entirely."

"I don't even know this man; I never did. My life is complete without him."

"Now, you're just getting *more* stubborn to try to prove your point. Why don't you just take a deep breath and think this through a little before you slam the door in this guy's face without even considering the big picture."

She let out a lengthy sigh that let him know she was possibly recovering from the initial shock of this discovery. He felt sure that once she had a chance to think it through and get used to the idea, she would see things differently.

Again they sat in silence for quite some time while Jackson hoped she might want to talk about this. "When I was a little girl," she finally said, "a day came when I figured out that I was being raised by my grandmother and I didn't have a mother and father like the other kids. Granny had told me all about my mother. Her dying in childbirth was like a legend. And Granny had told me over and over how much my mother had loved me, that she gave me life even though it had been a risk to her health because of her bad heart. But when I asked Granny about my father, I knew immediately that it wasn't good. She tried to cover it up, saying things like, 'Oh, he's just not around,' or 'You don't need to concern yourself about that.' After years of such answers, I got mad and made her tell me. I knew where babies came from, but I'd never imagined the possibility of such a thing being reduced to a crime. Many years later, Granny told me that she'd always feared the day she would have to tell me the truth, but I'd taken it even harder than she'd expected. She said that for a couple of years she feared it would be my undoing. I was so angry and confused over knowing where I'd come from that Granny feared she would lose me. My teenage hormones kicking in at the same time didn't help, I'm sure."

"You've never told me this before."

"No, it just never came up. Now you know that I had a rebellious stage. I didn't do anything horrible. I was just . . . angry; wouldn't talk to Granny about *anything.*"

"Obviously you got over it."

"Yeah, ironically I . . ."

"What?" he asked when she hesitated and looked as if she'd had a great epiphany. "I just . . . never made the connection before; probably because I've never even thought about this too deeply since I met you, but . . . ironically, it was meeting a man who was very much like *your* father that turned me around."

"What do you mean?" he asked, turning more toward her.

"I started hanging around with some friends that were a little rough. One day after school I went home with one of them. Her father was drunk, and mean, and foulmouthed. After I saw what kind of home my friend had been raised in, I realized she was actually pretty amazing; the cream of the crop. I left there thinking that no father at all was better than a father like that, and if my father *was* like that, I preferred not to know him. I also realized that if my friend could be as good as she was with that kind of father, I certainly didn't have to let my knowledge regarding my father determine my own behavior. I thought about it for a few days before it really sank in, then I had a long talk with Granny. We cried together, and things were better after that." She turned and smiled at Jackson. "And then I ended up marrying someone who was so much like my friend, without even thinking about it."

"How's that?"

"Look how you rose above the way you were raised to become such a good man."

"I think I still have a long way to go."

"We all do, Jackson. But you *are* a good man; you're certainly a far cry above what your father raised you to be."

"I can't dispute that. I'm grateful for whatever it is inside of me that gave me the desire and, well . . . the discernment, I guess, to want something better." He scooted his chair closer and took her hand. "And you also made a choice to rise above what you knew about your paternity and take hold of the good you had in your life, instead of using the bad as an excuse to mess your life up." He leaned forward and touched her face. "You're a good woman, Chas, and you deserve to be as happy as this world will allow. I've been thinking a lot about what I've learned, and I believe one of the things that's missing in our lives is extended family. I've got Melinda, but there are no other relatives I know or would care to know. But you have no one. I can understand why bringing this to light would be difficult for you, but I really think that it's worth meeting this man. There's nothing saying that you need to have a relationship with him. If problems come up, we'll deal with them. But I think he's a pretty decent guy, and it's worth a shot."

"What did you do," she asked lightly, "run a background check on him?" When Jackson didn't even crack a smile and made no comment, she realized that he had. "You *did?*"

"He said I was welcome to, so I asked Veese to do it. He's as clean as a guy can get. Not even a parking ticket." He paused for emphasis and added, "I invited him to Sunday dinner."

"Sunday?"

"But if you don't want him to come, I'll call him. He would completely understand."

"Good heavens," Chas said, getting a faraway look again.

"There's one more thing I'd like to say. You once told me that good things can come out of bad situations. I think you are living proof of that. What your father did to your mother was unconscionable. But I shudder to think where I would be without your existence. I'm sure Granny felt that way every day that you were a part of *her* life. And maybe your existence can bring some joy to a good man who has experienced more than his share of grief."

"I guess we have that in common; we both have fathers who caused a lot of grief."

"Yes, I suppose we do. And you know what? I think you need to sleep on it."

"If I can sleep."

"So, give it some time. Tomorrow is Saturday. I told him I'd call him by Sunday morning at ten if there was a problem. You give it twenty-four hours, and if you're not ready to meet him, I'll just call and we'll postpone it until you're ready."

"But you think I should meet him."

"I think you need to at least meet him, yes. But there's no time limit. And if you really decide you don't want to, I'll support you in that." He stood up and pulled her along. "Come along, Mrs. Leeds. You need to go to bed." He put his arm around her as they walked into the house. He locked the door behind them, hoping that this would all turn out the way he hoped.

* * * * *

Chas lay awake long after she knew Jackson was sleeping. While she had pondered the possible reasons someone might have been watching them, as Jackson had believed, something like this had never crossed her mind. She never would have considered the probability of a long-lost relative to even be a remote possibility. Then she recalled that Jackson had told her this man had children and grandchildren. If they were truly related—and they were—then she was part of a family. But her place there was very strange, to say the least. She wondered what they were like and felt something akin to a childlike excitement as she considered the doors that could be opened through this connection. She was still awake when Charles woke up in the night, but after he'd gone back to sleep she was able to fall asleep herself and woke up to find Jackson gone. She was only awake a few minutes before she heard him in the nursery, talking in a silly voice to the baby. Since he seemed to have Charles under control, she just stayed there and pondered once again what she'd learned the previous evening. It felt surreal and strange, but she had to admit that even in the hours since Jackson had told her that she had a grandfather, she was warming to the idea.

At breakfast Jackson said, "Here's a thought. I worked with a guy who had been adopted. He was well aware that his mother had been raped and had given him up for adoption for that reason. The parents who raised him were good people and he had a good life. That's not so different from your situation, except that you were raised by the most wonderful grandmother on earth."

"Yeah, she was, wasn't she."

"Still is, I suspect."

"You do believe in angels, don't you?"

"Yes, I do," he said with a conviction that gave Chas hope that one day his beliefs might broaden.

"What are we going to cook for dinner?" Chas asked.

"*I* will cook dinner," he said, and she knew that meant he wouldn't be going to church. "And my vote is for anything that doesn't involve turkey. I think we've had turkey overkill."

"As would nearly anyone two days after Thanksgiving. Don't worry, the remaining leftovers have gone into the freezer. I'll pull them out when we can stand turkey again; I'll make the casserole with the stuffing that you love."

"Sounds divine, but then . . . everything you make is divine."

"You're a pretty decent cook yourself, but I think tomorrow we should cook dinner together." She hoped he would get the implication that they should go to church together, too, but something kept her from actually saying it. "We'll have plenty of time."

"How about the beef and mushroom gravy stuff with mashed potatoes? *That* is divine. And it's not turkey."

"Okay," she said. "And I wouldn't have to go to the store. I have everything on hand for that." She paused thoughtfully and added, "I can't believe I have a grandfather. I can't believe I'm going to meet him. This all feels so weird."

"That's understandable," he said, wondering if she'd want to talk about it some more, but she insisted she had a lot of work to do. They had guests that would soon be arriving in the dining room for breakfast, and more guests would be arriving that evening. They'd been closed Wednesday and Thursday nights, but Thanksgiving weekend was always popular for some reason, and they were nearly full. As that thought occurred to Jackson, he said, "When I invited Mr. Stoddard to dinner, I wasn't thinking of what a busy weekend this is. Should we reschedule?"

"No, we'll manage. All of the guests will be checked out before I get home from church, and we only have two couples coming in tomorrow evening. Polly will be here to take care of that like she always is on Sundays. We'll manage just fine."

"Okay, if you're sure."

"Besides, next Sunday we'll be in Virginia."

"Ah, I forgot. Are we staying that long?"

"Six nights. We're flying home on Monday."

"Okay, this is your project. I'm just going along for the ride."

"No, once we get there, you're the tour guide. It's your city, you know."

"Not anymore. Now I'm a Montana man."

"So you are," Chas said. "Who'd have dreamed that I'd turn you into a Montana man?"

"I'm sure glad you did."

"Me too," she said and kissed him before she forced herself to get to work while Jackson watched out for Charles and helped with a few things here and there.

The following morning while Chas was sitting in sacrament meeting, she felt an unexpected rush of emotion at the thought of meeting her father's father. She could hardly call her father by that term, under the circumstances. But Nolan Stoddard was apparently a good man, and now that she'd gotten used to the idea, she could almost say she was looking forward to meeting him. Almost. She wanted to meet him, but she felt nervous. Still, she wasn't quite certain how to handle the tears, and she wasn't quite sure of the reason for them. While she was trying to figure it out, her mind wandered to the fact that Jackson was not sitting next to her. During the many weeks since he'd stopped going to church, she had struggled with coming to terms with his change of attitude, and she'd felt that it was best to keep her thoughts to herself for the time being. But today, for some reason, his absence felt more wrong and more hurtful than it ever had. She wondered if that meant it was time to discuss it with him. Did he even know how much it meant to her? Perhaps if he did, that knowledge had become lost in his other issues.

Chas's head began to hurt when it became difficult to hold back her tears. She took the baby out of the meeting and into the mothers' room, and she was glad to find no one else was there. Here she could listen to the meeting over the speaker wired into the room, and she could sit in a soft rocking chair and let the tears flow. She was glad to be able to get it out of her system before going to Sunday School and Relief Society, but Charles was so wiggly and noisy that she spent most of both meetings out in the hall. She started to feel a little nauseous and had to eat some of the Cheerios she'd brought in the diaper bag for the baby. She ended up going home before the meetings were completely over, and asked Jackson to watch the baby while she laid down for half an hour. She didn't sleep, but spent the time praying for guidance in her words to her husband, and an opportunity to be able to say them and move beyond this stagnancy. She also prayed that her meeting with Mr. Stoddard would go well. She concluded that he was probably at least as nervous as she was. It would probably only take a few minutes for the ice to break, and then they could all relax.

Chas got up and ate a little something to hold her over until dinnertime so she wouldn't get nauseous or lightheaded. Jackson put Charles down for his nap while she was eating, then he helped her work on dinner. The beef and mushrooms had been simmering in the slow cooker since early morning. Jackson worked on peeling and cutting potatoes while Chas made a green salad and prepared some fresh vegetables to steam. The raspberry cheesecake she'd made the night before was in the fridge, ready to serve.

"You okay?" Jackson asked when they hadn't shared any conversation at all for several minutes.

"A little nervous, I admit. But I'm sure it will be fine."

"I'm sure it will," Jackson said.

Once they had completed the food preparations and had cleaned up the kitchen, Jackson opened up the formal dining room, which had recently been used for Thanksgiving dinner. He helped Chas set three places at one end of the table, and he built a fire in the fireplace.

Chas was amazed at how efficiently the meal came together, in spite of her nerves. Of course, she was in the business of serving people food, and she had a lot of practice. Still, it all went surprisingly well, especially with Jackson's help. At five minutes to two, all of the hot food had been put into lovely serving dishes, covered with foil, and put into a warm oven, ready to be served. And the kitchen was spotless. At one minute after two, the doorbell rang.

"Okay, here goes," Chas said, putting her hands over her stomach to quell a sudden fluttering there. "You answer the door."

"I've got it," he said and kissed her quickly.

Chas stood back several paces in the entry hall while Jackson answered the door. She was able to get a good glimpse of this man as Jackson greeted him with a firm handshake and words that Chas didn't hear. He was nice looking and distinguished for a man who was old enough to be her grandfather. She realized how much younger he would have been at her birth than her grandmother who had raised her. Her heart quickened as Jackson closed the door and motioned toward her, saying, "Here she is. You both know each other's names, so I don't see any point in making an official introduction."

Chas watched through a kind of fog as Mr. Stoddard held out a beautiful bouquet of flowers. "Hello, Chas. I hope it's okay if I use your first name. In spite of the circumstances, I can't imagine us being too formal."

"Thank you," she said, taking the bouquet. "They're beautiful. Yes, of course. Please call me Chas. And we should call you . . ."

"Nolan, I suppose," he said with a nervous chuckle. "I don't suppose Grandpa would be appropriate under the circumstances."

"Okay, Nolan," Chas said. She was a little unnerved to hear him acknowledge their relationship, even though there was no reason to be. They were all fully aware of the situation. "It truly is a pleasure to meet you."

"Oh, the pleasure is very much mine," he said, holding out a hand. She gave him her hand, and he briefly held it instead of shaking it. "I only wish I had made the effort to get to know you sooner. I hope we can get past the awkwardness of the situation and get to know each other better." He said the words with a practiced efficiency that was coupled with apparent nervousness; he'd obviously memorized what he'd wanted to say and was hoping to get it right. "Please know that I would never want to impose on your life, but I would be grateful to have whatever association with you that you might consider comfortable and appropriate."

Chas cleared her throat. "Of course," she said, not knowing what else to say. Now that his speech was finished, he apparently didn't know what to say. "Um . . . I'll find a vase for these flowers," she said.

"Jackson, why don't you take Nolan to the dining room and we can eat; it's all ready."

She hurried into the kitchen where she was able to take some deep breaths and accept that the worst was probably over. She put the flowers in a vase and started pulling the serving dishes out of the oven. Jackson came in to help her carry them to the dining room.

"You okay? So far so good?"

"Yeah, I think so," she said. "Just . . . help me keep the conversation going. I'm a little tongue-tied."

"I can do that," he said and left with his hands full. Chas followed him with more food. Within a minute she had poured fresh water into the goblets, and the food was set out, including some of Charlotte's rolls she'd brought in the previous morning. Chas set the vase of flowers at the opposite end of the long dining table, then Jackson helped her with her chair before the men sat down. Jackson sat at the head of the table as he always did on the few occasions they ate in this room. Chas sat to his right, opposite Nolan, who sat across from her.

"It looks wonderful," Nolan said. "Smells wonderful, too."

"I hope it is," Chas said.

She was surprised when Jackson said, "Shall we bless it?" The prayer was always her idea, and she appreciated his taking the initiative at an awkward moment when he knew it was important to her. He asked Chas to offer the blessing, but she was fine with that. It gave her the opportunity to verbally express her gratitude for this meeting. She thanked Heavenly Father for having Nolan in their home and asked God's blessings to be with him in his life. After the amen was spoken, she looked up and caught a glimpse of surprise and some kind of emotion in Nolan's eyes, then Jackson broke the silence by passing the mashed potatoes to Nolan, declaring that Chas was a fabulous cook.

"But Jackson made the mashed potatoes," Chas said. "He's very good at it."

"It looks wonderful," Nolan said again.

While they were dishing food onto their plates, Jackson asked Nolan about the work he'd done before his retirement, his deceased wife, and his children that were still living. The subject of Chas's father didn't come up. Nolan then asked Jackson about his military experience and his years in the FBI. Chas was glad for their domination of the conversation, as it gave her the opportunity to observe this man and just accept the reality that they were related. The conversation steered more in her direction when Nolan asked about the history of the inn. Chas was glad to tell him; it was a topic comfortable to her and impersonal enough that she didn't feel put on the spot.

They finished eating but kept talking until Charles started making noises on the baby monitor that Chas had with her. She excused herself, glad for a little breather. By the time she'd taken as much time as possible to change the baby's diaper, she felt ready to face this man again, realizing that Charles was Nolan's great-grandson. She knew from what he'd said about his family that none of his other grandchildren had children of their own yet. She returned to the dining room to see that Jackson had cleared the table and was seated again. He was telling Nolan about the first time he'd come to the inn, and how his own personal interest in Dickens had attracted him to this bed-and-breakfast in particular. Both men stood up when Chas entered the room.

"There's the little man," Jackson said proudly.

"Yes, here's Charles," Chas said.

"He turned a year old on Monday," Jackson added.

"Oh, he's precious!" Nolan said with enthusiasm. He stepped around the table and asked, "Do you think he'd let me hold him?"

"He likes people," Chas said, "but once he gets wide awake, he's too wiggly to hold for long."

Nolan laughed gently as he took little Charles into his arms. The baby looked right at him as if to make an assessment. Nolan talked to him as if he were an adult, and Charles offered a smile that made Nolan laugh again. "My first great-grandchild," he said, and Chas took Jackson's hand.

Chas whispered to Jackson, "You take care of the guys. I'll get dessert."

He nodded, and Chas went into the kitchen. She could hear Nolan talking to the baby and the baby starting to jabber happily while she hurried to get the leftovers ready to go in the fridge, except for a plate of bite-sized pieces that she prepared for the baby. She rinsed the dishes for the dishwasher and loaded them. She got dessert out and put three servings onto pretty plates, which she put on a tray. Taking it to the dining room, she found the men sitting again, but Nolan was still holding Charles. She served the dessert and got a comment from Nolan about how she was spoiling him. She asked Jackson to get the baby's high chair from the other room so they could feed him while they were visiting. Nolan reluctantly let the baby go so that he could have his dinner, but he hardly took his sparkling eyes off of Charles, enjoying every little antic.

"It's been a long time since I've had a baby around," Nolan said. "My youngest grandchild is in high school."

Chas found she was feeling significantly more relaxed around him, and she had to admit that Jackson had been right. It was clearly evident that Nolan Stoddard was a good man, and she was glad to have him in her home. She didn't know exactly where the relationship would go, but she was very glad they had taken this step.

# Chapter Fourteen

When they were finished with dessert, Jackson cleaned up the baby and left him with Nolan while he took the high chair back to the kitchen and Chas hurried to put the few remaining dishes in the dishwasher. They all went into the parlor where it was more comfortable and where Charles could crawl around and play with some toys they kept there in a cupboard. Charles preferred walking around the coffee table over any other activity, and he was getting very good at it. They were all sure that he would take off walking any day now.

"And soon we'll have another one," Chas said.

"Really?" Nolan asked, clearly pleased. "You're expecting?"

"Yes, it's due in late June."

"That's wonderful!" Nolan said. "Are you feeling all right?"

"Oh, some days are worse than others, but nothing serious. I'm okay."

"You must take very good care of her," Nolan said to Jackson.

"I try," he said, "although I'm sure I could do better."

"No, he does just fine," Chas insisted.

When Nolan finally declared that he needed to leave, Chas was surprised at how quickly the time had passed. He thanked them both profusely and said that next time he'd have to take them out to dinner. They mentioned their forthcoming vacation to Virginia, saying they could set a date to get together when they returned.

"Is it all right if I call or come to visit again?" Nolan asked. "I promise not to make a nuisance of myself."

"You're more than welcome," Jackson said.

"And you don't have to feed me. I'd just like to see you once in a while."

"Of course," Chas said and impulsively kissed his cheek. "It's been a pleasure." He looked so pleasantly surprised by the kiss that she gave him a quick hug, and then feared he might start to cry and she wouldn't know what to say. He smiled instead, shook Jackson's hand, and made a graceful exit.

"Wow," Chas said after he'd gone and they were both back in the parlor where Charles was still playing.

"Yeah," Jackson said, and they sat close together on the sofa.

"You were right, you know," Chas said.

"About what?"

"About meeting my grandfather. I *was* being a hypocrite. You could see something I couldn't see."

"I guess turnabout's fair play, although I think you came to your senses a lot faster than I did."

"Well, I'm grateful. Thank you . . . for handling it so well, and for helping me see how important this was. He really is a wonderful man."

"Yes, he certainly seems to be."

"And so are you."

"Am I?"

"Oh, yes."

"I don't know. It sure feels like I fall short in a lot of ways. It seems like you should have a husband who shares your religion and supports you more fully in such things."

Chas could hardly believe what she was hearing, especially since the comment had seemed to come out of nowhere. Could this be the answer to her prayers? He'd not said a word in many months—if ever—that had invited any conversation on religion.

"There's a way to solve that," she said, not willing to pass up the opportunity.

He tossed her a skeptical glance. "I don't know if we should go there."

Chas took a deep breath and hoped she wouldn't regret saying things she'd wanted to say for a long time. "Why not?" He looked defensive, and she added, "Don't get angry; just tell me why we shouldn't go there. I told you I would never force my beliefs on you, and I would never make it an issue in our marriage. Does that mean we can't even talk about it?"

Jackson swallowed his temptation to get defensive. "Is there something you want to say?"

"Yes, but not at the risk of making you think I've broken that agreement. But then, you agreed to go to church with me, so maybe we're even."

"Touché," he said tonelessly.

"As I see it, you're wandering around in your life trying to find peace over some pretty tough issues. Even though you've made a lot of progress, I know you're still struggling, still searching, while the only true source of peace is staring you in the face, but you won't even look at it long enough to decide if it could help you or not. It's like dying of an infection while the unopened bottle of antibiotics is sitting on the table next to your deathbed. I don't know why you're so resistant to religion when you've had so many obvious blessings and miracles in your life. The problem is that I don't think you know either." She paused to take a breath. "That's all I have to say."

Chas walked away before he could dilute her words with his own retort.

Jackson felt as if he'd been slapped—twice. He *had* promised her he would always go to church with her. Was his own anger and defensiveness stronger than a promise to his wife? *Yes!* He'd proven that in many respects lately, and it was deplorable. He'd honestly never stopped to consider that his aversion to church had caused him to break his word to her, but it had. Surely he could endure sitting through church for her sake after all she'd been through for his. Beyond that, he couldn't avoid asking himself if she was right. Were the answers staring him in the face? He felt tempted to push the question away, but something more powerful lured him to look at it straight on. Perhaps he'd finally suffered enough that he was willing to do whatever it took to find peace. Maybe Chas was wrong. Maybe religion wasn't the answer for him. But he needed to test it enough to be able to look his wife in the eye and say with confidence that he had given it a fair shot. Her analogy about the antibiotics was effective. He felt like a part of him *was* dying. He'd worked hard and struggled to make peace with these feelings, and he'd come a long way. But he felt far from whole, and certainly not healed.

In spite of the logic of Chas's argument, it took him until the next morning to get up the nerve to take the next step. He thought of just waiting until next Sunday when he could surprise her by going to church with her. But the issue was weighing heavily on him, and he felt anxious to ease the tension. It wasn't that Chas was creating any tension over the matter. Once she'd said what she'd had to say, she had let it drop and had not behaved like anything was wrong at all. He appreciated that, but he needed her to know that he also appreciated what she'd said, and to know that he'd taken her advice to heart.

He went to the kitchen when he knew she would be busy preparing breakfast for their guests. Charles was contentedly playing on the floor. "I have a question," he said. "Actually, I have two. The first is . . . well, is it okay if I go to church with you on Sunday? We'll be in Virginia, but when you came out there to visit me, we went to church. I figured we should do that again; I know you wouldn't want to miss it. I want to go with you."

She stopped what she was doing and turned to look at him. He could see by her eyes how much that meant to her, and he felt the need to add, "I'm sorry I stopped going. Even though I was upset, I shouldn't have stopped going. You were right. I promised you, and I lost sight of that."

"I would love to have you go to church with me. I want to say that I don't want you to do it just for me; I want it to mean something to you. But . . . when it comes to raising our family right, I'll settle for having you do it for me. It means a lot. Thank you."

Jackson just nodded, feeling a little embarrassed, but glad that he'd apparently taken the right step and said the right thing.

"And the second question?" she asked, turning more toward him, completely ignoring her work.

He hesitated so long that he had to admit, "I don't know why this is so hard, but it is, so . . . bear with me."

"Of course."

"You said the only source of peace is staring me in the face, but . . . in spite of being a part of your life for three years now, I'm ashamed to say that I'm not exactly sure where to start looking." He was startled by the tears that rose in her eyes, then fell, and he had to ask himself what their source might be. Apparently this meant a lot more to her than she'd let on, or maybe she *had* let on, and he'd been too dense to see it. He felt the need to clarify, "I don't know if I can find peace through religion the way you do, Chas; I can't make any promises. But I figure I should at least give it a fair effort. I can't guarantee the results."

"Fair enough," she said and nodded, then she laughed softly and crossed the room to hug him.

He hugged her back and asked, "Does it really mean that much to you?"

"It really does," she said. "But I won't be pushy; I promise. You just go at your own pace, and we'll see what happens. But if you have any questions . . . or want to talk about it . . . you know where to find me."

"I do. But you haven't answered *this* question. Where do I start?"

"Just a minute," she said and left the room. "Don't go anywhere."

Jackson remained in the kitchen, eating a couple of the strawberries she had just washed. He was surprised to see her return with a small wrapped package. "What is this?" he asked, taking it from her. It was heavy.

"A gift I've been wanting to give you for a long time. But I had to wait until you asked for it."

"Okay," he drawled, then chuckled.

"I don't want you to open it right now, or at least . . . I want you to open it alone. I'll just . . . keep fixing breakfast, and you . . . open it whenever. Like I said, you know where to find me." She kissed his cheek and went back to work, adding nonchalantly, "I love you."

"I love you too," he said and kissed her cheek in return before he left the room. He debated waiting to open the gift, but his curiosity was too strong. He went to the bedroom and closed the door, sitting on the freshly made bed. Considering its shape and weight, he suspected it was a book. He tore away the shiny gold wrapping and silver bow to reveal a box. He slid the deep lid off and was surprised, although it made perfect sense, and if he'd stopped to think about it, he should have known this is what she would have wanted to give him. Still, he felt touched to think that she'd had it a long time, just waiting. He respected her for waiting until he'd asked, but he felt some regret that he'd not asked sooner. Only the front of the book was visible while still in the box; it was dark green leather, with nothing written on the front except at the bottom, in tiny gold letters.

*Jackson T. Leeds.* He knew what this was. He'd been to church enough times to know that many people had these fine sets of scriptures with their names engraved on them. He saw Chas reading from hers every day, although it was well worn and the name was fading. Since their marriage had changed her name, he was okay with that.

Jackson turned the box over to let the book fall facedown onto the bed, then he turned it over. It was what he knew they called a quad, since it contained the King James Bible, plus three other books of scripture that were exclusive to Mormonism. The edges of the pages were trimmed in gold, and the quality of the book was fine and elegant. It fell open to a page where a card in an envelope had been tucked. His name was written on the envelope. Leaving the book open to that page, he set it down and opened the card. On the front was a beautiful landscape photograph of a lake that reflected the mountains behind it, along with the words: *This world is a beautiful place . . .* Inside was printed: *Mostly because you're here with me.* But every bit of white space inside the card and on the back was filled with Chas's tiny handwriting. The date was only a couple of months after they'd been married. He took a deep breath and started to read.

*Today I took the long drive to the temple for the first time since I became your wife. The drive has never felt lonely before, but today it did. I could only think of you and how happy you've made me, and I wished that I had brought you along. After I was finished in the temple, I stopped at a Church bookstore, as I often do, and wandered around, looking to see if anything caught my eye. When I saw the beautiful scriptures, the thought came so strongly to me that I needed to get some for you, but they should be put away until you were ready for them. So, if you're reading this letter, I'm assuming that you've given me some indication that you have a desire to learn more about what is most dear to me. Just know that wherever I am and whatever I'm doing while you're reading this, my heart is filled with inexplicable joy that you've come to this place.*

*I'm grateful for your willingness to support me in my religious beliefs, and as I've promised, I never want to be pushy with them. I appreciate the mutual respect we share, in this and so many other things. But eventually you must know that my heart aches with the chasm that exists between us in this regard. I don't want you to take that statement as any kind of manipulation or attempt to guilt you. If you come to embrace my beliefs, it must be for the right reasons, and it must be from the heart, or it will be meaningless. Still, I pray every day that with time you may come to feel and understand the marvelous peace and joy that the gospel has brought into my life.*

*I want you to know that what I believe and what I want to share with you is not just about going to church together or sharing the basic belief that God is a part of our lives. I didn't find the gospel until after Martin was killed. At the time I felt so much regret that he hadn't been active in his beliefs, and that I hadn't embraced them sooner. I found myself wishing that I could go back and do things differently. Now, I find myself only wanting to go forward. As I grew to love you, I realized that I wanted nothing more than to be with you forever. It's most likely that one of us will leave this life before the other. When the day comes that we are separated by death, I don't want to have to wonder—or to leave you to wonder—if that separation will be permanent. I want to know that we'll be together again, that our children will be ours forever, that what we share will never end.*

*It is my wish that you will accept the enclosed book with all the love of my heart, and that you will have a desire to earnestly search its pages for whatever answers you may be seeking. You will find in the bottom of the box a list of some of my favorite passages, which I would like you to start with; I've also written some brief explanations of what they mean to me and why.*

Jackson noted the folded piece of paper that had also fallen on the bed. He picked it up and unfolded it to see a printed list of scripture references with notes. He set it aside and continued to read the letter from his wife.

*I know that you believe in God, you believe in miracles, and you believe in angels. I want you to know that these scriptures combined testify of the truth of these things. I want you to know that I know the principles you will find here are true. I know that Jesus is the Christ, that by Him and through Him we can find peace, we can heal, we can be together forever. My wish is for you to earnestly study these scriptures, and I would ask you to begin with the Book of Mormon. Read the passages I've listed, and then start at the beginning. I want you to start with Moroni, chapter seven (specifically the verses I have marked), which is where this letter was placed. I know that if you read with an open mind and an open heart, asking God to bless your search, you will get your answers. (See Moroni 10:4.)*

*I love you, Jackson, with all my heart. I pray that we will find much joy and happiness together, in this world and in the world to come. Love, Chas*

Jackson was fighting emotion by the time he'd finished the letter. He choked it back and picked up the book to the page that had been marked, and noted the verses marked in red pencil.

*And after that he came men also were saved by faith in his name; and by faith, they become the sons of God. And as surely as Christ liveth he spake these words unto our fathers, saying: Whatsoever thing ye shall ask the Father in my name, which is good, in faith believing that ye shall receive, behold, it shall be done unto you. Wherefore, my beloved brethren, have miracles ceased because Christ hath ascended into heaven, and hath sat down on the right hand of God, to claim of the Father his rights of mercy which he hath upon the children of men? For he hath answered the ends of the law, and he claimeth all those who have faith in him; and they who have faith in him will cleave unto every good thing; wherefore he advocateth the cause of the children of men; and he dwelleth eternally in the heavens. And because he hath done this, my beloved brethren, have miracles ceased? Behold I say unto you, Nay; neither have angels ceased to minister unto the children of men.*

Jackson thought of his undeniable experience while he'd been imprisoned, when he'd known that Chas's grandmother was with him. He thought of many other miracles that had occurred in his life, most of them since he'd met Chas. And he couldn't deny that she was right. Her words echoed in his mind again. *I don't know why you're so resistant to religion when you've had so many obvious blessings and miracles in your life. The problem is that I don't think you know, either.* Yes, she was right. He didn't know, either. But reading the highlighted words before him again, he felt something deep inside reaching toward their meaning, even though he felt that he didn't begin to understand what that was. But he wanted to know, and considering his attitude in the past, he believed that was a good start.

Jackson picked up the list Chas had typed, thinking he'd just look at a couple of references before he went to find her and thank her for this wonderful gift. It took him a little while just to get his bearings with the book and realize how to find the passages. He couldn't recall ever finding scripture references before in his life. His only exposure to the scriptures had been looking at Chas's book during Sunday

School to read along with what was being read. And he'd heard her read aloud here and there at home. But he'd never actually done this on his own. Once he got the hang of it, he found the references she'd listed, and found them all to be marked in red pencil. She had gone to a great deal of trouble to guide him to these passages. He found himself pondering and rereading, and thinking he'd have to come back to study more. He kept going down the list, fascinated and drawn to the concepts before him, even while he felt overwhelmed and unable to fully take in what he was reading. He was surprised to look up and see Chas peering into the room.

"You okay?" she asked.

"Yeah," he said and set the book beside him on the edge of the bed. "I was going to come and find you . . . to thank you . . . but I got reading, and . . . it's a wonderful gift, Chas. Thank you."

She smiled and stepped into the room. "You're welcome. You missed breakfast."

"Did I?" He glanced at the clock. "Good heavens."

"I've been busy, or I would have come to find you sooner. Now it's almost time for lunch."

"So it is," he said and chuckled. "Wow."

Chas found it difficult to speak and fought to keep her composure as she took in the situation. He'd lost track of the time because he'd been reading *the scriptures!* And even now his body language implied a hesitance to set them aside.

"I'm sorry," he said. "I left you alone to deal with the baby and breakfast and—"

"It's okay," she insisted. "Everything's under control, although . . . we need to be making certain everything is in order so we can leave in the morning."

"Of course," Jackson said.

"Wait," she said and stopped him from leaving. "Thank you."

"Me? Why are you thanking me?"

"For caring enough to ask, for keeping an open mind."

"I should have asked a long time ago." He kissed her forehead and went to the office. Chas had to lean against the wall and put a hand over her joyful heart. She had to remind herself to continue to allow him to follow this path at his own pace, and not to get overzealous.

He was studying with enthusiasm, his heart was open, her prayers were being answered.

Their day was busy as they made travel arrangements, but Chas felt a lightness in her heart that far surpassed her anticipation of getting away with Jackson for a vacation. That evening after everything was as ready to go as it could be, and the baby had gone down for the night, Chas found Jackson sitting in bed reading from the scriptures, his face firm in concentration. She just got into bed beside him and made herself comfortable as she prepared to read her own scriptures. She made up her mind not to make any inquiries, but to allow him to ask questions if he had them. But when they knelt together by the bed for prayer, he offered to say it—for the first time in many months. Chas felt so humbled, so happy, so grateful.

They were off to the airport early the next morning, and thankfully, Charles was a fairly tolerable passenger. By the time they landed in Virginia, collected their luggage, picked up their rental vehicle, and got away from the airport, they were all hungry so they stopped for a quick supper before checking into their hotel. They had no plans until the next day, since Chas knew that trying to cram too much into a day filled with travel would only make for a cranky baby, and, consequently, cranky parents. That evening in their hotel room, Jackson was reading from the scriptures long before Chas got hers out, and even after prayer he read until he knew he needed to get some sleep.

The following day they went sightseeing, going to places that Jackson had declared he'd always wanted to see, but because of the busy life he'd led, he'd never taken the time. He'd also never had anyone in his life with whom he'd cared to do such things. The baby seemed to enjoy the outing as long as they got him out of his stroller to move around here and there. He slept in his stroller while they explored an amazing art museum. That evening they went to a barbecue that Jackson's friends had arranged when they'd gotten word that he was coming for a visit. The gathering took place at the home of Agent Ekert, a man with whom Jackson had worked for many years, and who was also a good friend. Chas had only met him briefly on each of her two visits to Virginia. The last time she'd seen him, he had been sitting next to Jackson's hospital bed. She'd only known him as *Agent* Ekert; Jackson had always referred to him simply as Ekert. Now she learned his name was actually Shawn, and she met his wife, Karla, and their two children. Shawn and Jackson were so happy to see each other that it was almost comical. They'd obviously had a great many bonding experiences, not the least of which was Shawn being a part of the team that had rescued Jackson from his captivity.

Agent Veese arrived at the gathering, and Jackson was at least equally glad to see him. Chas knew that in a way, Jackson was closer to Veese; at least they kept in touch more. Now she learned that his first name was Elliott. She too knew Elliott better, even though with all the times she'd spoken to him briefly on the phone, she'd never known his first name until now. He too had helped rescue Jackson, and he'd been the one to help her see him when he'd been so sick in the hospital afterward. Elliott was in his late thirties and had never been married, and it was a running joke that he needed to go to Montana to find a wife and retire. Chas suggested that if Jackson stopped threatening to line him up with all of Chas's single friends, he might actually come to visit.

Over the next little while, a number of other people that Jackson had worked with arrived at the party. Jackson was pleased to see everyone there, and they were pleased to see him, but it was obvious that Veese and Ekert had been his true friends.

The company was enjoyable and the meal delicious. Everyone brought salads and desserts to share and their own meat to cook on one of the available outdoor grills. Chas had brought a store-bought cake since they were away from home without a kitchen, but it still tasted pretty good, and overall the meal was delicious. She noticed that most of the adults were drinking beer, and was proud of her husband for declining, even when he was teased about it. They ended up staying quite late, but Chas got the baby ready for bed, and he fell asleep in Jackson's arms while they visited with others who had also remained after most of the crowd had gone home.

While Jackson was sitting in the room with Veese and Ekert—and Ekert's wife—his mind went to the concept Callahan had proposed to him that had nearly stopped his heart. *Who would have gone in your place?* Well, Jackson knew who. It would have been one of these two men. While he mostly listened to a portion of the conversation taking place between the two of them, he considered what he knew of their lives. They were good men and great agents. But he wondered if they would have been able to survive it—emotionally if not physically. One stark difference stood out to Jackson, another point that he'd never considered before, and when he did, he had to excuse himself. Jackson went into the bathroom and hung his head over the basin. His chest tightened, and he found it difficult to draw breath as he tried to become accustomed to the idea that the way his father had treated him had actually toughened him up enough to be able to withstand the way he'd been treated. Was that why he'd been able to endure what Callahan had said a hundred other men wouldn't have? He'd also been a Marine. Ekert had no military background; Veese did, but not the Marines. It was different, plain and simple. But the disturbing point took him back to his father. Could he actually find a reason to be *grateful* for the unspeakable events of his childhood? The thought was incomprehensible, but he knew it warranted some discussion with his shrink when he returned home. In the meantime, he splashed water on his face and filed this away with other issues that were still difficult to confront. He blotted it dry, took a deep breath, and returned to find his friends laughing boisterously over some of their boyish antics that they'd indulged in to ease boredom on stakeouts.

The party finally broke up when it became ridiculously late, but they all had plans for more time together while Jackson was in town. On their way back to the hotel, Jackson said to Chas, "Thanks for bringing me back. That was great."

"I'm glad you enjoyed it. I did too. And I realized something tonight."

"What's that?"

"You don't have any friends in Montana."

"I have you," he said. "Contrary to how it might have appeared this evening, we really didn't do that much socializing outside of work. Ekert liked inviting us bachelors over for Thanksgiving and Christmas, and there was a rare thing here and there, but I was pretty much a loner. Now I have you."

Chas took his hand and squeezed it. She appreciated the sentiment, but she still wished that he had someone of his own gender in Montana to hang out with now and then. She had Charlotte and

Polly, and a few women she went to church with. She wasn't one to actually do a lot with friends, either, but she did go out with a friend occasionally for lunch or shopping. Of course, her deepest hope was that Jackson would eventually embrace the gospel, and perhaps he could find a more comfortable place among the men in the ward. But for now, that was just wishful thinking.

Back at the hotel, Charles was transferred from his car seat to his father's shoulder and then to the crib in their room without seeming ruffled at all. Chas and Jackson both went right to bed since it was so late, but Jackson was awakened by a nightmare a little after four, and he was dismayed to realize that it had awakened Chas.

"Sorry," he muttered through the darkness.

"It's fine," she assured him and urged his head to her shoulder. "You okay?"

"Yeah . . . other than wondering if I'm regressing."

"You do so much better than you used to."

"Yes, but not nearly as well as right after I got out of the hospital."

"You can talk to Callahan about it when we get back."

"Yes, of course," Jackson said, and his mind wandered back to his earlier thoughts. "I know we should get some sleep, but . . ."

"I'd rather talk to you than sleep anytime," she said. "We can take a nap when the baby does."

"Good plan," he said and eased a little closer to her. "There's something I've been wanting to talk to you about . . . something Callahan said . . . but it got lost in other things when I discovered you have a grandfather. I thought about it a lot this evening . . . and it kind of led to other thoughts that I just . . . I guess I just need to say them out loud."

"Okay," she said gently.

"He asked me if I'd ever wondered what might have happened if I *had* retired earlier, and I hadn't been the one to do the mission. I'm ashamed to say that I'd never looked at it in that context. I'd wondered how *my* life would have been if I hadn't gone; and I'd wondered how *your* life would have been. But I'd never wondered what might have happened if someone else had gone in my place. The mission would have happened; it was inevitable. And if I hadn't been there to take the lead on it, either Veese or Ekert would have gone instead of me."

Chas gasped softly as she perceived his meaning. Jackson continued, "As soon as Callahan said it, the strangest thing happened to me. A part of me actually felt *grateful* that it had happened the way it had. I was glad it had been me, and not one of them. And sitting there tonight, just looking at them, I wondered if either of them could have survived it, and I felt sick, and . . ." He paused to swallow a painful knot. "And then it occurred to me that . . . maybe I was tough enough to handle what happened to me because . . . because of the way my father treated me. And maybe, just maybe, a tiny part of me could be grateful . . . grateful for that, too." He let out a stilted chuckle, then his voice cracked. "I can't believe those words just came out of my mouth."

"It is rather amazing," Chas said in a voice that indicated she too was feeling emotional.

"So, what do you think?"

"I think it's a remarkable perspective, and I think perspective can make a big difference in many aspects of life. I think it's something you need to ponder and keep talking about until you can make peace with it."

"I'm sure you're right," he said, and Chas marveled at how far he had come. Following some thoughtful silence, she believed it might be a good time to share a thought that she'd considered many times. She uttered a silent prayer for guidance, took a deep breath, and said, "I've pondered this situation . . . your feelings about your father, specifically. I've thought about it a lot, and I have some thoughts I'd like to share with you . . . if you're interested."

"You know I'm always willing to listen to whatever you have to say."

"I know, but . . . this is a sensitive topic, and I know it's hard for you to talk about."

"You told me I only had to listen," he said, sounding mildly facetious.

"Fair enough," she said and searched for a place to start. "I want to make it clear that I am in no way trying to minimize your father's behavior or the way it affected you. There is no disputing that he was a very difficult man. I wonder, though, what kind of upbringing he had, or for how many generations the abuse had been going on. The good thing is that you have been strong enough to stop that cycle and put an end to it. That's no small thing, and it's one of many reasons why I love and admire you. I think that being the one to change it means that you're the one who has to learn to understand what happened and why. You can teach your own children to live a different kind of life. Are you with me so far?"

"I'm with you," he said.

"I have to ask you if you believe in life after death."

"You know that I do."

"I know, but . . . I'm wondering if you believe it in the respect that life continues to progress beyond death. There are some people who simply don't have the opportunities in this life to learn the really important things they need to learn. I truly believe, Jackson, that when life dishes out circumstances that people have no hope of rising above, God will give them another opportunity. I've believed that for a long time. I was worried when Martin died, because he died without being active in the Church, and he had some issues. But through study and prayer and the wisdom of a good bishop I came to understand this principle, and to feel peace over the matter. I believe he's progressing and learning. I believe the same about Granny. And I believe the same concerning your parents. I wonder what their perspective is from the other side of the veil. Do you think it's possible that they could overcome their differences when they don't have the dysfunctional behaviors of this world between them? Do you think your father might realize the damage his choices made? Do you think he's had contact with his own predecessors who might have been responsible for perpetuating the abuse? Obviously these are questions that don't have any concrete answers, but instinctively I believe it's possible. And I believe that if you could speak with your father now, he would likely express his regret, and maybe he would even hope for your forgiveness."

Chas stopped, leaving that word *forgiveness* hanging uncomfortably in the air. She hadn't intended to actually use that word, knowing that this very concept in regard to his father had once made Jackson very angry. She prayed that the mood between them wouldn't be shattered, that he would at least consider what she'd said. He finally eased the suspense by saying, "It's certainly something to think about." Chas wrapped her arms more tightly around him and kissed his brow. A long moment later he said, "You should probably know that Callahan told me I needed to forgive those who had hurt me."

She wanted to shout for joy, hoping that the doctor's influence might carry more weight than her own in that regard. She simply asked, "And what do you think about that?"

"You, of all people, don't need to wonder how I felt when he brought it up."

"But that was a while back, I take it."

"Yeah, it was."

"And now?"

"Now, I have a lot to think about . . . and a lot to sort out. And *right now*, I think we should get some sleep." Chas turned her head to find his lips with hers in the dark. "Or not," he said. She laughed softly and kissed him again.

# Chapter Fifteen

The remainder of their time in Virginia was a heavenly combination of sightseeing, visiting with friends, and just spending time together away from the busyness of everyday life. Chas was pleased to note that Jackson continued reading from the scriptures each day, and he seemed eager to pick them up and reluctant to put them down. They had no further conversations about psychology or religion, but he did attend church with her on Sunday. Just having him beside her at sacrament meeting made her feel blessed and hopeful. She knew he had a long way to go on many issues. She just prayed that the journey wouldn't be too long or difficult for either one of them.

It was starting to snow when the plane landed in Butte, and the drive home from the airport got a little scary the last few miles. But they arrived home safely to find Polly keeping everything perfectly under control, and the inn in pristine condition. Wendell had just arrived a few minutes before they had, and apparently his walk from school had rendered him wet and cold. Polly had him wrapped in a blanket by a fire in the parlor with a cup of hot chocolate while his coat, hat, boots, and gloves were drying out near a heater vent in the hall.

Over the next hour the storm worsened dramatically, and they were glad to be safely home. Their only scheduled guests called from Butte to say they wouldn't be coming, due to the storm. Polly announced that she might be spending the night. Since she always kept a few personal things at the inn for just such occasions, it wouldn't be a problem. After Wendell warmed up, he was put to work polishing the wood spindles that supported the banister rail on the staircase. Wendell's father called about ten minutes before he normally picked him up to say that not only had he been delayed at work, but he was doubtful that he could get there very quickly through the storm. Chas assured him that Wendell was fine and they would feed him supper. She also told him that if he ended up needing to stay the night, they would manage. Better that than taking risks to get there. He promised to call back a little later with a progress report.

When Chas told Wendell the news, he was thrilled, as if staying for supper—and the very possibility of spending the night—was a divine adventure. "Better than having to live with all those girls," he said in reference to his sisters.

Jackson chuckled and said, "If you're staying for supper, you'd better help fix it."

When Chas felt suddenly exhausted from the combination of traveling and her pregnancy, she left Jackson and Wendell to finish the simple casserole recipe that she had started. They also took care of Charles in the kitchen so that she could lie down for a while. She came to the table to eat, and was glad when Polly offered to clean up the kitchen. Since there were no guests at the inn, there were no preparations necessary for morning. Wendell got out his backpack and did his homework at one of the little tables in the guest dining room. When he was done except for needing to read, he took a book to the parlor where Jackson was reading and keeping an eye on Charles, who was making a mess of his toys.

"Can I sit here and read?" Wendell asked, and Jackson smiled at him. His overt politeness was endearing.

"Of course you can," Jackson said and went back to reading *Bleak House*. He noticed that Wendell was reading *A Tale of Two Cities*, and they talked about it for a few minutes before they both went back to their reading. Jackson had a funny thought come out of nowhere and chuckled.

"Is the book funny?" Wendell asked.

"Not at this moment, no."

"Then what's funny?"

"I just had a funny thought. Would you like to hear it?"

"That's why I asked," the child said as if he were ten years older.

"I think I told you about Chas's grandmother."

"Yeah."

"Well, she really liked Charles Dickens . . . a lot. She liked every-thing he'd written, but she'd also read a lot *about* him. She was a funny lady, and sometimes she would talk about Mr. Dickens as if they were good friends. I was just thinking that if she saw us sitting here like this, both of us reading Dickens novels, she'd say something like, 'Mr. Dickens would be pleased, boys. You just keep reading. It's good for you.'"

"Huh," Wendell said and went back to his reading. He obviously *didn't* think it was funny.

Jackson added, perhaps more to himself, "I guess you had to know her." He didn't go back to his reading, but rather indulged in memories of Granny, and how dear she had become to him in so short a time. It took no effort at all for him to recall her precious laugh, and how it had felt to hold her frail, aged hand in his. Then, out of nowhere, he recalled how he had known beyond any doubt that she'd been with him during some of the most difficult moments of his captivity. She had taught him to believe in angels. It occurred to him that maybe she was here with him now just as she had been then. As soon as he thought it, he figured it was a silly thought. There was no drama here, no need for her angelic comfort. But the feeling deep-ened, and he caught his breath. She *was* here. He didn't know why. He just knew that she wanted him to know that she was with him. Then the feeling was gone, and a moment later the power went out.

Jackson laughed at the coincidental timing of something that no one but himself could appreciate at the moment. With a fire in the room, it wasn't completely dark, but Wendell gasped.

"It's okay, kid," Jackson said. "I'm going to get a couple of lanterns. We might want to sit a little closer to the fire to stay warm, however. With the power out, the furnace won't run unless I start the generator. And I only do that when we get desperate, 'cause it's noisy and annoying. Will you watch Charles until I get back?"

"Sure," Wendell said.

Jackson lit some lanterns and checked on Polly, who had been watching TV, and Chas, who was still lying down. He left them each with a lantern and returned to find that all was well in the parlor. Wendell was sitting on the floor with Charles on his lap. With no source of light except the fire, the baby was fascinated with watching the flames. Jackson sat down beside them, and they sat in silence for several minutes before the power popped back on and Wendell let out a disappointed groan. Jackson chuckled and doused the lanterns that he'd set on the mantel. With the lights back on, they returned to their reading until Wendell had completed more than double his required reading time for the day.

Wendell was actually disappointed when his father called from his cell phone and said he would be there in a just a few minutes, and Wendell needed to be ready. Jackson assured him that sometime on a weekend when they had a spare room he could spend the night.

Once Wendell was safely on his way home with his father, Jackson locked up the house and got the baby down for the night. He made certain Polly was okay, then sat in bed next to Chas to read from the scriptures. When it became evident she wasn't asleep, he asked her how she was feeling.

"Just tired," she said. "I'm fine. How are you?"

"I'm fine," he said, then he remembered that strange moment in the parlor. He told Chas about it, then chuckled. "Is that crazy? Why would she let me know she was there?"

"I don't know, but it's happened to me a few times . . . very much like that."

"Really?" he asked. "Just . . . out of nowhere . . . for no apparent reason?"

"Yeah . . . it's like . . . she just wants us to know that she's there."

"It's remarkable," Jackson said.

Chas sat up next to him and pointed to the scriptures open on his lap. "You can read how it works."

"I can?"

"Moroni, chapter seven. Do you want me to find it?"

"Yeah," he said with enthusiasm, and Chas considered the moment somewhat surreal.

Chas took his book and shuffled through the pages to find the right place. She handed it back to him and pointed to the beginning of verse twenty-nine. It was a passage she knew well.

Jackson took the book back, noting immediately that she was pointing out a continuation of one of the passages she'd guided him to when he'd received the book, which was marked in red.

"Read it aloud," she said. "Just through verse thirty-three."

Jackson cleared his throat and read, *"And because he hath done this, my beloved brethren, have miracles ceased? Behold I say unto you, Nay; neither have angels ceased to minister unto the children of men. For behold, they are subject unto him, to minister according to the word of his command, showing themselves unto them of strong faith and a firm mind in every form of godliness. And the office of their ministry is to call men unto repentance, and to fulfil and to do the work of the covenants of the Father, which he hath made unto the children of men, to prepare the way among the children of men, by declaring the word of Christ unto the chosen vessels of the Lord, that they may bear testimony of him. And by so doing, the Lord God prepareth the way that the residue of men may have faith in Christ, that the Holy Ghost may have place in their hearts, according to the power thereof; and after this manner bringeth to pass the Father, the covenants which he hath made unto the children of men. And Christ hath said: If ye will have faith in me ye shall have power to do whatsoever thing is expedient in me."*

Jackson thought about it, then said, "I think I understand that, but I want to hear your interpretation. You've obviously given it a great deal of thought."

Chas wanted to pinch herself. She was having a spiritual discussion over the scriptures with her husband. She resisted the urge to let out a girlish squeal and calmly said, "In essence, it means that angels are subject to Christ, and their ministering to mortals is under His direction. They minister by the power of the Holy Ghost, and their purpose is to fulfill the covenants that God the Father has made with His children, and to bring people to Christ. I find it interesting that each member of the Godhead is included in the process."

"Yes, that is interesting," he said, and she gave him a minute to process it.

"Would you like to know my editorial on the subject . . . in relation to you?"

"I would," he said with no reservation.

"When you were in prison and you knew that Granny was with you, I think that God knew you had reached your limits and you needed something to give you hope and help you hold on. He knew hers was a voice you would recognize, and she had a personal interest in you, because you were meant to come home and marry me."

"Okay, that makes sense," Jackson said. "And it's funny how time has not made that experience fade for me. The memory of it is clear and real."

"I've found that's often the case with spiritual experiences. For me, that's how I've come to learn when it *is* a spiritual experience, as opposed to my own thoughts or emotion. The latter will fade with time."

"And why do you suppose Granny was allowed to let me know she was there this evening?"

"Maybe it has something to do with the searching you're doing, and it was important for you to know that she's with you."

Jackson looked at the book in his hands, then back to Chas. He felt as if something was coming together in his mind, but it wasn't quite connecting enough for him to form a cohesive thought. As if Chas understood, she said, "I guess that gives you something to think about."

"Yeah, thanks," he said and gave her a quick kiss.

She settled back into the bed, saying, "I'm exhausted. If you have any more questions they'll have to wait until tomorrow."

"Fair enough," he said, "but we need to have prayer."

Chas had honestly forgotten, but it was another pleasant surprise to have him initiate it. After prayer she drifted to sleep quickly, aware that Jackson was still reading. Her next awareness was the once-familiar realization that Jackson was caught in a nightmare and couldn't wake up. According to Callahan's suggestion, she didn't turn on the light, but she did take hold of him and speak to him firmly to urge him out of sleep. He came to his senses quickly, but it took him several minutes to breathe evenly. She just held him close and whispered reassurances until he was calm.

"I'm regressing," he said out of the darkness.

"Same dream?"

"No, it was different . . . mixed up . . . worse."

"Do you want to tell me about it?" she asked.

"No, and I'm not going to."

"Are you going to tell me why you think you're regressing?"

"I'll talk to Callahan about it."

"Okay, I can live with that."

Jackson never went back to sleep, but he was grateful that Chas did. He stared above him toward the dark shadows of the ceiling, wondering why his father had jumped headlong into his dreamed memories of imprisonment and torture. He'd understood from the very beginning of his PTSD that his experiences with his father had alarming similarities. He'd believed since his mother's death that they were more emotionally integrated than he'd wanted to admit. He'd realized since working with Dr. Callahan that the connection had been more complete in his subconscious mind than his conscious one. Repressed memories had been unearthed, and ugly dots had been connected into a hideous picture. And now he was regressing.

He had little to say to Chas or anyone else that morning. He knew she was concerned, but he didn't know what to tell her. He was concerned too. During the drive into the city for his scheduled appointment, he pondered what he knew as opposed to an ever-present unknown that still frightened him. He felt like he should know and understand the answer to this problem. But he just couldn't make sense of it.

Once seated in Callahan's office, Jackson got right to the point. "I'm regressing."

"Then we need to figure out why. With something like this, you can't really stand still, or you *will* regress. In other words, if you're moving forward, you can't move backward at the same time. But if you're standing still, sliding backward becomes a natural result. For example, I have a patient who is extremely obese; he always has been. He's working very hard to lose the weight, knowing it's a matter of life and death. He's actually done very well, but he's realized that if he lets off even a little with the strict diet and exercise, not only will he not *lose* weight, he will start to *regain* weight. In your case, I think we need to consider what the unresolved issues are that keep you from moving forward. With my obese patient, we've talked through a lot of emotional issues that are behind the extreme eating. With you, quite frankly, my friend, I think you are still hiding from things that tie into your PTSD, and until you face them and conquer them, you will continue to struggle, and yes, even regress."

"I was afraid you were going to say that."

"Why? Because you're afraid to face those things you're hiding from?"

"Maybe."

"Why, Jackson? What makes you afraid to let go of your ill feelings toward your father?" Jackson scowled at him, sometimes hating his perception. He added, "Do you think if you let go it will make him any less accountable? Or is your hatred toward your father such an integral part of you that you fear letting it go might undo you somehow?"

"I don't know," Jackson said. "I only know that just *thinking* of the things he did to me, makes me . . . *furious.* "

"Okay. But what is beneath the anger? I'm guessing you feel betrayed. A father should take care of a child, not harm him. You should have been able to trust him, but instead you were afraid of him. Perhaps you feel sorrow. A father should love his son, should care about his son's accomplishments and dreams. You never had any indication that he loved you. Is it really fury you feel? Or is it betrayal? Sorrow? Confusion? Grief?"

"All of the above, maybe."

Callahan talked Jackson through a visualization exercise, where in his mind he imagined a pile of rocks and a backpack. He had him label each of the rocks with his difficult emotions and memories and put them into the backpack. He had him imagine putting on the backpack and describing how it felt, and suggested that this was the way he'd been living most of his life. He was so accustomed to the burden that he didn't realize the damage it was doing. He then told him to imagine taking the backpack off and removing the rocks one by one. He told Jackson that in reality it wasn't as simplistic or easy as just throwing the rocks away and having an empty backpack that was no longer necessary to hold onto at all. He did say, however, that if he could define those rocks, perhaps even make a list of them, he might be able to sort out his feelings, as opposed to simply looking at the backpack as a whole and being unable to get rid of it. Callahan challenged him to work on it and asked if there was anything else he needed to talk about. Jackson figured he had way too much food for thought to last until the next session, so he left it at that.

Through the drive home, Jackson mentally tallied all those stupid rocks again and wondered if he could possibly pick it apart this way and make some progress. He returned home to find Chas pulling out the Christmas decorations. Their vacation had put them behind in decorating the inn, and it would soon be time for their annual Christmas open house. They had to get everything ready and in order. He dug in to help her and only said, "Fine," when she asked how the appointment had gone. When they took a break for lunch, and no one was around but the two of them and the baby, she asked, "Did you talk about regressing?"

"Yes."

"And what did he say?"

"He said there are issues I'm hiding from, and until I face them, I will continue to struggle."

"Does that makes sense to you? Does it feel right?"

"It's makes sense, but it feels *all* wrong. I don't know if I can do it."

"Do what, exactly?"

"You know very well what."

"Do I?"

"You're just trying to get me to say it."

"If you're talking about forgiving your father, I was *not* trying to get you to say it. I just wondered if that *was* the problem."

"It's the biggest one, I'm sure."

"And you don't think you can do it?" she asked while she was washing the baby's hands and face.

"You know what, Chas? I don't want to have this conversation."

"Why, so you can keep hiding from it?"

"You don't know the half of what I'm dealing with. You can't possibly understand or judge the situation."

Chas got Charles out of his high chair and set him free on the kitchen floor to play with the toys that were there. "I could never *judge* the situation; I wouldn't want to." She sat back down across the table from her husband. "I may not fully understand, but I've sure tried to, and I would like to understand it better. I don't need to know the grisly details to know enough to have some measure of understanding. I feel like you're holding back from me, and it's *not* just about wanting to spare me from disturbing images. I wonder if not telling me just makes it easier to hide from things you don't want to look at."

Chas expected him to be more defensive—even more angry. She feared having him retreat again into an emotional state where he was closed and unreachable. But he gave a heavy sigh and replied humbly, "Maybe you're right."

Chas took his hand and urged gently, "Just . . . tell me something, Jackson; tell me anything that will help me understand."

Jackson looked toward the window and took a minute to decide where to start and how much to say. He knew she was right, but he hated it. He cleared his throat and shifted in his chair. "Apparently I had repressed some of the worst memories. Callahan said they were emotionally triggered by the incident, but I didn't consciously remember them until I was in the hospital, spending all that time in the dark. There are details that I'm *not* going to tell you. But maybe you're right; maybe you do need to know why it's affected me so deeply, and why I have trouble letting go of it. You see, he . . ." Jackson hesitated, allowing the words to form in his mind. He measured them carefully and forced them to his tongue. "He'd get drunk, and then he'd get angry over some stupid thing. I'd try to stay out of his way, or hide, but that didn't always work. After he found me hiding in the closet once, he started using it against me. So, he'd get ticked off over something like . . . I had the TV too loud, or I hadn't gotten his beer for him fast enough. And he'd go off and start hitting me. Then he'd lock me in the closet. I was bruised and bleeding . . . and hungry eventually . . . and locked in the dark."

Chas swallowed hard but didn't try to hold back her tears. He needed to know how she felt. It all made so much sense that she nearly felt chills. When she realized he was waiting for her to say something, she took his hand and said, "No wonder, then. No wonder it connected so deeply into the incident."

"Yes, *the incident,*" he said with acrid sarcasm. "Of all the people in the world who could be thrown into a dark room and abused by lowlife criminals, it had to be a man whose father had done the same thing to him."

"You've already admitted to me that you were glad it was you and not someone else in your place. And you admitted that what your father had done to you had toughened you up. It may have made you more emotionally vulnerable, but I think it also made you physically more capable of enduring it. Would you agree with that?"

"Yes."

"But you can't forgive your father?"

He couldn't help expressing the anger he felt. "How could a man do something like that to his own son?"

"Did he do the same to Melinda?"

"No. He was hard on her, but it was mostly verbal abuse. He hit her occasionally, but he took the worst of it out on me. I'm glad he didn't hurt Melinda any more than he did. But I don't understand how he could do that to me. I look at Wendell; he reminds me of myself in some ways. I wasn't a bad kid, but I got punished beyond belief for *nothing*. How could a man be like that?"

"I don't know, Jackson. We've talked about the possibility of the abuse coming down through the generations. We don't know when or how it began."

"But he could have stopped it. He had a choice of whether to pass it on."

"Yes, he did, and the choice he made was not right. There's nothing that can ever justify his behavior or make it excusable. But somewhere in your heart, I think you can find a way to understand it enough to forgive him."

"How?" he practically snarled, but Chas was unaffected by his anger.

"Don't ask me. This is between you and the Lord, Jackson. I truly believe that with prayer and studying the scriptures with an open mind and an open heart, you will be led to the answers. Not some pat answer that's meant to cover all problems equally, but the answer that is custom-made for you from a God who knows your heart and knows your past. I know it's possible, Jackson; I know it. But no one but you can take that part of the journey. I can go with you, but I can't go in your place. Our Savior is the only one who was able to atone for the pain and suffering of others. He's the One you need to turn to. And I think a part of you believes it's possible. You've taken some marvelous steps, spiritually and emotionally. I think you just need to press forward on those paths, and you'll be all right. I really believe that."

Jackson shook his head. "I don't know how to do this, Chas; I really don't."

The humility in his statement made it easy for Chas to say, "All you have to do is ask, Jackson. Ask God to help you forgive those who have hurt you so that you can be free of the burden."

"Just like that? I ask and He makes it go away?"

"No, not just like that. I'm certain it will take some sincere effort on your part. You may not be able to comprehend how it's possible to forgive, but I think you've got to at least *want* to forgive. If you have that sincere desire to be free of it, then yes, I believe that sincere prayer and study and patience will bring you what you're seeking. God has commanded us to forgive, but He's also made it clear that He doesn't command something without making it possible. Is that making sense?"

He nodded but didn't comment. The baby started fussing, and Jackson rose to take care of him, needing an end to this conversation. Chas feared that her words had fallen on ears blocked by stubbornness and fears, but that evening he asked her a couple of questions about how to find something specific in the scriptures. She gave him a brief lesson on how the footnotes and topical guide worked. He thanked her and was still in bed reading from the scriptures when she fell asleep. She'd heard a lot of page shuffling and assumed he'd figured out how to search. She prayed that he could find what he was looking for.

The following morning Chas did something that she knew needed to be done. It wasn't that she didn't *want* to; it still just felt so strange. She phoned Nolan Stoddard to tell him that they had returned from their vacation and they would like to see him. He was so thrilled to hear from her that she felt deeply touched. He asked if they would mind coming to Butte so that he could take them out to a nice dinner at his favorite restaurant. They arranged it for the following evening, and Chas found herself looking forward to it. She was genuinely pleased to see him when they met at the restaurant, and he was so excited to see all of them that it couldn't help but make their efforts more than worth it. By the end of the meal, Chas realized she'd become very comfortable around this man, and she was pleased when he asked if they would like to come to his home for a short while before going home, just so they'd know where to find him. They followed him from the restaurant to a nice upper-middle-class home where they visited and enjoyed seeing pictures of his family. When it was time to leave, they all embraced and promised to see each other again soon.

On the drive home, Charles fell asleep right away, but Chas had anticipated this and had changed him into his pajamas before they'd left. After pondering the events of the evening for several minutes in silence, Chas reached for Jackson's hand, saying, "It's really quite remarkable, isn't it."

"What is?"

"I have a grandfather."

"It really is," he said and kissed her hand. "We should see what his plans are for Christmas."

"Yes, we should," Chas said.

The following morning, Chas called Nolan to thank him for the lovely evening, and she asked about his plans for the holidays. He told her he was flying to California to spend Christmas with his daughter's family, and that his other daughter who lived in New York would also be there. Chas then insisted that he come over for an early Christmas dinner before he left town. He was pleasantly surprised by the invitation, and they set a date. She also invited him to the annual open house for the inn, which she explained had become a Christmas tradition in the community. He promised to be there as well. When Chas hung up the phone, she was overtaken by a smile that was impossible to subdue.

Their days became very full with Christmas preparations, a busy inn, and much snowfall to contend with. It seemed they barely had the inn decorated and the Christmas tree in place when it came time for the open house. The event was a success, as always, but the highlight was Wendell bringing his family. He was thrilled to take his father and sisters on a tour of the inn, and to serve them refreshments that he had helped prepare. He told Jackson that he was still reading *A Tale of Two Cities,* but he didn't know when he'd be finished because it was such a long book. Jackson assured him that it didn't matter how fast he did it, as long as he didn't quit in the middle.

Nolan also came to the open house and thoroughly enjoyed Chas giving him a personal tour of the inn. He then insisted on looking out for Charles while Jackson and Chas were busy serving refreshments and overseeing the event. He was the last to leave, and even insisted on helping clean up. Polly and Charlotte, who were also there to help, had quickly bonded with Nolan, and they were all chatting and laughing together as they worked. Chas enjoyed his company and found his efforts helpful and very sweet.

With the open house behind them, they moved into the heart of the holiday season. Christmas with one-year-old Charles was far more fun for his parents than for him. They both agreed that their Christmases together just kept getting better, and they marveled that by next Christmas they would have *two* children. Charles took his first steps a few days before Christmas, and he was quickly managing to move around more on his feet than by crawling.

Christmas dinner with Nolan was a great success, and their exchange of simple gifts was touching. Jackson and Chas had decided to give him a picture of their family in a nice frame that he could add to his family collection at home. They hadn't wanted to set up any expectation of elaborate gift-giving that might have been awkward, and they were pleased when the gifts Nolan gave their family were also simple and more sentimental than extravagant. When he left, he promised to call them as soon as he returned home after the first of the year.

Chas was pleased to see Jackson maintaining a fairly pleasant mood throughout the holidays. He was still having occasional nightmares, and sometimes the effect was pretty bad. But she knew he was continuing to study, and he had started the habit of personal prayer both morning and evening. She was surprised the first time she'd gone back to the bedroom for something and found him kneeling beside the bed. But it was one of the best surprises she'd ever gotten. Occasionally he asked her a question regarding a scripture or doctrinal concept, but for the most part he just continued his quest very quietly.

Chas was understandably surprised when Jackson gave her a new set of scriptures for Christmas. Apparently he'd asked one of their home teachers for some guidance and had called a bookstore in Salt Lake City to order them. They were exactly like his, but blue instead of green, and he was pleased to point out that not only could she read her name that had been engraved on the front, but it was now the correct name. She had to agree that seeing *Chas Florence Leeds* on her scriptures was definitely a thrill.

At the first of the year, Chas asked if they could take on the goal of studying together a little every day. It was something Chas had always wanted to do, but she had never felt comfortable about making the request. Jackson eagerly agreed, and on New Year's Day they started reading the Book of Mormon together.

Nolan called as promised when he returned, and Chas invited him over for Sunday dinner. They had a pleasant afternoon together, and Chas especially enjoyed the way he got so much pleasure out of playing with little Charles. Without even thinking about it, Chas started calling him Grandpa, and it began to feel like they'd always shared this relationship. She looked forward to a time when she could meet the rest of the family, especially when he told her that he'd been telling the rest of them about her and they were all anxious to meet her as well. Spread across the country as they were, he didn't know when that might happen, but it was something to look forward to.

Jackson continued to study and search, but by the middle of January he was beginning to feel discouraged. He knew that patience was part of this equation, but it just seemed that nothing was happening. His symptoms felt no better and no worse, but it seemed that ever since Callahan had explained the backpack full of rocks theory to him, he'd become aware of an inexplicable weight on his shoulders that he was longing to be free of. Perhaps that meant something *had* changed. His awareness and desire had changed. He had taken Chas's challenge very seriously, and if nothing else, he could now look at himself honestly and know that he *wanted* to forgive his father and the others who had hurt him. The desire had fully come together for him when he'd been struggling with his own guilt over the things he'd done that had been hurtful to Chas. And there in the midst of his study, he had read in Third Nephi, *For, if ye forgive men their trespasses your heavenly Father will also forgive you; But if ye forgive not men their trespasses neither will your Father forgive your trespasses.* He'd heard the concept before, but that was the first time it had truly made sense. He searched further and found a life-altering passage in Mosiah: *Therefore I say unto you, Go; and whosoever transgresseth against me, him shall ye judge according to the sins which he has committed; and if he confess his sins before thee and me, and repenteth in the sincerity of his heart, him shall ye forgive, and I will forgive him also. Yea, and as often as my people repent will I forgive them their trespasses against me. And ye shall also forgive one another your trespasses; for verily I say unto you, he that forgiveth not his neighbor's trespasses when he says that he repents, the same hath brought himself under condemnation.* Jackson knew that holding on to his own senseless belief that he had the right or need to not forgive his father was only making it impossible for him to be forgiven of his own mistakes. It didn't matter that their severity fell into completely different spectrums. He had to forgive to be forgiven.

The forgiveness issue felt harder with his father, perhaps because it was more personal. He'd expect sadistic drug lords to be ruthless and unfeeling. But not his own father. He struggled every day with the feelings and wanted them to go away. He wanted to be free of this burden, and he'd prayed and prayed for it to be taken away.

As a result of his extensive study, Jackson had learned much about what Christianity really meant. He'd come to learn a great deal about the atoning sacrifice of Jesus Christ and what it meant. Intellectually, he could add it all up, and with a basic belief in Christ he could accept that it was probably true. But he didn't *know* it was true. And perhaps more importantly, he didn't know that it was applicable to him in regard to his own suffering. He kept waiting and hoping for some kind of experience like those he'd heard talked about in testimony meeting, but it just didn't happen.

Jackson woke on a cold, bright day and found himself pondering an idea that Chas had once suggested: the idea that his father had likely been abused as well; that the abuse might have been perpetuated generations before. Later in the day, he said to Chas, "I think I'd like to go to Arkansas for a few days. Do you think you can manage without me?"

"I'm sure I can," she said. "Is Melinda all right?"

"Oh, she's fine. She's busy with her friends, as usual. But she did tell me a few minutes ago that if I actually came to visit her she'd be thrilled to put everything else on hold."

"Then you should go," Chas said. "I assume you're going to explain this sudden need to return to your roots."

"Well, I guess that's it. I have a sudden need to return to my roots. When we went for the funeral, I didn't want to look at my past or feel anything related to it. Now, I think it would be good for me to do exactly that."

Chas smiled, then she hugged him and told him how proud she was of the progress he was making. She assured him that she would miss him, but she would gladly support him in doing whatever he needed to do.

That evening, Chas was surprised to enter the bedroom and find Jackson sitting on the bed, surrounded by the contents of the box that Melinda had given him when their mother had passed away.

"You're exploring without *me?*" she asked lightly.

"You're welcome to join me," he said, and she sat carefully on the other side of the bed, perusing the black-and-white photos, some odd pieces of Jackson's childhood schoolwork, and some simple drawings he'd done as a child.

Chas's eye was drawn to one photo in particular, and she picked it up. The handsome young man in it was wearing classic jeans, engineer boots, and a white T-shirt with a pack of cigarettes rolled into the sleeve. He was leaning against a truck and had a cigarette between his fingers. His smile was endearing. And the resemblance was striking. "Your father," she stated.

"Yes, that's him . . . although that was long before I came along."

"You *do* look like him; he's very handsome." Jackson didn't comment.

Chas picked up another picture of his parents together. They were young and looked happy and in love. "I guess it wasn't always bad."

"No, I guess not," Jackson said sadly.

She looked at a few photos of him and his sister, then asked, "Are you okay?"

"I think I'm getting there," was all he said before he put the contents back in the box, except for the picture of his parents together, which he tucked into the edge of the mirror on the dresser. Chas felt close to tears as she watched him gaze at the picture and ponder it. She couldn't imagine the irony and poignancy associated with what it represented, and the way that it surely affected Jackson. Knowing that he certainly had a lot on his mind, and that he was the kind of man who needed time to mull things over, she didn't say anything. She just put her arms around him with a tight hug that he eagerly returned.

# Chapter Sixteen

Three days later, Jackson drove himself to the airport and left his car in long-term parking. He didn't want Chas to have to come and get him when he came back because of the possibility of her having to drive in bad weather. Melinda was thrilled to see him when he arrived at her home. She fed him supper while they caught up on family and trivial matters. Brian was still in Iraq but doing well. Sasha and her family were also fine except for a little flu bug that the kids had struggled with.

Since Jackson had spoken to Melinda on the phone about what had been on his mind, she had already started doing some research and was eager to tell him what she'd learned. During the next few days, Jackson put his investigative skills to work and enlisted his sister's help in the associated busywork. They both felt a great mixture of emotions over what they discovered, but they were able to talk it through as brother and sister in a way they never had before.

On Sunday, Jackson went to church in the building where the funeral luncheon for his mother had been held. He was pleasantly surprised when Melinda declared that she wanted to come along. She even went to Relief Society by herself and told him afterward that the ladies were very kind.

Jackson arrived home late Monday evening. Charles was already asleep, but Chas was as happy to see him as she'd been when he'd returned from the hospital months earlier. He hadn't told her much on the phone, and she was waiting to hear about what he'd been doing in Arkansas. They sat close together on the bed and held hands while he told her about his needing to act on the idea that his father's abusive ways may have been a perpetuation of an ongoing tradition. The investigator in him had wanted to know more. He expressed varying emotions as he reported that the court records they'd found had indicated that Jackson's father and grandfather had both had multiple encounters with the law over drunkenness and violence. But most poignant for Jackson and Melinda had been the discovery that their mother had once filed charges against her husband for violence. It was clear from the records that she'd been trying to protect her son. But it had happened at a time when domestic violence had not been treated with the respect with which it was now handled. Her case had been dropped, probably because she was living with the guilty man who had likely threatened her into reneging on her charges.

"So, how does all of this make you feel?" Chas asked.

"I don't know. More confused in some ways. I think I need some time to sort it all out. Knowing the kind of upbringing my father had makes his behavior more understandable; not excusable, but understandable. And who knows how far back it goes? But what really matters now is how I'm going to come to terms with it. Sometimes I think that I'm just making far too big a deal of the whole thing. But I can't ignore how it's affected me. It might have affected other people differently, but it's me we're working on here."

"Maybe," Chas said gently, "it's affecting you so deeply because you're the one who came into this world to break the cycle. Maybe you're meeting with opposition for the same reason."

The principle struck Jackson deeply. He'd come to understand the principle of opposition through his studying, if only in concept. And he'd heard Chas talk about it some. But he'd never thought to apply it to his own struggle to become whole. The idea solidified further when Chas added, "If Satan knows you have the potential to change such destructive cycles, why would he want you to believe you can be healthy and happy?"

Jackson thought long and hard about that, and he continued to pray and study. He'd felt just enough growth in his understanding to believe that it was worth the effort to keep going. He had to believe that somewhere at the end of this road he would find the peace he was searching for.

A few days later, Jackson returned from doing some errands to see his wife smirking, as if she knew a secret that she was dying to tell him.

"What?" he asked, but kissed her in greeting before she could answer.

"Your sister called," she said. "You didn't tell me you went to church while you were in Arkansas."

He shrugged. "I went to church. I thought it went without saying."

"I thought you only went to church because I wanted you to. I wasn't there."

He shrugged again. "It didn't seem right not to go; habit, maybe."

"Maybe," she said, but she was still smirking.

"What?" he asked again.

"And Melinda went with you."

"That's right. Apparently she enjoyed Relief Society."

"So she told me. Apparently she was *very* impressed."

"Really?" Jackson said. "What did she say?"

"She said she wants to go back. She wanted to know how she could find out more." Jackson lifted his brows but didn't comment. "I told her to call the bishop who had conducted the funeral, that he could send the missionaries over to talk to her. She was thrilled."

Jackson smiled. "Apparently you are too."

"Would you expect me not to be?"

"No, I would expect you to be *very* thrilled."

"The question would be, how do *you* feel about it?"

"What do you mean?"

"How are you going to feel if your sister becomes a Mormon?"

"It works for you; why wouldn't it work for her? If it makes her happy, I think it's wonderful."

"Good," Chas said, wishing he would show the same kind of enthusiasm. But he had a very different personality from his sister. He was slow and steady, and she loved him for the man he was. She just needed to be patient.

They were interrupted by the baby's needs, but that night after they'd prayed together at bedtime, Jackson remained on his knees beside her and said, "Maybe I should do that."

"Do what?"

He turned to look at her. "Maybe I should talk to the missionaries. Maybe they can help me find the answers I'm looking for."

Chas took a deep breath and pressed a hand to his face. "It can't hurt any. They may not tell you much that you haven't already heard in church, but I think it would be great." She kept to herself the fact that she knew the missionaries would be much more bold than she'd ever dared to be about him seeking a testimony of the truthfulness of the gospel and taking the step of baptism. And maybe the timing was good.

Chas arranged for the local elders to come over for dinner the following week. Elders Debry and Otteson were both sharp and polite, and everything Chas would have expected missionaries to be. After the meal, they sat and talked with Jackson for more than an hour. Chas expected her husband to have some specific questions, but he just let them teach while he listened attentively, not saying much. He did invite them to come back in a week, and promised to give some serious thought to what they'd said. Chas quietly held in her heart the hope she felt, and left Jackson to work things out in his own mind, certain that with time he would.

On Groundhog Day, Wendell came as usual after school, except that he was thrilled to report to Jackson that he had finished the book.

"I knew I was getting close," he said, beaming, "but I didn't want to say anything till I was done and then I could surprise you."

"Well, that is amazing!" Jackson said. "Why don't you hurry and get the most important chores done, and then you can take some time off and we'll talk about it."

"Okay," Wendell said and dashed out to do what he knew was expected of him.

Half an hour before Wendell's father normally picked him up, Jackson sat down with the boy in the parlor and said, "So, tell me what you think now that you've finished the book."

"I liked it better than I thought I would," Wendell said, then nothing more.

Jackson probed him with questions about who his favorite character was and why, and what part of the story was the most frightening, or exciting, or funny. He felt like an English teacher as they talked, and he had to keep digging to get Wendell to actually be able to discuss the book. The conversation was warming up a little when Wendell said, "You told me you were gonna tell me about the ending. You said you were gonna tell me how it changed your life."

"I did say that, didn't I," Jackson said. He'd actually forgotten.

"So, tell me," Wendell insisted with the confidence of having kept his part of the bargain.

"Well," Jackson said, gathering his thoughts, "when I was a kid, things were pretty tough at my house."

"Like how? Did your mom die too?"

"No, but my parents weren't very kind; my father especially." Wendell furrowed his brow as if he couldn't comprehend such a thing. Jackson went on. "I wasn't doing very well in school when a teacher gave me a Dickens novel to read. I read it and wanted more and more. Those books helped me get through some tough years. When I was nearly eighteen and trying to decide what to do with my life, it was the end of this book you just read that helped me make that decision. I was thinking of becoming a Marine, but I have to admit I was kind of afraid to do that, even though it would solve some of my problems. I knew it would take hard work and sacrifice, and of course there's always the concern of the danger involved. But looking back, if I hadn't gone into the military, I don't know if I would have made anything worthwhile of my life. When I read that last line . . . 'It is a far, far better thing that I do, than I have ever done; it is a far, far better rest that I go to than I have ever known . . .' I knew that I could do it. I think I was in awe of the concept that Sydney Carton could go to the guillotine on behalf of Charles Darnay in order to give the woman he loved a better life. And that's when I knew that my life could have value in the military. I knew that if I could sacrifice and serve on behalf of my country to make life better for someone else, then my life would have meaning and purpose; it wasn't just a way to get out of town. It became a way of life. I lost my fear of dying when I came to believe that something good could come out of it. But as you can see, I didn't die. I did, however, make my life a lot better."

Wendell looked positively mesmerized, and Jackson gave him a moment to take it in. The boy finally said, "So, that kind of makes you like Sydney Carton."

Jackson smiled. "Only symbolically. I don't know if I would have actually had the courage to stick my head in a guillotine on behalf of someone else."

"But you did, didn't you?" Wendell asked with perfect innocence. Jackson was wondering how to respond to such a question when he added, "Chas told me she thinks you are the bravest man she has ever known. She said that some very bad men nearly killed you, and you were there so that other people wouldn't get hurt or die." When Jackson responded with dumbfounded silence, Wendell hurried to add, "Is it okay that I know?"

Jackson swallowed. "Of course it's okay. Chas wouldn't have told you if it wasn't okay."

"It's true, then."

"What's true?"

"That you are very brave."

Jackson looked down and cleared his throat. "I don't know about that." He chuckled tensely. "I didn't voluntarily agree to do what happened to me. It just happened."

"But you were in the Marines, right? You worked for the FBI, right? You did whatever they asked you to do, right? And if you hadn't done it, someone else would have had to go in your place."

"Did Chas tell you that?"

"No, I was thinking about it a lot while I was reading the book. You were like Sydney Carton. You changed your life for the woman you love, and you were willing to die for somebody else."

Jackson was stunned by the insights of a boy who was barely thirteen. But he was even more stunned by a strange burning in his chest that seemed to echo what Wendell had just said. He'd never thought of himself as brave, never considered himself to be a man who had made any great sacrifices or marvelous contributions to this world. But Wendell was looking at him with something akin to hero worship. He could laugh off the fantastical perspective of a boy, but he couldn't brush away the feeling consuming him. He couldn't speak for fear of being overcome by tears. He could barely breathe. The child sitting next to him, the room, the sounds of the house all became distant. In an instant he saw in his mind an image of the damage that would have been done if Jackson hadn't gone out of the country to finally see an evil drug lord behind bars. And while he'd been there, he'd been captured due to a case of mistaken identity. He saw it flash through his thoughts as if Ekert had gone in his place, as if he'd died there and his wife and children had been left behind. In a flash, a hundred other tiny incidents seemed to appear all at once in his mind and actually linger there. A series of seemingly insignificant moments throughout his service in the Marines and the FBI that had never seemed to him to be of much consequence were now being shown to him to illustrate a singular message: if he hadn't been there, putting his life on the line, a great many others would have been hurt to a greater degree, or even killed. While time seemed to stand still, he realized that a huge amount of information had poured into his mind in a matter of seconds, but it was the emotion accompanying it that he had trouble contending with. He was wondering what to say or do when Chas called Wendell's name, saying that his father was there.

"Thanks, Jackson," Wendell said and ran out of the room as if nothing was out of the ordinary. Jackson hurried in the other direction and went out the back door into the cold evening air. Once he was alone, he pressed a hand over the burning in his chest. He moaned, then he sobbed, and tears came hot and fast. Then, with no warning, the feeling intensified, and he heard the words in his mind, *Greater love hath no man than this, that a man lay down his life for his friends.* And in that moment, he knew. He knew the message he'd been given wasn't only to validate the fact that he'd done something great, even though he felt it was true. For the first time since it had happened, he fully and deeply could give himself credit for what he'd done—not with arrogance or to feed his ego, but to know that he could make peace with what had happened and know that he *had* prevented pain for other people. But that message was secondary to the one that really mattered. He knew that God had just used this very personal example to help him understand the most important message of all. It was as if Jackson could hear God speaking through his feelings, as if He were saying, *What you did to prevent your friend from suffering only gives you a tiny understanding of what I did for you. And I did it for your father as well.*

Jackson sat down on the cold concrete step and cried like a baby. The warmth inside him that left him feeling both powerful and weak dissipated slowly, leaving a residue that was alarmingly calm and brilliant. That weight he'd been carrying around all of his life was gone. He actually laughed aloud and wiped more tears as he realized the difference. *It was gone!* He sat there a long while, pondering all that had happened and everything he felt. His mind circled around through verses of scripture and dozens of different conversations and memories that all seemed to be pieces in the puzzle that had led to this epiphany that was far more remarkable than he'd ever imagined or anticipated. Chas had warned that some people didn't receive powerful answers. It was more common for the Spirit to speak quietly. And that's what Jackson had been looking for. He never would have believed that *he* could have been blessed with such a profound and undeniable answer to his prayers. Or maybe the credit belonged more to his wife's prayers. Whatever the case, he felt grateful beyond measure and bowed his head to express that gratitude to the God that had given him life, and then had given it back to him again.

Jackson heard the door and turned around to see his wife step outside. "Oh, there you are," she said. "I've been looking all over for you." She sat down beside him and took his hand. "Good heavens! You're freezing!"

"I'm fine," he said, then laughed.

She got a look at his face and asked, "Have you been crying?"

"It's a long story," he said and laughed again.

Chas took in his countenance and the evidence of his extreme emotions. Combined with how long he'd apparently been outside, she wondered what could have possibly induced such behavior. "Well, then," she said, "you'd better come inside and tell me. Not only is it way too cold out here for me, but your son is on the loose."

They went inside and found Charles pulling plastic lids out of a drawer in the kitchen. Both of his parents just laughed and sat down at the table, watching him finish the job.

Chas watched her husband while he was watching the baby play. Something had changed. Without taking her eyes from him, she asked, "What's happened?"

He turned to look at her, and the evidence of a change deepened. There was a brightness to his eyes she'd *never* seen before. Just seeing it took her breath away. He said in a raspy voice, "I don't know how to explain it; I don't know where to begin."

Jackson watched Chas's eyes widen then fill with moisture, and he felt like he didn't need to explain at all. He searched for a simple place to begin. "Wendell thinks I'm like Sydney Carton."

Chas smiled. "Does he? I can see that."

"You can?" he asked, genuinely surprised.

"Of course. What do *you* think?"

"Until a little while ago, I never would have put myself into such a comparison."

"And what happened a little while ago?" she asked, practically holding her breath.

He gave her a penetrating gaze. His voice cracked as he spoke. "Apparently God thinks so too." He chuckled tensely and wiped at a couple of tears that escaped without warning. "I can't tell you how I know that. I just do. Apparently He wanted me to see the comparison, because He . . ."

While he struggled to find the words, Chas began to grasp what had taken place. Warmth filled every nerve, and her heart threatened to burst open with the overflowing joy. She took his hand and waited eagerly for him to go on.

Their conversation was interrupted by a thud and the baby screaming. He'd fallen and bumped his head, but it immediately became evident it wasn't like the hundreds of other bumps he'd gotten. He was bleeding profusely, and Chas panicked when she picked him up. Jackson grabbed a towel and got it over the gash on his forehead before he spoke calmly to Chas, "It's just a cut, Chas. It's all right. Head wounds bleed a lot. If he was really bad off he wouldn't be screaming. Do you hear me?" She nodded and tried to breathe more evenly. He guided her hand to the towel. "Hold this tightly here. He's going to need stitches. I'll drive."

"Okay," she said and latched onto Jackson's calm example. Together they managed to get Charles into his car seat and keep the towel pressed over the wound. The baby had actually stopped crying by the time they reached the hospital.

When it came time for the shot and the stitches, Jackson took Charles and said to Chas, "Why don't you wait outside. I can handle this."

"Are you sure?" she asked, not wanting to leave her baby but nauseated at the mere thought of the needle going into his head.

"I'm a Marine," he said with a little smirk, but she felt sure it had something to do with his ability to remain so calm at the sight of blood.

"Okay," she said, certain her pregnancy was contributing to the lightheaded sensation overtaking her. She hurried to the waiting room and sat down, but she could hear Charles screaming in the distance, so she went outside and paced for a few minutes. When she went back into the waiting room she couldn't hear any wailing children and tried to relax. Then it seemed forever before Jackson came out holding Charles, who was holding a green sucker in his mouth.

"Oh," Chas said as she stood, noting the tidy stitches on his forehead. "Looks like we'll have a scar."

"Just a little one," Jackson said. "It'll just make him look more manly."

After Charles was down for the night with a dose of the liquid medicine the doctor recommended for the inevitable headache that would ensue, Chas recalled the remarkable conversation she'd been having with her husband when the accident had occurred. When they were both ready to go to sleep, she took his hand and made him sit beside her on the bed.

"Tell me . . . what you were going to tell me." She saw him smile, as if recalling it prompted a deep joy in him, then he glanced away almost shyly.

"I can't explain it, Chas," he said, looking at her directly again. "I only know that it's gone."

"What's gone?"

"The burden, the weight, the anger, the fear. It's just . . . gone."

"Oh, Jackson," she said with tears that couldn't begin to release the whole gamut of emotions tangled into the journey that had led to this moment. She took his face into her hands. "I can see it. I can see the change in your eyes." He smiled, and she added, "Tell me. Tell me what happened."

Jackson took both her hands into his and did his best to repeat the experience. Chas realized as he talked that he was not connecting the witness he'd just received to the truthfulness of the gospel. What he'd felt was purely and simply and beautifully a perfect testimony of the healing power of the Savior. She knew in her heart that with such knowledge in place, the rest would naturally flow after it. They talked until late, then read together and prayed before they fell asleep in each other's arms.

Charles woke up when his medicine wore off. Jackson insisted that Chas get her rest. He gave the baby his medicine and walked with him until it took effect and he drifted back to sleep. Jackson stood for several minutes over the crib just watching his son breathe evenly in gentle sleep.

Technically, life was the same as it had been yesterday at this time, but to Jackson it all looked different. He wandered back into the bedroom, not feeling sleepy. He just wanted to become accustomed to the new "him." He felt completely changed and altered. He'd never imagined that peace could be so tangible. From the light of the bathroom, he watched Chas sleeping, the same way he'd watched the baby. He wondered if a man had ever been so blessed in life as he was. He crawled into bed but left the beam of light shining so that he could just lie there and look at his wife while his thoughts wandered again through his spiritual experience. He considered it funny that he recalled a conversation between him and Granny about the book *A Tale of Two Cities*. She had lived in this room until Chas had taken it over following her death. He could close his eyes and recall vividly sitting side by side in front of the TV, watching a movie version of the Dickens classic.

*Granny dozed off toward the end and he had to elbow her to remind her to watch the best part. "Come on," he said, "you can't miss Sydney facing off the guillotine."*

*"No, I wouldn't want to miss that," she said with less humor than Jackson. "It's a very Christian story, isn't it."*

*"Is it? I'd never really thought about it that way."*

*"There's a lot of things you should think about, young man," she said. "Since you're reading it again, take notice of what a Christian story it is. I believe Charles was very purposeful with the way he filled it with Christian metaphors."*

*"Such as?"*

*She looked at him as if he didn't have a brain in his head, but her expression made him chuckle. "One man giving his life for another, with the only motive being love and sacrifice."*

*"Okay, I can see that," he said. "I've just never been very . . ."*

*"What?"*

*"Religious."*

*"Neither have I, but that doesn't mean we're not Christians."*

*"How exactly would you define being Christian?" he asked.*

*"Believing in Christ, living in a way that coincides with what He taught, which is simple: to be kind to other people, to have integrity. All the good things we can be in this world came from His example." She tightened her gaze on him. "So are you or aren't you?"*

*"What?"*

*"A Christian?"*

*"I . . . um . . ."*

*"You've never really thought about it?"*

*"No, I haven't."*

Jackson opened his eyes and came back to the present. He'd thought about it now, and now he knew what it *really* meant to be a Christian. He had accepted Christ into his heart, and it had been healed.

# Chapter Seventeen

Jackson drifted off to sleep and realized he was dreaming. It was the same old dream: a hazy but vivid re-creation of his imprisonment. Cold and darkness, hunger and pain. Then his captor merged into his father, and his surroundings became his childhood home. It was dingy and dirty, and he could smell the alcohol on his father's breath. And into the closet he went. He was sitting in the dark, crying quietly enough that he wouldn't draw his father's attention again. He knew his lip was bleeding and he was hurting in numerous places. He felt afraid and confused. Then he realized that he wasn't alone. A man was sitting next to him. Jackson couldn't see him, but he knew he was there. He felt no fear, only a strange kind of comfort from not being alone. The man spoke, but Jackson didn't hear words as much as he simply knew what was being said. "I know it's hard, Jackson, my boy, and I know it's impossible for you to understand, but one day you will, and you'll be able to make it right for all of us. You mustn't blame your father. All of this began long before he was born. It happened to me, and I passed it on to him. But between us, we're going to make it stop, and we're going to see healing in this family. You will be the one to stop it, my boy. Be strong, and a day will come when you will understand. You will understand that Elijah has come . . . Elijah has come."

Jackson came awake with a gasp. He recounted the dream once, twice, three times. It didn't *feel* like a dream; it felt like a memory. Had it been a repressed memory? He'd repressed the memories of being locked in the closet. But this? This was impossible. There couldn't have possibly been a grown man in the closet with him. But there had been. He fought to put the pieces together. *Elijah. Elijah.*

Why did it sound so familiar? Oblivious to Chas sleeping, he turned on the light and dug out the box that Melinda had given him after their mother's death. He knelt down and dumped the contents on the floor, sifting frantically through the school papers and crayon drawings. He gasped when he saw it. He couldn't believe his eyes. The page was yellowed more than the others. It had tape marks at the corners. He had hung it in his room, and it had stayed there long past the time that a child would have taken down such a childish drawing. But it had given him comfort, even though he hadn't known quite why. At least his adult mind hadn't known. When he'd seen this recently, he'd passed it off as something silly and irrelevant. But it wasn't irrelevant at all. It was evidence that during all those years when he'd believed he was alone, he hadn't been alone at all.

By the time he'd figured it out, Chas had come out of sleep enough to say, "*What* are you doing?"

"Look at this," he said, taking the paper to her. She took it, and he sat on the edge of the bed.

"I'm assuming you drew this," she said, trying to adjust her eyes to the light.

"I did. What does it look like to you?"

"It looks like . . . well, it's obvious. It's a little boy and a man sitting on the floor in . . . what? A box? A small room?"

"A closet," Jackson said. "I think that . . . I drew this when I was a child because . . . I knew I wasn't alone in the closet."

"I don't understand," she said through a yawn.

"I just dreamt this moment, Chas. I think it was my grandfather. He was there with me." She took a deep breath and had trouble letting it out. "He spoke to me," Jackson continued. "He told me that I mustn't blame my father. He said it started long before that. He said it had been passed to him and he'd passed it on. He told me I was the one to stop it."

"Good heavens," Chas muttered, so overcome with the miracles of the last several hours she could hardly breathe. She glanced at the paper again. "Was his name Elijah?"

"No."

"Then why did you write Elijah?"

"I have no idea. Does that name mean anything to you?"

"Well . . . it's a biblical name. Did you have a friend named Elijah, or—"

"No. In my dream, my grandfather said that I had to be strong, and one day I would understand that . . . Elijah has come. It must have left an impression. I wrote down the name. Did I spell it right?"

"Yes, I think so."

"How would I have known how to spell it when I'd never heard it before?"

"I don't know," she said. "I wonder if . . ." Chas gasped so loudly that Jackson was startled. He saw her eyes widen, then she put a hand over her mouth, which barely muffled a sharp whimpering noise.

"What?" he demanded.

She removed her hand. "Oh, Jackson!" she whispered in fervent reverence. "This is incredible!"

"We've established that. What do you know that I don't know?"

"Elijah. Elijah was a prophet. The very last verses of the Old Testament talk about Elijah. Malachi says that Elijah the prophet would come before the Second Coming of the Lord. As I understand it, the Jews have traditions of waiting for Elijah; watching for him. But he's already come. Your grandfather said that Elijah has come?"

"That's right."

"Well, he has; he did. He appeared to Joseph Smith in the Kirtland Temple. Through Elijah, keys were restored to the earth that would . . ."

"What?" he asked impatiently, hanging on her every word.

Tears rose in her eyes and spilled. "To seal families together. As the Bible puts it: *And he shall turn the heart of the fathers to the children, and the heart of the children to their fathers.*"

Jackson gasped the same way Chas had a moment ago. He let it sink in, then said, "I think I understand that, but explain it to me anyway."

"If your grandfather told you that you were going to stop the abuse, and that healing would come . . . and then he actually said that Elijah had come, then . . . I think it means that through you, past generations will be healed, and future generations will be free of the destructive cycles."

He thought about that and said, "What did you mean by 'seal families together'?"

"It's the work done in the temple, Jackson. Eternal marriage, eternal families. The work is done there for both the living and the dead."

He thought about that longer and harder. "So that means . . . if I . . ." He couldn't bring himself to say it; it sounded so strange, felt so foreign. He felt as if he'd lived on the border of a foreign country for years but had never actually crossed it, never taken in the scenery, never tasted the food, or spoken the language. And now he was longing to cross that line and wishing he'd paid more attention. There was a light beckoning him to the other side of that border, to experience what he knew Chas had experienced, to know what she knew.

Chas had no trouble being bold in her beliefs now. The time was right, the moment had come. She took his face into her hands and said it with her whole heart. "Not *if,* Jackson; *when.* When you and I are sealed together for eternity, not only will our marriage last beyond the boundaries of death, we will then be able to have all of our loved ones who have passed on sealed together as well. That's why Elijah came, so that we could all be bound together by that sealing power. You and I are going to be able to do for our ancestors what they could not do for themselves." She smiled, and the gaze they shared went deeper, as if they could see each other's spirits. "And you had an angel come to you in your childhood and tell you that you would do this. Do you have any idea what a *miracle* that is?"

"I have an idea . . . but I think it's going to take some time to let it sink in." He laughed softly and added, "I hadn't known you very long when you asked me if I believed in angels. I think my heart believed all along, even if my mind had forgotten."

"I would agree with that," she said and kissed him. "I love you, Jackson Leeds. Thank you for letting me be a part of the miracles in your life."

He chuckled. "I wouldn't have had any miracles without you to guide me."

"Then it would seem we are well matched."

"Yes," Jackson sighed, "it would seem so."

* * * * *

When the elders came for their next appointment, Polly was working late and volunteered to watch the baby in the office while they had their visit in the parlor. Jackson listened to the elders for a few minutes, then put up a hand and said, "Wait a minute. What about this challenge thing that you guys do?" They both looked as stunned as Chas, and he wondered what he'd said wrong. "Isn't that why you're here? You're working up to challenging me to get baptized, right?"

Chas couldn't believe what she was hearing. She honestly couldn't tell if this was a sincere question, or if he was somehow baiting them with sarcasm for some reason that she could never begin to imagine.

"Are you saying you're ready for baptism?" Elder Debry asked.

Chas held her breath. This was a turn of events she had *not* expected—or at least she'd not expected it quite so soon—and she simply couldn't believe that Jackson was actually going to answer this question the way they were all were hoping.

"Of course I'm ready," Jackson said, as if they all should have known.

Chas coughed. "What are you saying?"

"I'm saying I'm ready for baptism."

She wanted to say that she—his wife—had not been let in on this prior to this moment. She also wanted to say that in order to be ready for baptism he needed a firm testimony that the Book of Mormon was true and that this was *the* true church on the earth. For all of his amazing experiences, she'd never heard him saying anything to indicate that he'd felt either one.

Completely at a loss for words, she was relieved when Elder Otteson said, "Okay, that's great. Let's talk about it. Can I ask you some questions?"

"Of course," Jackson said. "Ask me anything." He seemed sincere enough.

"Have you read the Book of Mormon?"

"Yes."

"Have you had a personal witness from the Spirit that it's true?"

"Yes, absolutely," Jackson said, and Chas could hardly breathe.

"Do you believe that Joseph Smith was a prophet, and that he saw and spoke with God the Father and His Son, Jesus Christ?"

"Absolutely." Jackson laughed softly. "It's true. It's all true. And I know it's true. What next?"

Chas stood abruptly, needing to leave the room before she exploded into sobbing. When all eyes turned to her in question, she turned away and managed to mutter on her way out of the room, "Excuse me." She hurried through the bedroom and into the bathroom, where she closed the door and sat on the edge of the tub, hung her head, and cried tears that felt like they'd been bottled inside of her for years. She felt utterly elated to know that her seemingly endless prayers had finally been answered. This was what she'd wanted more than anything ever since she'd met him. And yet she felt so angry with him!

"What's wrong?" she heard Jackson say, and realized she hadn't heard the door.

Chas attempted to get enough control to give him an answer he could understand. She decided to get the anger out of the way first. "You know . . . you really need to learn to talk more."

"What do you mean?"

"How long have you felt this way? How long have you known? And you said *nothing* to me?"

"I didn't know it was that important to you," he said, and she had to look at him twice to realize he was serious. "You haven't said anything about it . . . not really . . . for a long time, and . . ."

"Because I thought you didn't want me to," she said.

Jackson couldn't hold back a little chuckle. But she scowled at him, and he quickly swallowed all evidence of humor. "I'm sorry," he said. "I know I need to talk about my feelings more. I guess I just . . . was lost in trying to make peace with my past. For me, that was the purpose of my quest. My realization that these things were true just kind of came on gradually. One day I just realized that I already knew it was all true. There wasn't any grand manifestation or anything. The experience that really changed me is the one I *did* tell you about. I just assumed that you would know that . . . if I knew that the Savior had healed my heart, the rest was just a given."

"There are a lot of people in the world who believe in Christ who don't believe *this* is the true church. There are a lot of people who think Mormons aren't Christians at all. I had no idea what you were thinking . . . or feeling . . . and I . . ."

Jackson sat down beside her and put his arm around her. "I'm so sorry," he said. "You're right. I do need to talk more."

Chas lightly hit her fist on his chest and took a minute to cleanse out the rest of her tears. Then she looked up at him and said, "You really mean it, don't you."

"I do. I'm very sorry."

"Not that. I mean . . . I know you mean that too, but . . . you really want to get baptized. You're ready."

"Oh, I am!" he said with perfect conviction.

Chas wrapped him in her arms and cried a different kind of tears. "I love you, Jackson. I'm the happiest woman in the universe."

He laughed softly and tightened his arms around her. "I'm pretty happy myself. But I think we'd better get back to the elders."

"Oh my goodness!" she said and stood up, frantically wiping her tears. She splashed water on her face and dried it while Jackson waited for her. "Do I look like I've been crying?"

"Yes," he said, "but I bet they're used to that kind of thing. Come on." He took her hand, and they returned to the parlor.

"Sorry," Chas said as they were both seated. "This is a big day for me."

"No problem," Elder Debry said.

Elder Otteson said, "Now, where were we?"

"I think we need to set a date," Jackson said. "How about the Saturday before Valentine's Day? That day is my mother's birthday. Is that possible?"

Chas squeezed Jackson's hand. He looked at her, and they exchanged a warm smile. She couldn't recall ever feeling so happy in her entire life. But there were visions in her mind of days ahead that would surely be happier, which only contributed to her present happiness. She laughed softly and laid her head on her husband's shoulder. Life was good.

\* \* \* \* \*

Becoming accustomed to the new man that Jackson had become, Chas felt as if she were falling in love with him all over again. Life went on as it always had. They were busy running the inn and caring for their son and each other. But everything had changed. Long before the first moment she'd bothered to look at Jackson Leeds as a potential husband, she had instinctively believed that she was meant to share the gospel with him. She clearly recalled when she'd first acknowledged her attraction to him, and she had prayed to know if it was a good thing to pursue such feelings, knowing he was not a member. Since the day she had gained her own testimony, the gospel had become the most important thing in her life, and she hadn't wanted to share life with someone who didn't share those beliefs. But she had prayerfully considered every step she'd taken with Jackson, and she had known that her Father in Heaven approved. Her patriarchal blessing promised that in this mortal life she would kneel at a temple altar with the man of her choosing, and together they would bring children into the world and do much good with their arms and hearts linked in living the gospel. Knowing beyond any doubt that it was right to marry Jackson, she'd naturally believed that this blessing would come to pass, provided she did her best to make righteous choices—which she had. And now it would! Nothing could make her happier!

Two days after Jackson had announced his intentions to be baptized, Chas rose early to get dressed for her monthly drive to Idaho Falls to attend the temple. She was surprised to come out of the bathroom and find Jackson putting on a tie. He turned to look at her and asked, "Do you mind if I come along? I know I can't go inside yet, but I'd actually like to get a good look at a temple."

Chas was too moved to speak. She'd invited him to come along more than once and he'd declined. She smiled and nodded, and he smiled back.

"I've already talked to Polly," Jackson said. "She's got everything covered for the day. We'll take the little man along. Us guys will go shopping or something while you do your thing. Then we'll go out to eat."

"It sounds wonderful," she managed to say, and then hugged him.

A few minutes into the very long drive, Jackson said, "I was also thinking that all of this time on the road would give us a chance to talk." He took her hand. "You did say I need to talk more."

"I did say that, didn't I."

"And I assume you meant it."

"Oh, I meant it."

"So . . . since we've got some hours to kill here, I thought maybe I should tell you the whole story."

"I can't think of anything I would like better," she said and turned more toward him. He started at the beginning, talking about how much she had impressed him when he'd first met her, how the way she lived her life was something he'd never encountered before. He repeated how she had taught him to believe in God and angels, and he talked about Granny's influence on him in that regard. In between Charles's occasional fussing and Chas trying to keep him happy, Jackson told her how he could see now the psychological reasons for his emotional trauma, how his childhood had tied into the violent episode that had damaged their lives. Then he talked about how he'd learned that psychology and spirituality seemed to have connected inside of him. He'd learned that he *had* been projecting his father's character traits onto God, and it had made it difficult for him to trust God or reach out to Him. And he'd learned that in order to heal emotionally, he'd needed to heed God's edict to forgive and to give those burdens to the Savior. He told her about his journey of reading the Book of Mormon and the Doctrine and Covenants, and how he'd slowly begun to feel the truth of their words penetrate his melting heart. He talked so much that he had to keep drinking water to lubricate his dry throat. He was so anxious to share every little detail of his experience, that he didn't run out of things to say until they were almost to Idaho Falls.

While Chas was guiding him to the temple, she said, "They do have a lobby where you can wait with the baby. Why don't you come inside with me for a few minutes."

"Okay," he said eagerly. He hadn't expected to be able to go inside at all, so this was a pleasant surprise.

As they approached the temple, he said, "Oh, it's beautiful."

"Yes, it is. The grounds are covered with snow, but when you come back in the spring you can see the flowers. They always have beautiful flowers."

"I'll look forward to that," he said and found a parking place. He carried the baby, and she carried her little suitcase. They walked through the front door holding hands, and he took in the lovely surroundings that exuded a nearly tangible peaceful sensation.

"Okay," she said, "this is where I have to leave you." She kissed him. "But one day soon . . ."

"Yes, one day soon . . ." he said and kissed her again. "Do you want me to meet you here, or . . ."

"I'll be done in about two hours. I've turned my phone off, but I can call you when I'm done, or . . ."

"I'll be here," he said, and she went farther into the temple without him.

Jackson stood there looking in the direction she'd gone until Charles started to wiggle, wanting to get down. He told himself he should just take the baby and go find a Wal-Mart or something, but he didn't really want to leave. They walked outside, and even though it was winter, the sky was blue and the air wasn't horribly cold. He walked slowly around the temple, pondering the changes in his life, and all he had to look forward to. Now that they were outside, the baby was more calm, looking around contentedly. Jackson went to the car and debated going somewhere, but a glance at his watch made it seem like just waiting for Chas was a more favorable option. He got the diaper bag and went back into the lobby where he was able to keep the baby occupied and fairly quiet, the same way he would at church.

Chas was surprised to return to the lobby and find Jackson and the baby waiting for her.

"You're still here," she said when he stood up. He'd been reading from scriptures that were always on the tables there. The baby was contentedly looking at a board book with pictures of animals.

"It's nice here; I didn't see any reason to waste my time going elsewhere. How was it?"

"Better than ever," she said.

"Why is that?"

"Because I know it's only a matter of time before I don't have to go alone."

He smiled and picked up the baby. "Shall we go?"

They drove past the falls that had inspired the name of the city. They were mostly frozen, but there were a few places where water was flowing through the ice. With the temple nearby, the view was quite remarkable. After sharing a nice meal, they stopped at an LDS bookstore where Jackson was like a sugar-deprived child let loose in a candy store. He was so preoccupied with perusing books and art that he didn't notice Chas making a discreet purchase that she slipped into her bag unnoticed.

When they finally started home with a bag full of books that Jackson couldn't wait to read, Charles fell asleep almost immediately. In contrast to their earlier drive going in the other direction, they both remained silent for many miles. Chas's thoughts kept coming back to the same place until she had to express them. She took Jackson's hand and just said it. "Will you marry me again, Jackson . . . forever this time? Now that we know the date you'll be baptized, we can set a date to be sealed. I want to put it on the calendar. I want to start crossing off days. We can pick a temple and start making plans. And then after we're sealed, we can do the sealings for everyone we love, whether we actually knew them or not. There's nothing I want more than that. I want it to be our biggest focus, and the most important thing we do. So, will you? Will you marry me again?"

He smiled, he kissed her, and he said with conviction, "I'll be counting the days."

She laughed softly, and together they drove on toward home.

\* \* \* \* \*

Jackson thoroughly enjoyed what he boldly declared to be his last visit to see Dr. Callahan. The doctor actually got tears in his eyes when Jackson told him how he had been able to completely get rid of that bag of rocks he'd been carrying around, and that he had fully and freely forgiven his father and others who had hurt him. He avoided too many spiritual details and focused more on the psychological aspects of the experience, although in Jackson's mind it was difficult to separate the two, and he told Callahan that as well. He felt complete confidence in telling Callahan that he knew he could handle whatever residue of his PTSD that might come up in the future, because he'd cleansed his spirit of the underlying issues, and he had the tools he needed to cope and not allow the problem to get out of hand. He also shared his gratification in knowing that he had finally been able to keep the promise he'd made to his mother at the time of her death.

The two men shared a brotherly embrace as they parted, and Jackson found it difficult if not impossible to fully express his appreciation for all this man had done to help guide him through his healing. He *did* give him a gift certificate for a weekend stay at the Dickensian Inn and said he'd look forward to seeing him whenever he decided to use it.

Jackson returned to the inn, trying to comprehend his life of not so many years ago, and the unexpected journey he'd taken to come to this day. "Wow," he said aloud as he parked the car. He laughed and hurried inside to see his family.

\* \* \* \* \*

Valentine's Day was always the busiest day of the year at the inn. It was the only night when every room was full, and Chas had made a point from the time the inn had first opened that this was a romantic place; therefore, if couples came here for a romantic getaway to celebrate a romantic holiday, she would go out of her way to make it memorable. The Valentine's Day traditions included frosted heart-shaped cookies in the office to enjoy when couples checked in. Each room had a long-stemmed red rose, a little box of chocolates, and a bottle of sparkling apple juice on ice, along with elegant goblets. She also went to extra trouble for the breakfast she served the following morning: heart-shaped waffles with strawberry sauce and chocolate-covered strawberries were the signature marks of the meal.

On the afternoon of the fourteenth, Chas went through all of the rooms to give them the extra finishing touches while Jackson listened for the baby, who was taking his nap. All of her preparations for tomorrow's breakfast had been completed as much as they could be until morning, and she had also prepared the beginnings of a nice dinner for her and Jackson this evening. She thought about how much nicer Valentine's Day had been since he'd married her and taken up innkeeping. The years she'd spent alone with no romance whatsoever in her life now seemed like a distant dream. Pondering her husband's baptism of a few days earlier, she couldn't hold back a smile nor suppress the warmth that filled her heart each time she thought of it. Everything that was good in her life had become better. She was the luckiest woman in the world.

Once assured that each room looked perfect, Chas went down to the kitchen. Passing through the dining room, she gasped to see a *huge* bouquet of red roses on the sideboard where breakfast would be laid out in the morning. A card with her name written on the envelope was leaning against the vase. She opened it to read a tender message of love and commitment that brought tears to her eyes. Jackson had written a personal message and signed his name, and underneath he had written, *Look in the bedroom.*

She turned around and was surprised to see him standing there with Charles in his arms; she hadn't known they were there. The baby had obviously just awakened from his nap.

"We love you," Jackson said.

"Then you must be responsible for the roses."

"We would be, yes," he said as if Charles might have initiated the purchase.

"And would you also be responsible for whatever is in the bedroom?"

"That was Charles's idea."

"Did your son tell you this?" she asked with a chuckle.

"Not him," Jackson said with complete seriousness. "It was Mr. Dickens."

"Oh, *that* Charles," she said and laughed again. "And how was it his idea?"

Jackson shrugged. "When I saw it I just thought Dickens would appreciate seeing this in the master bedroom, since the inn was inspired by him . . . and as Granny said, he was obviously a Christian."

Chas felt her intrigue growing into insatiable curiosity. She walked past them and into the bedroom, knowing Jackson would follow. The moment she stepped through the door, she saw the large, elegantly framed painting of the Savior on a wall that had always been empty.

"I think it was meant to be there," Jackson said.

"Oh, it's beautiful!" she cooed. "I would agree completely!" She laughed with delight as she examined it more closely. "How did you manage?"

"I ordered it when we were in Idaho Falls. I had it shipped to Charlotte's house, and I picked it up there this morning."

"You are very clever," she declared and dug into a drawer to pull out a card and a small wrapped box. "But you're not the only one. I bought this when you were looking at art that day in the bookstore."

He chuckled and took the gift at the same time she took the baby. He opened the card and read it before he kissed her and said, "That's all I would need."

"Maybe, but I think you need what's in that box, too."

Jackson opened it to find a CTR ring; it was very masculine and high quality. "I *do* need one of these," he said with a pleasant laugh. He slid it onto the ring finger of his right hand and declared, "The fit is perfect. How did you know?"

"Granny told me," she said, repeating what he'd said when he'd purchased her engagement ring. He smiled, and she shrugged, "I just knew. It sounds like a reasonable explanation to me."

"Very reasonable," he said and hugged her, which included hugging the baby as well. "Thank you. I love it."

"And I love this," she said, turning to look at the painting on the wall. "You really are *very* clever." She leaned against his shoulder.

He put his arm around her while they pondered the painting together. Even the baby seemed to be taking it in. "Yes," Jackson agreed, "and very happy."

# About the Author

Anita Stansfield began writing at the age of sixteen, and her first novel was published sixteen years later. Her novels range from historical to contemporary and cover a wide gamut of social and emotional issues that explore the human experience through memorable characters and unpredictable plots. She has received many awards, including a special award for pioneering new ground in LDS fiction, and the Lifetime Achievement Award from the Whitney Academy for LDS Literature. Anita is the mother of five, and has one adorable grandson. Her husband, Vince, is her greatest hero.

To receive regular updates from Anita, go to anitastansfield.com and subscribe.